Emmeline Lott

Harem Life in Egypt and Constantinople

Emmeline Lott

Harem Life in Egypt and Constantinople

ISBN/EAN: 9783337243494

Printed in Europe, USA, Canada, Australia, Japan

Cover: Foto ©Andreas Hilbeck / pixelio.de

More available books at **www.hansebooks.com**

HAREM LIFE

IN

EGYPT AND CONSTANTINOPLE.

BY EMMELINE LOTT.

LATE GOVERNESS TO HIS HIGHNESS THE GRAND PACHA IBRAHIM,
SON OF HIS HIGHNESS ISMAEL PACHA, VICEROY OF EGYPT;
AUTHORESS OF "NIGHTS IN THE HAREM."

"What precious things I found in Oriental lands,
Returning home, I brought them in my votive hands."
ALGER.

PHILADELPHIA:
T. B. PETERSON & BROTHERS;
306 CHESTNUT STREET.

DEDICATED

TO

HIS HIGHNESS ISMAEL PACHA,

&c.. &c.,

VICEROY OF EGYPT,

BY

HIS HIGHNESS'S MOST HUMBLE

AND DEVOTED SERVANT,

THE AUTHORESS.

PREFACE.

UPWARDS of a century has rolled away since that graceful, unaffected epistolary writer, the accomplished and "charming Lady Mary Montague," accompanied her *caro sposo*, Mr. Edward Wortley Montague, to Constantinople, when he was appointed Ambassador to the Sublime Porte.

In the eighteenth century, that "Princess of Female Writers" published in her Letters an account of her visits to some of the Harems of the *élite* of the Turks of that period.

She had no need to propitiate that all-powerful Sovereign Prince of the Ottoman Empire, "Baksheesh,"—who, whatever may be his demerits as a statesman, stands forth, in the present age, most prominently as the precursor of civilization in the Turkish dominions, and for whom a most brilliant future is in prospect—to obtain ingress. Her rank and position were the *Telecem*, "talisman," which threw open to her the heavy ponderous portals, drew back the massive double-bolted doors, and gave her access to those

(21)

forbidden " Abodes of Bliss " of the stolid, sensual, and indolent Blue Beards of the East.

Nevertheless, her handsome train, Lady Ambassadress as she was, swept but across the splendid carpeted floors of those noble Saloons of Audience, all of which had been, as is invariably the custom, well "swept and garnished" for her reception. The interior of those Harems were to her Ladyship a *terra incognita*, and even although she passed through those gaudy halls like a beautiful meteor, all was *couleur de rose*, and not the slightest opportunity was permitted her to study the daily life of the Odalisques. True, she had witnessed the

> "Strange fascination of Eastern gorgeousness, reverie, and passion;"

but yet, as she had not been allowed to penetrate beyond the reception halls, nor to pollute the floors of the chambers of those "Castles of Indolence" with her defiling footsteps, the social manners, habits and customs of the *Crême de la Crême* of both Turkish and Egyptian noblesse, and the Star Chamber of Ottoman intrigue, were to her all unexplored regions.

It was reserved to a humble individual like myself, in my official capacity as Governess to His Highness the Grand Pacha Ibrahim, the infant son of H.H. Ismael Pacha, the Viceroy of Egypt, the grandson of Mehemet Ali, and the son of that gallant warrior, the renowned Ibrahim Pacha, to become the unheard-of instance in the annals of the Turkish Empire, of residing within those *foci* of intrigue, the Imperial and Viceregal Harems of Turkey and Egypt; and thus an opportunity has been afforded me of, Asmodeus-

like, uplifting that impenetrable veil, to accomplish which
had hitherto baffled all the exertions of Eastern travellers.
The object of the following Work is to disclose to European
society " Life in the Harems of Egypt and Constantinople."
It has been my aim to give a concise yet impartial and
sympathetic account of the daily life of the far-famed
Odalisques of the nineteenth century—those mysterious
impersonifications of Eastern loveliness. With what success I have achieved this difficult task is left to the judgment of the public to determine.

HAREM LIFE.

CHAPTER I.

AFTER a quick but tempestuous voyage from the busy port of Marseilles, on board the *Peleuse*, one of the fleetest steamers in the service of the Messageries Impériales, I arrived in the land of the Pharaohs, at the harbor of Alexandria, in the month of April, 186—. I proceeded to the Peninsular and Oriental Hotel, where I took up my quarters for a few days. As a host of travellers have minutely but yet not, according to my impressions, very accurately described that Liverpool of Egypt, Alexandria—for *Egypt as it was* and *Egypt as it is* are vastly different—nevertheless I shall not attempt to give any topographical account of that wonderfully improving country and its ancient capital, the whole length and breadth of which I was enabled to traverse during my residence with the viceregal family.

The Viceroy's agent in London had consigned me, " bag and baggage," to the care of an eminent banking firm at Alexandria, who are also reported to be associated with Ismael Pacha in his private capacity as the *billionaire* Eastern merchant prince.

Upon forwarding my bill of lading—letter of introduction—I received instructions to proceed to Cairo by the express train, and there to report myself, on arrival, to Mr. B., who, independently of being associated with the Viceroy in mercantile pursuits, also holds the lucrative, yet by no means sinecure, appointments of Keeper of the Privy Purse and Purveyor General of His Highness's Households; for it must be observed that the Viceroy maintains numerous establishments, both at several palaces and harems.

After having visited every nook and corner of " *El Iskendereeyeh*," I proceeded to the railway-station, entered a first-class carriage, and was whirled away by the iron king *en route* for the capital. That journey has been so often described by abler pens than mine, that I shall merely give an account of my fellow-passengers and their conversation, which furnished me with an insight into the characters of many individuals with whom it was my fate afterwards to be mixed up.

Scarcely had I made myself comfortable in the carriage, when in stepped two gentlemen. Both were of middle age, most agreeable in manners, and rather chatty. The younger one was a Greek merchant, of the name of Xenos, who resided in Alexandria, and who was proceeding to Cairo, and thence up the Nile, to purchase cotton, which at that period was realizing most fabulous prices both in England and France. The other was much his senior: he was of the Jewish persuasion, and a native of the good city of Frankfort.

On our arrival at Tantah, where the annual fair was being held—and at which my two fellow-travellers assured me that slaves were sold in 186—, notwithstanding that there existed a treaty abolishing the slave-trade—the train was shunted off the line, to admit of the Viceroy's private despatch train passing on its route. Here we were detained twenty minutes; and as I watched that despatch train approach the terminus, thinking that I might be gratified with a glimpse of some of the Cabinet ministers, who I naturally concluded were seated in it, I was surprised at beholding the heads of several young ladies thrust out of the first-class carriage which was attached to the tender. My curiosity was considerably excited when I saw that their cast of countenance was either Levantine or German.   They wore no bonnets; long black veils were thrown carelessly over their heads; and they were attired in black *latarahs*.

Turning round to my fellow-passenger, Mr. Xenos— who sat, ruminating, perhaps, on the state of the cotton market, in the corner of the carriage nearest the main-line —I inquired of him why that train was designated " the Viceroy's private despatches."   He smiled, and said, " Well, I cannot exactly tell you; but, in all probability, it is because it is always appropriated for the purpose of conveying all fair damsels who may chance to come on *flying* visits to Ismael Pacha; and as foreign ladies are generally the very essence of intrigue, may it not be possible that they are the bearers of secret despatches?   But as it is not my province to unfold the mysteries of the Viceroy's private despatches, all I can say upon the subject is, that I hope that that courteous prince will enjoy the pleasure of their society."

The private despatch train rushed on at full speed, and we followed, about ten minutes afterwards, in its trail, at a snail's pace.

The ice having been broken between myself and my fellow-travellers, the conversation naturally led to the purport of my visit to the " Land of Dates " and its merchant ruler.   In reply to a few trivial questions I had put to the Greek merchant, Mr. Xenos very kindly explained to me that his twenty years' experience of life in Egypt led him to regard my position as one fraught with considerable perplexity; and, as I afterwards found that his observations were perfectly correct, I shall give them in detail, as their purport bears directly on Harem Life and the intrigues of the Egyptian Star-Chamber.

" But," added that amiable gentleman, " much depends upon the conduct of the Viceroy towards yourself, and that of his confidential advisers.   Perhaps I err in using that expression, for his Excellency Ismael Reschid Pacha, who is his confidential adviser, and a near relative, is, I am prone to believe, an upright Turk, who always has his hands full in counteracting the plots and machinations of the favorites and reputed partners of the billionaire merchant prince; for as Ismael Pacha receives you, so will His Excellency Reschid Pacha, his tried and faithful friend and relative, behave towards you.

"If you can manage to keep on good terms with that minister, all will go well with you; for no man in Egypt understands the difficulties of your position better than His Excellency, who has to combat in the day against all the arts and influences that are generally brought to bear upon the mind of the Viceroy at the reputed orgies which takes place at the Palace at night, when His Excellency is safely housed within the precincts of his own ' Abode of Bliss,' or very early in the morning, when Ismael Pacha—for he is up at the dawn of day—is steaming up the Nile at three or four o'clock, sitting on the sofa in the poop of one of his fairy-like yachts, smoking cigarettes, and sipping, not real Mocha, but full-bodied and refreshing Burgundy, though he be a *true believer*.

" It is the demeanor of the clique about his Highness and the reputed co-partners towards you, that I would have you watch and scrutinize most carefully. Life in the Harems of the Egyptian rulers has never been faithfully described by any authors, for the simple reason that no unbeliever has as yet been domiciled therein; to them it has been an unknown land, and one of myths; their pen-drawings, however, are far from encouraging, and the late lamented Dr. Abbott, who collected the most unique, most valuable, and perfect museum of Egyptian curiosities which the Americans possess, has left a very clever work, in which he describes them as being in his day 'the very focus of low intrigue, the scenes of profligacy of the most abhorrent nature, ah! and of crimes of the deepest dye;' but, thanks to the enlightenment of the age in which we live, a most wonderful and beneficial improvement has, I have been assured, taken place, even in those *sacred* places.

"The signification of the word *Harem*, is a perfect misnomer in our European acceptation of the expression, unless indeed we interpret it by its other and far more appropriate meaning, 'interdicted,' since it is considered by all Moslems as implying 'The Abode of Bliss,' and the type or model of that celestial paradise of houris, which the prophet Mahomet has inculcated into the minds of his followers will be their *Kishmet*, 'fate,' when they shall enter the seventh heaven in the world to come. Hence the reason why those monsters of men, those spectres of their sex, the chief eunuchs, are styled *Kislar Agaci*, 'the captain of the girls;' and also *Dar-us-seadet Agaci*, 'the guardian of the Abode of Bliss.'

"Besides, many of the recent Viceroys of Egypt finished their education in France, so that I am inclined to believe that a great amelioration has taken place of late years in their internal *ménage*; and Solyman Pacha the Magnificent introduced great innovations into the domestic habits and customs of the inmates of his Harem, as also among the manners and customs of the Princes themselves; and, if I am correctly informed, many of the late Pachas had not only their palaces furnished in the European style, but surrounded themselves with foreign attendants, and even had English nurses for their children. This is the case with Mustapha Pacha, the heir presumptive to the Viceroyship, who not only treats that person with respect, but contributes most liberally to all her wants and requirements *à la Européenne*; but then the manners, language, and habits of those domestics, could not have tended, in any beneficial degree, to ameliorate the characters of the children committed to their care, and none of them have been intelligent enough to give us an insight into Harem life. So I would fain trust that you will not find your position so unbearable as you may have led yourself to suppose.

"At all events you must keep yourself clear of the petty intrigues of the court cabals. Watch with a careful eye the manner in which the three Princesses, his Highness's wives behave towards you. Endeavor to gain, not only their respect and good opinion, but, what is of primary importance, *their confidence*, especially that of the mother of the young Prince; but, as she is only the second wife, she is not the Lady Paramount, for the first *épouse* claims that peroga- tive.

"Sad tales of the jealousy of Princesses in the Egyptian Harems have been circulated, and accurately too, as I can vouch for the veracity of my informant; so that it may be possible that, should you find it necessary to battle with his Highness's reputed associates to obtain European comforts about you, and to maintain your status as an English lady, the mere granting of those absolute necessaries for your in- dividual comfort, might arouse that green-eyed monster, jealousy, within their viceregal bosoms, as their entire igno- rance of your habits will make them regard such trivial attentions on the part of their liege lord and master as signs of his too pointed wish to become on terms of familiar inti- macy with you."

"Well done!" interrupted Mr. ——. "You are giving Madam a most truthful account of her position; but, my dear Xenos, you appear to forget that our fellow-traveller ought to learn to school her too-confiding mind to look upon the actions of all around her with the greatest distrust."

Then, addressing himself to me, he continued, "I would have you, Madam, alive to the well-established fact, that the whole *cotérie* into which you will be introduced is the very hot-bed of intrigue, jealousy, and corruption; but yet, let me trust, not of profligacy. The chief eunuch is generally supposed to possess absolute powers within the Harem, even over the Princesses; but as that all-powerful Egyptian, Prince *Baksheesh*, is the actual ruler of Egypt, you may take my word for it that most important personage is himself the abject slave of his reputed associates, for as long as they can command the favors of that omnipotent prince, and bask in the sunshine of viceregal smiles, to them is reported the sayings and doings of those 'caged birds' within the walls of the 'Abodes of Bliss.'

"I admit that your position as an English lady entitles you to receive every attention, yet at the same time you will be called upon to conform to many strange whims, fancies, and customs, which may appear most singular and outlandish to your European notions; nay, many may even seem quite repugnant to your naturally sensitive feelings; but you will, I hope, by the influence of your example, be able to graft a few civilized customs on their Arab and Turkish manners. Your apparent amiability of manner will, in all probability, cause you to be respected by the Viceroy, beloved by Grand Pacha Ibrahim, and esteemed by their Highnesses the three wives, and the Princesses their daughters. And no doubt your position will cause you to be feared by the slaves, among whom, I must caution you, commence those petty intrigues which have ruined favorites, gathered ruling concubines to their last accounts, led to the sudden disappearance, and, in many instances, most unaccountably strange deaths, of numerous vicreoys, who have falsely been reported to have died suddenly of apoplexy; to the unfastening of the bolts of the viceregal railway-trains; the poisoning of the dates that infant nephews have handed to their viceregal uncles : all these, and many more equally atrocious deeds, have been connected with the magic circle of a band of Harem slaves."

"I deeply regret," continued Mr. Xenos, "that any English lady should have accepted the appointment you have; and knowing, as I do, the strong antipathy that all Germans and Arabs entertain towards the English, I would strongly urge upon you, even at this the eleventh hour, the propriety of abandoning the idea of entering his Highness's service.

"In support of this suggestion I shall merely explain to you that I have resided many years both in Egypt and Constantinople, and from my dearly-bought experience of Egyptian and Turkish life, I lament that any European lady should contemplate domiciling herself within the influence of the viceregal Harem; for be assured that you will lack all the conveniences, much more the *agréments*, of a European residence. Ismael Pacha, Viceroy though he be, is a true merchant at heart, and squanders not away his *paras* in costly furniture for his wives. And yet you will find his palaces and yachts decorated in the most sumptuous style *à la Européenne*.

"That is not the only drawback that awaits you. The peculiar diet of the ' caged birds' of the Viceroy's Elsysium is literally *cuisine à l' Arabe*, which will be most unpalatable to your taste, even if it does not (of which I entertain great fears) prove most injurious to your health. The nature of the climate renders it obligatory on Europeans to imbibe much greater quantities of stimulants—such as pale ale and wine—than they have been accustomed to partake of in their own colder climate; and I do not imagine that those forbidden liquors, although quaffed so copiously by the Viceroy, will be provided for you. It is a well-known fact, that their Highnesses the wives drink quantities of Schiedam. Then again the entire atmosphere of the Harem and its grounds must necessarily be impregnated with the fumes of tobacco, into which powerful narcotics are introduced, so that the air which you will breathe will prove injurious to your constitution; besides, the loose and uncleanly habits of the attendants, more particularly those of the Arab nurses, will disgust you ; and the sad monotony of the daily life you will be called upon to lead will be of such a melancholy, convent-like nature, that in my opinion it were better far that you had immured yourself within the cell of a nunnery, than entered the precincts of a Harem."

I listened most attentively to Mr. Xenos's account of the difficulties of my position, and almost repented of having accepted the appointment ; still I could not help observing that I hoped he had overcolored the picture.

"Believe me," interrupted Mr. ——, "my friend has only given you a faint outline of Harem life in Egypt, and if anything, that delineation, dark as it appears to you, is really not overdrawn ; in fact, it falls short of the reality, even so far as we forbidden intruders into those castles of pleasure have hitherto been able to learn. You, who are about so soon to enter those 'sacred' recesses of viceregal life, will have an opportunity of judging of the correctness of my views on this head.

"I would, however, above all things, impress upon your mind the actual value which all Turks, Egyptians, Levantines, and (it is with feelings akin to shame that I affirm it) even Europeans who have been domiciled some time in the Ottoman dominions, entertain of the fair sex. They regard women, my dear madam, of every nation and of all grades in society, as the mere slaves to their sensual gratification. Hence the reason that they keep their wives, daughters, and concubines, caged up in lattice-windowed houses ; protect them by eunuchs, those atoms of mankind, whom they deprive of all social intercourse with the male sex and the outer world, and treat as abject slaves. Many erudite writers on Oriental life have gone so far as to question whether they are properly so termed, for it is certain that many of these guardians of the beauties of the East have married the wives of their lords and masters, whom they had previously sent to that 'bourne whence no traveller re-

2

turns '—and report adds, have even had large families by them.

"These remarks are not, however, so applicable to Harem life in Constantinople, as in Egypt; for, in the lovely-situated capital on the Bosphorus, the ladies of the Harems enjoy both carriage and caïque airing daily, and revel in a degree of freedom altogether unknown in Egypt. In the East the male sex think, as Butler has so naïvely expressed it in his burlesque poem of Hudibras :—

> "'Women first were made for men,
> Not men for them. It follows, then,
> That men have right to every one,
> And they no *freedom* of their own.'

"In Pharaoh's land, that sex, formed by the Creator of the Universe to become the solace and companion of the fallen sons of Adam, is prized by the stronger sex, whose duty it most unquestionably ought to be to protect them, only for the *price in gold* that they give or can obtain for them; they are viewed as marketable commodities, just as a chapman calculates the value of his bales of merchandize. Hence the reason why Turks and Egyptians will always remain semi-barbarians, until a radical change can be effected in their families by means of education, that slow but sure precursor of civilization.

"But most unhappily for the speedy amelioration of such a deplorable state of things, even Europeans, who have lived long in any part of the Ottoman dominions, imbibe the same laxity of morals and disreputable ideas." [Of the veracity of this assertion I had ample proof during my residence at Mr. B.'s, at Cairo, as there an acquaintance of that gentleman hesitated not to introduce into his apartment a person of most questionable character, at which I remonstrated, and threatened to return to Zech's Hotel, if such conduct was repeated.] "So that they hesitated not to tread in the footsteps of the votaries of the Koran, keep Harems, entrap European women into their clutches, and as calmly and coolly dispose of them, as if they had been born slaves.

"Would time permit, I could also disclose to you many instances of blank cheques, bonds, heavy mortgages on estates, most of which have been foreclosed, nay, most lucrative offices, under the Ottoman and Egyptian Governments, having been bartered away by licentious Egyptian and Turkish princes and millionaires, to unprincipled Europeans, for gems of female dots of humanity, many of whom, to their everlasting shame and degradation be it stated, even now rank as the *creme de la creme* of European society in the Ottoman dominions. Many are the instances I could enumerate of men, the scum of the earth, rising to enormous wealth, and holding high positions, both in Egypt and Turkey, by means of such infamy.

" The Crimean war produced a most baneful influence on the morals of the different Levantine populations of all grades. The requirements of the vast armaments that were concentrated there, brought untold sums of gold into the coffers of traders of all denominations. Prussian Jews, the very refuse of the good city of Frankfort, the Israelitish population of which is so celebrated for its craft, together with the scum of Italy, Spain, France, Malta, Greece, and the Levant, became suddenly enriched by that disastrous struggle. Many who at the commencement of that war were literally homeless, shoeless, and penniless, are now millionaires in Egypt—where they now roll about in their carriages, keep large establishments, live in *cuisine à l' Arbe*, and drink the choicest wines. Their tables, when laid out, would challenge the *chef-de-cuisine* of Gunter to make a handsomer appearance : the mouth of a *gourmand* would absolutely water at the sight of those inviting-looking viands. But be fully assured, kind reader, that the moment he tasted them, unless, indeed, he had been previously accustomed to Arab diet, he would become perfectly disgusted with those filthy messes. They keep large establishments, speculate in cotton, hold hundreds of bank, railway, and joint company shares, receive large deposits from Europeans, for which they give from twenty-five to thirty per cent. interest; and in short are the Hudsons of Egypt and the Ottoman Empire.

"Their banking operations are immense; the loans which they advance to the Arabs, who bury their gains in their Harems, instead of putting them out to interest, or using them to meet their current expenses, are most numerous and profitable. In short, these are the class of men who are all-powerful in Egypt; these are the reputed individuals who possess the contracts for every public work, from the opening of new railways down to the almost insignificant improvement of paving the roads of its ancient capital."

CHAPTER II.

"I HEARD you, my dear madam, complain of the manner in which you were jostled about on landing at Alexandria; how roughly the Custom-house officers examined your baggage, notwithstanding that they knew the position you came to hold?"

"Yes, indeed, I did, and can endorse the veracity of the statement made by a contributor to *Once a Week*, who most naïvely and truthfully asserts that 'The land of Egypt is ruled over by twenty Princes; one of whom is the Viceroy, eighteen of the others are known as Consuls-General of European nations, but the twentieth is the most powerful of all, and his name is Baksheesh ("Gift, Present, Bribery").

"'Very little, indeed, can be done without the aid or countenance of Baksheesh: *he* is the ruling power. Not a single package of a traveller's luggage (no, not even that belonging to the Governess of the Grand Pacha Ibrahim, the infant son of the Viceroy,) not a bale of goods can enter or be shipped out of the country without his leave; not a handful of cotton can leave it without paying him tribute.

" ' Do you want to set up a steam engine, to build a house, hire a lighter, to send goods off by train, to do something which you have no right to do, to get something which you have no right to get? Why, then, invoke Baksheesh; offer up a proper quantity of piastres on his shrine, and the thing is done. Imagine that you can get on without his aid, and you will soon find out your mistake. Put your faith in the most potent of his brother princes, and see how you will fare. Baksheesh will stop you in the corridor, as you approach the vice-regal presence, and if he frown, small profit will spring from your interview. Dodge past him, get your order, your permit, your judgment, concession, or what not, and the day of submission is but postponed. You can call spirits from the vasty deep, but will they come? Can you put what you have gained into execution, without the aid of Baksheesh? Not a bit of it. Let your own special "Prince" back up your petition, let the Viceroy grant it, let the Minister of State draw up the order, let the highest personage in the department be charged to carry it out on your behalf, and what have you got? Nothing—absolutely nothing. Get a firman from the sultan himself, and you are not any better off.

" ' Baksheesh has creatures, nominally filling some fifth-rate government post, any of whom can put a spoke in your wheel. Baksheesh is the very essence of bribery and corruption, and without his aid nothing can be done. As the Nile water is to the land, so is bribery and corruption to the rulers and people of Egypt. Nothing is produced without it.',

" Exactly so, madam," interrupted the Greek merchant, laughing most heartily. " That writer has hit the nail upon the right head, and I strongly suspect that he must have had considerable experience in Her Britannic Majesty's court at Alexandria, so admirably and faithfully does he describe the state of things in Egypt in this the nineteenth century. But come, ——, as I am quite certain that sooner or later our fair traveller will be brought in contact with the firm of —— at Cleopatra's ancient capital when next she returns thereto, if not with some of their partners at Cairo, pray give us a brief sketch of the autobiography of those reputed Rothschilds, as they have been, and most assuredly will be again, mixed up with many an intrigue of Harem Life."

"Well, as I trust that you will pardon the prolixity of my sketches of Egypt as it is, I will use my best endeavors to give you as graphic a sketch as possible of the eminent financiers of Egypt. They were born and bred in the pretty village of Oppenheim, on the banks of the far-famed Rhine. For years they struggled on, fighting the battle of life, and managed during the Crimean war to follow the occupation of suttlers in the British camp at Balaklava. There they drove a most lucrative trade, and greatly contributed to the comforts of our officers and soldiers. At a time when the British commissariat was in the most frightful disorder, the younger members of the firm might be seen driving their wagons about the camp in all directions; hence the reason that they are such 'good whips.' I remember a commissariat officer now resident in Egypt telling me that the Commander-in-Chief, Lord Raglan, had rated him pretty handsomely because he had allowed —— wagons to blockade, as it were, the leading thoroughfare in the camp. There they accumulated vast sums by selling pale ale, wines, and spirits.

"At the close of the Crimean war they hurried off to Egypt, and having been so fortunate as to attract the notice of Ismael Pacha, the Viceroy, that Prince is reported to have lent them a few thousands, and finding them thorough men of business, always intent upon making cent. per cent., they became his reputed associates in mercantile pursuits. The wealth which they had accumulated soon gave them a standing in the European commercial world; Egyptian loans were forced into the markets of London and Paris by their skill, tact, and manœuvring; that stock maintained its price. Then came the cotton mania. Taking advantage of the American civil war, they induced the Viceroy to plant cotton extensively; and by means of His Highness's command of forced labor, railway and telegraph communication, steam navigation on the Nile, taking forcible possession of the Nile boats, lighters, weighers; having orders issued to the Sheiks to lay heavy impositions on the lightermen, laborers, carmen, donkeymen; depriving the steamboat agents of the laborers whom they had procured at most fabulous wages, to the detriment of the interest of the whole of the legitimate commercial community of Egypt, both native and European; they raised the private fortune of Ismael Pacha from £600,000 per annum to upwards of two to two millions and a half pounds sterling.

"Their success as His Highness's private financiers (for none of them hold any appointments under the Egyptian government, but into the favor of all whose officials they have ingratiated themselves; of course their propitiation of the sovereign ruler of Egypt, Prince Baksheesh, has tended to place them upon a friendly footing with all parties, except the mercantile community, with whom they are generally at 'daggers drawn'), has been most amply rewarded, for they are reputed to be associated with His Highness not merely in his mercantile pursuits, but also to enjoy the benefit of the concessions that the Viceroy has made of railways, contracts for improving the city of Alexandria, the purchase of steam-boats, machinery, making roads, paving streets, forming steamboat navigation companies, forming existing railways, post offices, opening banks, &c., in nearly all of which His Highness, as plain Ismael Pacha, holds the greater number of shares. Independently of this, they are the purveyors to the Harems of all European condiments, and the miscellaneous medley of costly articles both of jewelry, china, clothing, &c., used therein, a monoply which is a fortune of itself. They have branch houses all over the Continent.

"The head of the firm, a gentleman of the Jewish persuasion, is much respected in the circle in which he moves. He, however, takes but little interest in the business of the house, and may therefore be looked upon as a sleeping or travelling partner, as he is like a locomotive engine, always on the move. His son, who generally resides in Alexandria, is the prop of the establishment. His manner is abrupt, curt, and anything but courteous to the fair sex, and he is an excellent man of business. He may most appropriately be termed the Viceroy's 'civil' aide-de-camp, if I may be allowed to coin the expression. He is disliked by the whole of the European mercantile community, whose interest he is continually thwarting.

"The member of the firm who passes the greater portion of his time on the banks of sapphire-looking Bosphorus, is one of the finest specimens of a Prussian Jew you can imagine. His look, shrewdness, and countenance, remind one most forcibly of

'The Jew that Shakespeare drew.'

He is the very impersonation of Shylock. Measure them all well by the standard I have given you; for their aim is to make a profit out of everything, to turn to account any article and baggage that comes into their net.

"These are the reputed associates of the Viceroy in his private capacity as Ismael Pacha, the merchant prince; and yet their influence is fortunately counteracted, in a slight degree, by the jus* and upright concessions of His Excellency Reschid Pacha, whose position is not a very enviable one, but on whom falls ALL the malignity that ought to be laid upon her shoulders. The ——, it is reported, have often aided the Viceroy in many private transactions when he was plain Ismael Pacha, and since his accession to the government; hence the reason of their possessing such influence over the son of the gallant Ibrahim Pacha, whose money-getting and avaricious propensities he inherits in a most remarkable degree.

"As Mr. —— seldom or ever visits the Viceroy, for why or wherefore we know not, unless it is because he is of the Hebrew persuasion, the abomination of the Turk, who will tolerate the intrusion of a Giaour, but not that of any Copek *dog* of an Israelite, in whose presence he feels himself defiled; for though —— may think, like Shylock, and say; ' Hath not a Jew hands, organs, dimensions, affections, passions ?   Fed with the same food, hurt with the same means, subject to the same diseases, healed by the same means, warmed and cooled by the same winter and summer as a Christian ? '—still His Highness most unquestionably considers, as all orthodox Ottomans do, that ' Dgehennum will be the portion of that accursed race, as there is but one Allah,' and therefore always kept his reputed but *trusty* friend and long-headed private counsellor at a respectful distance from him.

"As you have a letter of introduction to Mr. ——, of Cairo, I will make you *au fait* with the position of that gentleman. He is one of the Viceroy's oldest friends, but has, unfortunately, allowed his influence with His Highness to be supplanted by ——, and is therefore a *mere tool* in the hands of the clever young man. He is of Arab and Greek parentage; avarice and parsimony are his characteristics; and yet, had he been free from the thraldom of the firm I have mentioned, he would have been more respected."

Just as Mr. —— had finished his description of His Highness's associates, the collector opened the door of the carriage, took our tickets, and we alighted at the Cairo terminus. Thanking my two agreeable companions for their attention and information, I accepted their offer to accompany them to Zech's Hotel, which we soon reached, but experienced some difficulty in procuring the accommodation we required, as the whole establishment was in confusion, owing to rather an amusing incident which had just occurred there.

It appeared that an elderly French gentleman, whom I met afterwards at Pistoja, in Italy, had been staying there some time. During his sojourn, he had amused himself by travelling up the Nile, and into the interior of Egypt, in search of antiquities.

On one of these excursions he fell accidentally into the company of an Italian and Arab commissioner, to whom he stated his desire to become possessed of a mummy, perfect in every respect. Both expressed their doubts as to the possibility of his being able to procure such a specimen of frail humanity ; but upon his offering them the magnificent sum of six hundred sovereigns, they replied, after a short deliberation, that they would do their best to accomplish his commission.

It happened just at that time that an Italian apothecary, residing in the suburbs of Cairo, had died ; and the two rogues, taking advantage of that event, hastily repaired to the abode of the defunct. They represented to the old housekeeper who had superintended his frugal *ménage* that they had received instructions from his friends at Pisa—for he was the scion of an old noble family there—that he should be interred in the Catholic cemetery. By that means they gained possession of the body of the dispenser of drugs. They then procured the co-operation of a professional embalmer, who, steeping rags in those aromatic spices so well known to the Egyptians, bound the body up, and most skillfully formed it into a mummy. A case was then procured, on which was painted numerous hieroglyphics, *fac-similes* of those that are usually found on such antiquities.

Leaving their "treasure trove" at the residence of the deceased, they bent their way back to Cairo, proceeded to the hotel, and communicated to their unsuspicious dupe that they had discovered, in a village on the banks of the Nile, in Upper Egypt, a mummy, in a most perfect state of preservation, and which they had had transported to a hut in the village of Geezeh ; at the same time offering to conduct the antiquarian to inspect the same, prior to the bargain being concluded. The antiquarian accompanied the two commissioners, quite delighted at the prospect of being able to obtain the prize he had sought for with such research.

On the party arriving at the hut,—for the *morgue,* " dead-house," could scarcely be deemed worthy of any other designation,—Monsieur C., the antiquarian, examined the mummy most minutely once or twice. It seemed to him that the body was wrapped in linen which, although naturally very much discolored by the process of embalming, bore evident marks of modern manufacture ; and, turning round to his companions, he remarked that the cloth seemed to have been but recently wrapped about the different parts that he had examined. But' they explained to him that it was always customary to re-wrap any parts off which the linen had fallen or decayed away, with new pieces steeped in newly-prepared aromatics. The antiquarian examined the fingers, then the toes, and next the head ; all of which members he found in a remarkably fine state of preservation.

He then arranged that the commissioners should procure a case, have the mummy placed in it, and he would afterwards return with them, and see the treasure screwed down in its outer shell. Thus taking, as he imagined, every precaution that no deception could be practised upon him, by the substitution of any weighty substance being placed in the case in lieu of the "treasure-trove," he left the wily commissioners to arrange the matter ; and, after the lapse of a few hours, they all returned to the hotel at Cairo, where they sat down to a well-spread repast, quite delighted with the bargain each had made.

Three days afterwards, the two crafty commissioners called upon the antiquarian, and informed him that the case was quite ready to be screwed down, and begged him to accompany them to Geezeh, which he did. Then he had the satisfaction to see the mummy placed in the case, securely locked, directed, corded, and placed in a country *araba* (cart), after which they returned to the hotel.

In four days afterwards, the mummy was safely deposited in a spare room at Zech's, the six hundred sovereigns paid down in hard cash to the two rogues of commissioners, whom the dupe regaled with a most sumptuous luncheon, with copious libations of sparkling iced champagne.

Monsieur C. now amused himself by visiting all the different curiosities in Cairo, and as the time drew near for his departure for Pistoja, near Florence, he one morning entered the room in which the case was deposited, with the intention of nailing the address of his correspondent at Leghorn upon it. His olfactory nerves were assailed with such an offensive effluvia on his entrance therein, that he became quite electrified ; at first he thought that the disgusting odor proceeded from the bodies of some rats who might have been crushed to death in one of the drains. He approached the case, when the smell became much more offensive ; still, not thinking for a moment that it proceeded from the mummy, he unlocked it, but re-locked it in the twinkling of an eye, for the powerful and offensive effluvia gas emitted therefrom left him no doubt as to the fact that a recently deceased body had been embalmed in well-saturated aromatic rags !

and then he became fully alive to the trick that the two rogues of commissioners had played him.

It was bad enough to have been victimized of so large a sum, but he had no desire to become the laughing-stock of the Caireens, or to have the expense of interring the body, so he hastily locked the chamber, packed his "*penates*," paid his "*note*," told the headwaiter (for Mr. Zech was absent at the time) that he should return in a few days, as he was only going to Alexandria for a week. He then put himself into the train and reached that port just in time to take his passage by the Italian steamer bound for Ancona. Previous to his departure he forwarded a small parcel containing the key of the "*morgue*," to Mr. Zech, who had to incur the expense of the Italian apothecary's interment.

Through the kind attention of Mr. Xenos, I was shown up into an apartment. Hastily changing my travelling costume, I hurried off in a carriage to present my letter of introduction to Mr. B., but not finding him at home, as he had been summoned to attend the Viceroy at Boulac, I returned to the hotel. I had scarcely begun to unpack my *penates* when a waiter informed me that Mr. B. had sent his carriage to fetch me. Thereupon I requested him to bring my bill; and guess my astonishment when, in exchange for the Bank of England note which I had handed to him, he handed me not as I expected, the change in English or French money, but the following miscellaneous coins, viz., five and ten franc pieces, Spanish pillar dollars, several Russian coins of unknown names, valued at three francs each, francs, shillings, florins, Sardinian liras, half liras, Austrian quarter florins, together with a complete miscellany of smaller coins, both copper and silver, most admirably fitted for the cases of a private museum ; together with a collection of Egyptian, Turkish, Indian, and Arab coins ! Such is the change currently given for European gold pieces throughout the whole length and breadth of

Egypt, save and except in the Harems, where the gold effigy of her Majesty Queen Victoria and the Emperor Napoleon III. are the circulating medium.   So, taking a small travelling bag in my hand, I proceeded to the banker's, very loth to be hurried off in that unceremonious manner, after my journey from Alexandria, under the scorching heat of an Egyptian sun, and the *désagrémens* of whirlwinds of sand.

CHAPTER III.

ENTERING the brougham which stood at the door of the hotel, I was soon driven to Mr. B.'s residence, situated in the vicinity of the Esbekeeh Square.   It was a spacious, modern, stone-built three-storied house, having a good-sized balcony in front, which commanded a view of the square and its insignificant gardens.   The lower floor, or basement, was used as the bank and the upper part as the dwelling. The whole was furnished in the European style in an unostentatious yet comfortable manner.   The banker's establishment was upon a very limited scale, and consisted of a German housekeeper, black page, Arab cook, coachman and grooms. His mistress was a short, thickset, ugly Arab slave girl, about sixteen years of age, named Fatima, whom he had purchased when she was very young.

Mr. B. received me most courteously, apologized for having hurried me away from the hotel, but informed me that His Highness Ismael Pacha, the Viceroy, had requested that I should become his guest until the apartments were ready for my reception in the Harem.

I remonstrated at this arrangement, as I did not think it quite prudent that I should remain in the house of a bachelor who had his mistress under the same roof, and urged the expediency of my being allowed to return to Zech's.

This, however, Mr. B. overruled, by stating that, as he was a man of business and seldom at home, I should be well cared for by his German housekeeper, Clara, who would attend to all my requirements; besides, the Viceroy had particularly requested him to desire me not to form any acquaintances in Cairo. I therefore yielded to his persuasions, and there I remained almost in durance vile for a month, during which period I received every attention and respect.

Scarcely, however, had a few days passed, than I began to discover that my freedom of action was curtailed, and that I was as much a prisoner in my new abode as any surbordinate officer is when his commanding officer has placed him under arrest. I must confess that I was quite taken aback at being so unceremoniously deprived of my liberty. During the whole of that period I was obliged to vegetate *en cuisine à l' Arabe.* Fortunately, however, the kind Clara brought me a cup of coffee and a small roll early in the morning, but without any butter, which condiment I never tasted during the whole period I remained in the service of the Viceroy, none having ever been placed upon my table.

My breakfast was served me in my own room, at twelve P. M. and which, together with my dinner, at six P. M., consisted of the following *carte:*—

Soup, made of mutton, with strings of vermicelli floating in it. Rice, boiled plain, and served up with tomato sauce. —Boiled mutton (for beef, lamb, or veal, was *never* served up to me), of which soup had been made. A dish composed of tomatoes, with the insides scooped out, and filled with boiled rice and minced mutton. Boiled chicory, chopped up in imitation of spinach *à la Française.*

The whole of these dishes were absolutely swimming in fat.

Roast mutton, dried up to a chip.

No pastry, cheese, or malt liquor.

The dessert consisted of oranges, preserved and candied fruits.

Sauterne and claret wines.

Coffee was served up *à la Turque*, in small transparent *findjaus*, china cups, as small as egg-cups, placed in silver *zurfs*.

Of these refreshments I invariably partook alone, as Mr. B. never favored me with his company, being generally occupied in business, or else from home in attendance on the Viceroy, who is almost invariably accompanied by one of his associates in commerce, whether steaming up the Nile, or lounging at any of his palaces, as the Harems are all situated at some distance from the Viceregal residences.

After having submitted to this incarceration for several weeks I complained to Mr. B. of the diet; but the only answer I received was, that he regretted his inability to effect any alteration. Finding that my health was suffering from it, and the want of proper exercise, I requested to be allowed carriage airing, which was granted me immediately the other English lady—who had arrived previous to my coming out to Cairo—had taken her departure for Europe.

A few days after I had taken up my residence at the banker's, Mr. B. entered my room, and informed me, that if I would step out into the balcony about six o'clock, I should have an opportunity of catching a glimpse of the Viceregal family, as Ismael Pacha generally took a drive about that time.

Feeling naturally anxious to see what kind of individuals the Viceregal party were, I moved the easy chair into the balcony at the hour named. Scarcely had I been seated there ten minutes, when I observed a handsome European-built carriage, drawn by four noble-looking English horses, with postilions on their backs, advancing towards the banker's. The blue silk blinds of the carriage-windows were only half drawn down, which enabled me to obtain a good view of the Viceregal party. Its occupants consisted of the Viceroy, the Princess Epouse (the mother of the Prince), and the Grand Pacha Ibrahim.

As the *cortége* drew near Mr. B.'s, Ismael Pacha looked up at the balcony, smiled, and displayed his fine set of teeth. The Princess Epouse did likewise; while my *protégé* never moved his eyes off the packet of *bonbons*, out of which he was busily engaged in selecting those that pleased his palate best.

As the glimpse I caught of the party was but momentary, I had not time to scrutinize their features.

———————•◆•———————

CHAPTER IV.

THE next morning, Mr. B. introduced me to the Messrs. H., who, after having alluded to the vague contract that I had entered into with His Highness's agent in London, inquired of me if I were willing to enter the Harem; to which I merely replied, "Most certainly, as my object in coming out to Egypt was to take charge of the young prince; and I was quite prepared to enter on the duties of my appointment."

"Well, then, madam," replied Mr. H., "I think it necessary that I should explain to you the reason why you were spirited away, as it seemed to you from Zech's. It was owing to another English lady being resident there at the time. I cannot tell you exactly how it occurred, but Miss T. was so badly advised as to pay a visit to the Harem of Said Pacha, the late Viceroy; which imprudence, having come to His Highness's notice, he forthwith declined to allow her to take charge of the prince, and requested our mutual friend, Mr. B., to have the kindness to give up a part of his residence for your accommodation; as he did not wish that you should form any acquaintances at the hotel or associate with a lady who had so far forgotten herself as to 'peep and pry' into other Harems.

3

"Now, as that affair is finally disposed of no further restraint will be imposed upon you, and you are at liberty to take whatever carriage exercise you may think proper. My chief object, however, in calling upon you this morning, is to inform you what duties will be required of you. As you are necessarily ignorant of the manners and customs of Egypt, I must mention that the Viceroy labors under the delusion that he will be poisoned.

"The young Prince will be placed entirely under your charge. You must never lose sight of him; for it will undoubtedly appear strange to your unorientalized mind but, nevertheless, it is a fact, that apprehensions are also entertained that poison will be attempted to be administered to the boy, who is about five years old, in some form or other. So that he must never be left alone, nor be allowed to partake of any food which has not been previously tasted by the *Hekim Bachi*, 'Viceregal Doctor.' Besides, the Viceroy wishes that the lady, to whom he confides the charge of the Grand Pacha Ibrahim, should *never* quit the precincts of the Viceregal domains, without His Highness's special permission. That, however, you must understand, is but a mere matter of form, as you will always be able to obtain leave of absence whenever you desire to visit Cairo.

The Viceroy, with that forethought which characterizes him, has requested me to state, that as he considers his London agent has acted too parsimoniously in the matter of the pecuniary recompense named in the contract, he suggests that the stipend be doubled; that a fresh agreement should be drawn up; that the period should be extended to three years, and that the sum advanced should be allowed you in part payment of your outfit."

I replied, "That I was quite sensible of His Highness's kind offer; but that I could not possibly think of binding myself for any longer period than two years; and, besides, I requested that a clause should be inserted therein, so that in case of ill health, I might be able to resign the appointment."

"Most assuredly," replied Mr. H., "there cannot be the slightest objection to such an amendment; and our mutual friend, Mr. B., will have the contract drawn up forthwith; and as soon as the apartments in the Harem are ready for your occupation, he will kindly see you installed therein. As I am going to Constantinople, some members of my family there being rather seriously indisposed, I wish you good morning, trusting that I shall have the pleasure of seeing you on my return; or at Constantinople, should you accompany Her Highness the Princess Epouse to that city in the summer." Saying which, he, together with Mr. B took their departure.

Day after day passed away, and still I could learn no intelligence when it was probable that I should be installed in my office. The only reply that I could get to my inquiries was, that the apartments were not ready. The monotony of my daily life, the surveillance which was kept over all my actions, the want of a little social intercourse with Europeans, and the constant use of Arab diet, began to tell sadly upon my constitution; and at times I felt half inclined to resign that post, the duties of which I had not even entered upon.

After a great deal of perseverance I obtained a slight alteration in my diet, by the occasional change of boiled mutton for a little chicken broth, the chicken being served up whole after having been boiled in the soup; some potatoes, most wretchedly cooked, and a dish of mutton chops burned up to a cinder, and as hard as leather, without a spoonful of gravy or sauce of any kind. Fortunately, I had taken the precaution to bring out with me a small library of books, and in the hurry of my departure had left a little needlework to be finished, or else I really must have died of *ennui*.

For upwards of twenty days I was doomed to pass my

existence in that senseless, unprofitable manner.   True it is, that in the cool of the evening I took carriage exercise, which gave me an opportunity of examining every nook and corner of Cairo and its immediate vicinity.   At the end of about three weeks another of the Messrs. H. whom I will designate as Mr. C. H., called upon Mr. B., had an interview with me, and seemed quite surprised that the Viceroy had not sent for me to enter the Harem.   In the conversation that he had with Mr. B. he went so far as to express his opinion that Ismael Pacha must have forgotten my existence; and notwithstanding that Mr. B. informed him that His Highness was quite aware of my being his guest, and that my apartments were not yet fitted up, he flew off at a tangent, went poste-haste to the Viceroy, and on is return told me that I must go then and there into the Harem.

The abruptness and authoritative tone of his manner were something new to me.   I had not been accustomed to receive such treatment at the hand of persons of even exalted rank in my own country, about whose presence I had been brought up, and my sensitive feelings naturally rebelled at such behavior.   Stifling my anger, I coolly and calmly replied, that, as it was my Sabbath, I should most certainly not enter the Harem on that day, but that I would be ready to obey His Highness's behest on the morrow.

I was sorry to quit the hospitable roof of the banker, where I should have been exceedingly comfortable had Mr. B. only taken the precaution to have had my meals served from Zech's Hotel, as then I could have lived on European and not Arab diet, to the constant use of which latter my health eventually succumbed.

CHAPTER V.

I ROSE early on the morrow, and yet my spirits felt depressed. Mr. B. visited me, and expressed his deep regret that he was prevented from accompanying me to the Palace, as he was obliged to proceed to Alexandria; at the same time adding; "I could not possibly have escorted you beyond the precincts of the chief eunuch's apartments. As you must necessarily be quite ignorant of the importance of those officials in the Harem, especially the Grand Eunuch, who, by virtue of his office, amasses most fabulous sums of money, I will give you a brief account of them.

"Many of them become important personages in the country, hold high offices in the State, and even those who do not attain to such rank possess great influence. They are generally mounted upon richly-caparisoned Arab horses, the saddles and bridles of which are embroidered with gold. The horse wears around his neck, like an amulet, two silver wild-boar handspikes, with the points reversed, which form a crescent, and which are thought to possess the power of guarding the rider from the '*Evil Eye!*'" They are remarkably proud and haughty in their bearing, even when only of inferior rank; tenacious of the power they possess over the women of the Harems to which they are attached, and which authority they hesitate not to abuse or modify according to their individual appreciation of each lady's merits or demerits, which they calculate according to the quantity of *baksheesh* that each fair Peri hands them. They are exceedingly avaricious, and consider wealth must be acquired by any means, no matter however questionable; so that the majority of them are very rich. Their infirmity of body makes them despise all mortals, but especially women; so that it is a source of gratification for them to tyrannize over them as despotically as they can. Still, their love of the 'mammon of unrighteousness,' their idolatry of gold, makes them subservient to that all-potent sovereign Prince Baksheesh.

"Their contempt for the whole race of mortals is proverbial, but especially for all 'dogs of Christians.' You must have remarked, as they ride along upon their prancing Arab steeds, with what disdain they look down upon the passers-by. No Asiatic prince could possibly treat his subjects with greater imperiousness. I remember your asking me, one day, the name of that stately eunuch whom you noticed ride past my house last week, on a beautiful milk-white Arab. I cannot do better than narrate his history to you. He is called Dafay, is free, and is a millionaire; but how he acquired his wealth may appear to you a mystery. I will enlighten you on that point.

"There are exceptions to all rules, so that Dafay never was a woman-hater; on the contrary, like many of his race, he respects, nay, loves them. I know for certain that he has at the present time several female slaves in his service, one of whom ranks as his *ikbal* ('favorite'), and she is dressed and waited upon like a princess. She is mistress of the Harem of her fond and jealous husband; the apartments in which are furnished in grand style; nay, quite equal to any of the private apartments of the Viceroy.

"Well, I now come to his antecedents. He belonged to a very rich Bey (Colonel), who, being partial to him, placed him at the head of his Harem. The Bey had two legitimate wives, who lived together in the most cordial manner, and contributed reciprocally to their master's happiness. Dafay fell violently in love with one of them, and what is still more extraordinary, his passion was returned. It was, therefore, very natural that he should show *that* wife most marked attention, and neglect or tyrannize over the other. It is not necessary that I relate their quarrels and peccadilloes; suffice it to add, that the eunuch and his *inamorata* laid a snare for the other wife, and then, as an excuse that she had committed adultery with one of the Bey's servants who had left, Dafay stabbed her; but I have heard it stated that he actually allowed his *chère amie* to have the satisfaction of destroying her rival herself. What the Bey said on his return home I could never learn. Certain however, it is that the whole affair was hushed up, and that the eunuch, instead of losing his master's good graces, as might have been expected, rose higher in his favor.

"Not long afterwards the Bey died, having made a will, in which he bequeathed all his property to his faithful Dafay. At the time of his decease, many ugly reports were circulated, although the will was perfectly legal, and the Bey's death very sudden. Many of the gossips of Cairo state, that the eunuch became jealous of his master; that he coveted his wife, whom he loved most passionately; and that, as he had already committed one crime for her, he threatened to denounce her, unless she put her husband out of the way. An Asiatic's love stops at nothing, and he spares no cost to attain his ends. The mysterious doings in the Harems are generally enveloped in impenetrable darkness. It is utterly impossible for the Minister of Justice at any time to move in such delicate affairs.

"Shortly afterwards Dafay married the widow, and disbursed the 'talaris' (money) of the deceased with no niggardly hand. It is rumored that he is fearfully jealous; but not a syllable is ever uttered for or against his wife. They have a numerous family, and that fact speaks volumes with regard to all eunuchs."

I found that the duties of the Viceregal Grand Eunuch were almost legion. Independent of his daily attendance upon their Highnesses, he read prayers to his staff of attendants and the whole corps of eunuchs; the younger of whom he instructed, not only in their duties, but also in reading and transcribing the Koran. Many a time and oft

I have heard him, when passing his apartment, as Dr. Herbelot has so admirably expressed it, "reading the blessed Koran, with the seven different readings, and telling how seven different messengers were sent, at seven different times, to bring seven handfuls of seven different sorts of oil from seven stages of the earth; she (the earth) refusing all the seven messengers, for she said, 'I consent not that Allah make so bad a thing as man.'"

I found all these spectres of men most particularly anxious to obtain every information they could as to the manners and customs of us unbelievers; for whom, however, in their hearts they have the most sovereign contempt; and yet from all of them, but especially the *Kislar Agaci*, I received the most marked attention, courtesy, and respect. Not the slightest approach to any display of familiarity, or any overbearing behavior, was manifested towards me.

On the contrary, they were ever ready to discharge my commands with alacrity and fidelity. And yet I never propitiated them with *baksheesh*, though I have seen *my* Princess put purses of sovereigns in the hands of the Grand Eunuch, as their Highnesses had expressly forbidden me to place any offering on the shrine of that all-potent sovereign ruler of Egypt; so that, instead of finding those phantoms of men the crabbed, disagreeable apparitions I had been led to believe them, I had the pleasure of experiencing from them every politeness and civility.

So far as lie in their power and they could understand me, they supplied all my exigencies, notwithstanding that I was a Hawajee—a daughter of that accursed race, one of the banished Peris from their celestial Paradise, the Prophet's *seventh* heaven; and yet that erudite German Orientalist, Rückert, tells us that the true Moslem believes that

> "In the nine heavens are *eight* paradises?
> Where is the ninth one? In the human breast.
> Only the blessed dwell in the paradises,
> But blessedness dwells in the human breast.

> Created creatures are in the paradises,
> The uncreated Maker in the breast.
> Rather, O man! want these eight paradises,
> Than be without the ninth one in thy breast.
> Given to thee are those eight paradises,
> When thou the ninth one hast within thy breast."

All the inmates of the Harems believe that when young children die, they are turned into the flowers with which Paradise is decorated, and that birds and all animals are the spirits of their lost friends,—except dogs, which are spirits of the departed Israelites and unbelievers; hence the reason that they never allow them to caress them, or to become domiciled with them.

Having returned the banker my most grateful thanks for his kindness and attention, I entered his elegant brougham, and, accompanied by his page, who seated himself on the box with the coachman, we proceeded along an excellent road to the banks of the Nile, opposite Ghezire. There I alighted, and was handed into one of the Viceregal barges by the coachman, at the stern of which was a small cabin, into which I descended by two steps; around it was a divan, covered with red and white damask. It was manned by twelve Arab boatmen, dressed like the ordinary Arabs, but wearing turbans. The Viceregal standard, the everlasting crescent, floated at the stem and stern. On they rowed most vigorously, and, in less than ten minutes, I was landed at the stairs of the Harem.

The building is a very plain structure, the exterior of which is painted like the trunks of the trees at the Dutch model village of Broeck. In appearance it resembles the letter E, and is a large pile composed of five blocks of buildings. Proceeding to the one which faced the Nile, I entered *The Harem* (" sacred "), passed through a small door—the grating sounds of whose huge rusty hinges still seem to creak in my ears like the grinding of the barrel-organ of an itinerant Italian or Savoyard—which led into a courtyard, at that time lined, not with a corps of the Egyptian infantry, with their shrill brass band playing opera airs, but with a group of hard-working Fellahs and Arabs, toiling away like laborers in the London docks, and rolling into that immense space hundreds of bales of soft Genoa velvets, the costliest Lyons silks, rich French satins, most elegantly designed muslins, fast, gaudy-colored Manchester prints, stout Irish poplins, the finest Irish linens, Brussels, Mechlin, Valenciennes, Honiton, and imitation laces, Nottingham hose, French silk stockings, French and Coventry ribbons, cases of the purest Schiedam, pipes of spirits of wine, huge cases of fashionable Parisian boots, shoes, and slippers, immense chests of *bonbons*, in magnificent fancy-worked cases, boxes, and baskets, bales of *tombeki*, and the bright golden-leaved tobacco of Istambol (Constantinople); Cashmere, India, French, and Paisley shawls, of the most exquisite designs; baskets of pipe-bowls, cases of amber mouth-pieces, cigarette papers, and a whole host of miscellaneous packages, too various to enumerate, of other commodities, destined for the use of the inmates of that vast conservatory of beauty—all supplied by His Highness's partners. For, be it known to you, gentle reader, that the Viceroy of Egypt may most appropriately be styled, *par excellence*, the Sinbad of the age, the merchant prince of the terrestrial globe; but full well

> "He knows he cannot his treasure with him take,
> When forced of life's bright feast an end to make;
> His wealth then thus he gives away,
> To his lovely consorts day by day."

Here I was received by two young eunuchs, one of whom was attired in a light drab uniform, embroidered with silk of the same color. The other wore a similar costume, but of red. Both "sported" fezes. They salaamed me most respectfully in the Oriental manner, by putting their fingers to their lips, then to the heart, and finished by touching their foreheads.

I was then ushered through another door, the portals of which were also guarded by a group of eunuchs, similarly attired, but whose uniforms were most costly embroidered. Their features were hideous and ferocious; their figures corpulent, and carriage haughty.

They also salaamed me in the most approved Oriental style. Thence passing along a marble passage I entered a large stone hall, which was supported by huge granite pillars, which led me to the grand staircase, where I was received by the Chief Eunuch, who is called *Kislar Agaci*, "the captain of the girls," and sometimes *Darus-seadet Agaci*, "the guardian of the Mansion of Bliss."

This giant spectre of a man (for he was upwards of six feet high), who quite belied his caste, for he was a pleasing, affable, yet noble-looking personage, having a most diminutive head, almost as tiny as that of the great master of English composition, De Quincey, the celebrated writer of "The Confessions of an Opium Eater" (and who like that marvellous genius, I soon found out, had a mania for eating and smoking narcotics), advanced towards me, made his salaam, and ushered me, the *hated*, despised Giaour, into the noble marble hall of the Harem, which was then for the first time polluted by the footsteps of the unbeliever. The scene around me was so singular and strange, that I paused to contemplate it. The hall was of vast dimensions, supported by beautiful porphyry pillars, and the marble floor was covered with fine matting. I was now handed over to the Lady Superintendent of the slaves — a very wealthy woman, about twenty-four years of age, with fine dark blue eyes, aquiline nose, large mouth, and of middle stature.

She was attired in a colored muslin dress and trousers, over which she wore a quilted lavender-colored satin paletot. Her head was covered with a small blue gauze handkerchief, tied round it, and in the centre of the forehead, tucked up under it, a lovely natural dark red rose. She wore a beautiful large spray of diamonds, arranged in the form of the flower "forget me not," which hung down like three tendrils below her ear on the left side. Large diamond drops were suspended from her ears, and her fingers were covered with numerous rings, the most brilliant of which were a large rose pink diamond, and a beautiful sapphire. Her feet were encased in white cotton stockings and black patent leather Parisian shoes. Her name was Anina; and she had formerly been an *Ikbal,* "favorite." Beside her were grouped a host of slaves, all of whom appeared to be Arabs, and whose condition approximates to that of domestic servants in Europe, with this difference, that they cannot quit the precincts of the Harem without permission, but which is often given to them to go shopping, which they do unaccompanied by any of the eunnchs.

They are often sent to schools: some of them can read Arabic and Turkish—none, however, can write. As a general rule, they are condemned to *celibacy,* but it frequently happens that they are freed, given away in marriage, and, most horrible to relate, instances have been known of their having been united to their *own* children. They amass great wealth, by dint of hoarding up the *baksheesh* which has been distributed to them on grand occasions. The black slaves, who are chiefly natives of Nubia and Ethiopia, are generally employed in the mean and laborious duties of the household. They never obtain their liberty, but pass their old age in a state of idleness. The nurses to the Vice-royal family are an exception, since they are invariably emancipated, and many of them often marry some of the slaves who are engaged in the out-door work.

The Lady Superintendent now took me by the hand, led me up two flights of stairs, covered with thick Brussels carpet of a most costly description, and as soft and brilliant in colors as the dewy moss of Virginia Water. The walls were plain. Then we passed through a suite of several rooms, elegantly carpeted, in all of which stood long divans, some of which were covered with white and others with yellow and crimson satin. Over the doorways hung wide satin damask curtains, looped up with heavy silk cords and tassels to correspond, with richly gilded cornices over each, and the windows which overlooked the Nile had Venetian shutters attached to them outside. Against the walls were fixed numerous silver chandeliers, each containing six wax candles, with frosted colored glass shades, made in the form of tulips over them. On each side of the room large mirrors were fixed in the wall, each of which rested on a marble-topped console table, supported by gilded legs. The only other articles of furniture that were scattered about the apartment were a dozen common English cane-bottom *kursi,* "chairs."

Across one apartment a line was suspended, on which hung the Princess's jackets, wardrobes being totally unknown within the precincts of this "Enchanted Castle." Against the walls of another were piled up the beds, which heap was covered over with a rich silk coverlet. On the divan was placed a silver tray (as the use of both toilet tables and washhand-stands was totally unknown) containing the Princess's toilet requisites. These merely consisted of a plain black india-rubber dressing-comb, a white ivory-handled hairbrush, a very large-sized smalltooth-comb, two tooth-brushes, a glass box, containing tooth dentifrice from Paris, a small round silver bowl, into which poured the perfumed (rose) water with which Her Highness, the mother of the Grand Pacha, dressed her hair, the substitute for oil or pomatum (neither of which is ever used by any of the Viceregal family), and a large bottle of essences, all of which were covered over with a transparent crimson silk gauze cloth, bespangled with gold crescents, and bordered with gold fringe an inch deep.

In another apartment stood a large mahogany cupboard, containing the fumigating powders which are burned in the rooms, dried fruits, soaps, essences, boots, shoes, quantities of cast-off wearing apparel, Her Highness's cash-box, a small black ebony casket inlaid with gold, packets of cigarette papers, tobacco, pipe-bowls, silver braziers and dishes, zurfs, both in japan, china, and silver. Jewelry cases, candles, and a complete miscellany of sundry articles : in fact, it was a " curiosity shop."

At the extremity of those rooms I was led into a smaller apartment, where, on the divan (so called from the Persian word *dive*, signifying "fairy, gem ") which was covered with .dirty, faded yellow satin, sat the Princess Epouse. She is a wee dwarf of a handsome blonde, with fine blue eyes short nose, rather large mouth with a fine set of teeth, expressive countenance, but rather sharp and disagreeable voice ; her hair was cut in the Savoyard fashion, with two long plaits behind, which were turned round, over the small brown gauze handkerchief she wore round her head, in which were placed, like a band, seven large diamond flies.

She was attired in a dirty, crumpled, light-colored muslin dress and trousers, sat *à la Turque*, doubled up like a clasped knife, without shoes or stockings, smoking a cigarette. Her waist was encircled with a white gauze handkerchief, having the four corners embroidered with gold thread. It was fastened round, so as to leave two ends hanging down like the lappet of a riding-habit. Her feet were encased in *babouches*, "slippers without heels."

By her side sat the Grand Pacha Ibrahim, her son, so styled after the manner adopted by the renowned Mahomet Ali with the Princess Nuzley, " *Nuzley Hanem*." He was dressed in the uniform of an officer of the Egyptian infantry. On his head he wore the fez ; across his shoulder hung a silver-gilt chain, from which was suspended a small silver square box beautifully chased with cabalistic figures of men, beasts, and trees, enclosed inside which was another smaller box made of cypress wood, which contained verses of the Koran. He was about five years old, of dark complexion, short Arab nose, and rather tall for his age, and looked the very picture of a happy, round-faced cherub. When I approached towards the divan, he gave full proof that his lungs were in a healthy state, as he set up a most hideous shriek, buried his black head in his mother's lap, who laughed most heartily at the strange reception His Highness had thought proper to bestow upon his future governess.

In front of the divan, behind, and on each side of me, stood a bevy of the ladies of the Harem, assuredly not the types of Tom Moore's "Peris of the East," as described in such glowing colors in his far-famed "Lalla Rookh," for I failed to discover the slightest trace of loveliness in any of them. On the contrary, most of their countenances were pale as ashes, exceedingly disagreeable ; fat and globular in figure ; in short, so rotund, that they gave me the idea of large full moons ; nearly all were *passée.* Their photographs were as hideous and hag-like as the witches in the opening scene of Macbeth, which is not to be wondered at, as some of them had been the favorites of Ibrahim Pacha. But *que voulez-vous ?* It is their "*Kismet*" to remain for ever within the four walls of the Harem. It has descended to them from primeval days—the days of the Patriarch Abraham.

Some wore white linen dresses and trousers. Their hair and their finger-nails were dyed red with *henna ;* many of them looked like old hags, in the most extended acceptation of the expression. Some wore the *tarboosh,* round which they bound colored gauze handkerchiefs. They had handsome gold watches tucked into their waistbands, which were similar to that of Her Highness's, which hung suspended from their necks by thick, massive gold chains. Their fingers were covered with a profusion of diamond, emerald, and ruby rings; in their ears were earrings of various precious stones, all set in the old antique style in silver; while others only wore plain gauze handkerchiefs round their heads. They had been favorites in their youth. Behind stood half-a-dozen white slaves, chiefly Circassians, attired in colored muslins, their dress and trousers being of the same pattern. Their head-gear was similar to that of the ladies of the Harem, and the ornaments which adorned their persons were equally as costly.

The Mistress Superintendent introduced me to the Princess Epouse who kept me standing a considerable time, while she fixed her eyes steadfastly upon me and smiled.

CHAPTER VI.

THE private installation having taken place, I was conducted by Anina, according to Her Highness's orders, down the flight of stairs by which we had ascended on a tour of inspection through the Princess's suite of rooms. We proceeded across a small garden, then along two large stone halls, around which were ranged divans similarly covered with worsted damask, on which the slaves lounged about in the day and slept at night. A large deal table stood at each end. On each side are several rooms, in one of which is kept the drinking water. This is placed in large earthen jars, resembling, both in size and pattern, olive-jars; the key of which is in the charge of a black slave, whose office it is to dispense it daily. In another is made their Highness's coffee. Another is appropriated as the dormitory of the German laundry-maid and needlewoman.

Thence we passed along a stone passage which leads to Her Highness's bath-room, a small apartment entered by a red-baize covered door studded with brass nails. The marble bath is both long and wide, with taps for cold and hot water.   The water used for bathing actually boils, into which their Highnesses enter when taking their baths.   This only occurs when they have visited the Viceroy, and not daily, or even at any other time, as so many authors have erroneously stated.   The bath of the poets is a myth.

They are attended by two white slaves, who soap their persons all over before they enter the bath, on retiring from which they are shampooed and highly perfumed.   Leading out of the bath-room, is a small dressing-room, having a divan around it covered with red velvet.   Here a slave holds a toilet-glass in her hand, while Her Highness seated, on the divan, dresses herself.

Proceeding along a stone passage we passed into another pile of buildings, the basement of which was used as the laundry, in which stood numerous wooden tanks placed on the stones, as the slaves, who wash everything in cold water, perform that operation squatting on the floor.   After the clothes have been rinsed, but without blue being mixed in the water, they are hung up on lines in a large stone yard.   On Sundays the Viceroy's clothes are washed.   Mondays are appropriated for Her Highness the first wife's linen.   Tuesday for that of Her Highness the Prince Epouse (the second wife).   Wednesday for Her Highness the third wife's.   Thursday for that of the Grand Pacha Ibrahim.   Friday being the Turkish and Egyptian Sabbath, because their prophet Mahomet was conceived on that day, is kept holy.   On Saturday the linen of the ladies of the Harem, the children, and the domestic slaves is washed.   The ironing and getting-up of the linen takes place in the hall on the deal tables ; but I shall have occasion hereafter to enter into a minute detail of that process.

After we had inspected these apartments, I was led up a noble marble staircase covered with gaudy colored oilcloth, into the suite of apartments appropriated to the use of my

4

pupil, the Grand Pacha Ibrahim, who was, it will be observed, *not* domiciled in the Harem; although I must inform my readers, it was formerly the custom both in Egypt as well as at Constantinople, to have all the Princes brought up in a part of that isolated apartment in the Harem called *Cafess*, "Cage," which was surrounded by lofty walls.

There the Princes were kept from their cradle, without holding any communication with the outer world, or any officers of the palace, in order that every ambitious and magnanimous thought might be radically extirpated in the society of those Thugs of the Ottoman Empire—the mutes; those phantoms of humanity, the eunuchs (who now act the part formerly played by the mutes, as there are but one or two in the palace at Constantinople, and not *one* in Egypt); hags of women—most lascivious and disgusting harridans; and lewd, intriguing and aspiring slaves.   Thus both sultans and viceroys had no cause of fear.

From this gilded dungeon, for in fact it was no better, the successor to the throne issued upon the death of the reigning sultan, of course in utter ignorance, with no knowledge of men and of affairs, and quite prepared to vegetate upon the throne, as it was too late for him to learn anything; and the slothfulness in which he had been brought up too deeply rooted in his mind to be eradicated.   So that many of them became cruel, others besotted, while the rest of the Princes continued to vegetate for the remainder of their existence in the cage, where they were taught, as an antidote against melancholy madness, some mechanical art.   Many were employed in learning turnery, others in making bows and arrows; some in carving tortoise-shell and ebony, embroidering morocco leather or muslin.   The cleverest generally amused themselves by transcribing the Koran and other canonical works.

Whenever it happened (which, however, was of rare occurrence) that any of them were called upon to hold any distinguished post, they passed, as it were, from darkness into light; were generally overawed by the despotism of those around them; and when they managed to shake off that thraldom, they became steeped in cruelty and brutal lust, of which the erudite Dr. Abbott, in his work on Egypt, has left most painful yet faithful records.

I was then conducted into the Princesses' suite of apartments, which consisted of two large saloons, covered with magnificent Brussels carpet but completely besprinkled, as it were, with spots of white wax, which had been suffered to fall from the candles which the slaves carry about in their fingers. Around them were placed divans covered with red satin damask; the windows and door hangings of the same materials, a very large mirror, reaching down from the ceiling, which was painted with flowers and fruits, with the crescent, and numerous warlike instruments, and music placed in each corner, to the top of a marble table supported on gilded legs, on each of which stood a silver chandelier containing eight wax candles, with red-colored glass shades covered with painted flowers.

Out of each of these rooms doors opened into seven others, which are the dormitories of the young Princesses the daughters of the Viceroy, and the ladies of the Harem.

On the right hand side of the first room was the small bed-room which was assigned to me as my apartment, and which was to serve me, like

> " The cobler's stall,
> For chamber, drawing-room, and all,"

and into which my guide conducted me. It was carpeted, having a divan covered with green and red striped worsted damask, which stood underneath the window, which commanded a fine *coup-d'œil* of the gardens attached to the Palace and the Viceroy's pavilion. The hangings of the double doors and windows were of the same material. The furniture consisted of a plain green painted iron bedstead, the bars of which had never been fastened, and pieces of wood, like the handles of brooms, and an iron bar, were placed across, to support the two thin cotton mattresses that were laid upon it. There were neither pillows, bolsters, nor any bed-linen; but as substitutes were placed three thin flat cushions; not a blanket, but two old worn-out wadded cover- , lets lay upon the bed. Not the sign of a dressing-table or a chair of any description, and a total absence of all the appendages necessary for a lady's bedroom—not even a vase. Certes, there stood within that narrow cupboard-like uncomfortable-looking chamber a Parisian chest of drawers (rather a wonder, for the Turkish and Egyptian ladies invariably place their body-linen, &c., in the *youks*, cupboards constructed in the walls of their rooms), having a marble top, and a shut-up washhand-stand, to correspond with an elegantly-painted ewer and basin of porcelain.

I gazed at the accommodation assigned to me with surprise; and yet what could I have expected, as every apartment which I had passed through was totally destitute of everything that ought to have been placed therein? Not a footstool, no pianos, nor music-stools; not a picture adorned the walls. Being "The Bower of Bliss" of a descendant of the formidable Mahomet Ali, who so boldly repudiated the Prophet Mahomet's doctrine "that pictures were an abomination," it was but natural for me to imagine that I should find some beautiful paintings decorating the principal apartments. But no, none hung there. Not a single article of *vertu* graced the rich console tables.

In short, not any of the splendid rooms of the Enchanted Palace of the Crœsus of the nineteenth century contained anything, either for ornament or use, except the bare decorations. In fact, the whole of them seemed to me nothing more than places in which to lie down and in which to vegetate, aided by eatables and drinkables, and sleep. They were even destitute of *soofras*, "tables," whose shapes are very rude, height about a foot, breadth as wide as a plate; just large enough to hold a Turkish coffee-cup, "*findjar*," or the bowl of a pipe, and, although inlaid with some variegated pieces of mother-of-pearl, are only pretty, not having anything rich or elegant about them; still, none were to be seen. Accustomed to the elegant manner in which drawing-rooms of the nobility of my own country are set off with elegant *fauteuils*, superb occasional chairs, *recherché* nick-nacks, as well as a whole host of most costly things, they presented a most beggarly and empty appearance. The whole of the Harem looked like a house only partially furnished; in short, like a dwelling which either the poverty or the niggardness of its proprietor had prevented from being properly furnished.

At first I thought this proceeded from parsimony; for well do we know that a miser—and the Viceroy, like his strange character of a father, Ibrahim Pacha, who was one of the most notorious usurers of his day—loves bright golden sovereigns as dearly as his life : but I afterwards learned that it was *a la mode Turque,* for elegance is quite eschewed by all true Ottomans.

It most decidedly evinces a great superiority in remarkable characters, who have revelled in the midst of profusion, to be able—like that departed warrior of the nineteenth century, Arthur Duke of Wellington, who expired in his small apartment at Walmer Castle, plainly fitted up with that camp furniture which had been his only luxury throughout his most memorable campaigns—to resign, without a murmur, almost every luxury and convenience. It exhibits a healthy independence of externals; but it is a state of things that brings women down to the level of the brute.

Retracing our footsteps Anina led me into that vast regal-looking chamber, the Hall of Audience of the Castle of In-dolence; for it was much more spacious and loftier than the Long Room in the Custom House in London. The floor was beautifully enamelled, as it were, with that native product of the East, the glowing alphabet of that mystic code of signals, the language of flowers, woven on the finest carpeting which the looms of Belgium ever wrought. The lofty ceiling was as exquisitely painted with Egyptian landscapes as the Imperial saloons of Versailles, and an immense gilt chandelier hung suspended from the rich corniced roof. The walls were papered with floral designs, all in unison with that lovely bouquet, that blossomed, as it were, beneath the impious footsteps of my unbelieving self. The hangings of the lofty doors and noble windows, overlooking those perfumed gardens which had never before been trodden by any "dog of a Christian," were of the most costly description. They were composed of rich yellow satin damask curtains, over-topped with elaborately-gilded cornices, and looped up with massive silk cords and heavy bullion tassels. From the walls projected silver chandeliers, ornamented with colored tulip-shaped shades, the transparent wax candles in which, when lighted, threw forth a most agreeable pink shade over the whole of this superb and princely reception saloon. Long divans, covered with rich satin damask, bespangled with the eternal gold and silver crescents glittering about in all directions, like stars

"In the etherial firmament on high,"

were placed under the whole length of the windows.

Here, indeed, might be seen a few signs of elegance and refinement, as numerous richly inlaid console tables, which, in point of workmanship and design, might vie in splendor with those in the Pitti Palace at Florence, supported on richly-gilded legs, were scattered about, on which stood several beautifully-painted Sèvres and Japan china vases, filled with most lovely nosegays!

Ah! gentle reader! they were bouquets such as the hand of no European court florist could possibly have arranged; they were, in fact, mosaics of petalled gems, works of art, touches of genius, brilliant gewgaw, toy-like bouquets, which would outvie the far-famed taste of the flower-girls of lovely Florence, with all nature's fair charms at their command to construct, which only the fingers of the ladies of the Harem (for that is one of the special duties they perform) could pos-. sibly mingle together. The harmonious blending of the brilliant colors, the amalgamation of the delicious fragrance of their powerful perfumes produced nosegays which, while they charmed the eye, emitted forth a fragrance that quite intoxicated the senses. Between them were placed handsomely painted Japan china transparent drinking-cups, similar in shape to cordial vessels, standing in saucers as large as dessert plates.

In the centre stood mechanical Parisian gilt time-pieces, under large glass shades, marking Turkish time, which is counted from sunrise to sunset, and which are daily regulated by the timepiece at the Grand Mosque at Cairo, which is also set according to the setting of the sun. They played tunes in lieu of striking the hours, or chiming the quarters and half hours. Immense gilt mirrors reached from the top of the ceiling down to the floor.

But, oh! horror of horrors! the European innovation of a dozen common English cane-bottomed chairs, on which I afterwards beheld some of the ladies of the Harem endeavor to establish themselves, and at which exhibition not only myself, but the Viceroy and the Grand Pacha could not refrain from laughing outright! as one of their legs hung down, looking most miserably forlorn, while the other sought in vain for room to double itself up upon the chair like a hen at roost. This was not most assuredly, in keeping with the magnificent decorations of this palatial hall; and this constituted all the furniture. It looked bare, vacant, and miserably empty.

Upon re-entering the apartment, I beheld the Princess Epouse (the second wife), and whom I designated, in contradistinction to the other two wives, my Princess, as I was attached to her suite, seated on the Divan, doubled up like a clasp-knife, attired in Turkish costume, very plainly dressed, wearing the gauze handkerchief wound round her head, and fastened with a band, containing seven (the Moslem's magical number, as they believe there are no less than seven heavens) large diamond pins, forming as many of those scourges of Egypt, flies.

She was smoking a cigarette, for cigarettes have of late years almost superseded the use of pipes in this Elysium of Love. Perhaps the expense of those costly amber-mouthed and jewel-studded stems used by the élite of the Turkish and Egyptian ladies of rank, may have contributed in no slight degree to that innovation—for economy in the East appears to be the order of the day. Her Highness was smoking it most cleverly: she really seemed to puff away at it as if it were her amusement, and so it evidently was; but yet I soon discovered that my Princess, like the generality of all honorable Turks, was the *slave* to tobacco in the form of cigarettes. I cannot help thinking that such constant use of the weed vitiates their character, and renders stagnant the small stock of stability with which the Almighty has endowed the Ottomans of both sexes. Well, there she sat, just like one of the porcelain figures which ornament the chimney-pieces in Germany. Not a muscle did she move—she looked like wax-work, and her figure would have made an excellent addition to Madame Tussaud's celebrities.

How much did I regret that I had not been taught the art of taking photographs, for then I could have daguerreotyped the whole of the inmates of the Harems of Egypt and Constantinople. It was an opportunity missed of portraying, from life, the caged beauties of the East. This is much to be regretted, as no other European lady is ever again likely to have the chance. By her side sat the darling of her soul, the Grand Pacha Ibrahim, his person unadorned, by any jewel except the blue turquoise bead in the tassel of his fez.

Several of the young Princesses, the daughters of their Highnesses the first and second wives, sat close to her. The eldest of these was about sixteen years of age. Her name was Niemour; she was tall and slender in figure, of dark complexion, brown eyes, short nose, and was attired in white linen; her feet were encased in light-colored French boots, her hair was bundled up, uncombed, into a dark net, and round her head she wore a circlet of blue velvet, with a plume of red feathers hanging over the left side of her face. She wore no ornaments.

Around this group of the Viceregal family stood about fifty slaves, in the form of a semi-circle. There Arabs, Abyssinians, Ethiopians, and Nubians, were all mingled indiscriminately together, dressed in different colored muslins, all wearing handkerchiefs on their heads, and attired in satin, stuff, and silk paletots of almost every color in the rainbow; in short they formed a complete kaleidoscope. Their hands and ears were most profusely ornamented. On the former they wore numerous rings of diamonds, and other valuable stones; in the latter, large brilliant earrings, which were tied from ear to ear at the back of the head, with a piece of twisted colored cord so as to prevent them from losing them—as they are placed in the ear without rings, and hang down upon a piece of twisted gold wire, in shape like a watch-hook. All had valuable gold watches, which were suspended from their necks by thick massive gold chains stuck in their waistbands.

As I approached, the Princess Epouse rose from the divan, motioned to me to occupy her seat, and thus was I officially installed as governess to the Grand Pacha Ibrahim, the infant son of Ismael Pacha, Viceroy of Egypt.

CHAPTER VII.

As soon as the Princess Epouse had quitted the *oda* "apartment," I was surrounded by the entire motley group of slaves, both black and white. Most of them assumed singular gestures; some knelt and kissed my hands, others my knees, and many of them squatted down at my feet. The ladies of the Harem patted me on the back, a sign of their pleasure at seeing me; and almost all kissed my cheeks.

All of a sudden I was electrified at hearing upwards of fifty voices exclaiming simultaneously, "*Koneiis! Quiyis! Koneiis!*" "Pretty! Pretty!" While a whole chorus shouted forth, "*Gurzel! Gurzel!*" "Beautiful; Beautiful!"

Some of them took up the black straw-hat which I had taken off and laid down upon the divan at my side. This they passed from hand to hand, gazing with pleasure and delight at that specimen of English manufacture. After this they examined the whole of my costume from head to foot. What seemed to attract their notice the most was the crinoline I wore, which was by no means a large-sized one; and yet many Turkish and Egyptian ladies of the present day may be seen in the streets of Alexandria and Constantinople walking about in that appendage.

At the earnest request of some of the ladies of the Harem, I rose from my seat, and walked up and down that noble hall, in order that they might see how European ladies generally paced up and down their rooms.

Anina, thinking that I must require some refreshment after my journey from Cairo, clapped her hands, which is the Turkish and Egyptian manner of calling domestics, when two white slaves left the room, but soon returned, accompanied by two other black slaves, who carried in their hands a silver tray, on which was placed a *kebab*, a small piece of mutton on a silver skewer, which had been broiled upon charcoal almost to a cinder. It was highly spiced and sugared. A flat cake of white Arab bread, as salt as brine, was placed by it. There were no cruets, nor sauce, nor gravy of any kind, but a knife and plated fork. This they placed upon a *soofra*, at the side of the divan.

While I was endeavoring to partake of this specimen of viceregal hospitality—for I had been so surfeited with food cooked *à l' Arabe* at the banker's, that my heart turned against it—they kept gazing at me in as much astonishment as a child looks at the wild beasts at their feeding time in the Zoological Gardens in the Regent's Park, and watched the manner in which I used my knife and fork and ate my unpalatable refreshment, as if I had been a wild animal out of the depths of an Indian forest.

After I had partaken of a few mouthfuls, I made a sign that I had finished, for at that time I was unacquainted either with the Arabic or Turkish languages, both of which however, I picked up in a very short space of time. Then a *findjan*, a small cup, of the finest Mocha coffee in a gold *zarf*, was served me, and a handful of cigarettes, made of the golden leaf tobacco of Stamboul, handed to me on a silver tray. Not having as yet acquired the fashionable habit, for it has become one on the Continent, even among the American, Russian, and English ladies (who in that respect appear of late years to have fraternized with the Italian, Spanish, and Portuguese ladies), of smoking, I so far committed a breach of Oriental etiquette as to decline the fragrant weed, notwithstanding that Her Highness " my Princess " had sent them to me.

The Grand Pacha, who had now become accustomed to me, sat quietly enough by my side, playing with the charms that hung suspended from my watch-guard; for, knowing that I should find the meanest of the slaves bedecked with jewels of costly price, I had made up my mind not to wear my jewelry, and to dress as neatly and simply as my position would admit.

Soon His Highness became tired of those toys, rose from his seat, took me by the hand, with his *left* hand, while one of his little sisters clasped the other tightly in hers. They led me down-stairs, saying that they would take me for a *benich*, "promenade," as they termed it. We accordingly proceeded across the small garden, to the hard, sandy promenade on the banks of the Nile.

I was now styled the *Cocana*, "lady," and was attended by the two usual male attendants of the Grand Pacha, one of whom was a Turk, named Reschid, and the other a Greek, Spiraki by name, a man about fifty years of age, who had originally been a merchant, and was in the service of the late Viceroy, Said Pacha. Both were dressed in black frock coats buttoned up to the chin, and wore *fezes* on their heads. These, who walked behind myself and the Viceregal children, were followed by two soldiers, who kept at a respectful distance.

Scarcely, however, had I reached the promenade, when Spiraki, who spoke most wretched bad French, approached me, salaamed, and informed me that, as my *penates* had been placed in my chamber, I could return, as he would take charge of the Grand Pacha, and the little Princess his sister.

Consequently I retraced my steps alone, and passed into the reception hall ; but scarcely had I entered my chamber when His Highness's nurse, *dada*, whose name was Shayton, bounced into the apartment. She was an Ethiopian, as black as ebony, having the usual negro features, with very large broad lips. Her hair, which was like wool itself, was cut short, plaited into rows round her head, over which she wore a colored handkerchief. Her face was scarred with three large incisions on each cheek. Her countenance was one of the most artful, cunning, and malicious it is possible to conceive : she was, in fact, an admirable type of the lowest caste negress to be found in Ethiopa. She was afflicted with a most ungovernable temper. Revenge and hatred seemed to be depicted in her face, and it was an enigma to me how the Viceroy, or my Princess, could possibly have selected such a creature to nurse my pupil.

She was accompanied by half-a-dozen black slaves, certainly not very prepossessing creatures, but at all events rather more sightly than her hideous self. It appeared that they had been employed in placing my luggage in the room. Upon seeing me the whole of them stood by while I arranged my things, staring at both myself and luggage as if I had just been imported from the Gold Coast. Assuredly both myself, habiliments, manners, habits, and customs were a source of great novelty and amusement to them, so that I made all due allowance for their curiosity, and took their inquisitiveness in good part.

After having satisfied their innate desire of peeping and prying into every trunk, and handling some of the apparel I had unpacked, they salaamed and left me to myself, for which kindness I really felt thankful.

I can scarcely describe my disgust and disappointment on finding that, although I held the responsible office of *institutrice* to a prince, the only legitimate son of the wealthiest prince in the universe, the sole accommodation afforded me was a small wretchedly furnished dormitory, such a chamber as the lady's-maid of any of the wives of our wealthy commoners would not have slept in two nights. There I was, without a chair to sit upon, or a table to write on, with barely room to dress in, and totally destitute of anything to make myself comfortable—not even the convenience of what the French term a *vase*.

It was such a very different reception to what I had looked forward to, that, when I thought of the comfortable home I had left in my own native land, and the kind attention I had received at Mr. B.'s, at the hands of himself and his German housekeeper, I could not help giving vent to my feelings, as I threw myself upon my hard pallet. Ah! gentle reader, it was as hard as a board, and would have disgraced the meanest cottage of our humblest peasant; and I wished a thousand times that I had never set foot within the precincts of the Harem.

It had just struck six, European time, when Shaytan, the head-nurse, entered my room most unceremoniously, and informed me that the princess Epouse desired me to take the Grand Pacha for a walk into the garden.

Tired, vexed, and annoyed as I was, I hastily attired myself, proceeded into the reception-hall, and, taking the little prince by his *left* hand, I descended to the promenade, accompanied by the usual retinue. Hence we passed through a small wooden gate, then across a garden, all railed in with light iron fences, to another gate which led into the garden, *par excellence*, in which was a square sheet of water, also railed round with iron fencing, having in its centre a wooden pagoda, encircled with a terrace, which is ascended by three broad marble steps, with four large lions at each corner of the structure, from the mouths of which issued forth volumes of water. A pleasure-boat was at anchor on it; black and white swans were sporting about, searching for small fry; ducks and waterfowls, much more rare and beautiful than those that are to be seen in St. James's Park, were swimming about in all directions.

On the roof of the pagoda sat a number of birds; among which were several fine specimens of Egyptian crows, of black and grey plumage, which had there built their nests.

At one end of the water stood a beautiful white marble kiosk, having handsome damask cushions placed all round the inside. At each of the four corners of the raised marble-terraced walk around the sheet of water stood large vases, filled with odoriferous flowering shrubs and interspersed with beautiful blooming exotics: and at the sides of the corners were placed painted china cushions, so exquisitely finished that they had all the appearance of being *real* silk-covered cushions, having also china tassels suspended at each corner.

Four broad steps led down into the garden close to a plain white marble-columned gate, on the top of which stood out in bold relief the statues of two huge life-sized lions. As we proceeded along the path to the left, I examined attentively the different male and female statues that were dotted about among the orange-trees and myrtle hedges. Here and there were scattered rose-trees, the brilliancy of whose variegated colors and the perfume of their flowers were delightfully refreshing. Geraniums, of almost every hue,— jessamine, whose large white and yellow blossoms were thrice the size of those in England—and a variety of indigenous and Eastern plants, shrubs, and flowers, were so thickly studded about that they rendered the *coup d' œil* extremely picturesque, and perfumed the air gratefully to the senses. Verbena trees, as large as ordinary fruit trees; other plants, bearing large yellow flowers, as big as teacups, with most curious leaves; cactuses, and a complete galaxy of botanical curiosities, whose names the genius of a Paxton would perhaps be puzzled to disclose, ornamented these Elysian grounds.

At the end of this garden we entered a maze formed of myrtle hedges, then in full bloom; thence we passed along a path on the right-hand side, and came upon a " merry-go-round," on which the little prince took great delight in seating himself,

"Many a time and oft,

while I whirled him round for many a half-hour. It was similarly constructed to those I had seen in the Champs Elysées in Paris.

Close by was a large marble basin of water, in the centre of which, supported by four life-sized angels, from whose mouth played forth *jets d' eau*, sprung forth, as it were, another basin; and in the middle stood the colossal figure of the goddess Ceres, bearing on her head an open-worked basket of carved marble fruit and flowers, beautifully colored in imitation of nature; while in her exquisitely-wrought hand she held a cornucopia, filled with ears of corn and bunches of white and black grapes. The water that spouted forth from the mouths of the four cherubim was thrown up by means of an hydraulic pump, into the horn of the Goddess of Plenty, from whence it trickled down most gracefully. The lower basin was surrounded by a marble-paved verandahed walk, or terrace, interspersed with light iron fancy chairs, couches and tables. It was completely sheltered from the rays of the scorching sun by immense willow-trees planted round the basin, and numerous marble statues were scattered between their graceful drooping foliage.

Passing along another path, we reached the swings, which Tom Moore, in his "Lalla Rookh," describes as being "always a favorite pastime with the Orientals," which were erected in the shape of old-fashioned barouche carriages.

They were all fitted up with handsome cushions, wound up with a key, swung along by the aid of machinery, but were in a most dilapidated state.

Leaving these neglected sources of amusement, we proceeded along a path to the right, passed through a most superb marble-paved hall, the ceiling of which is in fresco and gold. It is supported upon twenty-eight plain pink-colored marble columns, surmounted by richly-gilded Indian wheat, the leaves of which hang down most gracefully. On each side of which, and also above (all of which are now finished—they were then in course of construction) are some very handsome lofty rooms, the ceilings of which are also in fresco, with superb gilded panels and richly-decorated cornices all round.

In the centre of this regal saloon hangs a magnificent glass chandelier capable of holding two hundred wax-lights. Thence we passed through a door which led us into another garden, at the extremity of which stands the Viceroy Ismael Pacha's pavilion. For we have all along been describing the Harem Gardens, in which, however, strange to state, their Highnesses the Princesses seldom if ever promenaded. Why or wherefore I am unable to say; perhaps indolence was the primary cause; but I strongly surmise that one of the chief reasons was, their Highesses' dislike to be attended by any suite, especially their guardians the eunuchs. Therefore they refrained from roaming about this almost earthly paradise; for it is impossible to conceive any idea of their beauty, and the skill with which they have been laid out.

The grounds of Frogmore, the Crystal Palace, St. Cloud, Versailles, the Duke of Devonshire's far-famed Chatsworth, and our national pride, Kensington Gardens, and Windsor Home Park, exquisite, beautiful, and rural as they are, most assuredly partake of the grand and magnificent; but then they all lack the brilliant display of exotics which thrive here in such luxuriance. The groves of orange trees, the myrtle hedges, the beautiful sheets of water, the spotless marble kiosks, the artistic statuary, are all so masterly, blended together with such exquisite taste, that these gardens, the execution of which was carried out under the personal inspection of that strangest of characters, the gallant Ibrahim Pacha, after his return from his tour in Europe, completely outvie them.

Then we came upon an immense lake, the sides and bottom of which are paved with stone, which is covered over with marble cement; the water, by means of large pipes laid down, is supplied from the Nile.

5

Passing along the marble walk we soon reached the Viceroy's pavilion—

> "Where in gay splendor and luxurious state
>   Mehemet Ali's proud descendant, on the Nile's shore,
>   Near old Cairo, populous and great,
>   Holds his bright court . . . . "

Murray, in his "Handbook for Egypt," states that "*none
of the Viceregal palaces are worth visiting.*"   I must beg to
differ, and to explain that no travellers have as yet been
able to inspect those on the banks of the Lower and Upper
Nile, several of which are not only situated in most picturesque spots, but fitted up in the most luxurious regal style.
In short, I hardly think it probable that sight-seers would
obtain access to them, as in most cases the Harems adjoin
them, and for that reason they would be inaccessible.

I shall now proceed to describe the one we were approaching.   It is a long two-storied, white-marble structure, most
admirably erected on a highly-polished black marble terrace,
and reached by a flight of three marble steps.   A broad
verandah runs along the whole length, shaped like a Chinese
pagoda and supported by sixteen red, green, and black porphyry columns; between which stand square blocks of beau-
tifully-polished variegated marble, on which are antique-
looking vases, having large rams' heads with horns as handles, and these are all filled with the choicest exotics.   Suspended from the roof of the verandah hung numerous gilt
lamps of exquisite design.

Entering the interior at the right-hand side, we passed
into one of the finest saloons I had ever entered.   The floor
was covered with an elegant carpet, the pattern of which
represented the most lovely moss imaginable, the brilliancy
of whose shades rivalled those of the exotics in the grounds.
The ceiling is most exquisitely painted in *fresco*, in squares,
in each of which were represented groups of various kinds,
such as men, women, and animals.   Some contained unique

sketches of Egyptain landscape, views of Alexandria, Cleopatra's Needle, Cairo, as seen from the citadel, the prettiest spots up the banks of the Lower and Upper Nile, Nubia, Ethiopia, Karnac, Thebes, Constantinople, Pera, the lovely Bosphorus, and the Cataracts. The walls were hung with costly tapestry,—

> " Where was inwoven many a gentle tale,
>   Such as of old the rural poets sung."

It was lighted by four enormously large, stained glass windows of the richest colors imagiuable, and also by an immense cupola-dome. The hangings of the doors and windows were of elegant flowered white satin, the exotics on which, especially the colors of the variegated selection of roses, were most exquisitely finished. The chairs and sofas —for divans were excluded from this luxurious apartment— were of white, ormolu and gold; the seats and footstools covered with the same material, as also the couches. Large mirrors hung down from the ceiling to the floor; in short, the walls were almost like a glass curtain. In the centre stood a superb round inlaid mosaic table, supported on massive gilded feet.

On the brown and red marble mantelpiece stood a handsome large modern timepiece, supported by gilt figures, on either side of which were placed two massively-chased candelabras, each containing twelve transparent colored wax candles.

Entering the small drawing-room adjoining, which was furnished in a similar manner, only with blue satin drapery and covers to the furniture in lieu of white, we passed into the dining-room, which was very long. It was covered with a thick green carpet, studded with raised moss-roses. In the centre stood a long carved oak dining-table, capable of accommodating thirty or forty guests. The seats of the chairs (which were of carved oak, and most singular to add, *mitre*-shaped) were covered with green velvet, and studded with gilt nails. The walls were of oak panels, also carved in mitre-shape, which would most assuredly have shocked the orthodoxy of any mufti, if such personages have ever entered its precincts, which I very much doubt.

The roof was of stained glass, from which was suspended a large gilt chandelier, containing no less than a hundred transparent colored wax candles. Against the sides of the walls, and at the extremities of the room, were fixed several silver branch candelabras, each containing twelve similar lights. The hangings of the doors and windows were of green velvet, lined throughout with white satin, looped up with gold bullion tassels. Leaving which we entered another apartment. This was covered with a crimson and black carpet, the walls and ceiling similar to those of the drawing-room, having likewise silver candelabras fixed to the walls, and a most magnificent gilt chandelier hanging from the centre of the ceiling. The chairs were rosewood, covered with crimson satin, as also the divans. The hangings of the doors and windows were of the same rich material, looped up with heavy silk cords and tassels of the same color. It was furnished with handsome ebony cabinets, inlaid with precious stones, on which stood elegant gilt cases of stuffed birds, the choicest selection of Egyptian, Indian, and American ornithology which could possibly be selected.

In the corners of this apartment stood several stuffed animals with glass eyes, which were rolling about by means of mechanism. In front of the fireplace lay crouched a full sized stuffed tiger, at the sight of which, the doors being open, the Grand Pacha Ibrahim screamed so violently that I could not pacify him, nor could I persuade him to enter the apartment. On several other occasions when I visited this pavilion, where I often passed much of my time, the Prince Ibrahim never could be induced even to walk by the windows of that to him most terrible " chamber of horrors," until he had seen the attendant carefully lock the door and draw down the transparent colored silk blinds before his face. Often have I smiled as I saw the little grandson of the renowned Ibrahim Pacha stand like a mute peering at the windows until his guard of honor had stationed themselves at the corner of each window.

Continuing my inspection alone of this elegant yet strangely arranged room, I walked across to the other end of it, where stood a large white polar bear. A small but most beautifully marked tiger-cat lay crouching down at its side, and close by was a fine group of cranes. Upon examining these animals, I found that they all could be put in motion by means of the mechanical power attached to them. But what rendered it more singular, was the fact that their natural powers of articulation could be made to issue forth from their mouths, so that, literally speaking, I found myself in a den of wild beasts; and I thought of Sir David Baird, and Tipoo Saib and his tigers—but in the case of the Mysorean Prince the animals were *alive*, and chained to a pillow near his Harem.

It is a well-known fact that Ibrahim Pacha was of a cruel and brutal disposition, and it is most probable that he had these animals collected together and set in motion whenever he had commanded the attendance of any Turkish or Arab dignitary from whom he desired to extort money, for avarice was one of his predominant vices. This vice was, however, of rather a refined nature, as from the immense wealth he had acumulated he must have been perfectly *au fait* in the art of turning his *talaris*, " money," to the best advantage, which tact Ismael Pacha, the present Viceroy, inherits in a most remarkable degree.

As soon as I had joined the little prince, who waited patiently while I explored the chamber, we opened a door on the right hand, passed through a small marble paved hall in which stood four life-size statues, each holding gilt lamps in their hands, which led us into the Viceregal bedchamber.

It was a noble-looking room, covered with a handsome Brussels carpet, with black ground and thickly studded with bouquets of variegated flowers of almost every hue. The whole was scrupulously clean. The gilt-iron bedstead was surmounted with gilded knobs, as also the foot and head plates. The musquito curtains were of fine crimson silk, gauze bespangled with gold crescents. The washhand-stand was of pure white marble, with ewer, basin, and the other usual appendages of beautifully painted Sèvres china, the bouquets on which were artistically executed, and matched the carpet admirably. A large pier-glass hung down from the ceiling. The divan (which was rather diminutive in comparison to those generally placed in the apartments of Turkish dwellings), and chairs were covered with crimson silk bespangled with gold crescents. The toilet-table, on which were placed His Highness's toilet requisites, all of solid gold, inlaid with most valuable precious stones, was covered with a similar cloth.

The ebony cabinet was inlaid with gold and costly jewels on each side of which stood two silver branch candelabras holding a dozen transparent colored wax-candles ; and in the centre was placed His Highness's jewel casket, a perfect gem of the same material, richly inlaid. The walls were covered with crimson paper, embossed with gold crescents. The ceiling was beautifully painted with Turkish and Egyptian landscapes. The chimney-piece was of white marble, and the handsome, elegant bronze stove on the spotless white marble hearth was constructed in the form of a kiosk.

Then we proceeded through a door that was left wide open, into another chamber, similarly fitted up, except that the furniture was of yellow satin bespangled with silver crescents, which was invariably occupied by that *Ikbal,* " favorite," whom the Viceroy from time to time delighted to honor. This was the guest chamber, and the history of its occupants would form a singular addition to the annals of Egyptian history. The beds in both of these rooms were encased in richly-figured satin, which matched the hangings in each apartment.

Passing out of the Pavilion by the same way we had entered, we turned to the left, and proceeded across a garden intersected with cuttings filled with the water of the Nile, by which means the grounds were irrigated. These extensive gardens are completely flooded, night and morning, by means of the river water which is allowed to pass through large pipes and is turned on by taps and sluice gates.

Crossing several of those cuttings, as also deep dykes in different places, which were bridged over with wide planks, we reached the barracks situated at the back of the pavilion. These consist of a long wooden shed raised upon piles, and the walls are constructed of mud. The roof and Venetian shutters (for there are no windows) are of wood, the latter of which are closed at night. They are divided off into two or three rooms, which are merely furnished with wooden divans, on which the soldiers sit by day and sleep on the floors at night, rolled up in their dark brown blankets. In a straight line with these rooms are the officers' quarters, erected in the shape of a Chinese pagoda. They are ascended by a flight of wooden steps, and consist of two rooms in each compartment. They are furnished with divans, the cushions of which are covered with common chintz. The floor is matted. The walls and ceiling are whitewashed. The sentries on guard presented arms to His Highness and myself.

As I passed the windows, or more properly speaking, the openings (for, as I have before observed, there were none, as the openings are destitute of frames and glass), I observed both officers and men lolling out of their respective loopholes; the former were in undress, but the latter I can scarcely describe. They never undress themselves, but sleep in their clothes, which are never taken off their backs, except on fête days, and at the Turkish fête of the Bairam! On that occasion they receive new uniforms. Many of them were eating onions, cucumbers, and other vegetables in their crude state. On another occasion, when passing by these wretched quarters, I heard one of the soldiers singing " The Turkish Sentinel's Refrain," of which the following is a translation :—

"I am a native of Rhoda, and since my birth I have beheld the Nile inundate my paternal lands no less than seven times.

There lived a man of the name of Abderahman, next door to me, who had a daughter, whose countenance had never been gazed upon by any other being than myself.

The beauty and symmetry of Fatima were absolutely incomparable.

Her eyes were as large as coffee cups, '*findjans.*' Her figure was stout and well made.

We loved each other, and we were waiting to be united in the bonds of wedlock;

When the Recruiting Sergeant, '*Fiachef,*' whom the devil take, haud-cuffed me, and lugged me off by the scurf of the neck, with fifty others, to the camp.

As both myself and neighbor were very poor, we were unable to give the Sergeant sufficient *baksheesh* to satisfy him, and may the devil take him!

The sound of the drums, trumpets, and fifes so bewildered my senses, that I soon forgot my peaceful hut, my goats, and my watermill; but I have never ceased to think of the joy of my heart—my beautiful Fatima.

Soon I had a gun, uniform, and wallet given to me; then I was drilled to turn my head to the right, then to the left, to hold my leg up in the air, stand upright, afterwards to shoulder arms, present arms, and many other manœuvres.

Soon I was ordered away with my regiment at Mecca.

When I gazed upon the *Kaaba,* ' Mahomet's Tomb.'

We bivouacked in the desert, in the rocks, in the mountains;

We slew the enemies of the prophet, and then I returned a *Hadje* ' Prilgrim,' from Mecca. May God be thanked!

I was soon made a corporal; and after three years' active service, we embarked on board a man-of-war, and returned to the country watered by the far-famed Nile.

There we encamped, and I longed to return once again to Rhoda, and behold my Fatima.

Still I was afraid to ask leave of absence, lest I should find things fearfully changed.

Then the fever seized me, and I became an inmate of the Hospital at Cairo, where the *Hekim Frandje*, 'Christian doctors,' prevented me from eating, and treated me much more cruel than sickness itself.

I was obliged to sell my *Tain*, 'rations.' May the devil take them.

Every day I became weaker and more sorrowful. I was on the point of death.

One morning the doctors brought me a medicine—the smell of which made me shudder—and I became worse. I had just raised the cup up to my lips, when I fancied that I heard a voice from without—the sound of which pierced my very heart—call to me, Mustafa, Mustafa, *in enui!* 'Oh, my eyes!'

I threw the cup at the apothecary's nose; my strength seemed restored to me, and the blood circulated in my veins. I rose up quite convalescent, and those fools of doctors thought that it was their physic which had cured me. My discharge! said I. They gave it to me, and I rushed into the arms of my Fatima, who had been most anxiously awaiting my release.

After we had embraced each other, she related to me how she had become acquainted with my return, and how she managed to enter the camp.

When I attempted to enter, said she, a black presented the point of his bayonet to my breast, crying out *dour*, 'stop.' As she did not understand the meaning of the word *dour*, 'stop,' so she did not answer, and the black fellow, crying out still more lustily, advanced towards her, when the Turkish officer came out and asked her what she wanted?

I wanted my *Mustafa*, replied she; my affianced, whom I have not seen for these three years. And then the Officer, turning his back upon her, exclaimed, I know nothing of him! The poor girl retired quite broken-hearted; but having met the sister of one of the sergeants, Your lover, said that noble woman, is lying at the hospital so ill that he is at the point of death.

Swifter than the fleetest gazelle, that dearest angel of my life, drawing near to the window of the hospital, exclaimed *Mustafa, Mustafa, in enui!* 'Oh, my eyes!'

Intoxicated with joy, I bore her in triumph through the camp. I pointed her out, like a madman, to my Colonel, my Commandant, my Captain, my Lieutenant, and my sergeant; and, having obtained a furlough, we went to Rhoda to get married, where the good old Abderahman was waiting to bestow his blessing upon us. May God be praised, God is great."

As His Highness the Grand Pacha Ibrahim began to complain of being tired, and I have no doubt that his little legs must have ached, we turned our footsteps towards the Harem.

I was rather taken aback after we had proceeded a short distance by observing the atmosphere become all at once dark and gloomy; but turning round I perceived dense volumes of black smoke issuing forth from a huge, tall chimney towering in the distance up to the sky. It raised its dark head a little beyond the whitewashed barracks. I inquired of Spirake, the Greek attendant, the name of the building, when he informed me that it was His Highness the Viceroy's sugar refinery. I then learned that immense quantities of sugar were manufactured from the cane which grew on His Highness Ismael Pacha's estates near Minich, which produce yields the billionaire merchant prince a most lucrative return, for the sale of sugar throughout the whole length and breadth of Egypt is monopolized by His Highness the Viceroy.

The refinery that we had seen towering in the distance yields upwards of 30,000 quintals annually, and there *coal* is used to clarify the sugar in lieu of bullock's blood. This explanation fully accounted for the huge pile of black diamonds that I had observed piled up on the sides of the landing-place when I first approached the gates of the Harem.

On my return I thanked His Highness the Grand Pacha Ibrahim for the very attentive and kind manner in which he had shown me all the lions of the Harem gardens, the Viceroy's pavilion and the barracks.

CHAPTER VIII.

As soon as I reached the Prince's suite of apartments, I found the head-nurse waiting to conduct His Highness to his supper, as it was about half-past seven, European time, I then proceeded with my pupil downstairs, then across the small garden into a large room on the ground-floor, which was usually occupied in the daytime by several of the ladies of the Harem. The floor was covered with a handsome Brussels carpet; the walls papered with a simple pattern; the ceiling was painted. The curtains of the windows and doors were of red damask; a divan extended along one side.

The five youthful slaves who formed His Highness's staff of domestics entered the room soon after we had seated ourselves. One carried the *soofra* (a kind of very low table), while the other bore the viands, of which the following is *la carte* :—

Soup, made from sheep's shanks or fowls, having rice and forcemeat balls (made of the crumbs of bread left on the trays) in it.

Legs of mutton (which are as small as the lamb of Italy) roasted, and stuffed with the kernels of ground-nuts, onions, raisins, spice, and sugar.

Tomatoes, scooped out and filled with meat, rice, and spice.

Cucumbers, dressed in a similar manner.

Boiled cucumbers, small vegetable-marrows, onions, and pieces of fowl, all mixed up together.

Broad beans, boiled in their shells, from which the bean is removed at table, and then eaten.

Boiled chicory, chopped up very fine, and then re-boiled in fat.

Cutlets, fried in syrups with spice.

Boiled fowls.

Pickles; salads, dressed with lamp-oil and water; onions, in their crude state; undressed cucumbers.

Lemons, sweetmeats, syrups.

Confectionery most tastefully formed into numerous devices, some like Banbury cakes, but which, in lieu of being made with jam in the centre, contained a quantity of whey, as salt as brine.

Jelly, with strawberries placed whole in it.

Pastry, consisting of batter fried, then opened, and sour milk poured into it.

Batter-balls, fried in syrups; hard bread balls, similarly cooked.

Large patties, filled with eggs and sour milk.

Pancakes, fried in grease, and eaten with syrups.

Bowls of sour milk; sour milk, with slices of crude cucumber swimming in it.

Thick rice-milk with sugar and jams, eaten with milk.

The dessert consists of all the various fruits in season; and the only beverage was water and sherbet, which the Prince and the other children drank out of silver mugs, each having one appropriated for his exclusive use.

The Grand Pacha was fed by Shaytan, who, squatting herself down upon the ground by his side, took the morsels out of china dishes and put them into his mouth. She used a spoon for the pilau, but broke the bread, dipped it into the liquid viands, and placed it into his mouth. At the same time the other Viceregal children sat in children's chairs round the *soofra*, and each was fed by the under-nurses in a similar manner.

If a piece of bread happens to fall upon the ground, it is picked up immediately, the word *Bismillah!* is repeated several times, the bread is kissed, and then placed up to the forehead; but if crumbs only fall, instead of leaving them to be swept up as Europeans are accustomed to do, they pick them up one by one and eat them. But should any pieces that have fallen be dirty, they are placed on the statues in the small garden, for the birds to eat.   All the broken bread at the meals is carried away to the kitchen, where it is moistened with milk, squeezed by the hands into balls, and then fried in batter and sugar.   Of those, however, I never partook.

The whole of the slaves are supplied with the dark Arab bread, and it not unfrequently happened that both myself and the German maids were kept on very short commons. In fact, time after time, I have actually been without any bread at all, as the slaves, who are all most adroit thieves, would, whenever they could find an opportunity, steal the European bread with which we Europeans were alone provided; for their Highnesses the Princesses, the Viceroy's wives, invariably partook of *white* Arab bread, which was also as salt as the briny ocean.   The inmates of the Harem have a perfect horror of dropping bread, and I have often heard them scream with dismay as a piece fell from their hands.

After the Grand Pacha had finished his supper, a large silver basin, shaped like a glass goblet, which had been brought into the room with the viands and placed upon the carpet, was raised up by a young slave, who knelt down and held it before the Prince.   The head-nurse then took a piece of rag (not a towel), soaped it with a ball of white soap (which, together with a piece of linen, is always placed in the centre of the strainer that stands by the side of the basin), and washed his face.   After this she wrung the rag and wiped him with it; then she held his hands over the basin, and water was poured upon them out of the silver ewer, which is shaped like an old-fashioned coffee-pot, but having a long spout, curved downwards.   The same ceremony was observed by the under-nurses with the other children, each of whom had separate basins and ewers.

It is hardly possible to give an accurate description of the appearance of the tray after their Highnesses had partaken of their meals. It looked just as if the whole contents of a few of those plate-baskets which are used in the kitchens of the first-class London hotels to place the pieces in collected off the plates that come down from the several dinner-tables had been emptied on to it.

Here and there lay morsels which had been torn asunder from the joint or bird, and, being unsuited to the palate of the guest, had been thrown down, after having been mauled about in their fingers; pieces of broken bread, crumbs of pastry, the remains of vegetables, both cooked and crude; in short, it presented a sight that would make the stomach of a cook-shop carver heave again. It was one of the most disgusting sights I had ever witnessed, and this was the scene enacted daily. Then the ladies of the Harem had their meals off it, just as it was.

After the Viceregal children had partaken of their repast, then the nurses, who in their turn were waited upon by their Highnesses' little slaves (for each Princess has two slaves to wait upon her, and act as her playmates), helped themselves.

When they had finished, then the group of little slaves (who, as I shall hereafter show, are near relations of the Grand Pacha) cleared the things away : and carrying them into the Stone Hall, placed them on the basement floor, and there squatted themselves down, and regaled themselves like the beggars of old, on the crumbs which had fallen, as it were, from the table of their superiors. These sometimes were very scanty, as no separate table was ever provided for them.

After supper was finished a little slave acted as marshal and led the way, holding a silver-gilt lantern, in which was placed a large wax-candle. Then Shaytan carried the Prince up into his reception-room, which at that time presented a most singular and novel scene. It appeared that during supper-time a number of other slaves had been busily engaged in removing out the "Bed Store-room" the beds that had remained piled up there during the daytime, and had placed them upon the carpet. Each of the Viceregal children and their nurse had two mattresses assigned them, which were encased in cotton covers.

On His Highness's bed was laid a sheet, then three flat cushions, also encased in muslin, the ends of which were embroidered in red worsted and tied with ribbons, for his head to rest upon, in lieu of pillows; and over the whole were placed two dark-colored wadded coverlets, under which the Prince slept. On one side were ranged the beds of his little sisters, and by the side of them those of the nurses, and on the other side that of the head-nurse.

The Prince and his little slaves played about for a short time amidst this "one full swelling-bed;" after which Shaytan undressed him, which she did in the following manner: first she removed his trousers, then the little coat and dayshirt, and then re-dressed him in his night-attire, which consisted of a pair of calico trousers, fastened round his waist by a long strip of muslin, with embroidered ends run through the broad hem, not unlike a pair of Indian "*pyjamas*," over which was placed a cotton dressing-gown, open all up the front, and over that a blue quilted cashmere paletot. His waist was girded with a silk handkerchief; his head was covered with a white cotton fez, with strings which were tied under his chin. His sisters were also similarly attired.

As soon as he was dressed in his night-clothes a silver brazier, filled with charcoal, was brought into the room. In it was thrown a quantity of wood of aloes, aromatic gum, and lumps of crystallized sugar. Then the head-nurse lifted up his Highness in her powerful arms, and swung him round it nine times, while she counted that number aloud in Turkish; but why that number was used I was unable to learn. After this she exclaimed *Allah ! Alla ! Bismillah !* ("God !

God!—in the name of the most merciful God!") The same ceremony was performed by each of the other nurses with their Highnesses the little Princesses; then he was laid down in his bed.

The nurses then took it in turns to repeat stories, or else sang himself and his sisters to sleep; their everlasting monotonous chant consisting of *Baba, Ni-na! Baba, Ni-na!* "father, mother;" *Nina! Nina!* "mother," in different tones of voice.

During the whole of this preparation for retiring to rest, the Prince Epouse sat upon the divan smoking cigarettes. All the nurses sat at the side of the beds, or else at the door. Those who were not engaged in telling stories were employed at needlework, which they executed with their left hands, until they retired to rest, which all did about ten o'clock, European time. At that hour the *Keslar Agaci,* Grand Eunuch, Captain of the girls, accompanied by several of his attendants, like the matron of an English house of correction,

"Goes his nightly rounds,"

locks the outer gates of the "Abode of Bliss," and then the guardians of the enchanted palace all repair to their respective apartments to smoke their pipes, and enact the farce of "High Life Below Stairs," which I shall subsequently show they did to perfection.

Above the whole of that most motley group, which was assembled together in the Reception Hall, hung suspended an enormous large colored muslin mosquito-curtain, made in the form of a canopy, similar to that which is daily seen carried in Catholic countries over the head of the dignitary, who walks along the streets when the Host is being carried to a dying person. Attached to the four corners of the square flat top piece, were sewn four large gilt rings, through each of which was run the crimson cord, which was fastened to the large brass hooks that were driven into the walls. It was then looped up to them; the long ends hanging down to the floor and being tucked underneath the mattresses, left the whole group of children and nurses snugly ensconced within its ample folds.

A large silver-gilt lantern, containing two lighted transparent wax-candles, as long as those used by mourners in Catholic countries, was left burning upon the floor all night.

This scene which brought to my mind the encampment of a party of gipsies on the stage, appeared to me most singular and novel, and it was some time before I could bring my mind to look upon it as a reality. At moments, when I gazed upon the group, I thought it was the idle phantom of a dream; but I was soon awakened from that delusion by the entrance of Clara, the German laundry maid, who came to announce that my own supper was ready.

Retiring from that noble apartment, now so strangely metamorphosed into the Viceregal nursery, I followed the German maid downstairs into the Stone Hall on the basement floor, which had but recently served as the dining hall of the little slaves, and there, to my disgust and astonishment, I beheld the little slaves bringing in the same *carte* as had been served up for the Viceregal children. I stared again in astonishment, and looking at the maid Clara, I found that she had seated herself at the table, and was prepared to *hobnob* it with me.

This was treatment I had never expected to receive. However, there was no help for it, and as neither knife nor fork had been provided for me, I was obliged to accept the German's offer to lend me those indespensable articles. Fatigue, disgust and vexation at the accommodation which had been provided for me, had almost taken away all my appetite; but at the sight of the Arab dishes I turned quite sick, and contented myself with partaking of a "*kebab*"—some bread, a little fruit, and a "zarf" of coffee —as nothing but water was permitted to be drunk, which

6

latter I found exceedingly acceptable. I hastily retired to my miserable pallet in the chamber which had been assigned me.

I can scarcely describe my feelings when I was alone. Being at that time totally ignorant of the apathy and absolute indifference with which the Turks, Arabs, and Egyptians treat all Europeans with whom they come in contact, I was at a loss to conceive why I had been subjected to such an indignity. The position I occupied about the Prince ought most assuredly to have saved me from such an insult.

I had inspected the Viceroy's pavilion that very day; and I remembered how accurately my intelligent fellow travellers, Mr. Xenos and Mr. ——, had described what would in all probability be my position and reception in this *Mansion of Discomfort*. I had seen a considerable display of European habits, in the manner in which his own private retiring-rooms had been arranged—everything bespeaking that His Highness was thoroughly Europeanized. At that I was not in the least surprised, for I knew that he had been sent to France in 1846, along with his brother, Achmet Bey, and his uncles Hassam Bey and Halim Bey, and this made me more annoyed, as I was confident that if either Messrs. H. or Mr. B. had merely taken the precaution they could easily have done, to let the good old German housekeeper enter the Harem and see what accommodation had been provided for me, that kind creature would have taken care to send in everything there for my convenience; and as she had been accustomed to wait upon ladies in her own country, she would have at once explained to her countrywoman the laundry maid, how she might have conducted herself towards me.

But no. I was bundled into the Harem like a bale of merchandise, and left, as Mr. C. H.'s sister explained to me before my departure from England to " fight my own battle,"—no easy matter among such a semi-barbarous set.

Now I was perfectly aware that I should have to vegetate on nothing but Arab diet. My health had begun to give way beneath the effect of that most unpalatable *cuisine* when at the banker's, and I was quite certain that it would be utterly impossible for me to keep body and soul together with such nourishment, with only water and coffee as drinkables. It was really unpardonable and unfeeling in the extreme; there was no excuse to be made. I had already remonstrated with Mr. B. upon the subject of my diet; and as the Viceroy had a staff of French cooks and attendants, there could not have been any difficulty or objection to my meals being prepared by them. Of this His Highness' *civil* aid-de-camp and associate in commerce was fully aware; but no—he was a Prussian, and as he hated the English, what had I to expect?

The entire blame must be attached to the hasty and inconsiderate manner in which Mr. C. H. overruled Mr. B.'s objection, who, knowing full well that nothing had been prepared for my reception, was anxious to postpone my departure from his hospitable roof until my apartment had been properly furnished. To such straits was I put that I was obliged to place different articles of body-linen as substitutes for bed-linen; fortunately, however, I had provided myself with a stock of Turkish bath towels. My room, as I have previously explained, led off from that of the Grand Pacha's. I had scarcely arranged my bed, for as yet not a slave had been appointed to wait upon me, when I heard the ponderous bolts and bars of the lower doors at the foot of the marble staircase drawn into their sockets, and the huge keys—for they are no less than nine inches in length —turned in the weighty wards, as the eunuchs locked the doors, let fly the secret springs, and then retired to enjoy their pipes in their own apartments.

Those grating sounds startled me; I could not for an instant realize my position; I thought I must be the inmate of some prison in a foreign land, and not a guest within the precincts of a prince's palace. My position was anything but enviable. Although I was conversant with several continental languages, still, strange to add, not any of the Princesses' ladies of the Harem, or slaves, could speak anything but Arabic and Turkish ; and the German laundry-maid had only just begun to pick up a few words of those languages. Well, there I was, among a crowd of nearly one hundred women, without being able to speak a word of their language, or to understand what they said to me. Then did I experience the worst of all loneliness,

"Solitude in a crowd."

So that when I found myself alone in my own chamber, I could not help exclaiming,

"Ah! why did Fate my steps decoy,
In foreign lands to roam."

Wishing, however, to divert my mind as much as possible, I resolved to keep a diary. But how was that to be accomplished, since I had no table in my chamber upon which I could arrange my writing materials? The top of my French chest of drawers had already been turned into a toilet-table, and even if I had removed my dressing-case and all the appendages thereon, even then I had no chair. Thinking that the slave who had arranged my chamber might, in the hurry of the moment, have forgotten both those necessary articles of furniture (as I had seen tables, and even English cane-bottom chairs in the apartments), I resolved to appropriate some to my own use; but, when attempting to do so, I was point-blank told by the eunuchs that I must not touch or take anything which had not been expressly given me. Thus I was checkmated, and powerless even to move a chair for my own accommodation. This was a kind of domestic tyranny I could not endure.

I abandoned the idea of making any substitutes for them

the first night; but finding upon inquiry that I was not to be provided with either, I had no alternative but to tax my ingenuity.

So, placing two of my largest square trunks upon one another, for a table, which I covered with my travelling-rug, and for a chair laying my travelling-cloak upon another box, and turning a larger one upright, I placed it at the back; which gave me a support for my back; and thus did I begin to dot down these incidents of my experience of Harem life in Egypt.

<hr />

CHAPTER IX.

THE following day I was informed by the German laundry-maid that I was expected to clean my own room, and wash my own linen, both of which I resolutely refused to do. Upon which the Princess Epouse ordered a slave to arrange my apartment, and the Greek slave, Spiraki, to find a laundress at Cairo, as none of the slaves would wash the linen of an unbeliever; and it was with the greatest reluctance that any of the youngest slaves could be forced to act as, what is termed in the *caste* phraseology of India, *Muhtur*, "sweeper," to empty slops, &c.

After these arrangements had been made, I had a most excellent opportunity of making myself *au fait* with domestic life in the Harem.

At five o'clock next morning, the eunuchs, who carry their bunch of keys about with them like the warders of an English prison, came round and unlocked all the doors of the outer rooms leading to the grand and back staircases. Then they called up all the slaves and the ladies of the Harem. The former, as soon as they were dressed (pardon me, kind reader, but I err in using that expression, for all Turkish and Egyptian women, as well as their slaves, never undress, but lie down with their clothes on, though they often change them in the daytime), took up and rolled their beds which they carried into the bed storeroom, and there piled them up in a corner, as I have previously described. Then they proceeded to sweep the rooms, each using the set of brooms and dust-pans which had been assigned her.

After this portion of household work had been performed, the members of the Viceregal family were called, and the nurses began to dress the children. The head-nurse, Shaytan, lifted the Prince out of his bed, sat him down upon the side, having previously had the mosquito-curtains looped up to the rings attached to the walls, tucked up his *pyjamas* as far as his knees, then water was poured over a piece of rag, placed in a deep silver dish, with which she soaped and washed his legs and feet. On each of the calves of his little legs there were *nine* incisions just above the top of the sock, some cabalistic superstition that I never had explained to me, but perhaps it was that he was considered as eligible for the *ninth* heaven, as Rückert, the Orientalist, has described as many. Then she removed his drawers, and began by putting on his stockings, then his boots, after which she washed his hands and face (his arms and neck never being touched), and his flannel shirt was removed.

Around his neck he wore, first, a thin black cord, to which was attached a small black silk pad, which lay upon his abdomen, that is *never* removed from off his person; then another one, on which were strung six black, carved cypress wooden acorns, which are supposed to be a *teleam*, "talisman," to keep evil spirits away from his august person. Then his flannel vest was put on him; after that a thin net one, then a linen shirt, all the ends of which were tucked inside his trousers; after which his coat was put on.

Around his neck he wore a small ribbon tie, and across his shoulders a silver-gilt chain, attached to which hung a small square silver box, about an inch thick, having a sliding lid, in which is enclosed a little cypress-wood box, containing verses of the Koran, and pieces of the coffin of the prophet Mahomet. The box is elegantly chased with palm leaves, elephants, and numerous other animals.

His head was washed with perfumed water, and his fez placed on it; in the tassel of which is fastened a small thin black silk cushion, or bag, containing some grains of a black seed, which are said to possess the power of warding off fits; also a piece of pink coral, shaped like a shell, which is worn to preserve His Highness from attacks of ophthalmia. At the top of the tassel is sewn a large turquoise, to guard him from all accidents.

The other nurses then proceeded to dress the young Princesses, who had narrow plaits of hair in front. They all wore the same charms, except the coral, black bag, and turquoise.

Their beds were then rolled up, removed into the bed storeroom, and the Reception Hall " swept and garnished." Then one of the eunuchs brought in a cotton sack, or bag, containing *symmets*, " buns made in the shape of rings, about the circumference of a tea-saucer," which the Grand Pacha counted, and allotted out a certain number to each of the little Princesses for their two daily meals, breakfast and supper.

If any had been purloined or a mistake made in the counting of them, His Highness invariably bundled them all into the sack, made the eunuch take it away, and return with the proper number; and until that was done, the Prince stormed and raved like a maniac. It was utterly impossible to pacify him.

If, however, I happened to jest with him, by secreting one or two of the buns, he would then calmly and quietly continue his distribution of them, without uttering a word of complaint. As soon as all the Viceregal children had assembled in the saloon, the brazier filled with live charcoal was brought in, and the same process gone through as had been practised the previous night when they retired to rest.

As the kitchen is situated at some distance from the Harem, in the vicinity of the Sugar Refinery, the dishes are all placed upon a large wooden tray, and covered over with thick white cloths, carried on men's heads into the small garden which separates the Harem from the Grand Pacha Ibrahim's suite of apartments; there they are laid down upon the path, and the shrill cry of the eunuchs exclaiming, *Dustoor! Dustoor!* "Out of the way! out of the way!" resounds from all quarters.

Then the slaves begin to run into their rooms; but should any of them linger about, then the cry of *Allah! Allah!* "God! God!" is shouted forth in stentorian tones, and the *courbache,* "whip made of bullock's hide," falls heavily upon their shoulders.

After the men have placed the trays down, and disappeared, then commences one of the most ludicrous scenes imaginable: for as I have previously explained, no regular meals are provided for the slaves, or, in fact, anybody else but the Viceregal family. They are necessarily obliged to purloin whatever they can lay their hands upon before the dishes are served up to their Highnesses the Princesses, or the Grand Pacha Ibrahim; hence they are accustomed, like hungry wolves, to rush down into the garden, and make a selection of what dishes they can, without fear of detection, and withhold them from the Viceregal repast.

It not unfrequently happens that the Princess Epouse would enter the Stone Hall, while the slaves were enjoying their purloining; then the cups, saucers, and gold spoons would be thrust into a pail, which a slave, who was always kept on the *qui vive,* and acted as sentinel, would whisk out of the room as if by magic. At other times Shaytan, the head-nurse, would be squatted very comfortably on the floor of the Grand Pacha's apartment, with a large flat patty, about twice the size of a Cheshire cheese, composed of vermicelli, fat, cheese, sugar, and spice—a most favorite dish in the Harem—which she had stolen off His Highness's tray, together with several large glass dishes full of strawberries, cherries, greengages, apples, pears, oranges, and lemons, all piled up like pyramids; also a dish of powdered sugar. The latter she generally hid away until night, but the former being hot, she usually began to partake of as soon as she had purloined it.

Sometimes the Princess would enter the room softly, and then the vermicelli pasty was pushed away under the divan out of sight; and in that case it frequently happened that another slave carried it off and consumed it.

Whenever the Princess caught any of them purloining the viands, she boxed their ears most soundly, and made them carry the dishes back again.

I cannot refrain from bearing testimony to their kindness and attention towards myself, as they invariably called me to go downstairs, and select my own dishes prior to any being served up to their Highnesses the Princesses; and this spontaneous act of their good will and sympathy towards me was not caused by any *baksheesh* that I had been in the habit of distributing among them, for I never gave them any, having been requested by my Princess not to propitiate them in that manner. It was their own attention towards me, and I always felt grateful to them for it, and never failed to grant them any little indulgence they required at my hands, or to do them a service in return.

The children's morning toilet being finished, the little slaves brought in the "*soofra,*" which they covered with a yellow satin cover, bespangled with silver crescents. On it they placed a round-rimmed green-painted tray, upon which they laid a white china soup-tureen of boiled milk, into which was put pieces of Arab bread.

Each child dipped its spoon into it, and helped herself; but if any one of them should so far forget herself as to place her spoon in the tureen before the Grand Pacha had helped himself, by taking the first spoonful, then His Highness would cast, nay, throw his spoon into the tureen, as well as those of all the Princesses, and order the slaves to move it away instanter. Child as he was, his word was law, and nobody dared disobey him.

The next course consisted of a small tureen containing a pigeon served up swimming in soup thickened with rice and flour: each one of the family party helped themselves to a spoonful of it. Then the head-nurse took the pigeon in her fingers, tore it to pieces, and then commenced a regular battle, as each of the children desired to have a leg, which ended on the morning in question, as was generally the case, in the separated bird making its exit without being touched. The Grand Pacha never partook of this dish, why or wherefore I was unable to learn.

Then followed a dish of mutton-chops, broiled quite dry, but highly spiced; afterwards some pigeons cooked in a similar manner, minus the spice. Each child took up a pigeon in her fingers, tore it to pieces, and ate whatever part she fancied. A salad, consisting of cucumber cut into slices and dressed with water and oil (for vinegar they never used), was then served up. Then followed a glass dish filled with jam; fried, greasy, pastry-like pancakes, literally swimming in fat and honey, and this completed the *carte*. The usual ablution followed as previously described as having taken place after His Highness's supper.

I lost no time in remonstrating with the Princess Epouse upon the impropriety of being obliged to take my meals with the German maid, and although unacquainted with her vernacular, still I managed to make Her Highness sensible that it was a degradation to me. Accordingly my breakfast was served up to me in my own room. It consisted of a cup of coffee, a small tureen of boiled milk, sweetened almost to a syrup, and a roll of European bread, but without any butter or eggs, of neither of which did I ever partake during my residence in the Harems. After I had partaken of that refreshment, I dressed, and proceeded, accompanied by my pupil, into the Harem.

The Grand Pacha, according to his usual custom, went to visit their Highnesses, the three wives, in their bedchambers. He first walked into the apartment of Her Highness the Lady Paramount (the *first* wife), who takes precedence of all, and without whose orders none of the other wives can interfere in the general internal arrangements of the Harem, save and except in their own apartments, and over their own slaves and families, with whom they act as they please. Her name was Ipsah; she was tall, stout, had a pleasing mouth, sinister expression of countenance, large blue eyes, but possessed a most violent temper; cruelty seemed to be marked in every lineament of her features.

When we entered she was dressing her hair. One slave held a looking-glass in her hand, another Her Highness's toilette-tray with its appendages, and a third stood by to hand her whatever she might require. She was not, as was her usual custom, squatted like a clasped knife, but sat on a cotton covered divan, attired in a dirty, crumpled, muslin wrapper, which had served her as her night habiliments. Her feet and legs were both stocking and shoeless, and hung down from the divan.

The Prince drew near to her, took hold of her right hand, which was jewelless, as also were her ears; for none of their Highnesses ever wore jewels except on grand occasions. He pressed her hand to his lips and forehead, then salaamed her, after which both of us left the room.

On reaching the chamber of the Princess Epouse (his mother), the Prince mounted the divan, saluted, as he had done the first wife, and then insisted upon having a cup of coffee. As soon as he had partaken of it, he asked the Princess to give him *baksheesh,* when she handed him a large packet of silver piastres, each valued at twopence half-penny. His mother took him on her lap, made a few inquiries of him in Turkish, which I did not understand, and asked him to go and fetch her a cigarette. Then we passed on into the chamber of the third wife, who is childless, but who has adopted a slave as a daughter, whom the Grand Pacha, on his visit to Constantinople two years ago, purchased for her. It was then nine o'clock, so making our salaams, we proceeded into the gardens.

We had not walked far, before the Prince espied one of the Arab gardeners, whom he requested to make him a bouquet. Three of the under-gardeners rushed off immediately to cull some flowers, but as they were, according to His Highness's idea, too dilatory (for like all Turks, whenever they require a thing, it must be brought to or done for them instantly), the little Prince put himself into a most violent passion. At length the head gardener came forward and presented him with the bouquet. His Highness scarcely deigned to look at it; threw it on the ground, stamped his little feet upon it, and then, in the paroxysm of his passion, after a slave had picked it up and handed it to him, he deliberately amused himself by tearing it to pieces. While thus giving vent to his anger, he kept scolding the gardeners for not having assorted the colors in a proper manner.

Turning round to the eunuchs who had accompanied the attendants, he ordered them, then and there, to cut sticks from off one of the trees, and to give the three gardeners a thrashing. Those spectres of men obeyed His Highness's instructions, and the three Arabs were laid down upon the path by some black slaves, and the eunuchs set to beating them. This they continued doing for some time; but as the Prince made no sign to them to discontinue the chastisement, I began to remonstrate with him at such a display of his ungovernable temper, and in an authoritative tone exclaimed, "*Bess! Bess!*" "Enough! Enough!" when the eunuchs ceased. The morning was extremely sultry, and the perspiration poured down the faces of the eunuchs.

This incident clearly gave me an insight into the Prince's character, which was evidently as cruel, overbearing, and brutal, as that of his grandfather, Ibrahim Pacha, whose private life was disgraced by the most barbarous pastimes; but I had satisfactory evidence, by his conduct in the pavilion, that he did not inherit that courage which obtained his grandfather such renown.

On our return to the Harem a novel scene presented itself in the noble Audience Hall. On the divan sat their Highnesses the Princesses, the Viceroy's three wives. They were elegantly attired in beautiful new muslin dresses, and very full trousers of the same material, with quilted satin jackets, of gaudy colors. Their heads were ornamented with large diamond pins; and all rose up from off their seats as a middle-sized gentleman, in a dressing-gown and slippers *à la Turque,* entered the room, bolding a white pocket-handkerchief in his hand, which was so large that I mistook it for a towel.

The Princesses formed a kind of semicircle round him; all salaamed him, to which he responded by an affable smile, patted the Grand Pacha on the cheek, and passed through without uttering a syllable. I followed the example set me by the Princesses, curtseyed to him, which salutation he returned by bowing.

As I had not yet been introduced to His Highness, Ismael Pacha, the Viceroy, I innocently enough considered that this gentleman must be the Viceregal barber.

The little Prince partook of his breakfast as usual at twelve o'clock, after which he amused himself by playing about the room with some of the English toys which I had presented to him.

While engaged in that occupation, one of the female slaves, whom I afterwards found was his half-sister, that is, the Viceroy's daughter by a slave (for his staff was composed of little girls and boys), offended him. He immediately seized hold of her by both her arms, pinched them most violently, and like a tiger bit them until he drew blood, after which he put his fingers into the poor little creature's mouth, and tore both sides of it, until the blood streamed down her chin like water. I scolded him well for such brutality, when His Highness burst into tears and walked away into another apartment.

Scarcely had the little Prince proceeded a few paces when he was met by the Princess Epouse, who inquired the cause of his grief, as it appears that all Turks and Egyptians have a perfect horror of seeing any person in tears.

The facts were explained to Her Highness, who made the poor little slave who had been so barbarously treated by her son, first kiss the skirts of his coat, and then the carpet. But when I pointed out to Her Highness that the slave was not to blame, the Princess merely laughed, exclaiming, " *Malesch, Madame,*" " it does not matter." Then the Prince became pacified, and resumed his amusements. Soon afterwards a middle-aged woman named Rhoda, the mother of the Harem, who was about fifty years of age, entered the apartment, accompanied by four women much older than herself.

This important personage, who acts as midwife, doctor, friend, and counsellor, is present in the bridal-chamber when any of His Highness's daughters or slaves are married. She is one of the most powerful and influential of the whole of the inmates of the Harem. To her is confided all the political changes which are hatched within its walls ; for it is the very focus of intrigue; as it is but natural to suppose that their Highnesses the Viceroys, when enjoying their *dolce far niente,* throw off all restraint, and chatter away as much as Turks are ever prone to do (and that is never very much) to their wives as to the sayings and doings of their ministers, associates in commerce, and favorites. But Ismael Pacha places his trust in and confides his secrets to the care of the Princess Validè, his august mother, the clever intriguing widow of that singular Prince the late Ibrahim Pacha. Still, all the Princesses belonging to the other members of the Viceregal family of Egypt, both widows, wives, and daughters, pay occasional visits to their Highnesses the three wives, with whom they generally pass the day; and their conversation, brief and curt though it be, naturally turns upon the plans and actions of their liege lords, and then the Harem became the arena of

"That vermin slander, bred in abject minds."

She was attired in white linen, was inclined to *embonpoint*, of agreeable countenance, and short nose *retroussé*. She inquired of me in Arabic whether I spoke Italian, and receiving a reply in the affirmative, she then asked if I were married? how long I had been so? where I had lived? what my parents were? and a number of other commonplace questions. Having satisfied her queries, she asked me to have the kindness to show her my wardrobe.

Conducting her into my room, into which I was followed by a whole bevy of white and black slaves, I placed in her hands several articles of wearing apparel, such as dresses, bonnets, hats, &c. She passed them over to the slaves, and coolly walked off with them into the Reception Hall, and there exhibited them to the Princess Epouse, who admired them, and seemed particularly pleased with the hats and bonnets, all of which she requested me to put on, so that Her Highness might see how they became me.

After she had amused herself in that manner, the Princess retired to her chamber to take her *siesta*. I then went down into the Stone Hall, where I partook of what was to me my luncheon, and was again subjected to the mortification of having the German laundry maid as my companion, notwithstanding that I had already complained to Her Highness of such treatment.

CHAPTER X.

His Highness the Grand Pacha partook of his supper at half-past five, after which we again promenaded in the gardens until half-past seven, when I took him in, and handed His Highness over to the care of the head-nurse. Then I retired to my own chamber, changed my dress, and descended into the Stone Hall to partake of my dinner, which was similar to that which had been served up to me on the first day of my entrance into the Harem, and so it continued till the day of my quitting the Viceroy's service.

While I was sipping my coffee, the little slave who had been appointed to wait upon me let the china vase containing the sherbet fall, and broke it to pieces. It was immediately replaced by another, which was handed me by an elder slave. Upon making inquiry of the head-nurse, who happened at that moment to enter the room, what had become of the Kaduyah, for that was the name of the slave who had broken the elegant china vase, she told me that I should not see her again for some days, as she had just undergone the usual punishment always inflicted upon all slaves who broke anything.

Reader, will you credit it?—the poor creature had actually been seared on her arms with a red-hot iron! And then Shaytan went on to explain that all the black slaves in the Harem bore their characters about them.

I had previously observed that there was not a single one who had not undergone that punishment; and, in short, many of their arms were literally covered with scars arising from such brutal treatment. All the black slaves were marked with three scars on their faces. The Viceregal brand being three marks distinguished them from those of private individuals, who were only marked with two scars. Singular to add not any of the nurses were branded.

Just as I had risen from the deal table, a young Arab woman entered the room; she was dressed in colored muslin, wore a red gauze handkerchief wrapped round her head; beautiful diamond earrings hung from her ears, a handsome gold hunting-watch suspended from her neck by a thick massive gold chain, having also a rich Albert chain attached thereto, was tucked into her waistband. Her fingers were covered with superb diamond rings, the value of which would have been almost a fortune to any European lady.

She was the Prince's *Dadu-nina*, wet-nurse, who had come to pay her respects to me. She remained but a very few minutes, asked several trivial questions, told me that she was married, that her husband lived at Cairo, that she was about to leave the service of the Viceroy to return to her home.

I was just on the point of entering my chamber, when Rhoda, the mother of the Harem, met me, and led me into the saloon occupied by the ladies of the Harem. There were about six or seven of them attired in different colored muslins sitting *à la Turque*, on cushions on the floor, which was covered with a rich Brussels carpet, playing at dominoes, their most favorite pastime; others were amusing themselves smoking cigarettes, and listening to the tales which each in their turn had been relating.

One of them, named Emina, rose from her seat and offered me a cigarette, which, however, I declined with thanks; and, knowing full well that I never smoked, she did not feel in the slightest degree offended at my breach of Turkish etiquette, but returned to her cushion.

7

As soon as I had seated myself in the divan, Rhoda related the following incident of the manner in which marriages are frequently arranged in Turkey :—

" Some years ago, on one occasion," began the mistress of the Harem, " when I accompanied the Princess the Lady Paramount to Constantinople, I became acquainted with a Turkish family who had an only daughter, named Sarata. She had just turned eleven ; had been affianced when in her fifth year to a young man of the name of Reschid, who was then about sixteen, and to whom she was on the point of being united.

" Reschid had never seen her since they were children together; so that he had no recollection of her features. Sarata had also lost all idea of the photograph of her betrothed. She therefore entreated her mother to allow her to have an opportunity of seeing him before the marriage took place.

" The old lady, who was a very indulgent parent, so arranged it, one day when Reschid was paying a visit to the father, that Sarata should conceal herself behind a *macharabieh*, and thus she obtained a full view of her future husband's features. Curiosity prompted her to remain some time in her hiding-place ; and she heard her father say, in reply to a question that Reschid had put to him, respecting the day on which they were to be married, ' *Quail im* ' ('I give my sanction,') and the day was named.

" It now only wanted about eight days to the period when Sarata, who was then called *Kutchuk Hanem* (miss, or little lady), would be addressed by the long-coveted title of *Bruick Hanem* (mistress, or great lady).

" Singular to add, Reschid also expressed to his mother a desire to obtain a peep at the features of his future better half, for, as she was continually lauding the beauty of his little bride, he felt rather dubious whether he ought to believe all that his parent had said in her favor. Her anxiety to hasten the match made him dubious as to the personal appearance of Sarata.

"Determined, if possible, to gratify his desire, he had recourse to a Levantine Jewess, who was in the habit of supplying many of the harems of the *élite* with jewelry. She was an old, cunning creature; and knowing how completely she was the slave to that sovereign ruler of the Ottoman dominions, Prince Baksheesh, he endeavored to persuade her to introduce herself into the hall of the Harem in which Sarata was domiciled, in order that she might be able to give him an accurate delineation of the features and appearance of his betrothed.

"The sly faggot of a maid of Israel returned to his residence two days afterwards, and gave him a most flattering account of Sarata, whom she designated as the 'Star of beauty'—compared her teeth to pearls, her eyes to stars, and the arches of her eyebrows to the *arc-en-ciel* (rainbow).

"It appeared that she had been in the habit of taking quantities of jewelry into that Harem on several occasions, and that, on that very morning, she had visited Sarata for the purpose of calling for some watch-charms, keys, &c., that required to be repaired. And it is no uncommon occurrence, where valuable ornaments are taken away by such individuals out of the Harems, that some of less value are substituted for them, or else they are purloined.

"It happened only at the latter end of last year that Hawwaia Hanem, a member of the late Viceroy Abbas Pacha's Harem, brought an action in the British Consular Court at Cairo, before Albany Fonblanque, Esq., H. M. late Vice-Consul, against Barbara Maggi and Luigi Maggi, to recover a valuable ornament, called *girlandu*, worth 2,500*l.*, which she had entrusted to the defendants to repair.

"The bride had found great fault with the quality of those articles, for, like a great portion of the modern *bijoux* generally sold to the inmates of many of the Harems by those kind of women, they were perfect rubbish, being neither more nor less than metal covered with a thick plate of gold, and for which the slaves pay almost fabulous sums.

" Reschid, thinking himself extremely fortunate in the selection that his mother had made for him, exclaimed, ' *Allaha chukur el hamdu billah pèk éyou ûn* ' (' Very well; God be thanked ! '), and at the same time handed her a packet of gold. He also gave her several pretty boxes of fruit and bonbons, and two handsome vases, filled with artificial flowers, to present to his bride.

" As soon as the marriage contract was signed, the costly bridal presents were sent. They consisted principally of a parcel of rich silks and jewelry, a dressing-glass, and a pair of slippers for the bath-room, which latter is always considered an indispensable article.

" Reschid, in return, received from Sarata's parents a quantity of body-linen, napkins fringed with gold, silver, and silk. Then each of the parents exchanged presents among themselves.

" A considerable period elapsed between the signing of the marriage contract and the bridal day, during which time Reschid was occupied in getting together the amount of the settlement, while the bride's parents were preparing her *trousseau*.

" At length the joyful day arrived, and the festivities lasted four days—that is from Monday morning until sunset on Thursday. The marriage night was fixed for Friday, which is considered the most propitious day, on account of that being the day on which Mahomet the Prophet was conceived, hence the reason why it is our [the Turkish] sabbath.

" The bridal ceremony was celebrated by both families, the women according to their manner, and the men in theirs. The rejoicings consisted chiefly in grand banquets, during the intervals of which large quantities of coffee, sherbet, preserves, perfumes, pipes, and cigarettes were used.

"A most lively hilarity characterized these re-unions, which were at one time varied by the feats of jugglers and dancers, and at others by the exhibition of *Kara-kioz,* the Turkish Punch. The parents and their acquaintances passed twenty-four hours in each other's residence; and so numerous were they that the divans in the rooms and the Harems were their seats by day and their couches by night.

"Each day had its peculiar ceremony. On the Tuesday Sarata's *trousseau* was carried in state to the bridegroom's house. On Wednesday evening the bride was led to the bath-room, and there underwent the luxury or torture of a bath. For to my idea and feelings it is nothing more nor less than a punishment to be scalded with *boiling* water like a dead pig, and then to be kneaded about like a lump of dough until your whole body looks like a mummy. The hands of the slaves who soap your person and rub you are shrivelled up like those of a washerwoman just taken out of the scalding suds, and in that state they remain. Then an incredible number of cosmetics, salves, dyes, &c., are used, my utter abomination (for my mother's daughter has never used anything but healthy cold water), which they apply before quitting the bath-room, where the whole of the lady guests and the poor women of the locality were assembled to meet her.

"The latter had divested themselves of their rags, which they left in the hall, and attired themselves in new garments which had been bought for the occasion out of the sum appropriated for the festival. Early the next afternoon, Sarata, accompanied by her mother, sisters, and suite, left her parental roof for that of her husband. Then the parents, the guests who had been invited by both families, the men and the women belonging to both Harems, all assembled there. The festivities lasted the whole day, and ended with a grand supper.

"At the silent hour of midnight, Reschid, after having

taken leave of his father, whose hand he kissed, as also those of his brothers and relatives, repaired to his own Harem, into which he glided more like a snake than a human being. There he found Sarata, closely veiled, seated on a divan, awaiting his arrival. The mother of the Harem, who stood in one corner of the room, introduced him, as was her office, to his bride, who on his entrance rose up off her seat, and as he advanced to take hold of her hand, seized his and kissed it as a token of submission. Reschid then lifted up the mysterious veil. The old mother of the Harem still occupied the corner, as motionless as a statue in its niche.

"'I must send that baggage away,' thought Reschid to himself; but this was easier said than managed. 'Here,' said he, drawing forth from his pocket a silk purse, 'are two hundred piastres, take them and begone.'

"The old hag did not move a muscle.

"'Take any one of these!' exclaimed the bridegroom, holding out his hand, in which lay several purses, some with five, six, eight, and ten hundred piastres.

"Still the old creature did not budge an inch. Sarata was smiling all this time beneath her mask, yclept veil.

"At length, Reschid thinking that it was quite time to put an end to this farce, pushed the old hag out of the chamber. Then he turned round and looked upon Sarata's face for the first time. But, alas! he was most wofully disappointed; for Sarata was not the beauteous Peri the crafty Jewess, who had taken *baksheesh* from all parties, had led him to believe."

As soon as Rhoda had thus finished this reminiscence of her visit to Stamboul, I regained my chamber, and added a few pages to my journal. It was a most lovely night. I sat on my box by the open window, but my reverie was soon disturbed by the sound of the beating of muffled drums falling on my ears, which brought to my mind the "Dead March in Saul" played at a soldier's funeral. Leaning out of the window, and glancing in the direction of His Highness's pavilion, I perceived a female figure enveloped in a large black *hubarah*, shuffling (for no Turkish or Egyptian woman can walk) along towards the gate that leads into the pavilion gardens. She was preceded by two eunuchs; then followed several boy eunuchs beating their muffled drums, which I was afterwards in the habit of hearing of a night, almost as frequently as the beating of the tattoo in India, and

> " I hated its mournful and discordant sound,
> Parading round, and round, and round."

I looked with astonishment at this midnight march. For some moments my glance was riveted upon the procession, it had such a novel and singular appearance; but turning my eyes towards His Highness's pavilion I beheld it lighted up. Then, looking through my achromatic opera-glass, and at the same time placing my ear down on the window-sill, I

> " Heard through the pavilion melodious music steal,
> And self-prepared the splendid banquet stands;
> Self-poured the champagne sparkles in the bowl;
> The lute and viol, touched by unseen hands,
> And the soft voices of the choral bands."

Then full well did I know that Ismael Pacha, the Viceroy, was giving a fête that evening: and the idea struck me, as afterwards proved to be the fact, that the veiled figure was one of His Highness's "*ikbals*" (favorite slaves), who had gone to pass the night in the far-famed "guest's chamber," in the Pavilion. I afterwards learned that whenever the Viceroy required the presence of any of the favorites, they invariably proceeded to his presence in that manner; and proud, indeed, were they whenever His Highness delighted to have their society.

A few nights afterwards, about eleven o'clock, when I had closed my window, and had sat down to continue my journal, I was disturbed by the sounds of loud revelry. At first

I was at a loss to conceive whence the noise issued, as I knew that the eunuchs always locked the outer doors leading down to the staircases at ten o'clock. Still, as the romping and laughing appeared to come from near the Harem gardens, at first I thought that, perhaps, some of the Viceroy's guests had become rather jovial, and had rambled about in the Pavilion gardens, in the vicinity of the Harem.

" Listening, however, for a few moments, I heard the well-known laugh of one of my own slave attendants. Rising from my seat, I extinguished the wax-lights, opened the window softly, peeped out into the grounds, and, lo! there, to my utter amazement, I beheld a motley group of black female slaves. Moving about them were figures closely resembling the soldiers, when muffled up in their cloaks, who usually mounted guard at the outside gates of the Harem. Looking through my opera-glass, I immediately discerned several of the eunuchs " tripping along the verdant green ; " others were dancing and singing as merrily as if they were an " elfin band."

I had heard much, and read a great deal about the impossibility of men entering the Harems of the East, considered so " sacred " by all Moslems, that no true believer has ever been known to visit the " Abode of Bliss " of a true Mussulman. But now that I had seen the female slaves of the Viceregal Harem rambling about at night with the eunuchs, "the guardians of those girls," and other muffled figures, I could not help giving credence to the assertion of a celebrated writer on Oriental life, that, crabbed and cross-grained as the eunuchs may be, still there are many of them who bow the knee to that sovereign ruler of Egypt, Prince Baksheesh, and that golden keys do sometimes throw back the rusty hinges of the doors they guard ; or else how came the slaves and their partners, those muffled figures,

" To be dancing on the verdant lawn,
In the bright moonlight."

Then I remembered Mr. B.'s narrative of the eunuch, Dafay, whose wife had a numerous family; and having myself witnessed several of these spectres of mankind " toying and wooing" with the black female slaves, I doubted their infirmity of body, and kept a watchful eye over them. I would never allow any of the female slaves to sleep within my chamber, the door of which I both locked and bolted within nightly.

I had an excellent opportunity of remarking the immense sums of money squandered away in the Viceregal Harems of Ghezire and Alexandria. The annual supply of the richest silks, satins, velvets, laces, muslins, and numerous articles of female attire, together with boots, shoes, slippers, confectionery, *bonbons*, golden-leaved tobacco, Schiedam, perfumes, and a whole host of miscellaneous European articles, could not have cost less than 100,000*l*. per annum. The amount that their Highness expended in jewels alone averaged 3,000*l*. per annum; the sum sacrified upon the altar of Prince Baksheesh cannot fall far short of 70,000*l*. per annum, and the bare expenses of the household must amount to 44,000*l*. per annum; so that it may be estimated the Viceregal Harem costs the Viceroy no less a sum than 250,000*l*. to 300,000*l*. per annum, or 250*l*. to 300*l*. per head; and this is, I feel assured, considerably within bounds, because it must be borne in mind that their Highnesses the Princesses distribute *baksheesh*, and a supply of both plain and costly attire, to those around them with no sparing hand.

The census of the Harem is 150 to 200 slaves and eunuchs included; and the profits of those who supply the Harem must be enormous; for every commodity is purchased in bulk, at wholesale prices, and charged to the Viceroy at the *marketable* rates.

CHAPTER XI.

ONE morning when I was quitting the Grand Pacha's Reception Saloon, accompanied by my pupil, to take our usual ramble in the gardens, one of the eunuchs approached, and after having made his ordinary salaam, informed me that the Viceroy Ismael Pacha requested me to take the Prince on board his beautiful yacht, *The Crocodile*, and that I should find the Grand Pacha's yacht, the elegant *Fairy*, lying off the Harem landing-place, which would convey us on board His Highness's steamer, which had proceeded farther up the Nile.

Returning to my chamber, I attired myself in a silk walking-dress, while Shaytan took the Prince into his room, and dressed him in grand tenue as a Turkish General. His uniform consisted of a pair of grey trousers, fastened round his knees with a strap, patent leather knickerbockers, laced up outside, a grey cloth kilt, buckled round his waist by a broad white web band, over which was placed a jacket of the same color, most richly embroidered with silver lace and silver buttons. Then a black silk velvet paletot, trimmed with gold lace and gold buttons, and lined with crimson satin, the skirts of which were drawn back by a strap of gold lace fastened behind to the waist with a gold button, completed his dress. On his shoulders he wore two gold epaulets. In his pockets were placed two handkerchiefs, one of red silk and the other of finest lawn, each corner of which was embroidered with white silk and gold thread, neither of which he ever used. They were never washed, but when crumpled, ironed out.

Leading the Grand Pacha by the hand, I took him down stairs, proceeded across the garden into the Harem, and passed forthwith into the room occupied by the ladies of the Harem. There I found their Highnesses the Princesses, the three wives, congregated together, each of whom took hold of the Prince, kissed him several times, and gave him messages to deliver to the Viceroy.

As soon as the Grand Pacha had bid them adieu, I proceeded with him to the landing-place, where we embarked on board the *Fairy* accompanied by his usual attendants, and the yacht steamed away up the Nile. The Prince, as soon as he went on board, where he was received with the usual honors, hurried down the stairs into the saloon, and most kindly took me all over the yacht.

The saloon was most elegantly fitted up. On its gilded panels were painted several pleasing landscapes of Alexandria and its suburbs. The ceiling was painted white, with gilded beading and cornices. The floor was covered with a rich Brussels carpet. The sofa was of ormolu and gold, covered with figured white satin. Large mirrors reached down from the ceiling to the floor. Ormolu tables, with marble tops, were placed about in different parts, as also cane chairs. The cushions of the divans were of white figured satin, trimmed with brilliant massive gold tassels. Some black satin cushions, ornamented with gold thread and pearls, also lay upon the floor.

The six plate-glass windows on each side, which reached from the ceiling down to the floor, were fixed in rosewood frames, that could, as well as the wooden jalousies, if necessary, be drawn over those openings when the glass windows were drawn back into the sides.

At the farther extremity were two immense glass mirrors, which formed, as it were, folding-doors, and when these were drawn back the whole appeared as one immense saloon.

The doors having been pushed back, I entered the other compartment, which I found similarly furnished to that I had just quitted. Proceeding along it, I reached a mirror that formed a door on the right-hand side, and pushing this back, I discovered that it led me into a lavatory. Opposite to it was the water-closet — not *à l' Anglaise,* but *à la Turque*—which consisted of a marble floor, in which was a hole cut, in the shape of a carpenter's plumb-line. I had seen similar ones at Troyes, in France, on the line from Paris to Basle. In one corner stood a silver ewer filled with water. At the farthest extremity of the saloon were two immense mirrors, reaching down from the ceiling to the floor, which formed folding-doors, and on sliding them back into their sockets, both myself and my pupil walked out on to the semicircular poop-deck, which was carpeted and covered with an awning, and encircled by a gilt rail.

After steaming up the river some distance, the tender, as the *Fairy* was often called, soon reached the Viceroy's yacht, *The Crocodile,* and was hailed by the Captain Bachi, to bring-to.

A long narrow rowing boat then approached the yacht. It was covered with an awning, manned by fourteen rowers, having crimson velvet-cushioned seats on both sides, the bottom being matted and richly carpeted.

At the stern, which was raised, sat the captain and four of the crew, holding the cords of the red satin awning, lined with white satin and trimmed with gold fringe. We both entered it, seated ourselves under the awning, and were rowed alongside *The Crocodile.*

As the boat neared His Highness's yacht, the band of the regiment on board (for Ismael Pacha, who may be said, like the Chinese, to live the greater part of his time on the water, always carries a band with him), struck up the Sultan's March as the Grand Pacha and myself ascended the ladder, which was covered with crimson cloth. The officers then advanced, saluted him, and the soldiers presented arms.

As the Viceroy had visitors, we proceeded into the first or audience saloon, on the panels of which were exquisitely painted several scenes of the most interesting places on the

Nile. Between these were let in, as it were, in richly gilded frames, peacocks with their magnificent tails spread out at full length, and several other specimens of the varied ornithology of Egypt, all formed of precious stones. Also numerous bouquets of flowers and clusters of fruit. The ceiling was painted white, having a beautiful centre-piece representing a battle-scene, one of Ibrahim Pacha's victories in Syria; the most conspicuous objects in which were several wild-looking horses, held by Arabs. It was edged with gilt beading and ornamented with rich cornices.

The floor was covered with matting, over white was placed a rich-looking drab-ground carpet, interspersed with rose and large blue convolvuluses. The divan in which His Highness sat is covered with red and white silk and gold thread, which gives it a most gorgeous appearance. The framework of the chairs were gold, and the seats covered with the same material as the divan, as also were the hangings of the doors and windows. In the centre stood a superb round inlaid table. Mirrors were placed on each side of the entrance, and also behind the divan, which was ranged across the saloon on which the Viceroy generally sat, so that he could see every person as they approached. Passing through a panel door, which was painted with a fine view of the cataracts up the Nile, we entered another saloon, whose sides, ceiling, and carpet were similar to those of the compartment through which the Prince and myself had just passed, except that between the painted panels were placed gilded frames containing figures of wild animals and birds, all having jeweled eyes.

The seats to the chairs, &c., were covered with red satin, the framework, chairs, and sofas were of ormolu and gold, the hangings and doors were of the same material as the covers of the furniture. In the centre stood a square sliding dining-table, covered with a crimson cloth richly embroidered with gold thread, fringed with a deep border of bullion, and at the corners were the everlasting crescent and star. Mirrors reached from the ceiling, on which was painted an Egyptian landscape, down to the floor.

Then I pushed back the folding glass-doors into their sockets, and we walked out on to the poop-deck, which was covered with a handsome thick carpet. Large easy rosewood chairs and footstools, covered with green velvet, were scattered about. It was protected from the rays of the burning sun by a snow-white canvas awning, under which was placed a square one of thick crimson silk, lined with white satin and trimmed with bullion fringe, with curtains of the same material hanging down from a gilt rod. Having remained for some moments enjoying the refreshing breeze which had sprung up, and which at that season of the year was a luxury, we descended into the saloon, opened a door on the right hand and walked into the Viceroy's bedchamber. The ceiling was richly gilded and beautifully painted in fresco; and the panels were of rosewood highly polished, between which hung in superb gilded frames figures of numerous animals. This constant display of figures of the inhabitants of the forest impressed me with an idea that the whole of the descendants of Mehemet Ali with whom I had not as yet come into contact, were naturally cruel, overbearing, and even brutal in their tastes. In short, barbarity appeared to be a legacy which had descended to them, as I had already seen the Grand Pacha manifest the utmost indifference to human sufferings, and take delight in the exercise of wanton cruelty towards his inferiors and the companions of his daily pastimes.

The floor was covered with a crimson carpet interspersed with white Japan roses. The gilded iron bedstead was surmounted with gilded knobs; on the top in the centre stood a large gilt crescent. The hangings, which slid upon gilded rods, were of rich crimson silk. The coverlet was of white corded silk superbly embroidered with gold thread and trimmed with bullion fringe. At the foot, resting on an ormolu table on which was placed a magnificent Sèvres toilette service, stood a large mirror. At one side of the chamber was placed a superb inlaid ebony wardrobe, and opposite to it stood a rich cabinet to match. The latter was a most exquisite piece of workmanship, a perfect gem. On this day it so attracted the notice of the Grand Pacha, who must have observed it " many a time and oft," that he stopped to examine every part of it. On this morning, however, its golden key had been left in the lock, and the Prince's curiosity to examine its interior was so intense that I could not restrain His Highness from unlocking it, who immediately commenced rummaging its contents. Among numerous other objects of rare *vertu* which attracted the little Prince's attention, was a gold-clasped red morocco book, about the size of an ordinary note letter blotter. Taking it up and handing it to me he requested that I would open it for him.

Acting according to his commands I turned the elegantly-chased gold key that was fastened to its handle, in the Bramah-like wards, and then handed the book over to the Prince. He took it in his tiny hands, turned it over and over again, admired the elegant manner in which its covers were embossed, opened it, turned the leaves over, apparently expecting to find that it contained some pictures or photographs.

Great, however, was his disappointment, when he found only a few pages covered with what he termed characters *à la Franca*. Placing that precious "Red Book," which, though not the Egyptian Court Guide, might most appropriately have been termed, *minus* its color, the Viceroy Ismael Pacha's "*Blue* Book," into my hand, I scanned the pages, and—guess my utter astonishment, when I saw that it contained a list of the "eighteen other Princes" who govern Egypt.

I could scarcely believe my eyesight. It appeared to me

as if I were under the delusion of a *mirage*. Again I ran my eye down that list. Then I became convinced that it was a reality; for at the head of the first page loomed forth, in a bold, clear handwriting, the title of that sovereign ruler of Egypt, Prince Baksheesh, and underneath, in regular order, were placed the names, at full length, of all those special Princes and their subordinates; and opposite to each, in the red-ink column, commencing with that of my own special Prince, were placed sums beginning with 3,000*l.* down to 300*l.*, and at the bottom the significant words "*per annum.*" Then I fully understood the force of the expression of that clever contributor to " Once a Week," when he states, " Let your own special Prince back up your petition," &c., and what have you got? Nothing! I repeat, that at that moment I only understood the force of that expression, but I can now affirm that I have lived to experience its veracity.

I relocked that valuable *souvenir*. Kind reader, it is indeed a precious volume! for no less a sum than 17,000*l.* was offered for its abstraction. I then explained to H. H. the Grand Pacha that it contained an account of the *baksheesh* which I supposed the Viceroy was either accustomed to, or else intended to, distribute to those Europeans whom "he delighted to honor," and safely lodged it in its place. I had held a fortune in my hands; but as " honesty is the best policy," I left the tempter, and walked away from the cabinet—a wiser, although decidedly not a richer woman.

On the top of this matchless cabinet stood a most magnificently inlaid square ivory box, which also attracted the Prince's attention; but finding it was locked, he turned round to the Viceroy's *Tchiboukdji,* " pipe-bearer," who may be termed His Highness's factotum. The individual holding this office is one of the most influential persons about his person, since he possesses the power to refuse all admittance to the Viceregal presence, and can at all times command the ear of his august liege. In short, it may be remarked, that he seldom or never quits the Viceregal presence by night nor day.

I have often been with His Highness, Ismael Pacha, when the world may have thought that we were "all alone, all alone!" but you may take it for granted that, as my footsteps approached towards the Viceregal sanctorum, the *Tchiboukdji* vanishes, Asmodeus-like, out of sight, undoubtedly exclaiming to himself, like Oberon in the "Midsummer's Night Dream,"—

> "But who comes here? I am invisible,
> And I will overhear their conference;"

and snugly ensconced himself behind the hangings of either the doors or windows, as was his wont. Had that drapery been drawn aside, there would that faithful being have been found standing as motionless and as breathless as the spectre in "Don Giovanni;" so that you may believe me when I say that, shrouded as it were in his invisibility, he is ever present at all interviews which take place between His Highness and his male favorites, associates in commerce, ministers, ah! and even when "our own Prince," or any of the other seventeen Princes who govern Egypt obtain audiences.

Thus does he become the depository of both private and state secrets. His smile to all about the Viceregal person is like the "new born day," but his frown is like the impenetrable darkness of night. The Grand Eunuch is his bosom friend, and when smoking their golden-colored tobacco together (rendered still more acceptable by the addition of a mite of opium) is it not possible that he may have exclaimed, in the beautiful language of the Prince of Poets—

> "But that I am forbid
> To tell the secrets of the prison-house,
> I would a tale unfold, whose lightest word
> Would harrow up thy soul, freeze thy young blood;
> Make thy two eyes, like stars, start from their spheres;

8

> Thy knotted and combined locks to part,
> And each particular hair to stand on end,
> Like quills upon the fretful porcupine."

The *Tchiboukdji* immediately produced a small key and opened the box.

The Grand Pacha gazed with delight upon the contents of both the compartments. The top one contained numerous small purses filled with Egyptian silver *paras*, and sovereigns, both Egyptian, English, and Turkish, French napoleons, and gold ten and five-franc pieces. Lifting up the tray, the second compartment was filled with jeweled hilts for swords, buckles, inlaid with crescents and stars of diamonds, which had evidently been used for sword-belts, many of which must from their antique settings, have belonged to the renowned Mehemet Ali and the gallant Ibrahim Pacha.

There was another tray filled with an immense quantity of large loose precious stones of great value, of which the little Prince took up a handful, seated himself upon the divan, and began to play with them. After he had amused himself for a considerable time in that harmless manner, he made the *Tchiboukji* hand him all the large purses of money which stood in the top compartment, one by one, while he emptied their contents on to the divan, and then set to playing at keeping a bank, his most favorite pastime. Thus early did he develop that he inherited his father's genius of understanding "the art of making money produce a proper return."

As soon as he became tired of that amusement, he rose up, leaving to the *Tchiboukji*, who was of an amiable disposition, the trouble of re-sorting all the different coins, and putting them back into their respective purses.

After we had examined the whole of this princely yacht, we proceeded into the grand saloon where we now found Ismael Pacha, the Viceroy, who had been closeted with His

Excellency Reschid Pacha on our arrival, alone, dressed *à la Européenne*, sitting on a divan; and whom I now discovered, to my discomfiture, to be no other than the individual whom I had mistaken in the Harem to be the Viceregal barber. I curtseyed and remained standing, until he motioned me to be seated on the divan on his right side.

His Highness, who is most affable both in his manners and deportment, has a pleasing yet thoughtful expression of countenance, an excellent type of *bonhommie*, and yet the very picture of the celebrated Rothschild when leaning against the pillar on 'Change, minus the Jewish cast of contour. He scanned my lineaments and attire from head to foot, and, as is his custom, "he slily lifted his eye's blue windowlet," and looked intently at me for a considerable time. Then he placed the little Prince on his left hand, and despatched the *Tchiboukdji*, who had now entered the agartment, to fetch a purse of *paras*, which generally contained about 5*l.*, the contents of which he emptied into the Grand Pacha's pockets to distribute as *baksheesh* among his attendants, the whole of which I was surprised to see on our return to the Harem was taken possession of by the head-nurse, who handed the greater portion to myself. At first I declined to accept any of the coins, but being informed that it was the custom to receive such, I always afterwards took whatever pieces of money Shaytan handed to me; the rest, as a matter of course, she kept to herself.

The Viceroy then turned round to me, and inquired if I would like to make an excursion up the Nile. Replying in the affirmative, and thanking Ismael Pacha for his attention, I curtseyed and retired with the Prince, who salaamed his father, as was his usual custom.

On descending the gangway we were rowed alongside another yacht, called the "Ibis," on board of which we were received with the customary honors, and passed the day steaming up and down the Nile, during which excursion we passed within sight of the palaces of Kasr Dubarra, Kasr El Ainée, and the celebrated island of Rhoda, at the southern extremity of which stands the Nilometer, at the point where the river branches off into two streams, one of which passes by Ghiseh, and the other by Old Cairo. A portion of the island was at that time covered with the slime of the Nile, through which, however, several shrubs had thrust, as it were their branches; while ibises were on the surface, dipping their beaks into it in search of prey; huge sycamores spread their grateful shade around.

Those beautiful gardens, the delight of Ibrahim Pacha, which stand on its northern extremity, were at that season of the year just bursting forth in all their splendor. There the stately palm-trees of the Antilles waved their lofty, slender branches; the gigantic Indian bamboos, upwards of ten feet high, grow as luxuriantly as if they reared their heads in the jungles of Bengal. There also were to be seen specimens of foliage quite foreign to the soil, but cut in most singular fashion, as also fruit-trees, whose forms are as peculiar as the taste of their fruit, all of which give a most curious and unique aspect to those exquisite gardens, which are interspersed with long and wide shady avenues, and surrounded by almost impenetrable masses of masonry. There flower-beds flourish filled with brilliant exotics, and emerald spots irrigated with streams of clear water, and large patches of vegetable-gardens in the highest state of cultivation. A small white marble kiosk reared its tapering roof above the dark green foliage of the sycamores, and a stone bank stood by the river-side.

The next morning, as soon as the Prince had returned from his usual walk, I obtained permission from the Princess Epouse to pay a visit to Mr. B.'s, at Cairo. Orders were accordingly given by the Grand Eunuch for a state barge to be prepared to convey me across the Nile, and a messenger was despatched to Cairo, to order a carriage to be sent down to the landing-place, on the Cairo side, as there are no carriages or horses kept at the Harem or Pavilion.

After I had been kept waiting several hours, I embarked in the barge, landed on the other side of the Nile, entered the Viceregal carriage, and forthwith proceeded to the banker's.

Fortunately I found Mr. B. at home. He received me very kindly, and listened attentively to my description of the inconveniences to which I had been subjected.

As I found it utterly impossible to adopt any regular system as to the educational surveillance of the Grand Pacha, I deemed it prudent to explain in detail to Mr. B. the difficulties which I had to encounter.

The irregularity which prevailed in the domestic arrangements of the Harem had totally frustrated all my endeavors to carry out any regular system. Sometimes I received orders from the Grand Eunuch which were issued at the caprice of the Princess Epouse, who, as a matter of course, was perfectly ignorant as to the manner adopted in Europe of training up young children, to take the Grand Pacha out walking at six o'clock in the morning; on other occasions at seven, eight, and nine o'clock. And when once the little Prince was in the gardens, it was exceedingly difficult to get him to return. His will was law; and no matter how singular and unreasonable his whims were, still he must be indulged in them.

I drew up a scheme for his education, and endeavored to obtain the Viceroy's sanction to its execution; but that Prince explained to me that he did not wish the Prince to be taught from books or toys, as he would pick up English quickly enough by being constantly with me; so that I abandoned all idea of educational training.

Then I explained to Mr. B. the numerous degradations to which I was subjected, and called his attention to the fact that I was unprovided with either chairs or tables; that I was obliged to use my trunks as substitutes for such necessaries, which were liable to, and actually did, before I retired from His Highness's service, produce spinal complaint.

Again and again, as I had previously done, when remaining as a guest, nay, I should rather add as a caged bird, under his hospitable roof, I pointed out to him that not only did I find the Arab diet so nauseous to my taste as to oblige me to live chiefly upon dry bread and a little pigeon or mutton, but that, owing to the want of more nourishing food, and especially European cooking, I found my strength gradually sinking day by day; and that the constant use of coffee, and the total deprivation of those stimulants, such as malt liquor and wine, to which I had always been accustomed, and of which it is absolutely necessary that Europeans should partake in warm countries to counteract the hostile debilitating effects of the climate, would, I fear, soon throw me on a bed of sickness.

Besides, I was constantly being sent out with the Prince into the gardens during the intense heat of the day, the thermometer often ranging from 99° to 100°; it really seemed as if the Princess Epouse considered that I had been thoroughly acclimatized before I entered the Harem.

Then the very atmosphere that I breathed was continually impregnated with the fumes of tobacco, into which large quantities of opium and other deleterious narcotics were infused, which so affected my constitution that my spirits began to flag, and I felt a kind of heavy languid apathy come over me, that scarcely any amount of energy on my part was able to shake off.

The irksome monotony of my daily life had produced a most unpleasant feeling in my mind. Not only had I lost much of my wonted energy, but a kind of lethargy seemed to have crept over me; a most indefinable reluctance to move about had imperceptibly gained ascendancy over my actions;—to walk, to speak (and here I must not forget to mention that my voice had become extremely feeble)—to apply myself to drawing, reading, or in fact, to make the slightest exertion of any kind whatever, had become absolutely irksome to me.

It was not the feeling of what we Europeans call *ennui* which I experienced, for that sensation can always be shook off by a little moral courage and energy; but it was a state bordering on that frightful melancholy, that must, if not dispelled, engender insanity. And my experience of such feelings is not to be wondered at, if my position in the Harem is thoroughly examined.

CHAPTER XII.

WELL, kind reader; there I was, totally unacquainted with either the Turkish or Arabic tongues; unaccustomed to the filthy manners, barbarous customs, and disgusting habits of all around me; deprived of every comfort by which I had always been surrounded; shut out from all rational society; hurried here and there, in the heat of a scorching African sun, at a moment's notice; absolutely living upon nothing else but dry bread and a little pigeon or mutton, barely sufficient to keep body and soul together. Compelled to take all my meals but my scanty breakfast (a dry roll and a cup of coffee) in the society of two clownish disgusting German peasant servants; lacking the stimulants so essentially necessary for the preservation of health in such a hot climate; stung almost to death with mosquitoes, tormented with flies, and surrounded with beings who were breeders of vermin; a daily witness of manners the most repugnant, nay, revolting, to the delicacy of a European female—for often have I seen, in the presence of my little Prince.

> " A lady of the Harem, not more forward than all the rest,
>   Well versed in Syren's arts, it must be confessed,
>   Shuffle off her garments, and let her figure stand revealed,
>   Like that of Venus who no charms concealed ! "

Surrounded by intriguing Arab nurses, who not only despised me because I was a Howadji, but hated me in their hearts because, as a European lady, I insisted upon receiving, and most assuredly I did receive, so far as the Viceroy and the Princesses, the three wives, were concerned, proper respect.   The bare fact of my being allowed to take precedence of all the inmates of the Harem, even of the *Ikbals*, " favorites," galled them to the quick ; and there is no doubt that they were at that time inwardly resolved to do their utmost to render my position as painful as possible, nay, even untenable.   Then my only companions were the ladies of the Harem, whose appearance I have already described as being totally at variance with that glowing myth-like picture that Tom Moore gives of retired beauty. so erroneously supposed to be caged within the precincts of the *Abodes of Bliss*, in his exquisite poem of " Lalla Rookh," for therein I failed to find

> " Oh, what a pure and sacred thing
>   Is beauty curtained from the sight .
>   Of the gross world, illumining
>   One only mansion with her light."

They were composed of old *Ikbals*, favorites of Ibrahim Pacha, and some of those who had ceased to rank as such, or as the slaves emphatically termed it, to *please* the " Baba Efendimir."

I was struck with their use of the expression, " please the Viceroy," for it was one that had been used to me, when I had an interview in London with Mr. C. H.'s sister prior to my leaving for Egypt, by that lady.   At that time I did not heed the expression ; now that the *Ikbals* had used it I understood their significance of its meaning, and I was perfectly convinced in my own mind, that, taking it in that sense, they meant that I should *not* please His Highness, no matter how long I remained in the Viceregal service.

Many were very old, as no woman is ever ejected from this supposed type of the Mahometan Paradise, as poor Hagar was repudiated of old; except when the " green-eyed monster," jealousy or envy, sends her to her "long account with all the imperfections on her head." When she is doomed, however, with calm resignation,

"She hears the fatal news—no word—no groan;
She speaks not, moves not, stands transfixed to stone;"

but how she went, or when, no one within that mystic Castle of Indolence dare tell; and yet the depths of the slimy Nile, could they but speak, " would many a tale unfold." When questioned all shake their heads, and utter that significant Arab expression *Malesch! Malesch!* "No matter, no matter!"

White slaves and black were mingled indiscriminately; the former, though young, were not beautiful. Black slaves were there, disgusting-looking negresses with low foreheads, sure sign of cunning, malice, deceit, and treachery, sunken over the eyebrows, not unlike those hideous-looking beings the Cretins, with large, rolling, heavy, inexpressive eyes, the mark of want of intelligence which renders women almost akin to animals; flat, misshapen noses, wide mouths, projecting jaw bones, black broad lips, long-fingered hands, filbert nails, orange-colored by the use of *henna*, spindle legs, projecting heels, and not very large but flat feet. The color of their skin varied considerably. Some had bright glossy black, others rather brown, and all possessing bad teeth, a rare thing with the regular negress; and to sum up all, their *tout ensemble* was very repulsive.

Their occupation during the best portion of the day consisted in lolling or rolling about the divans and mattresses which lay upon the ground, or squatting upon all fours, doubling themselves up like snips upon their boards, or clasped knives, which *pose plastique* I was for ever doomed to behold. These were proceedings far more appropriate to beasts than human beings.

Then my head ached again with the incessant clattering of the tongues of upwards of two hundred women and children, jabbering away like monkeys—some in Arabic, others in Turkish; while the Ethiopian, Nubian, and Abyssinians were constantly hooping and hallooing out most indecent language in their own vernacular, since they do not, like Europeans consider that

> " Immodest words admit of no defence,
> For want of decency is want of sense; "

but made such a hubub that it was like " Bedlam let loose."

Pray, kind reader, just picture yourself surrounded by such a motley group of beings, gabbling, chattering to me in their unknown tongues (for at that moment I did not understand either Arabic or Turkish), and making grimaces like monkeys from four o'clock in the morning until ten at night incessantly; and then you may form some idea of life in the Harem—that myth-like Elysium of the fertile imagination of both western and eastern poets.

My conduct in this " Mansion of Bliss " had to be marked with the greatest circumspection, in order not to awaken the jealousy of the Princesses, the three Wives, and the Viceroy's Ikbals, favorite slaves. Their Highnesses watched my actions and movements with the closest interest; I should rather add with *alarm*, lest the Viceroy should bestow upon me what they in their total ignorance of European manners and customs might be led to construe with attention too marked.

All were Arabs, and many of the favorites Nubians; and well did I remember the account that Warburton has given of the revenge taken by that Nubian, Malek of Shendy, surnamed "The Tiger," who burned His Highness's uncle, Ismael Pacha, Mehemet Ali's second son, on a funeral pyre, because that young prince struck him with his pipe across the face, and yelled triumphantly with delight when he heard his dying screams.

I had also heard the slaves in the Harem talk of the sudden disappearance of a favorite slave some short time before I entered that "Castle of Pleasure;" and as I had been particularly instructed by one of the Viceroy's "partners" (as the ladies of the Harem styled him) not to allow His Highness to partake of anything that had not been previously examined by the "*Hekim Bachi*" (Viceregal doctor), lest he should be poisoned, I very naturally kept a sharp look out, in case an attempt should be made to remove me by similar means.

I knew that the head-nurse hated me, simply because more respect was paid to me than was shown to herself. On one occasion that negress offered me an apple; but looking round I perceived a slave, who had been one of the Viceroy's favorites fix her large blue eyes upon the nurse, who changed color—for, "although black as ebony as she was," still she blushed—and recalling to my mind the circumstance, as told me in the Harem, of the little nephew handing a Viceroy the poisoned dates, I declined the fruit, and after that Shaytan ever afterwards abstained from offering me any more. The vile wretch had betrayed herself by her own countenance, and henceforth I was on my guard.

I soon became aware of the dangerous position I occupied, and resolutely determined, by tact and prudence, to gain not only the esteem but the confidence (as Mr. —— had advised me) of their Highnesses the Princesses; and I can say, with feelings of satisfaction, that, after I had fought "the battle" on my first entrance into the Harem, I was esteemed by the Viceroy and his three wives, beloved by my Prince, and respected, yet feared, by the whole of the inmates of the Harem, from the Grand Eunuch down to the meanest slave; yet I never propitiated them with that sovereign ruler of Egypt, Prince Baksheesh.

No attempt was ever made by Mr. B. or the Messrs. H.'s to ameliorate my position. Mr. C. H. termed my complaints fastidious, and added that " we English people never would accommodate ourselves to circumstances." But, Prussian as he was, I can assure you he very much resembled a first-rate Parisian exquisite. One thing which I can vouch for is, that at the Hotel du Rhin, at Paris, and in his own house in Alexandria—for I had visited it—he took special care to have everything provided for his own convenience, as in all probability he had, in the capacity of a Crimean sutler, like his partners, roughed it in the war, where he had reaped the first fruits of his wealth from the purses of the English officers, whose countrymen he so thoroughly despised, not feeling (to use his own expression) " disposed to accommodate themselves to circumstances." I think he would have shown much better taste had he allowed the Viceroy's orders to have been carried out; for the Prince, whom I had heard styled by that immaculate Prussian as a " barbarian," perfectly understood

> " That when a lady is in the case,
> Everything else gives place."

It is due also to the Princess Epouse to state it was through her kindness and attention that I was supplied with a chair and table, and night commode; had a slave appointed to attend upon me, and the Viceroy sent me a case of claret, a chest of tea, soup from his own table when I was ill, ordered his *Hekim Bachi*, "Doctor," to attend upon me, and placed a carriage at my disposal to take airings with the Grand Pacha. Orders were given to supply all my wants. But His Highness's partners stepped in, and, like one of Prince Baksheesh's creatures, "put a spoke in my wheel," and I got nothing. Absolutely nothing!

His Highness the Viceroy learning that I had complained of my diet, with thorough kindness of heart sent to Europe for a cook ; and a German from Frankfort—the most accommodating of all foreign cities—was engaged. She arrived on the eve of my departure for Constantinople, so that I derived no benefit from her gastronomic services, as she remained in the Harem at Alexandria, and I was the only European who accompanied the Viceregal family to Istamboul.

The next morning I was surprised by the German laundry maid entering my room, after breakfast, and asking me if I would do her the favor to speak to the Princess Epouse, and obtain permission for her to visit Cairo ; but as I had been cautioned not to interfere or meddle in the slightest degree with the domestic arrangements of the Harem, I declined, at the same time advising her to apply to the Lady Paramount, to whose suite she belonged. After that I was never troubled with any more applications, except to read the contracts which had been entered into by herself and sister, who afterwards came into the Harem as needlewomen. Their duties consisted in keeping the linen of the Viceroy, and that of the Grand Pacha, in order. These contracts were drawn up by a gentleman in the office of one of His Highness's partners, and then I learned, to my astonishment, that their stipends were nearly double the amount which had been assigned to me in the vague contract that I had entered into in London, and that circumstance at once conveyed to me the appreciation in which English ladies are held in the eyes of this Frankfort clique.

The offices of these two German maids were perfect sinecures, as they were not employed more than two, or at the most, three days in the week ; but the airs and graces which they gave themselves were most unbearable, and I was often obliged to reprove them for the free and easy, nay disrespectful manner in which they intruded themselves into the presence of their Highnesses the Princesses.

One morning when I entered the reception-hall with the Prince, I was informed by the grand eunuch, that the barge was waiting at the landing-place to convey us to the other side of the Nile, where a carriage would take us to pay a visit to the Harem occupied by the widow of the late Viceroy, Said Pacha.

After having been rowed across the Nile, we landed, entered one of the Viceregal carriages, and, attended by an escort of cavalry, proceeded to the Gate of Bab-el-Hadid; then we passed across the bridge erected over the canal, and proceeded through a beautiful avenue of sycamore trees. They were originally planted by the French, but trhough the fertility of the soil, have grown up to an enormous size, so that they closely resemble a dense forest; forming a most agreeably shady avenue, assuredly the prettiest promenade to a European's taste, in the vicinity of Cairo: and yet it is by no means so fashionable as that leading to Boulac and old Cairo. When we had proceeded halfway down, as the day was extremely sultry, we stopped at an old café to let the horses draw breath.

This drive afforded me an opportunity of seeing a little of the suburbs of the capital, which are very interesting. Among many other objects we caught a glimpse of the fort which that unfortunate French General, Kleber, erected; it is prettily situated amidst several unique country houses. Soon afterwards we approached that magnificent palace built by Mehemet Ali. Alighting from the carriage I took the Grand Pacha by the left hand, as the Viceroy had explained to me that such was their custom, as the right hand was left liberty to salaam with.

Our path lay through some very pretty but by no means very extensive gardens. They are arranged in the European style, and scarcely partake of anything like Orientalism, except the foliage and exotics. A German gardener keeps them in a high state of perfection. They are intersected with straight walks, some of which have a most singular appearance, being paved with mosaics.

The myrtle and jasmine hedges are very pretty, and in the grounds there is a greater variety of sweet-scented roses—the perfume of which is almost overpowering—than is to be found in any other part of Egypt.   Here grows the banana beside the orange, the golden narcissus hides its tender head from the scorching sun, the Mexican tuberose germinates as well as in its native soil, and impregnates the atmosphere with its delicious odor.   Here bloom the odoriferous lemon-trees, and the lofty acacia Nilotica rears its head amidst the numerous fountains.

In the centre of the gardens stands an elegant octagonal kiosk, and what is singular, of European architecture.   It has beautiful stained-glass windows, over which hang rich yellow satin curtains, handsomely arranged with unique European furniture to correspond.   Proceeding farther on we reached the Grand Kiosk, an elegant, highly-finished, modern structure.   It has a large white marble basin, with huge sculptured lions. *couchant* at each corner, from'which spouted forth streams of clear water.   The fountain, decidedly the real lion of the place, is roofless ; but a covered gallery, supported by elegant alabaster columns, extends all around it, and leads into the apartments.   These are furnished in truly regal style *à la Européene,* put having handsome divans extending underneath the windows *à la Turque.*

Numerous very pretty kiosks hang, as it were, over the water, and yet the entire structure has the semblance of being neither more nor less than a facsimile of some other Oriental building.   The singular style of its architecture, which is only partly Eastern, renders it a most interesting object to gaze upon, although it then contained neither baths nor odalaks.   Its pleasing effect is considerably diminished by the walls being covered with some very mediocre Italian frescoes, which would be utterly unworthy of notice, were it not that the subjects are of a very interesting nature.

Here it was that a celebrated French artist most admirably painted the portrait of its celebrated founder, Mehemet Ali, who passed almost all his leisure time at this agreeable retreat; and here it was too that, when pointing to that full-length portrait that now adorns the apartment in the palace of Ras-el-Tin, at Alexandria, the venerable octogenarian regenerator of Egypt delighted to amuse his guests by impressing upon their minds how boldly he had set at nought that ridiculous prohibition of the Prophet, who forbade every Mussulman to sit for his portrait or to hang up pictures of figures in their dwellings.

Murray states, in his "Handbook of Egypt," that the fountain "had gas lamps, and that such was actually in use here long before any part of Paris was lighted with it," but I failed to perceive any. The kiosk called *El Gebel,* "the Hill," is most commandingly situated, and affords a superb vista of the whole grounds, the Nile, the lovely terraces, all studded with fragrant exotics, and the distant verdant hills.

We soon entered the palace, a large but rather indifferently-built structure.

Passing through the gates of the Harem, which were immediately closed after us, and the massive bolts drawn, we traversed a small court-yard. Then the eunuch unlocked a small door, and we ascended a broad staircase, the steps of which were covered with fine matting, which led us into a large apartment, covered with a thick variegated-colored Persian carpet. The ceiling was ornamented with well-executed arabesque designs, the walls were whitewashed, and the lower part had a skirting, from four to five inches deep, round it, of Dutch tiles.

The windows, which were in the French style, reached down to the floor. The hangings both of them and the doors were of rich colored silk and muslin, looped up with massive bullion cords and tassels. In the centre stood an elegant inlaid colored marble fountain, whose waters spread a delightful and refreshing coolness all around, for the thermometer then stood at 120°.

Her Highness, the widow of Said Pacha, one of the handsomest women I had yet seen in any of the Harems, sat reclining on a divan, smoking cigarettes. She was of middle stature, her full brown eyes were lustrous and still full of expression—for she was rather advanced in years—her features regular and of the Circassian type. She wore no corset, although rather stout, but her carriage was erect. Her dress was composed of a very long maroon-colored silk dress, which trained upon the ground, very full bright crimson silk trousers, over which costume she wore a chocolate colored velvet jacket.

Her head was covered with a dark silk handkerchief, a plume of ostrich feathers hung down over the right ear, and a beautiful artificial damask-rose, highly perfumed, drooped down, as it were, on the left.

A black spot was painted in the centre of her forehead· In her small ears hung magnificent diamond drops; and her alabaster-looking neck was encircled with a necklace of brilliants. Her small hands were as white as snow; her finger-nails were tinged with *henna;* and several large diamond rings of the finest water sparkled on the little fingers of each hand.

Her Highness sat quite motionless as we were ushered into the room. I curtseyed to her, while the Grand Pacha salaamed her in his usual manner. She motioned to us to be seated. The Prince, whom she kissed several times, sat on her right hand, and I on the left. A whole bevy of slaves, both white and black, stood about Her Highness, in the form of the everlasting crescent, awaiting the orders of their mistress, who still maintained an almost interminable silence. After a lapse of about ten minutes the Princess inquired of me, how long I had been in Egypt? How many sisters I had? And whether I liked Cairo? To which interrogatories I replied briefly, yet with the greatest politeness. She then asked the Grand Pacha whether he liked me, upon which he replied in the affirmative.

The semicircle of slaves now receded a little, as a number of black ones entered the room bearing silver trays, which they handed to some of the white ones. On the trays were placed small glass dishes filled with Turkish and Egyptian sweetmeats, having three small gold spoons in each. These were handed to the Princess and ourselves. Other slaves served us with glasses filled with iced water. After this we partook of coffee, which was handed to us in elegant small *zarfs* or transparent Japan china, egg-shaped, footless cups, inlaid with diamonds and other precious stones, which stands they held between the thumb and fingers of their right hands.

While we were indulging ourselves with that refreshing beverage, light, beautifully cut-glass cups with covers, similar to those used in Europe for custards, only having two handles to them, placed in small saucers filled with different kinds of sherbet, were passed round on frosted silver trays of exquisite workmanship, over which were negligently thrown embroidered rose-pink silk napkins which the slaves removed as they drew near to us.

In conformity with Oriental etiquette, we drank about two-thirds of that deliciously cool beverage. This refreshment being over, the Circassian slaves then knelt down and presented each of us with a gold salver, on which was placed a fine embroidered muslin napkin, fringed with a deep border of gold lace, with which we just touched our lips according to the custom of the country.

Then commenced a short running conversation between Her Highness and myself, which simply embraced a few commonplace questions as to my opinion of the country and the newest fashions, the details of which seemed to afford the Princess much pleasure, as all Oriental ladies of rank take great delight in learning how European ladies attire themselves.

After the lapse of half-an-hour the Princess rose from the divan and took me on a tour of inspection through the whole apartments. The Circassian and Greek slaves followed us at a respectful distance, while the black ones grouped together and brought up the *cortége*. All the rooms were meagrely furnished; I should rather add, that they contained absolutely nothing more than elegant divans.

Returning to the audience saloon which we had quitted, Her Highness seated herself on the divan, and motioned for us to do likewise. She then clapped her hands, when the Circassian slaves brought the veil and *habarah* which I had worn; for European ladies when paying visits to any of the Viceregal Princesses, out of respect invariably adopt that portion of the Turkish costume, and fail not to attire themselves in a black silk *habarah*, and wear a muslin veil, doubled at the upper part over the face, which had been laid on a small rose-pink colored Cashmere shawl, richly fringed with a deep border of bullion lace.

When I was attired in, to me, my *bal masqué* costume, I touched my lip and forehead with Her Highness's dress, who pressed my hand, saluted me on the cheek, lowered her right hand, then touched her lips and forehead, and graciously descended the staircase leading into the first courtyard, walked across the yard to the suspended colored Egyptian mat that hung before the door of the Harem like a curtain, which was then lifted up by the eunuch in attendance. Her Highness having retired, we found the Grand Eunuch standing upon the raised stone platform at the grand entrance awaiting our arrival.

The Prince bestowed baksheesh upon him, and we entered the carriage, re-crossed the Nile, and returned to the Harem. I was very glad that I had this opportunity of visiting Her Highness the widow of Said Pacha, and from

the conversation which I had with that Princess I came to
the belief that Miss T 's visit to that lovely creature had
not been the *real* cause of her not having been, as Mr. C.
H. stated, allowed to enter the Viceroy's service. From all
that I had heard and seen, it appeared to me that she had
actually been *in* the Viceregal Harem, but why or wherefore
she did not enter upon her engagement is a mystery that I
cannot solve, especially as my own "Special Prince" told me
"that she was well remunerated." Hence there must have
been some *fracas*, or how could *he* have known anything
about her contract? But perhaps, like myself, she had
occasion to call at the British Consular Court at Alexandria
to obtain her passport, which document is taken from all
foreigners when they enter the Ottoman dominions, and
being questioned by the English Vice-consul or his subordinates, as to the purport of her visit to Egypt, she at once
entered into a full explanation of her position, and was
called upon to pay a fee of five shillings for registering herself as a British subject, a monstrous imposition, when the
Foreign Office passport fully proved her nationality.

CHAPTER XIII.

A MOST erroneous impression has been drawn by authors
as to the manner in which the inmates of the Harem pass
their social life. It is certainly true that the greater portion
of the day is spent in doubling themselves up on divans.
Not attired in costly silks of China looms, nor bedizened
with gems of Golconda's mines, the Peris within the Viceregal "Castle of Indolence" generally wore dirty, filthy,
crumpled muslin dresses, just as one might imagine the
greatest slatterns in the back slums of St. Giles's would be
seen walking about in when all their finery had been
pledged.

There they were to be seen smoking their *Tchibouks*, or cigarettes, and drinking coffee *à la Turque*, as dark as porter, but yet most delicious.

I was quite astonished to find that their Highnesses were about and stirring as early as four o'clock in the morning, which was indeed *matinal*, as I have before mentioned that the Turks count their time from the setting of the sun, and it was then only a little after daybreak.

At the dawn of day the Princesses partook of coffee and smoked cigarettes: then they remained quite motionless, apparently in a dreamy state, as they never uttered a syllable. About seven o'clock they received a visit from the Grand Eunuch. A crowd of old and young ladies of the Harem, and slaves wearing fashionable Parisian colored satin shoes down at heel, and stockings almost heelless and footless, were squatted on the floor, like snips on their boards, in the form of a semi-circle facing their Viceregal mistresses, while others had gone and shut themselves up in their own apartments, which they invariably did when affected with any ailment however trivial, as they considered solitude to be Nature's best nurse and the body's safest physician. The former had been arranging bouquets, which are fresh gathered every morning, as they are never placed in water, and the latter had been occupied in household duties, sweeping, dusting, carrying water, and arranging the apartments.

The morning toilette began by the slaves bringing into the Grand Pacha's room several small silver pans, not deeper than soup-plates but considerably wider, as also several small pieces of rag and balls of soap. Their Highnesses now squatted themselves upon the floor and tucked up their trousers (I and the Head Eunuch being also present), and began to wash their own feet, as they will not allow a slave to touch them under any circumstances whatever, and they wiped them with towels. After which silver ewers and basins, similar in shape and size to that which has already been described as being used by the head-nurse when dressing the Prince, were brought in by the slaves. Then they washed their faces with pieces of rag, which they had previously well soaped.

The slaves then held basins before each of them, while others poured water from the ewers over their hands as they kept soaping them; after which each held basins before them, into which water was poured, and which fluid they threw, or more properly speaking jerked, into their mouths, and then cleansed their teeth (which were not only irregular but much discolored) with tooth-brushes and powder of French manufacture.

They only combed their hair (which was full of vermin) once a week, on Thursdays, the eve of their sabbath (Friday, *Djoumà*), when it is well combed with a large small-tooth comb; and pardon me, but " murder will out," the members of the vermin family which were removed from it were legion! It was afterwards well brushed with a hard hair-brush well damped with strong perfumed water. The tail at the back was plaited and turned up round over the handkerchief with which each covered her head, and fastened with small black dressing-pins to the handkerchief. Their Highnesses never wore stockings in the morning, nor did they change any of their attire till the afternoon.

On Mondays they employed themselves in cutting out pantaloons, dressing-gowns, &c., for their liege lord, which were then given to the German needlewoman to make up; and the slaves made up flannel things for themselves, sitting on cushions laid down upon the carpet. The Princesses attended to the domestic occupations of their own slaves, over all of whom they possess the power of *life and death*, but with whom they live on terms of the greatest familiarity, and yet are at times most imperious and overbearing to them, so their motto seems to be

" *Nemo me impune lacessit.*"

With the *cuisine* they had nothing to do, for, as we have previously explained, it was situated near the barracks, and only men were employed therein. The Grand Eunuch waited upon them in the morning to know if they had any orders; but that was a mere matter of form, as I scarcely ever remarked any particular change in their diet or in the number of dishes served up, during the whole period of my residence at the Palace.

Those who performed the duties of washerwomen were occupied daily in their avocation, except on the sabbath, Fridays. But that was not very laborious work, since neither bed, table, nor chamber linen are used. Thus they were engaged until twelve, when their Highnesses partook of their breakfast separately. It was served up on a large green lackered tray *minus* table cloth, knives and forks, but with a large ivory tablespoon having a handsome coral handle, the evident emblem of their rank as Princesses. It was placed upon the *soofra*, "a low kind of stool," covered with a handsome silk cloth. The courses were similar to those I have already described as having been placed before the Grand Pacha. That repast occupied about twenty minutes. Then *Khanum Khaleouns*, "pipes," into which are placed small pills of opium, or more often cigarettes and coffee, were handed to them, and each Princess retired to her own apartment. Thus they became confirmed opium smokers, which produced a kind of intoxication, but in a less brutal or offensive form than that of drunkenness, yet of a much more powerful nature.

Oftentimes after the Princesses had been indulging too freely in that habit, to which they had become slaves, their countenances would assume most hideous aspects; their eyes glared, their eyebrows were knit closely together, no one dared to approach them. In fact, they had all the appearance of mad creatures, while at other times they were gay and cheerful. In short, all depended whether, during their *kef* " *dolce far niente*," they had been transported in imagination into the seventh heaven of their paradise, and had enjoyed the bliss of delightful visions.

Then they drank off the contents of a glass, apparently filled with water. The Princess Epouse had often asked me to taste it; in truth, she had so frequently solicited me to do so, that one day I complied with her request, as I was fearful she would feel offended if I did not. I took the proffered beverage, and when I put it to my lips, guess my utter astonishment at finding that it was not water but wine. Yes, actually and truly the veritable beverage so expressly forbidden by the Prophet.

I could hardly believe my senses, but did not utter a syllable, neither did I attempt to express any surprise, but told Her Highness that it was very good—and thanked her. But subsequently, when I visited Constantinople, I learned that it was Carnabat wine; the *Khismet,* "fate," of that extract, not to be drunk by Mussulmans, and yet of which the Turks swallow most copious draughts.

Then the Princesses took their *siesta,* as also did the ladies of the Harem and the slaves, who went and hid themselves in the most out-of-the-way places imaginable. Shaytan, the head nurse, who had no idea of being disturbed from her "dreams of bliss," generally laid herself down in the bed store-room, and sinking down, literally, on her " downy couch," fell off into the arms of Morpheus most happily.

One day, however, the Princess Epouse happened to enter the Prince's apartment, clapped her hands several times, but receiving no response to her Viceregal summons, became impatient and passed into my apartment. Then we both began to hunt everywhere for the head-nurse. At length I bethought myself of the bed store-room, and leading Her Highness up to the pile of mattresses, showed her " the Sleeping Beauty " in her " Bower of Bliss."   But the

Princess, who was an Arab, thinking in all probability that it was a pity the "Sleeping Beauty" should lack the "Beast," rushed at the nurse like a Tigress, pulled her by the ears, and boxed her cheeks until her hands tingled again.

Shaytan jumped up affrighted, and looked at me with such an evil eye, as if she meant to say

> "But never shalt thou know, destroyer of my sleep,
> What I alone can tell, my hiding-places keep."

Having taken their *siesta*, the Princesses rose at five in the afternoon, and performed their evening toilet, which consisted in merely changing their outer-garments, and attiring themselves in *new* muslin dresses, as they never wear them after they have been washed; for when crumpled or soiled, they are ironed out, and when too faded, they use them as morning-wrappers. The slaves also adopted the same plan, hence the consumption of clothing of every description was enormous. For even the Princesses, as well as both the ladies of the Harem and the slaves, lacking wardrobes, are obliged to keep them in their *sarats,* "trunks," or *youks,* "cupboards in the walls," or else hang them up suspended on lines across the rooms; like a laundress drying her linen in the laundry when the weather will not admit of its being hung out in the open air. Silk coverlets are, however, thrown over them.

At six o'clock they partake of their supper, which consists of the same courses, with the addition of crude vegetables, which they eat like beasts of the field, and it is served up in the same manner as the breakfast.

Then their Highnesses sometimes took a promenade in the small garden which separates the Grand Pacha's apartments from the Harem; after which coffee, poured into *findjans* placed in *zarfs* studded with diamonds and other precious stones, cigarettes, and *tchibouks,* "pipes," were served them.

At half-past seven the Princesses amused themselves by playing at dominoes, and passed the remainder of the evening in having tales related to them, which often comprise incidents which had transpired in the Harems of the late Viceroys and their widows or daughters, by the ladies of the Harem, who generally select the most lascivious about women and their immoralities. Listening to these stories may be seen the then demure and solemn-looking slaves, sitting, or more properly speaking, squatting, down in the form of a crescent, during which they are constantly sipping *zarfs* of pure Mocha coffee, of which they drink no less than twenty-four daily (but then it must be borne in mind that the *findjans* are not larger than an egg-cup); munching away at *bonbons*, fruit, and most luscious sweetmeats, and smoking cigarettes.

Almost every slave has her daily occupation assigned her, for each Princess employs one in arranging the cigarette papers, another in preparing the tobacco, a third in making the cigarettes, a fourth hands them on a silver tray, and a fifth attends with the light, which consists of a piece of live charcoal held between a pair of silver tongs.

At ten they retire to rest; but I have known them to remain as late as eleven, when the Princess Epouse would at my request, make some of the Ethiopian slaves sing their own melodies. To use a vulgar expression, the London itinerant Ethiopian serenaders are *fools* to them; their gesticulations were so comic and original, that none but the writer of a comedy with the pencil of Hogarth could possibly have daguerreotyped them, and they would have afforded Mrs. Howard Paul a most excellent subject for imitation.

One Tuesday as I was passing through the Stone Hall on the basement-floor of the Grand Pacha Ibrahim's apartments I was surprised by the appearance of that apartment, which served as servant's hall, the governess's dining-room, and dormitory of the black slaves—who are all huddled indiscriminately together as in an hospital-ward. It presented a scene which beggars all description; for there they lay upon mattresses on the marble-floor, with a large silver-plated lantern standing in the middle, in which burned a thick wax taper. For the Viceroy does not allow what us Europeans term *plate* to be used at his Viceregal " Mansion of Bliss," at least I never saw anything of the kind except the salvers which are used for the service of their Highnesses the three wives. There they pass half the night in smoking cigarettes, and chattering away like magpies, and telling stories to each other; some talking Arabic, others Turkish, and by far the greater portion their own vernacu lar, especially the Greeks, Circassians, Nubians, Abyssinians, and Ethiopians. It is a perfect "confusion of tongues," and it would puzzle the most learned European polygot to interpret their conversation. The echo of their gabbling has often, night after night, thrown me into a nervous fever.

Well, on the day in question, that most useful apartment was converted into the Viceregal laundry, in which I stopped a considerable period, looking at the German laundry maid and her half-dozen slave-assistants ironing.

On the floor a square piece of matting was laid down, and a large piece of calico as big as two ordinary sheets was placed over it. Kneeling down on it were eight slaves with two rolling-pins, similar in length and thickness, not an inch larger than those used by cooks for making pastry. After having first damped the pieces of washing, they folded them, then rolled them tight round one of the rolling-pins, which they laid down upon the sheet, and with the other rolling-pin in their hands, they kept rolling the end of it. For they held it straight up in their hands like a stick against the other one round which they twisted the linen. This process, which they called mangling, being finished, the German maid began ironing the Viceroy's and the Grand Pacha's body-linen.

At eleven o'clock the Lady Paramount (the first wife) under whose superintendence the whole of the household arrangements were carried on, entered the laundry. She smiled at seeing me and the Grand Pacha watching the slaves at their work.

She was both shoeless and stockingless; but her feet were incased in a pair of polished wooden clogs, standing as it were upon two wooden bridges, like the strings of a fiddle. The parts on which she rested her feet were lined with red velvet, the ties were of the same material, and the clogs were studded all round with silver-headed nails.

Her hair, hanging loosely about, was tucked under the handkerchief bound round her head; and the sleeves of her dirty cotton wrapper were turned up to the shoulders, and there tied.

And thus behold Her Highness, the first wife of Ismael Pacha, the richest Prince in the universe, save his Imperial Majesty the Emperor of All the Russias, in her domestic circles.

Here Her Highness remained all the livelong day every Tuesday, merely leaving the laundry to partake of her meals and to indulge in a short *siesta*.

Not a slave is allowed to utter a syllable. Her Highness enforces the silent system most admirably.

On that same afternoon, while I was passing through the hall on my return from our ramble in the Pavilion gardens, I had just time to preserve the life of my Prince. It appears a slave had been very refractory, and would not refrain from chattering. So making no more fuss about it, the Prince took up a shovel full of burning charcoal, and flung it into the poor creature's face, which almost killed her, several pieces of it falling upon the Prince's coat and setting him in a blaze. Fortunately, I had presence of mind to seize hold of a flannel petticoat, which was hanging over one of the washing-tubs or troughs, and wrapping it round His

Highness, I extinguished the flames, with no other damage than the burning of his uniform in several places. Had it not been a very sultry day, or had the evening breeze set in from the Nile, the Grand Pacha would have fallen a victim to the silent system.

The Lady Paramount often scolded the German maid because she did not act in the same barbarous manner; but I am glad to bear record that that "bore of a peasant," as she was, still possessed a little more of the milk of human kindness than did her Viceregal mistress.

None of the other Princesses ever entered the laundry, or superintended the *repasseuses*. Each of the young Princesses the Viceroy's daughters by his wives (for there are no less than twelve of the children in the Harem who justly claim Ismael Pacha as their *baba*, and who have themselves openly told me so), with the assistance of their slaves get up their linen in their own apartments, where a rug is laid down on the floor, over which is placed a sheet. There they squat down on the carpet, and both mangle, in the manner I have previously described, and iron their own linen, following the maternal example set them.

The irons used are very large, made in the shape of an English box-iron, with a spout at the back of the handle, in which live charcoal is placed, which has this advantage, that they are kept hot a very much longer time than in the European constructed box-irons.

Whatever may be said about religious toleration in Egypt, certain it is that, while the inmates of the Harem always observed their religious rites, so as to abstain from work on Friday (their Sabbath), yet, when first I entered therein, I was not permitted to enjoy rest on my Sabbath.

CHAPTER XIV.

I HAD to battle for the privilege to attend Divine worship; as, being ignorant of the Turkish habits, no stipulation had been inserted in my contract that I should not labor on my Sabbath-day (which Europeans now take the precaution to have done): but I eventually gained it. Their Highnesses never thought that "the unbeliever of Hawajee" would require this; since, according to the doctrine of their creed, I had no paradise assigned to me in heaven. But yet, woman like, their curiosity was excited to learn how I prayed; and what my Bible (Koran, as they termed it) was like. When I performed my devotions before them, and read aloud the Holy Scriptures, upon me was fixed many a sly eye, but on the whole they behaved most decorously; not a smile, not a syllable was uttered. But when I had finished, a whole chorus of voices exclaimed, " *Quiyis! quiyis!* " (Pretty! pretty!) " *Guzel! guzel!* " (Beautiful! beautiful!) They seemed surprised that I did not use any *tusbee* (rosary) like themselves and the Romanists.

When in Cairo, they had often passed all the European places of worship, and a most singular idea haunted their imagination. They insisted that, unlike their own "call" to Evening prayer, the bells, the hated Giaours' call to prayer, was the summons to *Shaytan* (devil).

At first I was quite at a loss to interpret the meaning of their conversation; gradually, however, I began to understand them, but still the expression *Shaytan* perplexed me, especially as that was the patronymic of the Prince's head-nurse.

Her Highness the Princess Epouse, perceiving my embarrassment, sent Anina, the superintendent of the slaves, into my chamber, who quickly returned, bringing with her my little silver hand-bell, which I had brought out from Europo with me, and which stood upon one of my trunks which I had converted into a table, since it was not until the eve of my departure for Constantinople that I was supplied with that necessary appendage. Then about fifty slaves shouted forth *Shaytan! Shaytan! Batala! Batala!* "The Devil! The Devil! Bad! Bad!—that is our abomination." I was absolutely astonished at the energetic manner in which they shouted out, and the demoniacal gestures they made; but by maintaining my usual equanimity I coolly replied, that we Europeans always summon our domestics by ringing a bell just as orientals call their slaves by clapping their hands.

It is almost impossible to imagine the celerity with which their Highnesses the Princesses, the whole of the ladies of the Harem, and the slaves, even down to the lowest scullery-girl, effect their transformation from slatterns to "Peris of the East," the instant that substitutes for the wires of the electric telegraph in the Harem announce the approach of Ismael Pacha. It seemed like a pantomimic feat; as if harlequin with his magic wand had touched them all with his galvanic battery, for in the twinkling of an eye, their dirty, soiled, and crumpled muslins, their Monmouth Street and Petticoat Lane finery was exchanged for gorgeous silks and glittering diamonds. The transformation was not effected like that of harlequin, columbine, pantaloon, and clown, by a total change of garments, but by placing them over their habiliments.

The scene was acted most inimitably; it would have been an excellent study for Hogarth, one to which his pencil would have done ample justice; and the clever inventor of that chair-trick, so admirably placed on the stage of the Princess's Theatre, during Charles Kean's able management, would have represented it capitally in a pantomime.

I had the pleasure one evening of witnessing such a scene, on the occasion of the Viceroy having informed his wives of his intention to pay them a visit. Of this, according to Turkish etiquette, he was obliged to give them time-ly notice, lest any of their female acquaintances should happen to be in the Harem, or visitors expected, as no Turk ever enters his own " Abode of Bliss," if his wives have visitors with them.

It has always been asserted that no Turk has entered the Harem of his brother Mussulman, but I know an instance of an exception to that rule. On my return to Alexandria, previous to leaving for Constantinople, I was located in the Harem facing His Highness's Palace of Ras-el-Tin, where I found great difficulty in persuading any of the young slaves to go about when it became dusk. They assured me that there were *fritz*, " spirits," in that Harem, and, as an instance, related to me that at the time His Majesty the present Sultan visited Egypt after his accession to the Throne, one evening, when the Viceroy was in the Harem with his three wives around him, a Ferindjee, for it was His Majesty the Sultan, dressed in European costume! was seen sitting by his side. All the inmates of the Harem were astonished, yet none dare say a word. The appearance of that *ghost*, as the little slaves, His Highness's daughters by his concubines, called His Majesty the Sultan (for it could be no other personage), so frightened them that they have never forgotten the circumstance, and in all proba-bility never will; and the sudden disappearance of a pretty slave soon afterwards left no doubt but that she was spirited away to Constantinople. The Sultan intended to do them the honor of partaking of their hospitality, *yclept* to dine, in the Harem, an event of some moment, as such occurrences were previous to my arrival, " Like angel's visits, few and far between."

On this, as on all occasions when their Highnesses had to dress to receive visitors, or any particular festivals, such as the Bairam, (when they were attired in magnificent courtly costumes, and wore jewels that would have been the ransom of an Empress), they asked my opinion of their costume, the manner in which they had adorned themselves with those priceless jewelled "jems of art," which they never wore except on such occasions, and when the "*Baba*" came to visit them, the ladies of the Harem and slaves, as on this evening.

They are well trained in the art of hoarding, for they are extremely careful of their wardrobes, and those I have already described as shuffling about on ordinary occasions in such crumpled gaudy-colored finery (as we are accustomed in England to see strolling actresses bedizen themselves at the theatres at country fairs), make themselves beautiful with cosmetics, the use of which they understand quite as well as any Madame Rachael of London celebrity. They wore the most costly silks, richest satins, and softest velvets; adorned themselves with the treasures of their jewel caskets, so that their persons were one blaze of precious stones. That crescent of females (for they always ranged themselves in the form of the Turkish symbol) was then a parterre of diamonds, amethysts, topazes, turquoises, chrysoberyls, sapphires, jaspers, opals, agates, emeralds, corals, rich carbuncles, and rubies.

In short the profusion of diamonds with which the latter adorned their persons from day to day, became so sickening to me, that my eyes were weary at the sight of those magnificent baubles, to which all women are so passionately attached.

It seemed to me quite a monstrosity, an absolute sin, that such immense wealth should be expended on those brilliant gewgaws, merely to sparkle on the tawny and ebony skins of slaves, many of whom were repulsive in their looks; and whose habits, manners, customs, and appearance in general were totally repugnant to European feeling.

It was bad enough in all conscience to behold the white *oustas*, "slaves," bedecked with gems of almost priceless

10

value, many of whose *sarats*, " trunks," contained *parures* far more valuable than most of the elegant gems of art which ornament the jewel-cases of the noblest and wealthiest of the lovely beauties of the European Courts ; but to know that upwards of from 30,000*l.* to 40,000*l.* was annually expended by the billionaire of the world, who much of his surplus wealth

> " For Cupid's sake he gave away,
>   For bags of gold came to the Harem every day,"

in jewels for distribution among such a motley group was indeed monstrous.

As all gallant knights were excluded from the precincts of this Castle of Indolence, such a lavish profusion of wealth I could not unriddle, except that they were offered up as sacrifices on the altar of that immaculate sovereign ruler Prince Baksheesh.   I could perfectly well understand the pleasure which Ismael Pacha felt in expending vast sums in the purchase of those valuables which the collectors of precious stones, the wealthy diamond merchants of Constantinople, and the expert divers for pearls had procured ; because, at his death, those priceless " gems of art," into which the genius of man had converted those valuable stones (small caskets filled with them being treasured up by almost every member, both young and old, of the Viceregal family), constitute the sole private fortune of their possessors, except the quantity of *paras*, as they term the packets of Napoleons, Turkish, Egyptian, or English sovereigns.   The latter of these they prefer, for the best of all reasons, because they are the *weightiest*.   And I can understand why His Highness displays such liberality to his consorts, for no one knows better than the Viceroy Ismael Pacha how the families of defunct rulers of Egypt have been despoiled both of their personal property and hereditary possessions.   But I never could see why such valuables were presented to the slaves of all denominations.

I will now describe the Viceregal dinner-party. The courses were the same as those partaken of by their Highnesses when alone, with the addition of a roast turkey, soup extremely rich, *entremets*, and some pastry. It was laid out in the Viceroy's private sitting-room in the "Abode of Bliss," which was similarly decorated and furnished as that in the pavilion. In the centre stood a moderately-sized dining-table, which was covered with a tablecloth, the first and only time that I ever saw such an appendage used in the Harem. White slaves, dressed *en grande toilette*, brought the dishes up on large silver trays, placed them upon the floor, then handed them to their Highnesses the Princesses according to their rank. The lady paramount taking precedence set the first dish on the table; all of them stood in attendance upon Ismael Pacha, while I and the Grand Pacha sat upon a divan playing at dominoes.

After the Viceroy had finished his repast, to which he appeared to do ample justice, being a *bon vivant*, the Princesses set themselves down upon cushions which had been placed upon the carpet, and partook of their dinner separately off *soofras*. Ismael Pacha then amused himself by smoking cheroots and playing at dominoes with whichever of his wives he took it into his head to select; coffee, sweetmeats, and sherbet being handed round, as is customary, the Grand Pacha and I salaamed the Viceroy, and I retired.

A few days afterwards, the little Prince having complained of a violent headache, I informed Her Highness that it would be advisable to send for the hairdresser to cut his hair.

"*Malesch! Malesch!* Madam," replied the Princess, "you can easily do it yourself."

Following her instructions I cut the Prince's hair, every single atom of which was most carefully picked up off the ground, placed in a large sheet of white paper with a quantity of white pebbles, and cast from a window into the Nile, where an Arab, standing up in a boat knocked it three times under the water, exclaiming each time, *Bismillah! Bismillah!* "In the name of the merciful God!" "In the name of the merciful God!" If it floats, which it did not, owing to the stones tied up in the paper, which had also been well saturated in water, *evil* is prognosticated to the boy; if it sinks (which as a matter of course it did), then it is looked upon as a good omen.

It was often quite ludicrous to behold their Highnesses the Princesses, who could neither read nor write, the Ladies of the Harem, and slaves, as they came shuffling into my small room, and which was frequently crammed full of them, to ask my opinion of nearly everything they received.

If the Princesses had opened any boxes of new dress-pieces they had had brought up into the Audience Hall, they handed them to me, at the same time appealing to my taste to decide whether they were *quiyis,* "pretty," or *batal,* "ugly," and my verdict was final. The instant that any of the slaves received presents from their Highnesses, they came and showed them to me, almost stunning me with the same interrogatories. If, as frequently happened, I examined the dress-pieces and found them damaged (for many of the boxes contained the last year's fashions), some of the pieces soiled, and others deficient in quantity (for having been purchased in that condition they had been obtained at cheap rates), I condemned them, when the recipients returned them to the Princesses, who bestowed others upon them.

In short, the whole of the inmates of the Harem soon began thoroughly to appreciate my European ways and habits in many respects. If they were taken ill they consulted me, followed my remedies, and did their best, poor ignorant, deluded, and neglected creatures, to abandon any habits which I explained to them were repugnant to delicacy,

especially when I told them that such were not *à la Franca,*
"European."   They had all become so attached to me before
I left for Constantinople that, from their Highnesses the
Princesses down to the very *Mihtur,* "sweeper," all treated
me with the greatest kindness, attention, and respect, which
enabled me to gain that insight into their sayings and
doings, without which it would have been utterly impossible
for me to remain within the walls of the Harem.   But perhaps, kind reader, you will say,

"How hast thou so profouud a lore attained?"

My reply is, that I was never ashamed to ask; and then,
amidst all my discomfiture, I took care to dot down every
occurrence in my journal.   I adopted the precaution to abstain from appearing to take the least notice of their singular habits, and to me, outlandish customs.   I was careful
never to incur their jealousy.   I showed all their Highnesses
the same attention, made them presents of the same things,
abstained from passing the slightest remark upon anything I
heard or saw—unless the Princesses, ladies of the Harem,
slaves, or eunuchs, which not unfrequently happened, drew
my attention to any particular object—then, when asked,
but not otherwise, I candidly gave them my opinion, at
which they never seemed offended.

Thus I gained their respect, esteem, confidence, and, what
was everything to a person in my critical position, their pro-
tection; and in this way I gained my object; consequently
I became no stranger to them, and the terms of familiarity
in which I stood with them afforded me the opportunity of
seeing the *Odalisques* as no European lady has ever done or
is likely to do again, what we empl.atically call—"At
home."

As to the ladies of the Harem and the slaves, I kept
them at a most respectful distance, not daring to allow them
any approach to freedom : no, not even so much as we Eng-

ish people permit our domestics. Neglect or want of respect was never tolerated for a moment. I invariably maintained the greatest reserve, remembering the Oriental proverb which I had read in Algier's " Poetry of the East ":—

> " Do thou thy precious secrets to no other lend:
> Thy friend another has: beware of thy friend's friend,"

and by so doing I acted judiciously; for well did I know that the Greeks and Germans in the Harem were the emissaries of parties who were then doing their utmost to surround the Viceroy with creatures of their own. Of course this was done from private as well as political motives, for when did Prussians ever lose the opportunity of supporting English influence?

It was not long before I had the opportunity of witnessing the *First* Wife at her orisons. Just at that moment of sunset I and the Prince entered Her Highness's chamber. She was engaged spreading a very large handsome Persian carpet, or, more properly speaking, rug, in the centre of the room. Then she knelt down, turned her face towards Mecca, and repeated her *Namaz*, " prayers." On her head she wore a long white muslin scarf; in her hand she held a string of large gold beads, here and there interspersed with several diamond ones, which precious ones count as two, and which she counted like a monk telling off his rosary, exclaiming all the while, " Allah! Allah! Illah-as-la-Illah il Allah!" " There is no deity but God," but being a Princess she never performed the *Souddond*, the bowing of the head on the ground.

The Grand Pacha, whose powers of imitation are wonderfully acute, frequently interrupted Her Highness, who, smiling good-humoredly at him, threatened to box his ears; at which the little Prince only laughed, and kept kneeling on the rug, bowing his head to the floor in genuine Moslem style.

It was with the greatest difficulty that I could refrain from being guilty of a breach of decorous propriety. Fortunately, however, the Princess did not remain long at her *Namaz*. After she had finished she folded up her rug, and placing the scarf and beads in it, put them into a *sarat*. Then a slave handed her a superbly ornamented *tchibouk*. The mouthpiece was of clear, transparent amber, and the rosewood stem was thickly encrusted with precious stones of great value. It must have been worth from 1,000*l.* to 1,500*l.* The bowl was filled with golden leaf tobacco, and a small piece of some narcotic, the name of which I never learned, of a bright rose-pink color, was placed in it, which Her Highness continued to smoke with considerable zest.

A short time previous to our departure for Alexandria, at the commencement of the hot season, one of His Highness's daughters, who resided with the Validè Princess, his mother, the widow of the gallant Ibrahim Pacha, died; and owing to her demise the whole of the Viceregal family shut themselves up in their own private apartments for three days. During this period they received no visitors, and would not allow even their own children nor any of the slaves to approach them. Their meals were placed at the doors of their rooms, of which they hastily partook, and then retired into their solitude.

The divans were covered with lavender-colored satin, fringed with a deep border of silver lace, the cushions of which had black gauze handkerchiefs, bespangled and fringed with silver lace thrown over them. On their heads they wore black handkerchiefs. Their persons were attired in lavender satin quilted jackets, and white linen dresses.

When the sad intelligence of the young Princess's death reached their Highnesses the Princesses, the three wives, together with the whole of their establishments, squatted themselves down upon the floor, and absolutely set to howling like wild beasts.

At first I thought they had all gone demented. The Grand Pacha, who was almost frightened out of his senses by the uproar, in his haste to see what was the matter, tripped up against one of the little female slaves belonging to his staff. This slave I subsequently learned was also one of the *daughters* of the Viceroy, who has no less than fourteen children, four of whom are sons, the eldest being about twelve years old. These children reside at another place, under the care of a French tutor, but *my* Prince was the only legitimate one. The Prince fell sprawling on the carpet. A glass of water was immediately brought in by the head-nurse, who sprinkling some over his face exclaimed, "*Bismallah! Bismallah!*" ("in the name of the most merciful God!") and then threw the contents of the glass upon the spot where His Highness had fallen.

Singular to add, the Viceroy, whose presence in the Harem had not, contrary to Turkish etiquette, been announced, entered the Audience Hall, and, looking round at the little Prince burst out into a hearty laugh at the child's discomfiture and my endeavors to pacify him; but seemed highly amused at the solemn manner in which Shaytan performed her superstitious observance.

CHAPTER XV.

I HAVE already given an instance that Ismael Pacha is a Prince who acts upon the spur of the moment, and does not adhere to the rigidity of Turkish etiquette, as he very often entered the Harem without giving any notice of his approach.

One day, after I had returned from my morning walk with the Grand Pacha, I inquired of the Princess Epouse where I could find the Lady Paramount. Upon being told that Her Highness was in the bath-room, the atmosphere of which was almost suffocating, I proceeded thither, knocked at the door, and entered, but almost as quickly drew back; not until, however, I had perceived the Viceroy, seated on a divan, dressed in his *pyjamas*, " drawers."

He was attended by a complete hevy of women; for, like the Sultan, females always assist at his toilette when he visits the Harem. Her Highness, the first wife, and several of his *ikbals*, " favorite slaves," were acting as his valets: they also put on his shoes or boots, stockings, fan away the mosquitoes, and watch him as he slumbers, for no others can attend upon him. Of them he may have as many as he likes; but were he to take a fancy to any of the slaves belonging to either of his wives, even though

" Her eyes were sapphires set in snow,"

the Princesses could obtain a divorce, and marry again. For among the Ottomans, the prince as well as the peasant is amenable in this respect to the laws laid down in the Koran in which the injunction respecting a plurality of wives runs thus: " You may, if you like, marry two, three, and 'even four women." And that favorite's life would not be worth an hour's purchase. This has lately been clearly shown by the fact, that a princess, one of the near relatives of His Majesty the Sultan, having suspected—nay discovered —that her husband had had an intrigue with one of her slaves, had the unfortunate creature's head cut off by her Grand Eunuch, placed it upon a dish, covered it over with a cloth of gold, and served it up to him.

As she was of royal blood, her husband was in point of rank her slave, so that Her Highness did not wait upon him at his meals.

As soon as he sat down at the *zoofra*, he drank off a cup of sherbet, as was his custom, which had heen poisoned; and when the dish was uncovered, he stared wildly at the gory head, and dropped down dead. Nothing was done to Her Highness the Princess; and I can affirm that any Turkish woman would have recourse to that expedient, upon receiving the same amount of provocation. It is dangerous, as the Proverb says, " to play with edged tools," but doubly so within the mysterious walls of a Viceregal Harem.

Well, to continue my description of His Highness in his bath-room, all I saw was, that the Lady Paramount and several *Ikbals* were drying his Viceregal person with bath towels. His Highness smiled, exclaimed " *Approchez, approchez, madame.*" But I let go the Grand Pacha's hand who advanced towards his august parent, then curtseyed, and retired.

That same day, when the Grand Pacha returned from the bath-room, the head-nurse, according to her habitual custom took him into his apartment to change his uniform; upon which occasion she rifled his pockets and reaped a golden harvest, as the Viceroy had emptied several purses of small gold Egyptian coins into his pockets, telling him that there was plenty of baksheesh for him to give his governess.

I should have taken no notice of this circumstance, and, in fact have known nothing about it, had not Shaytan asked me to give her my tin cash-box, which was a moderate-sized one such as is generally used by ladies when residing on the Continent.

I was rather astonished at her presumption in making such a demand. However, being anxious to learn what had caused her to make that request, I asked her what she wanted it for. Leading me into her room, she opened her *sarat*, " trunk," and guess my surprise, when she took out an English workbox, all the compartments of which had been removed, and I saw it was as full as ever it could hold of napoleons, half-napoleons, gold five-franc pieces, Turkish,

Egyptian, and English sovereigns; in short, she had the greatest difficulty in lifting it out of the trunk. It was fastened or bound with thin cord, was very heavy, and must have contained several hundred pounds; in short it was so full that it could contain no more. All was packed in rolls closely together.

Then she showed me several hundreds of the smallest gold Egyptian coins which have ever been put in circulation. They were about the size of an ordinary gold pencil-case seal, and as thin as a wafer cut into two slices. As they were all new, I inquired of her by what means she became possessed of them; and then I learned the trick she had played me. Taking no notice, for *baksheesh* had always been her perquisite prior to my arrival in the Harem, I declined to give her my cash-box, which I could not conveniently spare, but handed her a tin tooth-powder box out of my dressing-case, into which she placed her purloinings, and salaamed me for the gift.

This circumstance naturally led me to inquire what became of the slaves' hoards after their decease; and I was told (but I can scarcely believe it) that it was expended in what they term giving them " a grand funeral; " that is, in paying for torches 'and hiring a vast concourse of professional mourners, as is customary in Egypt, to cry most bitterly over the body at the interment. But I should rather think that the bulk of their savings found its way into the coffers of the Kislar Ayaci's iron chest, as he has to superintend their obsequies.

Scarcely had this little incident occurred than the Grand Eunuch entered the apartment, and informed me that I was to accompany the Grand Pacha on board the *Ibis* yacht, as the Viceroy had placed that steamer at the disposal of the Princesses to convey them on an excursion up the Nile.

Hurrying on my hat and cloak, I took the Grand Pacha down to the landing-place, where we all embarked in barges and were quickly rowed to the yacht, whose steam was up. There I found their Highnesses assembled on the deck, under the spacious awning, squatting on the divans, smoking cigarettes, and looking the very picture of delight at the idea of enjoying a pic-nic on the bosom of the far-famed Nile.

Soon I found that it was to be a general treat; for, on looking round, I found that the whole of the inmates of the " Abode of Bliss," ladies of the Harem, and slaves, even to the meanest, were on board. Their meals were prepared for them, just as if they had been in their gilded cage. There they smoked, sipped their coffee, enjoyed their *kef*, and appeared to pass their time most agreeably. And I should have enjoyed the trip myself, if I had not been frightened at the manner in which the captain of the steamer (a Turkish officer, who spoke English very well) gratified the singular whim of my Prince, the Grand Pacha Ibrahim, who on this occasion, as on several others I have already mentioned, evinced an innate cruelty of disposition which appears to characterize the descendants of the renowned Mehemet Ali. Still, I cannot but think that he might have been taught to be merciful, had not bad example been set him.

I remember, when first taking charge of him, that I had great difficulty to make him mind me when checking any of his bad propensities. One day, when Her Highness, his mother, was sitting on a divan, and he would not obey me in something, she took hold of his hand, and then taking a diamond pin out of her hair, she pricked him gently with it, at the same time explaining to me that that was the manner in which I was to punish. I looked at her, said not a word, but nodded my head. Thus the Prince himself was taught to be cruel to others, which may, in some degree, account for that characteristic in him.

I never did correct His Highness in that manner, but one day, when I requested him to discontinue a very bad habit he had of forcing, as it were, his fingers up his nose, which caused it to swell, and which would, if persisted in, have made his nasal organ unseemingly wide, he rose up from the cushion upon which he was seated, stood quite upright, as if he had been on drill, and drawing his figure to its full height, he stamped his little foot upon the floor, exclaiming, " *Grand Pacha, madame! Grand Pacha, madame!*" as much as to tell me that he was the Grand Pacha Ibrahim, and that I was not to order him to do anything that he disliked.

I desired him to do as I bid him, but to no purpose. Knowing that it was necessary that the Prince should learn to obey me, I bethought me of the Princess's instructions; so I walked up to him, took hold of his tiny hand—not, kind reader, with the slightest intention of hurting him— then took a hair-pin out of my hair, placed the points on it, and the Prince withdrew it, at the same tine exclaiming, " *Evvét, madame! Evvét, madame!*" "Yes, madame! Yes, madame!" and that was the first and last time that I ever tried the Princess's mode of punishment, for it produced a lasting impression on the Grand Pacha's mind; and yet His Highness was not angry with me. But I knew, as a positive fact, that Shaytan the head-nurse, used to pinch him until His Highness shrieked again with pain; and I did all in my power to prevent her from acting in that cruel way, and had, prior to my departure, put a stop to it altogether.

The young Prince, who had often witnessed from the windows of his apartments some of the sailors belonging to the Viceroy's yacht, the *Crocodile*, plunge into the Nile, and whose agility in swimming had afforded him much amusement, happened, as he stood on the poop-deck, to perceive several crocodiles basking in the sun on the low banks which shelved down to the river: he ran up to the captain, and told him to order a young slave, who was passing by at that moment, to be thrown into the river.

I did all in my power to prevent this order from being carried out; but as His Highness put himself into a passion, and the captain assured me that the slave could swim, to use his own expression, "like a water-fowl," I let him act upon his own responsibility.

Two sailors then laid hold of the lad, and plunged him into the Nile, not on the side, however, on which the formidable crocodiles were enjoying themselves; and I had the heartfelt satisfaction to see the slave swim to the boat which was hanging to the rope at the stern.

The Prince laughed heartily at the lad's acuteness in getting into the boat, and ordered him to be cast into the river, which was done, but the boat was sent adrift. The cunning slave swam to it, jumped into it, and was soon alongside the yacht, which had just heaved-to in order to return off the Harem stairs.

I gave the lad a handful of *paras* as *baksheesh*, who salaamed me and went away to join his companions, quite delighted with his prize. Poor fellow! had it not been for the humanity of the captain he would have been swallowed up by the crocodiles; for had he been flung on their side of the stream, nothing could possibly have saved him.

The sad monotony of my daily life was often relieved by the pastimes of the Grand Pacha, a merry little boy, who, had he been left alone with me away from all the disgusting manners of the ladies of the Harem and the slaves, might have been "made a man of," and even a gentleman, like his illustrious parent, whose manners are courtly and amiable.

I had been interdicted from affording him any instruction through the medium of books, except so far as to teach him the alphabet, which I did by means of an illustrated primer and a box of toys. I therefore took a lively interest in his games and amusements. I found that he possessed most excellent abilities, dull and heavy-looking boy as he appeared to be; nevertheless the prominent features of his disposition were three of the worst vices that a child could possibly demonstrate, namely, cruelty, avarice, and greediness.

He had been accustomed, as soon as he could talk and toddle about, to have his pockets filled with *paras*, " silver coins," by the Viceroy, which as I have previously related, were purloined by the head-nurse, who doled out *miles*, of them, as it were, to the under-nurses; hence the manner in which she had accumulated her treasure. That practice being constantly before the Prince's eyes, it had engendered in him the vice of avarice, which a distinguished author has most accurately described as " begetting more vices than Priam did children, and which, like Priam, survives them all."

It is a passion full of paradox; a madness full of method. Its votary falls down and worships the god of this world, but will have neither its pomps, its vanities, nor its pleasures, for his trouble. He kept constantly urging me to play at banking with him. One day we were both seated on cushions upon the carpet in the Audience Hall, and after he had finished cutting up (for he was particularly fond of handling a pair of scissors) some card-board into a number of middling-sized and small circular pieces, he piled them up in parcels of twenty, as if they had been sovereigns, then placed them in rows upon a cushion which was opposite to him; beside them were several empty packets. Then squatting himself down in imitation of the Arab money-changers, who are to be found at almost every corner of the streets in the Egyptian towns and large villages, he began to personate the character of a banker, or, more properly speaking, the money-changer.

The peculiar manner in which he so inimitably set, as it were, his feathers to represent those of the stolid, calculating " dealer in rupees," as the Indian ruler so emphatically designates a banker, was a fine piece of acting.

I sat down facing him, as he had removed his "stock in trade" to his right-hand side. He then gave me several packets of the card-board pieces he had cut, at the same time telling me that I was to count them as English sovereigns. I then stood up before him and asked for change.

As soon as I had done so he looked at the counter I had handed him, poised it in his tiny hand to see that it was full weight, turned it over and over again, to examine whether it were cut or cracked, said not a syllable, placed it on the cushion beside him, and began counting the *paras*, as he termed the change, in English, for he had soon acquired a knowledge of the numbers in my vernacular, and then handed a number of small card-board counters to me, by simply placing them in piles upon the cushion before him.

I took them out and counted them, but I found that he had not given me the proper change, even after having deducted a few *paras* for the exchange. I looked at him full in the face. His countenance still retained its rigidity of expression—not a smile, not a muscle had he moved; he looked the very impersonation of a usurer; his close resemblance at that moment to the portrait of his grandfather, which hangs in the palace at Ras-el-Tin at Alexandria, was very striking. There sat the prototype of that Viceregal usurer who so thoroughly understood the art of making money to yield its best value, a gift which has descended to his descendants.

I remonstrated with him, and told him that he had charged me too much for the exchange. His Highness wishing to gain as much as he could, and having no desire to part with the *paras* now that he had once fingered them, held rather a long argument with me, for a Turk seldom talks much, as to the scarcity of change. When he found that I was not satisfied with his explanation, he demurely stroked his chin, as if it were his beard, and left me to walk away and put up with my loss. The Grand Pacha Ibrahim laughed most heartily, and chuckled within himself to think how cleverly he had mulcted me of a few *paras.*

"Now then, Madame," said His Highness, as he rose up off his cushions, at the same time taking due care to remove close to him that which contained his treasure, "You must take my seat, and act the money-changer."

According to his instructions I repaired to the seat he had vacated, at the same time placing my cushion with the counters by my side. As soon as I had arranged myself, the Prince, who had cunningly clipped the corners off several of the counters, probably with the intention of placing them among those that he had given to me at first, handed me one of those pieces. I examined it, pointed out to His Highness that it had been cut, and therefore was deficient in weight, and refused to change it, except at a considerable reduction ; but he would not agree to that agreement. Then he put himself into a towering passion, threw himself upon the floor, screamed out most hideously, and brought the whole staff of the establishment, princesses, ladies of the Harem, slaves and eunuchs, into the apartment, to see what was the matter with the Grand Pacha; for at the very sound of his voice the whole of the establishment was always on the alarm.

The head-nurse took him up, and began performing her superstitious observances, by sprinkling water on the floor, as a slave had attended her with a silver basinful, naturally thinking that His Highness had met with some accident.

When the matter was explained to the Princess Epouse, she laughed most heartily, and exclaimed, "*Malesh ! Malesh !*" and retired from the apartment, accompanied by the whole retinue.

The Viceroy, Ismael Pacha, happening to be in an adjoining apartment, entered the room a few minutes after I had managed to pacify the little torment, who had set himself down, and was once again quietly playing with me at the

11

same pastime. I was not aware of His Highness's presence ; but as I sat counting out some *paras* on a cushion on the floor, I suddenly felt the breath of some person fan, as it were, my cheek. Thinking that it was Shaytan, I raised up my hand, with the intention of boxing her ears, as I thought that, according to her custom, she had slipped into the apartment unperceived, and was watching us at play.

Suddenly, however, I saw the Grand Pacha smile, and, turning round, I perceived the Viceroy, bending, as it were, over my shoulder. I sprung to my feet, blushed, curtseyed to His Highness, who smiled, and playfully exclaimed, "Pray, Madame, as I am a poor man,"—and the marked emphasis with which the billionaire of the world uttered that expression was so peculiar that I shall never forget it (for the tone of voice was that of a professional money-lender),—"allow me to take possession of your stock-in-trade." Saying which, His Highness seated himself on the cushion I had just vacated, and began to play with his darling son.

After having amused himself for some time, His Highness rose up, approached me, for I was standing at one of the windows looking out into the garden, and thanked me for the judicious manner in which I had managed to amuse his refractory heir, and then left the apartment.

I had flattered myself that when he rose up from the banking department, the Viceroy would have left some packets of golden *paras* on the cushion. None, however, were deposited there ; for, like his son, he was reported, and I believe the fact, to be fond of accumulating treasure as a means to happiness, and by a common but morbid association, he continued to accumulate it as an end. This attachment to wealth must always be a growing and progressing attachment, since misers and usurers are not slow in discovering that those same ruthless years which detract so sensibly from their bodies and their minds serve only to augment and consolidate the strength of their purse.

Sometimes His Highness the Prince would order all his young slaves to come into his apartment, when he would make them go through the whole military exercise (many of whom were girls, and his half-sisters too) just as efficiently as if they were battalions of infantry. He gave the words of command in a most clear and distinct voice, and made them go through their manœuvres as admirably as if he had been a drill-sergeant. If any one of them did not stand up or march properly, he immediately ordered the eunuch who was in attendance upon him to give the refractory private several strokes of the *courbache* (a whip made of buffalo hide); and if the offender repeated the offence, he ordered him treble punishment, which was immediately inflicted.

Thus, while the Prince displayed a strong passion for military glory, like his renowned ancestor, Mehemet Ali, he also demonstrated his possession of that vice, cruelty, which had so often sullied the fair name, not only of the rengenerator of Egypt, but which had also tarnished the renown of his courageous grandsire, Ibrahim Pacha; both of whom were neither more nor less than most remorseless tyrants.

At other times the Prince would make his retinue sit down on cushions on the floor, which he had arrranged in rows; and then he commanded them to imitate the boatmen rowing boats on the Nile. If any one of them did not move their hands and arms in unison with the rest, he would order them to be bastinadoed upon the soles of their feet.

His powers of imitation and mimicry, as I have previously stated, were very great, and his favorite pastime consisted in imitating the Mussulmans at their prayers in the mosques. In the first place he went himself and fetched a Persian rug from one of the rooms, which he placed on the carpet, close by the elder slaves, who were busy cutting out their dresses, &c. Sometimes, however, he would have it laid in the centre of the room ; then he took the silk cover-lets off the beds out of the bed store-room, and placed them on each side of the room.

Personating the Mufti, which he did to perfection, he knelt down on the rug and made all the little slaves kneel down by his side on the coverlets. After which he began muttering some words, which I did not understand, but which the slaves repeated after him. Then he bowed his forehead down on the rug, the slaves following his example. After this he stood with his face towards Mecca, put his two little hands together, bowed his head down to the ground, and continued repeating such gestures for upwards of fifty times, the slaves imitating him. Then he placed his thumbs behind his ears with his fingers, and extended them upwards to the ceiling, in a devotional attitude, ex-claiming at different times, " Allah ! Allah ! Amin ! Amin !" " God ! God ! Amen ! Amen ! " He then bowed his bead and smoothed down his chin, in imitation of the Turk stroking his beard.

At other times His Highness would collect a number of small pieces of wood out of his toy closet, in which were stored toys of the most costly and varied description, for it is almost impossible to estimate the sums which had been ex-pended in this manner. During my sojourn with him, up-wards of 500*l.* worth arrived from Paris of the latest nov-elties, and I am sure upwards of 400*l.* were already in the Pal-ace on my arrival. Yet most oddly enough, those of the most simple kind, and which are most commonly in use among European boys, had not been provided for him. Hoops, skipping-ropes, trap, bat and ball, football, and more especi-ally a rocking horse, had been omitted ; but as to drums, fifes, whistles, and those of the noisiest, their names were legion. The majority were, however, most costly mechani-cal inventions. I presented him with a small pistol, with percussion caps, rather a noisy though harmless weapon, but the use of it was prohibited, lest he should hurt himself, which was impossible. All gymnastic amusements had been neglected. But in making the slaves pretend to be carpenters, he himself acted as foreman and taskmaster, an office in which, like the Egyptians of old in the time of Pharoah and the Israelites, he was a proficient. Many a time and oft did he turn bricklayer himself, by getting flat pieces of wood, with which he made the slaves scrape the walls, while to others he gave long sticks, and pretending to mix up mortar, he placed the pieces of paper moistened with water upon flat pieces of wood instead of hods, and made the slaves carry it to those who were engaged in erecting his temporary palace.

At other times he would enact the pilgrims going to Mecca. Then he made the little slaves take their handkerchiefs, one of which they bound over their faces, concealing the whole of their countenances except the eyes, and spreading the other open, they placed it over their heads. Then, taking the thin coverlets, they made *habarahs* of them, in which they attired themselves. Their handkerchiefs were then converted into wallets, in which he placed paper to represent their provisions, and card-board counters for their money. This being done, he started them off down the apartment two by two, while he himself attended one of the little Princesses, who was carried on the shoulders of some of the slaves, seated in a chair, the substitute for a palanquin (for, singular to add, none are ever used in Egypt), and then the procession moved up and down the apartment, while several of the other slaves kept beating their drums in the most discordant manner. Sometimes His Highness would imitate the *Hammals*, "porters," by making the slaves carry the cushions of the divans on their shoulders, he himself walking in front of them, holding a long and rather thick stick in his hand, at the same time hallooing out, *Hum ! Hum ! Allah ! Allah ! hout iyam,* "God be thanked for this daily burthen," which all the slaves were obliged to repeat under penalty of receiving several knocks with his stick. Occasionally he would also personate the *Hekim Bachi*, "Viceregal Doctor," and then he made one of the little slaves run before him, shouting forth, *Allah! Allah! Dustoor! Dustoor!* "God! God! Move away! Move away!" when the slaves, both young and grown up, many of whom mingled in his pastimes, covered their heads with their dresses, or with anything that they might be making up for themselves, which made him laugh most heartily.

Then he walked up and down the room, accompanied by a little slave, looked at the hands of the female slaves, some of whom were obliged to pretend that they were ill, and had bad fingers or wounded legs. Then he gave orders to his little assistant to bind up the part affected, and administered bread pills to them for medicine, but to those who were his *Ikbals* "favorites," he gave *bonbons*, as immense baskets filled with them are monthly imported from Paris by one of His Highness's partners there for exclusive distribution in the Harems. I repeat Harems, because his Highness the Viceroy has several others up the Nile both in Lower and Upper Egypt, besides that in which I resided with the Prince.

CHAPTER XVI.

WHILE dilating upon the admirable manner in which His Highness enacted the physician, I may as well mention that His Highness the Viceroy has a staff of medical men, chiefly Italians. When I fell ill at Cairo, His Highness Ismael Pacha sent his own physician extraordinary to visit me; but it appeared evident to me that, from his treatment of myself, they do not understand the constitutions of Englishwomen.   They are seldom or never called into the Harems, except to attend upon the Prince.

The mother of the Harem are skilled in the practice of midwifery; they are generally old, ugly women, who bend the knee to that sovereign ruler of Egypt, Prince Baksheesh, and are ever ready to commit any crime or forward any intrigue, as the annals of Egyptian history ever since the rule of Mehemet Ali testify.   They have all kinds of narcotics at their command, are well versed in the use and abuse of the deadliest of vegetable poisons; are skilled in making up *philtres*, sometimes administered as draughts or powders, and which they affirm have the power to produce love or hatred.

One of their principal charms is *Haschachir, Haschisch,* which has been known to have the most extraordinary effects on the brain.   When taken it causes violent palpitations, followed by excruciating pangs and qualms, which produce an hallucination of the senses that makes the mind fancy all kinds of improbable things.

If taken at night, even if the darkness be ever so intense it often causes the patients who are under its influence to fancy that they see a most brilliant sunset.   If the chamber is as silent as the grave, most singular noises are heard; sometimes the ringing of bells, the Moslem's abomination, although none are used in the East except in the dwellings of the Europeans, and in their places of worship; the striking of clocks; at other times the chanting in the distance of beautiful sacred music by sweet and melodious voices. And yet, what is most curious, the individual who is under its pernicious influence is perfectly aware that those distortions of the imagination are but the effects of the *Haschisch* which gives the mind, as it were a double existence.   Even the taste and smell seem effected by it, for the nostrils imbibe, as it were, perfumes which do not impregnate the atmosphere, and the palate flavors that exist not.

Should the individual be taking a promenade, when under its influence, the thoroughfare through which he is passing seems to have no outlet, and every object around appears double, and to assume the most grotesque shapes and forms. At times his memory becomes impaired. and he sinks into a deep lethargy, which feeling I experienced myself during my illness at Constantinople. He loses all idea of time; a minute seems to him an hour. He is consumed with a burning thirst, which nothing seems to assuage.

In order to experience these effects, or many other most singular delusions, it is only necessary to take half a tea-spoonful of it, drink a cup of pure Mocha coffee, partake of a meal afterwards, and the potion will soon begin to operate.

The *Haschachir*, like the *Bang* drunk by the Sepoys in India, is said to be destilled from the leaf of a kind of hemp called *Konnab Hindi*, "Fakir's Weed," or "Fakir's Keff," hence the derivation of the Turkish word *Keff*, or *Kef*.

These harridans attribute great efficacy to the marrow of the ostrich, or portions of a dried hippopotamus, when it is powdered and taken by their patients in that manner. But their *forte* lies in procuring abortion. European physicians are not unfrequently conducted into the Harems, but the greatest precautions are taken to prevent them from seeing the faces of their patients, as the whole of the face, except the eyes, is covered with a *habarah* whenever they enter the palace, and the eunuchs cry out with most stentorian lungs, *Allah, Allah! Dustoor, Dustoor !* "God ! God ! Away ! Away !." when all the women run into their rooms, in the twinkling of an eye. It really is most amusing to see the singular manner in which they managed to let the *Hekim Bachi*, "Viceregal doctor," examine the diseased part.

Once an operation had to be performed on a slave, and then the face was most carefully concealed. At another time the tongue had to be examined, and that was thrust out of the mouth, the lips being covered over.   One day, it happened that a slave was on the point of death, and it was necessary to see her face, which was managed by a thin colored gauze being thrown over it.   I know an instance of an Italian doctor being called upon to attend a young married Turkish woman, who did not seem to have much the matter with her.

"*Hekim effendi*" (Doctor), said she to him, "I want to know what ails me."

The peculiar manner in which she made that interrogatory gave the doctor the key to what she wanted.   He assumed a very serious countenance, and after a few moments' deliberation, exclaimed, "*Hanem*" (Lady), said he, "you do not appear to be very unwell; but there is one thing . . . ."

"What is that?" inquired the lady, hurriedly.

"*Hanem*, you are as ladies wish to be who love their lords."

"*Pek-ein*" (Very well!) said the young lady's mother, who was present, as was usual, at the consultation.   "But how long has that been the case?   Pray tell us, I beg of you."

After a few moments' pause, and by the aid of some indication which had been revealed to him, the doctor told her that the *Hanem* had been *enceinte* about four months. He then thought that his visit was ended: but the mother pressed the *Hekim* to tell them whether the child would be a boy or a girl.

Any other medical man but that Italian physician would have burst out into a fit of laughter; but he without moving a muscle, looked intently at the *Hanem*, stroked down his beard several times, and then replied in a firm tone of voice :

"*Inch Allah!*" (By the blessing of God!) "the child will be a boy, and the very picture of his father."

"God grant you a long life, *Hekim effendi*," exclaimed

both the women; and the doctor left the apartment loaded with blessings and a purse full of Turkish sovereigns.

One of His Highness's favorite pastimes was playing at dominoes, which he did with great skill. When he became wearied of that amusement cards were introduced, and he played numerous Turkish games with his little playmates. At other times he would have a fantasia enacted. Then he ordered the slaves to pile up several cushions, which he called a *Musnud,* "throne," on which he seated himself with the little Princesses, his legitimate sisters, arranged on each side. The young slaves sat about him in the form of a semi-circle, and a slave named Rosetta commenced singing in a very pretty manner the following verses in Turkish :—

"The complexion of my love is like the freshness of the velvet-looking jasmine; her face is as resplendent as the bright, bright moon; her lips were as rosy as the choicest Burgundy, and her lily white bosom the fairest and softest-looking that an amorous youth ever beheld.

"Oh! beauteous creature, the perfume of whose breath is like the grateful odor of the musk rose, allow me to sip sweets from thy ruby lips, and pour forth into thy ear the passion that consumes my heart."

All the slaves joined in the chorus, and sang the last verse. Their Highnesses the Princesses encored; then the Grand Pacha, quite elated at his success as director of the fantasia, ordered another slave, named Damietta, to approach the musnud, and the little girl poured forth, in a plaintive voice, the following strain :—

"My mistress wears a beautiful gold embroidered dress; her wide trousers are of azure blue silk; her waistband is a costly cashmere shawl worth two hundred Egyptian sovereigns. All the richness of her attire is nothing in comparison to the beauty of her face!

"There is nothing either in heaven or earth half so lovely as her beautiful sparkling orbs."

At other times he would give orders for a banquet. Then

two slaves were ordered to fetch all the *soofras* they could find, which they placed down the whole length of the apartment. Then His Highness commanded them to ask the eunuchs to give them a number of the prettiest *bonbon* cases, filled with those condiments, which they brought up into the room. Emptying their contents into one of the silk coverlets, the Prince mixed them all together, replaced them in some of the handsomest baskets at hand, and ordered the slaves to hand them round to the Princesses, the wives, and to his little sisters; also to his *ikbal*, "favorite," for he had one, young as he was.

She was a slave who had been purchased at Constantinople, and was placed in the Harem to be educated with His Highness. Had that plan been followed out, some good results might have been produced; but like most others adopted by many of the Viceregal family, it was abandoned. The only distinction which was made between this child and the young Princesses was that she was obliged to eat her meals with an iron spoon. Upon this occasion, imitating the example set him by his Viceregal parent, he took it into his head to honor her that day, and therefore ordered the slaves to hand every basket to her first, after they had served their Highnesses the Princesses, the wives. She was distinguished from the other slaves by wearing a fez; which was not on account of the position she would probably be called upon to take, but simply from the fact that the cleanliness of her hair had been so much neglected, that she had not only lost the greater portion of it, but that the vermin had eaten sores into her skull!

After this sherbet was served.

The entertainment, however, did not pass off without one of the Prince's favorite slaves having purloined a basket of *bonbons*. The Princess Epouse, upon being informed of it, ordered the girl to be punished. But the Grand Pacha put himself into such a paroxysm of rage, that he lay upon the floor and foamed at the mouth, and exclaiming at intervals that she should *not* be punished except by *himself;* and nothing would satisfy him until his mother countermanded the order. When that was done he took up a small cane which was near at hand, and laid it lightly across her shoulders and thus ended the affair.

It afforded me considerable pain to observe that His Highness always evinced, at these feasts, the utmost greediness, by setting apart for himself the largest basket of *bonbons;* and if any of the slaves (and several of them were in the habit of doing so) teased him by exchanging their own baskets, cakes, &c., for his, he would break up the entertainment *instanter,* have all the *soofras,* &c., removed immediately, send the slaves away, and dismiss the company.

One day, when it was too hot for the Prince to take his usual morning walk in the garden, I was playing with him at football, the ball being a middle-sized India one, enclosed in network; the hangings of the doors being looped back to admit of a free circulation of air. His Highness happened to kick it with rather more force than usual, it bounded into the corridor, and rolled into a room, the door of which I had never seen open before, and disappeared.

The Prince followed in pursuit; but hearing him halloo out, I hastened to his assistance, and, entering the unexplored chamber, I found that the tails of his little coat had been caught in the leg of a Broadwood's grand piano. I instantly liberated the little captive, who, as soon as he had snatched up the ball, threw it into my hands, which were extended to catch it, and proceeded (as he was exceedingly curious) to examine every nook and corner of that room, which was to him an undiscovered region.

Hand-in-hand, we proceeded to take an inventory of the miscellaneous articles which were huddled up together in that "Old Antique and Modern Curiosity shop." I cannot do better than compare it to the show-room of an extensive furniture-warehouse, with half-a-dozen parlors, of Wardour-street *vertù* dealers.

There we found beautifully executed full-length portraits of Her Majesty the Queen, the late Prince Consort, Napoleon III., the Empress Eugenie, and many other of the crowned heads of Europe; elegant gilt time-pieces, large bulky rolls of handsome carpet, marqueterie tables, spring easy-chairs, sofas, ornaments for mantelpieces of the most costly description; clocks, with birds which, as I wound some of them up, began singing, instead of striking the hours. Some had fish swimming round and round the dials, which stood in the centre on imitation lakes; all of them were most artistically inlaid, with large figures on the tops. There was one far more beautiful than the others which attracted my attention, which had the figure of Venus in a shell drawn by swans : it was a magnificent piece of workmanship. Others had chariots drawn by wild horses—one with Mazeppa and the wild horses. There were stood up against the wall suits of old armor, beautifully inlaid. On lines hung quantities of old clothes, consisting of suits of uniforms which had belonged to Mehemet Ali, Ibrahim Pacha, Ismael Pacha, the Viceroy's uncle, and other defunct Egyptian princes. Saddles, bridles, silver bits, and stirrups; immense mirrors, evidently of English manufacture ; superb large glass lustres, services of old Sèvres china; fire-irons, richly gilt; children's toys in abundance, of the most expensive kind, all fitted with mechanical movements ; musical instruments, and a host of miscellaneous articles that it would take a catalogue of twenty pages to enumerate.

It was a very large apartment (not in the Harem) and happened to be open on that day, as the Viceroy's *Tchiboukdji* was standing there, while several slaves were dusting it. I then determined to ask the Viceroy, when an opportunity offered, to allow me to have the furniture which was in it (for therein I had found everything that even a European lady of rank could desire to make her rooms comfortable) placed in the rooms above it, which would have enabled me to keep the Prince apart from the host of slaves, whose disgusting ways tended to counteract my best endeavors to bring him up in European habits and manners.

But most unfortunately, our sudden departure for Alexandria prevented me from carrying out that *beau projet*, as also did my subsequent illness at Constantinople, which obliged me to repair to Europe. I never again returned to the Harem, for which I was not sorry.

On my return to the Prince's reception-hall, into which His Highness had hastened some time before me, I found one of the little eunuchs (for there were then eight of them in the Harem, whose ages averaged from four to ten years) who were to accompany us to Constantinople as presents to His Majesty the Sultan, crying most bitterly.

Upon making inquiries, I found that he had been dreadfully frightened by the Prince with a snow white lamb, a toy, who bleated by mechanism, and had run his horns against his private parts. The blow had so exasperated the little eunuch that he rushed on the Grand Pacha, who, doubling up his fist *à l' Anglais*, had struck him in the same part near the abdomen, and sent him sprawling on the floor. The head-nurse had rushed in, and performed her incantations, and the mother of that little " spectre of a man " was tending that offspring whom she had sold for filthy gold, like a farmer sells his sheep.

When I had complained to Mr. B. and the Messrs. H. of the scanty accommodation of one tiny little room, not more than twelve feet long by twelve feet broad, and about fourteen high, I was met with the reply that His Highness had no other accommodation to give me. Now I had found out the contrary, and learned that not the slightest efforts had been made by the Viceroy's partners to contribute to my comfort. But as I was one of mother Eve's daughters, all of whom they looked upon as handmaids and slaves, born to be bought and sold, anything was good enough for me; for I had found a whole suite of noble rooms unoccupied, and plenty of useful elegant European furniture to adorn and befit them for the occupation of His Highness and his Governess, close by my own chamber.

Perhaps had I been a Frankfort lady, or a denizen of the lovely village of Oppenheim, on the banks of the beautiful Rhine, my comfort would have been better cared for, and I should have found my position much more endurable; but I was *Kopek*, "a dog" of an Englishwoman, a Howadjee, an unbeliever, a Pariah, whom both Moslems and Jews despised and spat at, therefore, as I was told before I quitted my own dear bright land of liberty, "I must fight my own battle," I determined to do it, my motto being, "*coûte qui coûte.*"

⬤

CHAPTER XVII.

NOTWITHSTANDING the sudden demise of Ismael Pacha's daughter, and the intense heat of the season, we passed the festival of the Grand Bairam (*Courban*), held in celebration of the three days' pilgrimage to Mecca, in the Harem at Gehzire. I should have observed that there are two festivals called *Bairam ;* the other, named *A'idfitr*, corresponds to our New Year's Day. On the former occasion, and the festival I am about to describe, all the shops kept by Turks are invariably closed, and both they and the Egyptians dress themselves in new attire, feast most immoderately, sacrifice lambs (the scraps of which, after they have finished their repast, are given to the poor,) pay visits to one another, as also do the inmates of the Harems.

Well, this festival so anxiously looked forward to by the

Peris of the Viceregal Harem, began on the Monday, and continued until the following Wednesday until sunset; during the whole of which period the sound, the sight, of fez, girdle, robe, and scimitar, and tawny skins awoke contending thoughts of surprise, astonishment, and wonder in my mind.

On the Sunday night, three large fat sheep, which would have done credit to the show of cattle in Baker Street at Christmas time, with their horns gilded and blue ribbons tied round their necks, were brought into the court-yard of the Harem.   Early on the Monday morning, between three and four o'clock, they were killed, and their blood besprinkled on the posts and thresholds of every outer door. The sight made my heart heave again.   Then they were cut up and cooked, the greater portion of them being cut into steaks, and broiled upon live charcoal, portions of which were distributed to every person in, about, and in the vicinity of the Harem.

At the doors of each apartment were placed Sèvres china bowls of sour milk, and custards on trays, when every one as they entered took some of them, and helped themselves to the Turkish sweetmeats, *bonbons*, cakes, fruit, &c.

In fact, the whole time from morning to night was one continual scene of gourmandizing and paying visits.   At five o'clock in the morning the inmates of the Harem arrayed themselves *en grande toilette*, and went to pay their Highnesses the Princesses, the three wives, a visit, at the same time presenting each with a gift, the value of which they returned tenfold by bestowing baksheesh, in the shape of sums of money, jewelry, and dresses, upon them.   When dresses were given they invariably comprised three muslins and a silk one.   Upon this occasion I took the Grand Pacha with me into their Highnesses' rooms, when they all saluted me with the expression, "*Bairum Madame*," and each handed me a small packet of *paras*, gold coins, as baksheesh.

Her Highness the Lady Paramount wore upon this occasion a pink satin robe, trimmed with black lace and silver thread ribbon, with full trousers of the same material. Around her head was a white gauze handkerchief embroidered with gold. On her forehead she wore a tiara of large pansies in diamonds; round her neck was a costly necklace of the same flowers with emerald leaves, and pear-shaped pearl drops, as big as pigeons' eggs, were suspended from the centre. Her arms were ornamented with two massive gold bracelets, on one of which, contrary to the express command of Mahomet, their Prophet, was the portrait of the Viceroy Ismael Pacha, dressed in his rich Turkish uniform with fez, set in brilliants, which she very kindly took off and handed to me. I looked at them some time, and when I returned them His Highness inquired of me how I liked them? To which I replied that they were *Guzel!* *Guzel!* "Beautiful! beautiful!"

Her armlets were of large pear-shaped opals, which hung suspended like drops, between which was set a large diamond. On her little finger on the right hand, she wore a magnificent sapphire ring, about the size of a walnut, and on the same finger of the left was a rose pink diamond ring. Her waist was encircled with a gold band fastened with diamond clasps, into which was tucked her gold watch encrusted with brilliants, the Albert chain of which, an inch broad, was composed of diamonds and emeralds. The watch was fastened to the side of the gold band by a gold watch hook, attached to which was a very small silk bag, studded with brilliants, containing the keys of her cash-box and jewel-cases, with which she never parted by night or day. Her feet were encased in pink silk stockings and high-heeled embroidered white satin shoes. In her left hand she carried a richly gold embroidered muslin handkerchief, and in her right hand she held a pink satin purse, more like a bag than anything else, richly embroidered with pearls, containing small gold Egyptian coins for baksheesh.

12

I must here observe that I have often seen their Highnesses amuse themselves by sticking a number of these coins all over the Pacha's face, and then sending him laughing out of their apartment, and, as a matter of course, they were eagerly picked off by the head nurse, whose perquisites they became.

Her Highness the Princess Epouse, the mother of my Prince, was attired in a rich blue figured silk robe, trimmed with white lace and silver thread, with a long train; full trousers of the same material, high-heeled embroidered satin shoes to match the dress. On her head she had a small white crape handkerchief, elegantly embroidered with blue silk and silver, and round it was placed a tiara of May blossoms in diamonds. She wore a necklace to correspond, having large sapphire drops hanging down on her neck. Her arms were ornamented with three bracelets composed of diamonds and sapphires, and an armlet entirely of sapphires of almost priceless value. This was *par excellence*, the veriest *bijou* I had yet seen amidst all the galaxy of jewelry of precious stones which adorned any of their Highnesses' persons, although at times my eyes, when looking at the bedizened Peris arrayed in all their gems, have become as dim as if I had been fixing them on the gorgeous noonday sun in any eastern clime. In her bosom she wore a brooch containing the Viceroy's portrait in European costume, with —hear it not, ye Moslems!—a hat on, having two circles of diamonds around it. Upon looking at it, it recalled to my recollection Ben Johnson's celebrated lines:—

" This figure that thou here seest put,
  It is for Ismael Pacha cut;
  Wherein the graver had a strife
  With Nature to outdo the life;
  O could he but have drawn his wit
  As well in brass, as he hath hit
  His face, the portrait would then surpass
  All that was ever writ in brass;
  But since he cannot, reader, look
  Not on his picture, but in this book."

On the little finger on her right hand she wore a large bright yellow diamond ring of almost untold value, and on that of the left an enormous white diamond. Her waist was encircled with an elastic gold band, having as clasps two crocodile heads in diamonds and emeralds. Her gold watch, encircled with brilliants, had appended to it an Albert chain composed of sapphires and diamonds; to it was attached a small gold bag, containing the keys of her cash-box and jewel-case, and in her left hand she held a small sky-blue satin bag embroidered with pearls, containing the gold coins which she purposed distributing as baksheesh. The third wife was attired in a similar manner, except in a robe of different color, as also were the young Princesses, but all were resplendently ornamented with precious jewels.

The ladies of the Harem, and the whole of the slaves, were dressed in the richest silks, and were adorned with jewels, almost as costly as those of their Highnesses.

It was to me rather a novel sight, to observe that the German laundry maid and needlewomen had, upon this occasion, dressed themselves up as Turkish houris. It is almost impossible to conceive the nondescript figures they cut in their *bal masqué* costume; as, being naturally very bad shapes, they looked more like the scarecrow figures one is accustomed to see placed in cornfields, to keep the crows away; and their awkward manner of imitating the *Turkish shuffle* was ludicrous in the extreme.

After I had paid my respects to them, I returned with the Grand Pacha, and handed him over to Shaytan, who proceeded to dress him *en grande tenue*. He wore black trousers, striped with red, with a narrow slip of gold-lace down each side. His coat was black, richly embroidered with gold-lace and ornamented gold buttons. I then placed on each of his shoulders a massive gold epaulette, buckled around his waist a gold band, which was fastened with a diamond clasp, in the shape of a crescent, from it dangled a diamond-hilted sword. In the heels of his patent-leather boots, were fastened gold spurs; and in èach of his pockets was placed a purse, filled with *paras*, for baksheesh, which was invariably called *sish* by the inmates of the Harem.

I then led him into the Grand Eunuch's apartment, which was fitted up on that occasion as the Grand Audience Hall; the hangings of the doors and windows being of crimson silk; and the chairs and divans covered with the same material. There the Grand Pacha held a levee of the Ministers of State, the Consuls General, at which were present the most distinguished military and naval officers, as well as a host of the *élite* of Turkish and Egyptain *noblesse* and the European community.

His Highness, the Prince Ibrahim, was seated on a divan, while I sat by his side, on the left, plainly attired, as not the slightest intimation had been given me that I should be called upon to take part in this ceremony, which was extremely fatiguing. All the Ministers of State, the highest in rank taking precedence, advanced towards His Highness, kissed his right hand, then placed their foreheads upon it; the next in rank kissed both his hands, and then, likewise, placed their foreheads upon it. To their Highnesses, the Princesses, *findjans* of the finest Japan china, placed in gold filigree *zarfs*, encrusted with precious stones, and filled with coffee, were handed round, and pipes were presented to those distinguished guests.

When this *Besa los manos*, for it was tantamount to that ceremony at the court of Spain, was over, the Grand Pacha Ibrahim, attended by myself, the illegitimate sons of the Viceroy, and the Ministers of State, proceeded with a brilliant escort of infantry and their band, to receive the Viceroy Ismael Pacha, at the landing-place of the Harem. Immediately on our arrival, the band struck up the Sultan's March, and the Viceroy landed from his yacht.

On the promenade, facing the Harem stairs, close to the

edge of the hill, stood the Prince, myself, and His Royal Highness's illegitimate sons, on the right hand, with a host of attendants behind, while the Ministers, &c., lined the left side. As the Viceroy passed up this line, he took the little Prince by his left hand, and saluted the Ministers with his right, then, dropping the Grand Pacha's hand, I took hold of it, and we walked by the side of the Viceroy Ismael Pacha, up to the entrance gate of the Harem, when the Ministers and Officials saluted, and went their way.

Entering the Harem, the Viceroy stopped at the outer gate to take a few *bonbons* out of the gold filigree-basket, in which they were placed, as also did the Prince and myself, as it is customary for all visitors on that occasion to partake of something on entering the precincts of the Harem.

Then the Grand Eunuch and his corps, dressed in richly-embroidered uniforms, threw open the doors of the Stone Hall, that most useful of all the rooms in this " Mansion of Bliss," and there stood, ranged in double lines, like files of infantry, the whole retinue of slaves, much more superbly attired than has been already described in the transformation scene, on His Highness's first visit to the Harem after my arrival. In short, they constituted two such dazzling and brilliant lines of sparkling jewels, as perhaps it never fell to the lot of an European lady to behold. There stood upwards of two hundred women, with their persons decorated with the most resplendent precious stones which the mineral kingdom had produced, and then to have a photographic sketch of the appearence of these houris of the East. And as the Viceroy walked slowly on, according to his custom between them, with the Prince and myself, all salaamed him, at the same time exclaiming, *Bairam Effendimiz* " Bairam your Majesty! " at which His Highness smiled, and waved his hand.

The Viceroy was received at the foot of the staircase by the Princesses, the three wives, to each of whom he presented his right hand, which they kissed. The steps of the grand-stair-case were lined on each side by the ladies of the Harem; and *Ikbals*, who also salaamed the Viceroy as he ascended, and the Princesses as they followed. On his Highness reaching the Audience Saloon, he sat down on the Divan, *à la Européenne*, while the Prince stood at his knee.

I had been particularly struck, on my first introduction into the Harem, with the repugnance which the Grand Pacha Ibrahim invariably manifested when called upon to make visits to the *Baba*, "father," as the Viceroy was familiarly termed in the Harem. Notwithstanding that His Highness showed him the greatest kindness and affection still the Prince did not appear to return it. I repeat *appear*, for, Turks are never very demonstrative, it is almost impossible to know when they are pleased or vexed, so that their sayings and doings are like those diplomatic avalanches which are constantly taking place in all parts of the Ottoman dominions. Whenever he approached his august parent, he cast his eyes down upon the carpet. Sometimes the little Prince would hand things to him from off the *soofraz*, at others nothing could induce him to do so. Whenever he addressed the Viceroy, he called him *Effendimiz*, "Monseigneur," but the *Baba* designated his son as plain Ibrahim.

Between the Grand Pacha and his sisters there also existed a kind of restraint; as owing to the Prince being the legitimate son, the heir to the billionaire's vast wealth, but not to the Viceroyalty (as that honor passes in a direct line to the descendants of Mahomet Ali, and therefore would fall to the lot of Mustapha Pacha, the Viceroy's brother, the surviving son of Ibrahim Pacha,) he made the little Princesses show proper deference to him, in the demonstration of which His Highness was most exacting.

In a corner of the divan, but at some distance from the Viceroy, sat the Lady Paramount; and on another divan, opposite to the *Baba*, sat the other two wives.

Then their Highnesses rose, and offered him coffee, sweet-meats, sherbet, and cheroots, which the white slaves had handed to them, after which the eunuchs entered the room, bearing several trays, covered with cloth of gold, containing His Highnesses's presents of gold coin and jewelry, of the most costly description, to the Viceregal family. After this a grand repast took place, at which the Princesses according to their precedence in rank, received the dishes from the hands of the slaves, and placed them on the table, which was elegantly laid on that occasion in the European style. Then the viceroy, and Lady Paramount, accompanied by two of his daughters, went through the *muayédé* that is, proceeded in state to the *Moosky*.

On the return of the Viceregal party, the Princesses went and paid visits to other members of the Viceregal family, who resided in the different Harems.

On the Tuesday following, at six o'clock in the morning, the Grand Pacha and myself, both dressed *en grande tenue* proceeded to the Harem. The Viceroy had not yet risen: but, after waiting a short time, the *Baba* passed through the reception-room, into his dressing-room, attended by his two *Ikbals*, and several other slaves, who assisted at his toilet. They had been preceded by the Lady Paramount who has the privilege of handing the *Baba* his sword (which is similar to that worn by the Grand Pacha, only of full size, and more thickly encrusted with diamonds,) and placing the broad blue ribbon that His Highness wears across his shoulder.

The toilette of the Viceroy being finished, he re-entered the apartment. He was dressed in full uniform, and appeared one mass of gold lace. When Ismael Pacha entered the Audience Hall the Lady Paramount was standing conversing with me, holding the Viceroy's sword in her hand. At this moment the *Ikbal*, the reigning favorite of the day, came out of the dressing-room, pushed rudely up against the Princess, and touched her on the arm (their Highnesses have a perfect horror at being touched by any of the slaves;) upon which she became crimson with passion, stamped her feet, and exclaimed *Wallah! Wallah-el-Azeem!* "By the most merciful God!" (the Arabs' mode of swearing, for she was an Arab,) and raised the sword, with the intention of striking her down to the earth.

Fortunately the *Baba,* whether designedly or not, had moved towards her, girded with his *trusty steel,* and the blade, for Her Highness had drawn it, fell mechanically into its glittering scabbard; while the *Ikbal,* with a smile beaming upon her countenance, which was not unlike that of an ordinary-looking English peasant girl, went her way unscathed, not disconcerted in the least by this display of Arab mettle. The appearance of the *Ikbal* was so totally different to that of any other of the slaves, that it struck me she might be of European origin, if not a European herself. I had seldom or ever heard her speak, and then it was in Turkish; but there was a bold, defiant, don't-care manner about her, that did not savor of Asiatic parentage.

A few days afterwards, when I was standing on the landing-place, arranging the Prince's sword, as we were going to take a promenade with the Viceroy, the *Ikbal* came running (for she walked much better than any of the others) out of the Reception Hall, and rushed by me, in the same unceremonious manner in which she had passed by the Lady Paramount. But just as she approached, the *Baba* waved his hand, reproved her, point blank ordered her to return, exclaiming, "The Grand Pacha and Madame are always to take precedence." After that we had no more scenes, and she was amiable enough to me ever afterwards.

Then Her Highness, the first wife, whose peculiar privilege it was to wait upon her liege lord on this grand occasion, hastily snatched out of the belt of the slave who officiated as light bearer, a small pair of silver tongs, similar in size to a pair of grape-scissors, as used at dessert in Europe, quitted the room, but returned almost in a moment, holding between them a piece of live charcoal, which she held up to the Viceroy, who lit his cheroot with it. After the lapse of a few minutes the *Baba* made a move, and, attended by the Grand Pacha and myself, left the Harem, unaccompanied by any suite, proceeded on board the yacht, which landed us at the Palace at Boulac, which is a magnificent structure, superbly furnished, but still in an unfinished state. Here it is that audience is generally given, as was done on this occasion, to the Ministers, Foreign Consuls-General, and where His Highness's men of business privately arranged all commercial matters with the *Baba*.

On our disembarkation a double file of troops was drawn up, through which we passed into the Grand Audience Hall, while the band played the Sultan's March. There all the officers stood ranged in two rows, who presented arms to His Highness, at the same time exclaiming, *Allah umerlez were Effendimir!* "May God grant our Lord a long life!" Upon receiving the announcement that His Highness the Grand Pacha's carriage was drawn up, I, together with the Prince, salaamed. The Viceroy left the Palace, and we were driven along at a most furious pace through the narrow streets of Cairo, lined with old, dilapidated, Oriental-looking houses, having wooden balconies and projecting windows, absolutely encrusted with dust, near one of which the horses kicked a poor Arab off his donkey: but whether he was killed or not I know not, as the carriage dashed along at a most terrific rate. Soon afterwards we entered the gates of the Harem in the citadel, the residence of Her Highness the Validè Princess, the Viceroy's mother.

There we were received by seven eunuchs, who conducted us through a small stone hall covered with matting, which led into a marble-paved walk, open on the side facing the gardens. It was covered with a verandah which formed the winter promenade, at the extremity of which we were ushered into a large stone hall also covered with matting, and having divans ranged around it. Then we passed up four steps covered with matting, and entered a large uncarpeted apartment, containing no other furniture than a divan covered with faded straw-colored satin, ranged under the three large windows overlooking the lovely, well-kept gardens. After this we descended some steps, and entered into another uncarpeted room on the right-hand side, quite destitute of furniture. All presented the picture of misery and discomfort; all looked most disconsolate and empty; just such rooms as you would imagine the widow of a usurer, who, by discounting bills, exacting most exorbitant rates of interest, and thoroughly understanding the art of buying and selling rupees, would delight to occupy.

A divan was ranged underneath the windows; but seated on a cushion on the floor was a lady dressed in Turkish costume, whom I immediately recognized as a European, and when her history was subsequently told to me in Italy, near Pistoja, by a gentleman who knew her, it brought to my recollection those Europeans whom I had passed at Tantah, looking out of His Highness the Viceroy's private despatch train; and I could not help wondering to myself how many more European women were " caged up " in the chambers of the *Baba's* other Harems situated on the banks of the Upper Nile. I learned that she was a Belgian, that her name was Caroline, and that she was the mother of the illegitimate sons of the Viceroy; and it is not improbable but that the Princess, whose death I have narrated, was also her daughter.

She was a very handsome woman, rather stout, and between thirty and forty years of age, and dressed in black, *à la Turque*, but unveiled, as all are when within the Harem. When we entered she was smoking a *Tchibouk*. She rose off the divan, took the Prince by the hand, placed him by her side, kissed him, bowed to me, then clapped her hands, and handed the Grand Pacha over to the slave, who had responded to her call, to carry him about. Then we all proceeded up the broad staircase, which was covered with matting, at the top of which, on the landing, as it were, we found several of their little Highnesses, his sisters, who had preceded us, in charge of the eunuchs, sitting down (squatting would be the most correct expression) awaiting his arrival, close to the door of the chamber of the Validè Princess. She was a Princess by birth, the mother of Ismael Pacha, the widow of the gallant yet avaricious Ibrahim Pacha, and who, by some deep researches into the genealogical records of the sultanas of Turkey, has lately discovered that she is closely related to the Validè Sultana, the mother of His Majesty Abdul Aziz, the present Sultan.

CHAPTER XVIII.

Her Highness, who takes precedence of all the wives, who stand in awe of her, had not yet risen from her downy couch, and so there the young Princesses waited like a band of slaves until their imperious grandmother had finished her toilette, as she never would receive them in her chamber. Why or wherefore I know not. Perhaps there were other visitors there, whom it did not suit the Validè Princess to allow her grand-daughters to see: perhaps her Grand Eunuch, a shrewd, crafty individual, who was a very sinister looking personage, but who appeared thoroughly to understand the ways of his Viceregal mistress, was closeted with Her Highness, communing with her on affairs of state, or private matters. At all events there I found them squatting down at the door-sill.

But His Highness the Grand Pacha (who was her pet—

her Ibrahim—the very prototype of her lamented husband, the gallant yet cruel Ibrahim Pacha,) broke through all ceremony; and I soon found that this "dot of humanity's" word was law here as well as at Ghezire; for, passing by the Princesses, he exclaimed, "Come along, Madame," pulled aside the dismal, funeral-looking, black curtain, ornamented with a silver crescent in the centre, which hung across the doorway, and bounded like a gazelle into the apartment, where he remained some time with the Validè Princess, as I did not presume to enter her presence.

I stood talking to the young Princesses, all of whom were rather intelligent, tractable, and amiable girls, and would, had we remained longer together, have become considerably Europeanized, as I found them anxious to learn, and particularly attached to me, poor, dear, neglected creatures! a circumstance not to be wondered at, as, extraordinary as it may appear, neither Turkish fathers nor mothers seem to like having a posse of daughters. Perhaps it is from avaricious motives; for with them they are obliged to give dowries suitable to their position in society; whereas boys, so to speak, are made to shift for themselves. Thus the Viceroy, or their mother, the lady Paramount—whose first child was a son, who had been dead many years, but who would have been eighteen years old had he lived (for they were her children)—took not the slightest interest in them. Consequently they were allowed to grow wild and uncared for; but as I thought it was a pity that such noble females should be brought up in that barbarous manner, I took an interest in them, and began to teach them English, and to cause them to adopt many European modes and customs.

As soon as the Viceroy's mother had finished her morning toilette, she came forth out of her chamber. She was a short elderly person, a most courtly dame, and perfect lady in the fullest acceptation of the term, with grey hair and large piercing black eyes, but commanding in her manner, often too imperious and stately in her carriage. Her manners were courtly, at which I was surprised; in short, I never beheld anything but what was ladylike in her behavior. She appeared to have sprung from quite a different stock to that of the *Baba's* three wives. Perhaps she was brought up at the Imperial court of *Is-tam-bol,* "Constantinople;" but I never could learn anything reliable about her history, except that Ibrahim Pacha, when desperately in love with her, wrote some beautiful verses to her at the old palace of Bebek, a copy of which I have given elsewhere. That perhaps may account for the Sultan naming the Palace of Bebek as that Princess's residence during her visit to the imperial Court in 1864, and which was considered by her as a very great compliment. About these grounds she must have rambled with infinite delight, but perhaps mingled with sorrow for the loss of Ibrahim Pacha, to whom she was devotedly attached; all appeared to be mystery, doubt, and conjecture. All I know is that at first I found her exceedingly imperious towards me; she even went so far as to expect that I should kneel at her feet and squat down at her door like a slave.

I had often, when a child, been found by Her Most Gracious Majesty the Queen and the late Prince Consort playing about in the private grounds at Frogmore and Windsor; and when I had encountered the royal pair, who took flowers from my basket which I had gathered in the grounds and smiled, I had stepped aside, stood still, and curtseyed—no more. I did the same to the Validè Princess of Egypt, and I thought that was quite sufficient respect to show her, and I never did anything more; nay, I positively refused to do more.

Gradually, as we became better acquainted with each other, her haughtiness diminished; still there was a lack of that amiability and suavity of manner about her which most certainly characterized their highnesses, the three wives, always making you uncomfortable in her presence. She was a fitting partner for such a prince as Ibrahim Pacha. She possessed great intellectual activity; hence there is no doubt but that she meddled indirectly in the weightiest affairs of the State; weightiest, I repeat, because I suppose Her Highness considered, in her eyes, the relations between the Sultan and the Viceroy to be such; in those matters she appeared at home, as I shall afterwards have occasion to explain.

She was extremely penurious—nay, mean would be the more appropriate expression—and as an illustration, I need only adduce the fact of her Harem being the most beggarly arranged of any I ever entered. Her staff of attendants was very limited; her habits were frugal; her attire, upon ordinary occasions, extremely plain, while on grand ones it was regal and queenlike. She was avaricious to a degree, imperious in her manner, and exacting in the extreme.

The finest trait in her character was her devoted affection for her son, the Viceroy, which was truly riciprocal. She loved the Grand Pacha with the same enthusiasm, and spoilt and indulged him in every way possible. As regards myself, when Her Highness began to uuderstand my European ways better, she treated me with respect. I never received a present, or baksheesh, of any kind from her, although to others she distributed gold and jewels with no sparing hand; but when illness overtook me, she manifested great sympathy—and did everything in her power to contribute to my comfort, so far as she understood how, and Heaven knows, that was little enough! about our European ways and habits; for she had never been in England, although Ibrahim Pacha, when he visited London, took with him some women. They were Armenians, and not Turkish, whom European travellers, because the former adopt at pleasure that mask, *the veil*, always take for the latter, a most common error.

The Validè Princess was attired in a robe of white satin on this occasion (for be it remembered that it was the *Bariam*, the Turks' greatest festival), having a breadth in front and behind, about two yards longer than the rest of the dress, which was on this day, being a state occasion, held up by four of the ladies of the Harem, or four of her *Ikbals*, but which, on ordinary times, is turned back like a three-cornered handkerchief, one of the corners being tucked in the waist-belt. Over that was placed a blue satin paletot, trimmed with sable fur. On her head she wore a small handkerchief; and in the centre of the forehead was a large diamond fly. In her hand she carried her small gold watch, encircled with diamonds; and her feet were encased in white satin shoes.

When she reached the landing-place, the young Princesses and myself salaamed her. Her Highness then descended the staircase (the slaves holding up her train in front and behind) which led into the room where we had found the Belgian lady, passed between two rows of the ladies of her Harem (many of whom were very aged,) and then walked majestically through four rows of slaves, and sat herself down in the centre of the divan, under the window (the Belgian lady had vacated the apartment). Then she took her darling pet, the Prince, placed him beside her on the right hand, while on the left sat a lady whom I was afterwards informed was the widow of Said Pacha, the late Viceroy. By the side of the Grand Pacha sat his sisters, and then, lower down, a bevy of Princesses belonging to other members of the Viceregal family.

After all were seated in due order, according to their rank, each of the ladies of the Harem approached this viceregal dame. Those of the highest rank kissed her right hand, and bowed their foreheads upon it, exclaiming, "*Allaha emanet oloun!*" "May God be with you!" The others kissed the hem of her robe; upon which all the slaves bowed their foreheads.

After this ceremony had been gone through, coffee and pipes were handed round (to the Princesses only) by six slaves, dressed in black cloth jackets, wearing black trousers, embroidered shirts, like men, and black silk neckties, over which were turned white collars. Their heads were covered with fezes; their feet were encased in patent leather shoes, with bows of black ribbon. All were of the same height, and, what was singular, their complexions were nearly alike.

The Grand Pacha then kindly took me on a tour of inspection through the whole suite of apartments. They were large, noble, lofty rooms, but all carpetless, and destitute of every kind of furniture, except divans; having suspended from the centre of the ceilings chandeliers, quite as large and elegant as that which hangs from the roof of the Italian Opera House, in London.

Before the Grand Pacha took his leave, Her Highness filled his pockets with several packets of gold coin, as *baksheesh;* of which he was despoiled by the head-nurse, on his return to the Harem, who on that occasion must have pocketed upwards of twenty to thirty pounds.

This visit to the Harem in the citadel had initiated me into some of the secrets of Harem life, and I failed not to profit by them. I learned that the Messrs. H. were the *Inan divan end*, the Genii of those "Abodes of Bliss," and that Madame Caroline had been, at one time, the three wives' *Karagueuz*, ("Evil Eye").

I now looked upon Egypt as a strange country. I regarded my own position as a dangerous one. I had to guard against being looked upon by the Princesses as an "Evil Eye;" for although the Viceroy only treated me with that consideration which my position entitled me to receive, still, as one European woman had supplanted them in the *Baba's* affection for a time, I had no desire that a similar mark of his favor (honor, all in the Harem consider it to be) should be shown to me. I had been engaged to take charge of the heir presumptive to all his wealth, as I had been led to suppose, to educate the Prince, and prepare him for a preceptor. I had thought it rather singular when the Viceroy and his reputed partners had told me not to care about his instruction; but now I thought it more so than ever. I resolved to keep my standing in that character. I trusted that my own habitual reservedness of manner would save me from any advances being made, and determined not to become a loadstone of attraction to the Viceroy.

I had remarked how dull, melancholy, ah! and even dejected, Madame Caroline looked when I glanced at her, and my curiosity was naturally wakened to know what really were her feelings at being "caged up," as it were, in the Harem of the Citadel.

Had she been entrapped, "caught," bought or sold like a parrot? If so, who were the white slave-dealers? Thereby hung a tale. In after times I obtained, at Constantinople, a solution of all these queries which now floated on my imagination; and now I believe that Turks, Jews, and Europeans, who have become domiciled in the East, are not only traffickers in every kind of merchandise, but also in *live* as well as dead stock. Did she ever think of her European home? What a dull, monotonous life she must have led there! Poor creature! I wondered how the Validè Princess treated her and her sons, noble, intelligent European-looking boys, also called Princes. I recall to mind the imperious look of that haughty dame. I longed to know her antecedents, her manners were so stately and court-like.

Above all other beings in the world, I, who had always been accustomed to have my own will, and to enjoy my liberty, should not have liked to be at her beck and call. Oh! no, indeed; I had, before I saw Her Highness "at home," witnessed enough of the proud Validè Princess.

13

I had no idea of being treated like an *abject* slave, by the widow of that overbearing ruler, Ibrahim Pacha, nor to be at Her Highness's command, nor by her caressed, flattered, and then cast off as whim or fancy led her. I was the Grand Pacha's *Institutrice*, and not the Validè Princess's slave or subject. I had no idea of passing the best years of my existence within such a "a gilded cage;" and so I always kept a respectful distance from the Viceroy's mother, as I knew her to be a most shrewd and accomplished intriguante, one who, to advance the interest of her son and grandson, would " stick at nothing," absolutely nothing.

A few weeks afterwards, I accompanied the Grand Pacha to witness the return of the Pilgrims from Mecca. This was rather an imposing spectacle; but as the main object of this book is Harem life, I shall abstain from describing it.

Not long afterwards, we proceeded with the Viceroy in his yacht, to open the canal at Old Cairo. His Highness was accompanied by the Ministers of State, military and naval officers. When the billionaire waved his hand, a number of fellahs cut with their pickaxes an opening in the dam, in the centre of which stands the *Aroost-é-Neel*—"Bride of the Nile"—a large earthen pillar; and as the water flowed into the canal, the *Baba* scattered handfuls of *paras* into its bed, which were most eagerly scrambled for by the host of Arab *gamins* and donkey boys, who had assembled there for that purpose. It was highly amusing to the Prince to see them floundering in the mud.

As soon as the water rose to a tolerable height, an immense number of boats ascended it. The decks were crowded with men, women, and children, all dressed in holiday attire, with native music; and as they squatted themselves on the decks beneath the awnings, the boats and river presented as gay and lively a scene as I had ever witnessed on its placid bosom : for there were hundreds of them, and several steamers puffing away at full speed.

As soon as the ceremony was finished, coffee and pipes were served on board the Viceregal yacht, and we returned to the Harem in time for the Grand Pacha's supper, and my dinner—a most frugal meal, consisting of the everlasting, kebab and dry bread; but now, thanks to Ismael Pacha's courtesy, washed down with a glass of his own imported full-bodied claret.

CHAPTER XIX.

WHEN the hot season began to set in, I fell sick, and was assailed by frequent attacks of intermittent fever and cholera; but having providentially taken the precaution to bring a medicine chest with me, I began to doctor myself. The weak state of my constitution, owing to the want of proper nourishment (for I had been living upon Arab diet ever since my arrival in Egypt), naturally gave way, and the Viceroy sent his Physician Extraordinary to attend upon me.

He did not prescribe for me, as he found that I had literally "cured myself;" however, instead of leaving me some stimulants, which any other European medical man would have done, to restore my strength, he very coolly told His Highness that I had taken all that was needful. The Viceroy, from his knowledge of our habits, knowing that we drank tea, and as the "Validè" Princess also partook of that beverage, very kindly made me a present of a small chest of gunpowder tea, and a few loaves of sugar from his refinery, and frequently sent me soup from his own table. Finding however, that I did not get much better, orders were given to hasten the departure of the Viceregal family to Alexandria, whither they always proceed to pass the hot season, as the palace of Ras-el-Tin and the Harem are situated on the Mediterranean, the breezes from which are very refreshing at that time of the year.

Of this I was extremely glad, as I had no nurse to attend upon me, and was totally unable to obtain the most simple diet, such as gruel, arrowroot, or beef-tea, although they could all have been purchased, at the English Italian warehouse in Cairo, had the Hekim Bachi only taken the trouble to order the Grand Eunuch to procure them; nay, it would not have been much trouble for him to have sent them himself by one of his own servants.   Then he was an Italian, and troubled his head very little about any of the patients within the Harem, except the Grand Pacha.   I was a "poor governess," and a foreigner, besides an Englishwoman.   I know not why, but my country-women are not, as a general rule, very great favorites with any foreigners, especially those residing in the East, unless they have a well-lined purse.   I could not help thinking what a deep debt of gratitude the British Army owes to those bright ornaments of my sex, Miss Nightingale and her staff of nurses, who tended their heroes with such unremitting attention.

Their Highnesses the Princesses frequently visited me, and asked me what I required; but although I explained to them that all my illness arose from the bad and poor diet which had been provided for me, they knew not how, and, therefore, could not alter it.   They might have sent the German laundry-maid into the city of Cairo to have procured me what I needed; but then they had at all times the utmost repugnance to allow even myself to have free ingress and egress, so that was quite out of the question—consequently I had to trust to chance.   God be praised, however, I recovered sufficiently to be able to travel to Alexandria.

As soon as orders had been given to the Grand Eunuch to hasten the departure of the Viceregal family to Alexandria, and that their Highnesses knew it was time to depart, there was bustle all day long.

One morning, when I returned from the gardens into which I had been strolling for a short time, I entered the Grand Pacha's reception room, and there I beheld one of the most extraordinary scenes imaginable. It was one of those nondescript tableaux to which only a Hogarth could have done justice. My feeble pen-drawing must necessarily fall very short of the original; for there were their Highnesses the Princesses, squatted on the carpet amidst a whole pile of trunks, most of which were much deeper than carriage imperials—a host of portmanteaus and carpet bags, of small and large dimensions—jewel cases and immense red leather sacks capable of holding from six to eight mattresses.

They were all attired in filthily dirty crumpled muslins, shoeless and stockingless, their trousers were tucked up above their knees, the sleeves of their paletots pinned up above their elbows, their hair hanging loosely about their shoulders, as rough as a badger's back, totally unencumbered with nets or handkerchiefs, but, pardon me, literally swarming with vermin! no Russian peasants could possibly have been more infested with live animals.

In short, their *tout ensemble* was even more untidy than that of hard-working washerwomen at the tubs; nay, almost akin to Billingsgate fishwomen *at home*, for their conversation in their own vernacular was equally as low. They all swore in Arabic at the slaves most lustily, banged them about right and left with any missile, whether light or heavy, which came within their reach.

Well, there they were, doubled up like clasped knives, sorting and packing up their *penates*, jewelry, pipes, *zarfs*, *findjans*, large gold and silver salvers on feet, together with numerous other displays of Viceregal magnificence. I had never beheld before sets of gold vegetable dishes, each of the wives having a set for her separate use, pipe-stems encrusted with diamonds and other precious stones, most valuable amber mouth-pieces, all ornamented with gold tassels.

These were counted over before the Eunuchs, then packed in boxes and delivered over to their care. Between whiles they sipped *findjans* of coffee, and all the time kept puffing away at cigarettes.

It was highly amusing to see the slaves bundling their Highnesses' beds into the large thick red leathern sacks, and much more ludicrous did the scene become when they attempted to remove them out of the apartment, as it was found that they were too large to pass through the doors. So that, when the Princesses (as they often did) hit them rather sharply with anything they might happen to have in their hands at the time, exclaiming, " *Destour, destour, yu mobarakee!* "—" Get in, you fool ! "—the slaves cried out most lustily, and hastened to take all the beds out of the cases. Then they carried them one by one into the Harem's small garden, and there replaced them in the huge red sacks. Close by sat the *Ikbal* of the period, superintending the packing up of the beds and bedding of her Vice-regal liege lord.

The whole of the reception rooms, as well as the spacious hall, looked as if the Sinbad of the nineteenth century had given orders for the shipment of his cargo to some distant land, or that the magic wand of harlequin had instantaneously changed the scene into Tilbury furniture and luggage warehouse in Marylebone Street. For it was no exaggerated statement to affirm, that " within those marble halls '' were piled up hundreds of bales, boxes, trunks, portmanteaus, carpet bags, jewel and pipe cases, &c., &c. Yet amidst that *mélée* there sat not " the rough mariner who had weathered many a storm," with bronzed countenance, but the Prince of merchants *par excellence*, the billionaire of the world, Ismael Pacha, the Viceroy of Egypt, in his shirt sleeves, looking quite as fagged, not through over bodily exertion, but on account of the heat of the thermometer, which was then at 110o in the shade. His Highness has become very stout of late. He was as "dead beat" as the packer of a Broad Street warehouseman, when about to ship his costly ventures to Alexandria or Constantinople; not casting up the pounds, shillings, and pence columns of an invoice (which he so well knows how to do, as long as the taxed bill of a chancery suit solicitor, nor calculating the probable golden returns that those bales, had they but been of fine Egyptian cotton, would have brought into his coffers,) but playing dominoes with one of his lovely wives, and laughing fit to crack his sides, and puffing away at some of the choicest Havannahs that a Pontet had ever imported from the far-famed Cuba Isles with all the good-humor imaginable, and evidently quite *at home* amidst that commercial-like bustle and turmoil, delighted beyond measure at the *gaucherie* of the slaves, and particularly amused at the ludicrous manner in which those *oustas* bobbed their heads, and dodged round the trunks and bales to avoid being struck by the missiles which were aimed at them, right and left, by Princesses.

I too, ill as I was, had to pack up my own traps; but scarcely had I done so when, although at that time suffering from attacks of spasmodic cholera, I was awoke at half-past one in the morning (for weary and faint I had fallen down upon my bed exhausted with pain and suffering) and was ordered to get up immediately, as the slaves wanted to take and pack up my bed. I opened the door, let them carry it away, and threw myself down upon the divan, where I remained, not sleeping—for that was utterly impossible—as the slaves were hurrying to and fro all the livelong night; some carrying their beds, others bales, boxes, &c., many running about with wax candles between their fingers; others lying on the floor dead tired, snoring away like great grampuses, whom nothing could possibly awaken from their dreams of bliss.

At five o'clock in the morning, the whole houshold were

about and stirring.   Then was enacted a truly comic scene. Many of the slaves, it then turned out, had sent away the attire which they required to wear; so that they were obliged to borrow some things from one and some from another, which rendered them, when dressed, the most extraordinary looking beings imaginable.   It was fortunate, indeed, that they were able to dress themselves at all decently.

The young Princesses began their morning toilet by throwing the whole of their things at the slaves.   After they were tired of that amusement, they sat upon their divans and commenced crying and bellowing away like town bulls, kicking each other, and screaming as if they had gone demented.   When they became a little mere reasonable, they soon finished dressing themselves by simply placing their silk dresses over their dirty crumpled habiliments, and enveloped themselves in their *habarahs*.

I partook of my usual breakfast very early.   At seven o'clock the whole of the juvenile members of the Viceregal family had proceeded down to the landing-place, and there they embarked on board a yacht, which steamed down to Boulac, and at eight o'clock we all entered the Viceregal state railway carriages at the back of the palace.   The state saloon carriage was occupied by the Grand Pacha, myself, the young Princesses, the Mother of the Harem, the nurses and the Prince's usual attendants.   The carriage was divided into three compartments, consisting of one large and two small saloons.   The former was fitted up with easy spring chairs, carpet divans covered with brocaded silk, and mirrors; the latter was similarly furnished, but covered with green velvet and brown morocco.   The windows were of plate glass, with movable net wire blinds; the former were taken out on this occasion, but the latter remained.

As soon as the train started, the Mother of the Harem threw herself down upon the carpet, and placed one of her bundles under her head as a pillow; for singular as it may seem, all Turkish women, even the Princess, when travelling, have almost every thing, even silver ewers, basins, and "vases" (which latter appertain only to the children, as the Princesses never use such indispensable appendages) packed in bundles formed of a round piece of cloth or silk, hemmed all round with a cord run in it, which when drawn tight forms a round bag not unlike a seaman's clothes-bag. Even when "at home," after every toilette their things are packed up in square pieces of thick wadded cotton.

As soon as the eunuchs had seated themselves in their carriage, all the Princesses and slaves threw off their *haba-rahs*, unveiled, took off their silk dresses, all of which they piled up in a heap in one corner of the saloon, removed the wire blinds, and then put their heads out of the open windows.

At half-past ten the train stopped at Benha, when breakfast was served up just as if they had been in the Harem, for the cooks and whole staff of domestics and *batteries de cuisine* had been placed in the train. During that repast several tin stands holding porous clay water-jars, having gold stoppers, which had been placed in the saloon, were replenished; the eunuch taking the precaution to taste the water in every jar, lest any should have been poisoned. Then the whole party squatted themselves down upon the carpet, and as neither plates nor *soofras* had been provided, they tore the meat with their fingers like a set of cannibals, which was served them on metal trays similar to those used by *trattorie* in Italy; and after the Princesses had partaken of what they fancied, the remnants in the trays were handed over to the slaves for their breakfast.

The Princesses asked me to partake of some of their *entremets;* but I declined, first, because my health would not allow me to eat Arab diet; and, secondly, because it would have been utterly impossible for any European lady to have felt the slightest inclination to partake of the refreshment in such a barbarous style.

During the journey, the young Princesses made their toilettes no less than half-a-dozen times, putting on one dress and then another. Then they ornamented their heads, by tying a piece of ribbon round their foreheads, and placing crimson and blue feathers around them in bands, and encircled their waists with broad and long ribbon sashes. After they had finished attiring themselves, each began to dress up their favorite slave, as if they had been dolls.

The Validè Princess on this occasion unloosed her purse-strings, and bestowed baksheesh of gold watches and chains upon all the European engineers, drivers, and stokers, who were employed on the train in which she travelled. The three wives went into another carriage, and did not start at the same time as we did.

The Princesses were most disgusting in their habits, and so totally devoid of decency, that they did not hesitate to empty the contents of their "*vases*" out of the window, as the train was passing along. I thought their manners bad enough in all conscience at *home;* but now I have seen them *abroad,* and I never wished to have the honor of travelling with them again. Then they laid themselves down on the carpet, and fell fast asleep, like wild beasts after a gorge.

About four o'clock in the afternoon the Viceregal party, after having been no less than eight hours in their transit, only a distance of a hundred and thirty miles, on account of the Viceregal children being afraid of proceeding at express rate, reached their destination. During which period the whole traffic on the line was interrupted, to the great inconvenience of the mercantile community.

When we arrived at the terminus of Alexandria, we met with a most regal reception. The platform was covered with crimson carpet, and decorated with flowers and flags. The Grand Eunuch, who had preceded us by three days, met our party here. He handed the Grand Pacha and myself out of the carriage, and conducted us to the waiting-room, which was also covered with crimson carpet; while the band played "The Sultan's March." The troops who lined the platform presented arms as we walked across it.

The Ministers of State paid their respects to the Prince, and accompanied us to the Viceregal state-carriage, which was in attendance. It was drawn by eight fine grey horses. Three outriders preceded us in front; *sais*, "grooms," ran on before to clear the way, and also by each side of the carriage; we were also attended by an escort of Cavalry to the Palace of Ras-el-Tin, situated on the ancient Isle of Pharo, which was built by Mehemet Ali, and where that celebrated prince held his court much oftener than at Cairo, which latter city he disliked. There we alighted and passed into the Harem, which stands facing it, and from which it is only separated by a large court-yard. In short, much more respect and ceremony was shown to the little Prince on this occasion than is generally shown to his illustrious "*Baba.*"

The Princesses had led me to believe that there I should find everything arranged for my convenience; but alas! I was doomed to be most wofully disappointed. On entering the gates of the Harem, so replete with many an historical reminiscence, we passed through three spacious marble halls; then proceeded up the grand staircase into His Highness's apartment. It was a very spacious three-windowed room, overlooking a large marble-paved court-yard, around which were situated the Princesses' rooms. It was excessively dirty; the windows and frames were nearly broken; totally destitute of hangings, with the exception of pieces of white calico, which were nailed up at each window as substitutes for blinds, with a piece of cord hanging down in the centre, by which they were drawn up or down. The floor was covered with common country matting; the walls and ceiling were whitewashed. It was totally destitute of furniture, with the exception of a divan which stood under the three windows, covered with cotton chintz.

"Well," thought I to myself, "if this is all the arrangement which has been made for the comfort of *my* Prince, what can I expect has been made for me?" I soon had an opportunity of seeing this as I was shown into my chamber, which certainly was a large room. It was one consolation, after the cupboard in which I had been cooped up in at Ghezire, which at best was only fit for a lumber-room, in such a hot place, with the thermometer standing at 110°. It was filthily dirty, lighted by three windows, at which were hung up six tattered brown calico curtains, and three dirty calico blinds. The walls and ceiling were whitewashed, the floor matted; and the furniture consisted of a divan, as damp as if had been soaked in water, covered with brown cotton, to match the window-hangings: this was placed underneath the three windows. And there kind reader, you have an accurate description of my lady's chamber!

I was tired, suffering from attacks of my recent illness, and weary after my journey, and this was the apartment in which I had to vegetate, after having entered Cleopatra's capital, in viceregal splendor. I really was quite disgusted with Harem life; and I will lead you to imagine what were my feelings to find that there was nothing whatever for my convenience, not even a *bed* to lie upon, for it was utterly impossible that I could sleep upon that damp, mildew-covered divan.

I sought to lie down upon the floor, but that was equally impracticable, for it was only matted, and as damp as the deck of any of those wooden walls I beheld from its windows as they commanded a good view of the roadstead, in which many vessels were at anchor, and among which I espied two or three Egyptian frigates. I looked round my apartment and longed to possess Harlequin's magic wand or Aladdin's Wonderful Lamp, that I might bid some fair spirit to transport even the few conveniences I had left behind me at Ghezire; but alas! neither were there, and so I had to put up with it.

When the Superintendent of this Harem, who was a great tall hoarse godmother of a black, most meanly attired, entered to pay her respects to the Prince, I inquired where I was to sleep? Her answer was, "On the divan;" and at the same time she told me that she was quite surprised that I should feel dissatisfied, as I had the same accommodation which had been provided for the Grand Pacha. I had no idea of being treated in that manner, so I walked down into the marble paved hall, where some of the baggage had arrived, and made the slaves, *nolens volens*, carry up my bed and bedding into my apartment and lay it upon the matting.

At eight o'clock I clapped my hands, and Zenana, a Turkish girl about fifteen years of age, not very prepossessing in appearance, and most assuredly not gifted with more sense than she knew what to do with, responded to my summons, as she had been newly appointed at Ghezire to attend upon me. I ordered her to fetch my dinner, but she soon returned and very coolly informed me (it will hardly be credited, but it is a fact), that there was neither European bread nor any meat in the Harem, so that, sick as I was, and after travelling from seven in the morning until seven at night (for it was about that time when we reached Ras-el-tin), I had not had a meal provided for me. Then I was obliged to content myself with what I could get within this "Mansion of Discomfort" of the billionaire of the world, the wealthy scion of the usurer, Ibrahim Pacha.

Well did I verify the truth of the old saying that " hunger requires no sauce ;" so I sat down on my pallet, not "on the cold flinty rock," but upon the damp matted floor ; and there I selected a meal from the *cart*—a piece of Arab bread as salt as brine, and some salad, which consisted of a lettuce dressed with oil and water, without either pepper, salt or vinegar, and a slice of boiled fowl, of which the soup had been made which had been served up to the young Princesses, who had already partaken of their supper, and a *findjan* of coffee; and that constituted my repast. Then I was obliged to give the Grand Eunuch money out of my own pocket to purchase me an ewer, basin, and vase, and in this manner I installed myself on that memorable day in the Harem at Alexandria. There seated at the window, my thoughts naturally wandered over the reminiscences of all the varied scenes I had beheld, and the inconveniences to which I had been subjected ever since

"I trod the pestilential soil of Egypt's shore."

Then I recalled to mind the day of my arrival at the Pacific and Oriental Hotel, where I had found excellent accommodation, plain *auberge* though it was, and gladly would I have returned to it again. For although I was an inmate of the stately marble halls of a Viceregal Palace, the residence of the Crœsus of the East, I had been unable to procure a crumb of European bread, though loaves in abundance might have been procured in the city almost within a stone's throw of the Harem, and everything was at hand; yet not any of the conveniences enjoyed by the meanest villager in my own country had been provided for me. With whom did the fault rest? Surely not with that good-humored, jovial Prince H. H. Ismael Pacha, whom I had left not many hours before in his splendid palace at Burlac, surrounded by every luxury that wealth could command, who had said, "Madame, whatever you want, ask for and you shall have it."

I had taken the Viceroy at his word, I had asked for—mine had not been a very unreasonable request—bread to satisfy the cravings of hunger, but I could not procure even bread.

I exclaimed to myself as I then remembered the words of the writer on Egypt in *Once a Week*, "You may call spirits from the vasty deep, but will they come?" I had tried the experiment, and found that they would not respond. Was I then to consider that H. H.'s words were to use a very significant Turkish (but of late years turned into English slang) word, *bosh*, and meant nothing, absolutely nothing? How little did His Highness imagine that the companion, guardian, and instructress of his heart's idol was actually wanting bread to eat, and was lying on the floor in a damp room, absolutely destitute of every comfort; sick, weary, and uncared for! And yet these were the *luxuries* that I had been told I ought to be thankful for; I had been treated like a Princess. My reply was: " Like what kind of a princess? " Perhaps their Highnesses might at one time have considered what I termed inconveniences as *luxuries*, but I did not. I had learned much of the antecedents and doings of the whole of Mehemet Ali's family and his descendants.

Well did I know that only a few short years had elapsed since that very room in which I lay was furnished with every luxury which the most fastidious dame could have required. Ah! and even later than that, for Said Pacha was a prince of great taste, whatever may have been his demerits as a ruler; and there his lovely Princess had resided with every regal luxury around her. I soon became weary of lying down. It was a lovely night: the sight of the placid ocean as the bright moon cast her reflection on it brought to my recollection Southey's beautiful lines in his ' Thalaba.'

> " How beautiful is night!
> A dewy freshness fills the silent air;
> No mist obscures, nor cloud, nor speck, nor stain,
> Breaks the serene of heaven.
> In full orb'd glory, yonder moon divine,
> Rolls through the dark blue depths."

I rose up, walked to the window, and gazed at the calm scene around me. I noticed that the depth of the sea there would even admit of ships of war sailing close up to it, and wondered what tales, could it but speak, that depth could tell, what bodies it could cast up to it, were they once again "filled with the breath of life!" the doomed victim of a licentious and cruel wanton of a Turkish Princess—that bold, cunning, and subtle Nuzly Hanein Effendi.

I remembered that that beautiful Princess (and if she had been only as handsome as the little daughter of Said Pacha is, she must indeed have been *most angelic*—for that little Princess is the only being I have yet seen in the East who could be termed "to come up to" Tom Moore's description of a *Peri*), the right hand of her astute father, Mehemet Ali, had often sat where I then stood gazing intently on that fleet, the command of which had been held by Ibrahim Pacha, when he went to seek glory in the Morea. I had visited the palace which she occupied in the vicinity of Cairo, and the old Frenchwoman, who had been in her service, and who now lived within this Harem, where she passes her time in taking care of H. H. the Viceroy's wardrobe, when he is at Ras-el-Tin. She related to me the following strange, yet true incident, in the life of that extraordinary Princess :—

" It appears that Nuzly Hanein was very intimate with a Levantine lady, whose husband was in Mehemet Ali's service. A young Italian nobleman, whose countenance and manners were very effeminate, offered that Levantine a large sum of money, if she would assist him to visit the interior of the Princess's Harem at Cairo, which he had heard was most superbly furnished.

" Accordingly, it was arranged that Madame Otto should inform Her Highness that a lady of rank, who was on a pilgrimage to Jerusalem, and who had been most highly recommended to her from Europe, was extremely anxious to see her Harem, of the splendor of which she had heard so much when in Italy, and pay her respects to a princess whose renown was spread all over the world.

"'You must ask her,' added Count Luigi, 'to give the lady an audience; you will be sure to obtain permission, and when the appointment is made, you must lend me one of your richest dresses, which I am certain will fit me admirably You must superintend my toilette, and then I am sure that I shall pass muster, and that the keenest eye will be unable to recognize my sex under that disguise.'"

I could not help exclaiming to myself, as the old Frenchwoman, for she was an octogenarian, related the Count's conversation, "Silly, silly young man, how little did he know the power of an Arab, or Turkish woman's eye, or how quickly they can detect an imposture of that kind." Well, to continue the narrative :—

"Saying which, the Count, who was then sitting in Madame Otto's boudoir, added, 'Come, let us try how I should look,' and hastily metamorphosed himself as one of the fair sex, with the aid of one of the fair Levantine's dresses. The disguise was so complete, that Madame Otto could not keep her eyes off him, and seemed quite bewildered at the Count's first *debût* in female character.

" Soon, however, she became more accustomed to his metamorphosis, and then burst into a fit of laughter at the droll idea which he had taken into his head, and which she looked upon as a dangerous enterprise, knowing as she did the formidable character of that *Grand Lady*, as the Egyptians call her to this day; for after that title of *Grand* bestowed upon her by Mehemet Ali, all the eldest sons of the Viceroy are styled *Grand Pachas*. Madame Otto again burst out laughing. However, in a short time, she accorded the Count her coöperation.

" It is certain that the lovely Levantine did not possess much firmness of character, for even the Count's mad whim which, however, had *method in it*, was wisdom itself, when compared with many of that volatile lady's vagaries. She carried out all the Count's instructions to the very letter, and

14

her embassy proved as successful as he desired. The audience was granted, and the day appointed, on which occasion she acted as lady's maid, with such taste and tact that the Count, when he looked in his mirror, was really unable to recognize himself. He acknowleded that he had the vanity to think that he really looked like a very pretty woman. The success of this rehearsal gave them both great hopes that the attempt itself would realize their most sanguine wishes.

" The Count, who related the adventure to me," added the old Frenchwoman, " did it so naïvely, that I cannot do better than repeat his own words. ' I wore,' said he, ' for I can still remember it as plainly as if it were only yesterday, a very pretty white chip hat, a rich crape bertha covered my thin shoulders, and an ample merino velvet dress, trimmed with deep rows of Mechlin lace, which helped to conceal any defect that I might have otherwise shown in my mean and slender figure. My transformation was performed with the greatest secrecy ; no mortal being, except our two selves, having been entrusted with our secret. My male attire was carefully concealed, and when my toilet was finished, I availed myself of the absence of all the domestics, whom the Levantine lady had sent out on some distant errands, to take my place in the drawing-room, as if I had been a stranger, who had come to pay her a visit.

" ' A handsome carriage which I had hired for the occasion, together with two footmen, to whom I was unknown, were waiting for me at the door. It would, perhaps, have been far better if I could have prevailed upon my charming hostess to accompany me ; but all my entreaties to do so proved unavailing. I really felt that I should never be able to keep my countenance, and the semblance of a smile, however slight, might place both our lives in jeopardy. I waived that point ; for, to tell you the truth, I did not care much about her company on that occasion. Although I had planned the whole affair without having any particular object in view, my mind was agitated with many a foolish hope and romantic idea. Hence I preferred being alone; for, perhaps, had the charming Levantine accompanied me, I should not have had a *tête-à-tête* conversation with the Grand Princess. I promised to make some excuse for her; to acquaint Her Highness that she had been taken suddenly ill; to tell Her Highness any falsehood which came uppermost in my mind at the moment.

" ' My dear friends, I can assure you that Signora Rosina (for that was the name of the Levantine) had never before appeared so lovely in my eyes. She almost overwhelmed me with precautions. " Take care, above all things, to be-ware of the snares and captivating manners of that most formidable of syrens." I remarked to her that she need not entertain the slightest jealousy, since I had now become a woman : and if it should unfortunately happen that the Princess were to entertain the least suspicion, she might be certain that she would sooner have me empaled than fall in love with me. " Who can tell ? " replied she, as she shook me affectionately by the hand; " for that woman is of such a whimsical disposition."

" ' Preceded by two handsome *sais*, with their flowing garments, who ran nimbly along before the horses, I soon reached the Esbekiëh, in which quarter the Princess's new palace was situated. To say that I did not experience considerable trepidation when I found myself on the threshold of that princely dwelling, would be untrue; on the contrary, my heart palpitated very much. Like the hunter, I could not behold the tigress in her den without experiencing considerable alarm; for I remembered that if that was the Grand Princess's palace, it was also the residence of her husband, the cruel and merciless Defterder.

" When far away from its precincts, I had only thought of the wife; but now that I found myself within it, my thoughts naturally dwelt upon the husband, and the remembrance of his bloody exploits awakened anything but pleasing reminiscences in my mind. I had forgotten that, being much inferior in rank to his wife, he was, according to the Oriental custom, her slave rather than her liege lord and master, and that she alone possessed sovereign power within her domain. I had also overlooked the fact, that a husband, no matter who he may be, never enters the Harem when his lady has visitors, and that the eunuchs, or grooms of the chamber, who always stand at the door, are placed there expressly to say to him, "You must not enter." Therefore it was, morally speaking, quite impossible that I could beard the lion in his den, or awaken his suspicions.

" 'I was evidently expected. On alighting from the carriage I was received by about half-a-dozen fierce-looking eunuchs, black as ebony, wearing the fez, and richly clad. The younger ones wore red jackets, embroidered down the shoulders at the back and front, which terminate in a point at the centre of the back, at the waist; and the others large flowing white muslin robes. With the exception of one or two, who were very handsome, these "phantoms" of men were stout, paunch-bellied, and puffed up; their eyes betokening haughtiness and cunning of the deepest dye.

" 'I was conducted by them through a courtyard; then we passed into a second one, which opened into a large octagonal vestibule, paved with beautiful white marble, where I was handed over to six white slaves, all of whom were young, well made, and extremely pretty. They wore on their heads small velvet richly embroidered fezes; and their dark jet hair hung in flowing ringlets down their backs. They were attired in wide trousers, hemmed at the bottom, through which ran a string drawn up and fastened round the leg just above the ankle, like a garter. The trousers were then pulled down over the feet (which they concealed); they are made of the stoutest and richest blue and red silk, between which and the bottom lining rolls of muslin are placed.   It is that weight which causes that shuffling manner of moving about they have, for their carriage hardly deserves the name of walking.   Their waists were encircled with costly Cashmere shawls ; they wore long jackets beautifully embroidered with gold thread and lace, which were open at the chest, but reached down to their hips ; their small feet were encased in elegant Oriental slippers ; their wrists were ornamented with most costly golden bracelets, in which were set many almost priceless diamonds, some white, others pink, yellow, and black.

" Escorted by them, I ascended the beautiful staircase, on the landing of which stood ten other slaves ready to receive me : they were all white, and in the same costume. There my shoes were removed from off my feet, and a pair of handsome Turkish boots replaced them.   Then I was muffled up, I hardly know how, but believe it was in a superb Cashmere shawl ; and, thus swathed, I was led through three or four saloons, each one more spacious than the last, and more superbly decorated ; but the style partook more of European than of Oriental luxury.   The mirrors, the lace curtains, and the hangings were of Parisian workmanship.   The divans, which were covered with the richest damask, embroidered with gold and studded with pearls, were alone of Oriental craft ; and as to the carpet, it was perhaps, one of the finest ever woven in Persia.   When the Princess left it for any other residence, all the carpets were taken up, the curtains unfastened, the divans covered, and everything turned topsy turvy.

" Thence we proceeded into a small room, but much more cosy, more congenial to my ideas than the others, because it was more frequently occupied.   There I was requested to be seated to await the Princess, who soon made her appearance.   I was highly delighted to have a few moments to prepare myself for the dangerous interview and the perilous adventure in which I had engaged. The fresco of the ceiling of that room was wretchedly painted; the chairs were European, covered with red morocco, but very shabby. Double deep scarlet curtains hung over the open windows which looked into the beautiful gardens, and cast a dark shade upon my person.

"Here were assembled several other slaves; some of whom, from their dark ebony complexions and regularity of features, were evidently Abyssinians. Their costume resembled that of the white slaves, except that they were not so rich. Several of the latter were attired in robes open at the sides, all of whom were bedizened with emeralds, topazes, turquoises, and several other precious gems of great value. Some of them wore plumes of feathers; others, butterflies made of diamonds, which, as they moved their heads, flitted about, as it were, sparkled and seemed as if they were on the wing.

"There was no mistaking the Georgian, Circassian, and Greek white slaves. And yet you must not imagine that the black ones were ugly: this was by no means the case, as many of them were extremely well made, nay, handsome, and possessed pleasing countenances. There was even something rather attractive in the variety of the color of their complexions. Besides, the eye soon becomes accustomed to those beautiful ebony skins of the slaves, when their features are regular and their forms faultless. Nearly all their black orbs were fixed steadily upon me; but if my presence there attracted the curiosity of those lovely creatures, I was equally struck with theirs.

"I shall not attempt to describe to you all the old women, as well as the other slaves and harridans of the Harem, who, as they stood grouped together, alone formed a pleasing outline in that interesting scene. The quick and searching glances of those *fates* caused me considerable annoyance; but in the twinkling of an eye my attention was riveted upon the Grand Princess, who had just entered the room. If I use the expression *grand* when speaking of her, I merely do so out of etiquette, and because that was the title which had been given to her, for that appellation could not be applied to her person; as the Princess Nuzly was of small stature, though beautifully made.

" As to her costume, I remember it as well as if she now stood before me. She wore, over a pair of bright amaranthus-colored silk trousers, a large white cashmere dress, the loose sleeves of which displayed her well-formed arms, and which, being open in front, made her a train a yard and a half in length. A waistband of splendid large pearls, fastened with two large diamond clasps, encircled her waist. Her tiny feet were incased in a pair of satin slippers, almost as small as those of a child, embroidered with costly pearls. Her head-dress consisted of a large fillet of golden-colored crape Cashmere, which were twisted very prettily around her 'head. Her long black hair, neatly plaited, was rolled up behind and fastened with large diamond pins. Her bracelets consisted of strings of enormous pearls; her necklace was composed of some of the finest pearls imaginable, which fell negligently on her clear alabaster skin, and half disclosed her bust. This enchanting figure did not shuffle, but glided rather than walked, towards a red satin divan, on which she threw herself down.

———————— ✦ ————————

CHAPTER XX.

" When persons visit each other in the East it is the custom for them, on entrance, to observe the strictest silence. It also appears to be the same with women, for the Princess was a long time before she addressed me, and etiquette prevented me from taking the intiative. You can well imagine how narrowly I scanned her features. How incomparably beautiful she appeared ! How haughty and tapered was her nose ; what a sweet, pretty mouth ; what pearly white teeth ; the whole of her lineaments were perfection itself !

" I fell desperately in love with her at first sight. Her eyebrows were painted in the true Oriental style, just as they are delineated in the Holy Scriptures, and as Racine describes Queen Jezebel to have used antimony to conceal the ravages of age. Her filbert nails, I mean those of the Princess Nuzly, not those of Jezebel, (although in features both those women bore a close resemblance to each other,) were stained red with henna. But her eyes, my friends, ah! what eyes ! they were the most piercing I ever beheld; at one glance they seemed to scan me from head to foot, to read my thoughts and cause my heart to palpitate most violently. In short, they shot through the very innermost recesses of my mind. Every time that her penetrating glance was fixed upon me I felt my countenance change, and I could have sunk into the earth. Is it possible, thought I, that those scrutinizing orbs can read the audacious lie that I had framed ?

" In the mean time the slaves had brought into the room, according to custom, two pipes with amber mouth-pieces, encircled with gold and ornamented with a broad ring of magnificent diamonds. They handed one to the Princess and the other to me, and while a slave knelt down and lighted Her Highness's, another, a beautiful Circassian girl, performed the same office for myself. Then coffee was served us in beautiful thin Japanese cups (*findjans*), placed in golden filigree *zarfs*, and each time we sipped it the Oriental salutation of placing the hand to the forehead was performed. It is generally whilst partaking of that beverage that the conversation begins, by passing compliments to each other and inquiries touching the health of the visitors.

"I have omitted to explain to you that Providence had endowed me with a wonderful facility for acquiring languages. Having already resided at Constantinople, and formed an intimacy with several members of the Turkish Embassy in Paris, I could speak Turkish sufficiently well when I arrived in Egypt to be able to keep up a conversation, and as Turkish is the language of the conquerors of Egypt, it is generally spoken at Cairo, but more especially by the goverment officials and the *beau monde.*

"Mehemet Ali knew no other. I therefore naturally thought that no other ought to be spoken in his daughter's palace, who being Turkish like her father, was very proud of being thought so; so I presumed, perhaps it was rather too presumptuous on my part, to dispense with the services of an interpreter, and at once enter into conversation with my viceregal hostess. As soon as the usual compliments had been exchanged, and, Heaven be praised! they did not last long, I conveyed to Her Highness the fair Levantine's deep regret that her sudden indisposition had prevented her from accompanying me. I told her that she was extremely ill, almost in the last agonies of death, and I am really astonished that I did not even go so far as to state that she was dead.

"When once we begin to tell lies we hardly ever know where to stop. The excuses that I made for that lady's absence were graciously accepted by the Grand Princess, and our conversation passed on to other subjects.

"'Have you any family?'

"That is always the first question which an Oriental lady asks her visitor. I answered as a matter of course, in the negative.

"'Therefore I suppose you are journeying to Jerusalem to pray to your prophet to give you some?' added the Princess.

"'Your Highness, with singular aptitude, has guessed the object of my journey.'

"'May Allah grant you your desire! for then your husband will love you more affectionately. Does he go with you?'

"'No, your Highness, business detains him in Europe.'

"'I am sorry for that : for it must be very dull to have to travel all that long way alone. For when a woman has to endure loneliness it is almost as wretched as death!'

"Her Highness's language was very impressive; an appropriate gesture accompanied every sentence. You must allow my dear friends, that the subject which she had mooted was a very delicate one for me to answer; so that I endeavored to turn the conversation upon some other topic. But to do so was no easy task, as that of all the daughters of the Prophet is always of a very mediocre nature. Thus the interchange of visits among themselves is scarcely anything more communicative than pauses of interminable silence. But Mehemet's daughter was, for a Turkish lady, a very superior person : she appeared to possess something more than a mere smattering of general knowledge. Dearly beloved by her extraordinary father, possessing his unlimited confidence, she had, literally speaking, been the companion of his misfortunes and active life, and, therefore, had become quite a politician.

"It very seldom happens that women in the East meddle with politics, but especially the Princesses; nevertheless she had become quite *au fait* with them, and her beautiful mouth often uttered both very pleasing and terrible truths. I gathered this outline of her character from the hints which she let fall about some very serious affairs which had happened at that time, showing me clearly how well and deeply she had studied the art of government. No topic appeared to come amiss to her. Notwithstanding, however, that politics had always been my own peculiar *forte*, still it was evident that I ought not to appear to take much interest in the subject, seeing that I myself was then but a woman.

"Wishing to act my new character to perfection, I turned the conversation as skillfully as I could, and began to display my feminine weakness by praising, in the most fulsome Oriental style possible, the lovely pearls, large diamonds, and jewelry, with which the Grand Princess had adorned her person, at the same time taking care to assure her that her taste in those matters had been the theme of general admiration in Paris and in London; and I expressed to her how great would be my delight if she would so far honor me as to let me see her casket of jewels.

"Alas! how little did she suspect that the brightest jewel she possessed, in my estimation, was her own lovely self! But I dare not for worlds have expressed those sentiments to her. I found out, however, at a later period, that I had been guilty of an act of very great indiscretion in asking Her Highness to show me her jewels. But she did not express any astonishment at my rudeness; for she was above taking offence at such a slight infringement of etiquette by a stranger. Therefore making a signal to an old Abyssinian slave, who probably held the office of 'Keeper of the Jewels,' she left the room immediately.

"She re-entered it shortly afterwards, accompanied by several other slaves of the same caste, who came loaded with an immense iron chest, covered over with red satin, richly spangled with gold. It was opened, and the jewels were taken out of the cases.

"It was impossible to describe their magnificence and splendor! My sight was actually almost as much dazzled by looking at them as if I had been fixing my eyes upon a glaring midday tropical sun, for blindness seemed suddenly to have come upon me. Aladdin's wonderful lamp, I am quite sure, could never have given its fortunate possessor a sight of anything like those precious gems. Among them were pearls as large as pigeons' eggs, topazes as big as fowls' eggs, emeralds as large as pears, rubies, diamonds, and—I really cannot enumerate the name of half the other uncut precious stones; but there were quite enough of them to fill a bushel measure. How many countless millions of pounds sterling in jewels did that chest contain! Just picture to yourself a superb chain of diamonds, mounted transparently, all of the same size, without spot or blemish, and as big as large Barcelona nuts. You can imagine a beautiful full-blown rose, with its blossoms, buds, and leaves all composed of diamonds; a very large one formed the heart of that queen of flowers, which was only fitted to have been plucked by a fairy from the garden of the Peri.

"Then I was shown a splendid waistband, about half a foot wide, and of good length, and so heavy that my hands trembled beneath its weight. Do you wish to know what rendered it so heavy? Well, my dear friends, it consisted of diamonds, and such diamonds that it actually appeared as if it were one solid piece. It is utterly impossible for me to describe to you all the head-dresses, bracelets, clasps, rings and smaller articles contained in that chest.

"As to the quantity of gold and less valuable precious stones, all of which would have made the eyes of a London belle of the season sparkle with delight, they were countless, although scarcely any slave in that Harem would have considered any of them worth her acceptance. I cannot omit stating the fact, however unpalatable such may be to the French nation, that within that iron coffer were to be seen a superb crown of diamonds and several most costly trinkets which had formerly belonged to that amiable Empress Josephine, Napoleon the Great's consort; but by what chance they had become buried as it were, within the precincts of an Egyptian Harem, I was unable to learn.

"The Grand Princess, at a latter period, I believe, presented them to one of the little princesses, so that the costly Imperial crown passed away into the hands of a less worthy and less distinguished personage. Now it is the property of the Validè Princess of Egypt, and she wore it on her last visit to Constantinople. The princess Nuzly hardly deigned to bestow a glance upon all these priceless treasures.

" 'Your Highness,' inquired I, after having greatly extolled the beauty and workmanship of these wonders of art and nature, ' does not often wear them ? '

" 'Never replied she, very curtly. ' No, never; they are too heavy; and of what use would it be for me to adorn my person with them ? '

" Then there was a long pause : the silence at length became so painful, that my embarrassment was extreme, more especially as the Princess never removed her eyes from off my face.

"Not daring to presume to break the silence, for fear I might be considered too loquacious, I endeavored to conceal my perplexity, by smoking a little, and drinking coffee; a slave, the same who had attended upon me on my entrance into the room (for each has her office allotted to her), that handsome Circassian, of whom I have already spoken, kept continually replenishing my pipe.

" ' I have been told that you have a great desire to visit my Harem ; your request shall be gratified.' Upon a sign being given, I was immediately surrounded by half-a-dozen slaves, all equally pretty, who took me with them. They were preceded by an older one, who led me into the interior of the apartments.

" The Mother of the Harem, who wore a large diamond necklace, appeared to have supreme command over all the others ; she was a funny, jovial creature, as nearly all the old slaves generally are; the young ones, on the contrary appeared sad, with downcast eyes, like weak plants, which have been kept away from the sun, nay, even shut up from the fresh air, and doomed never to enjoy either liberty or love.

" We ascended a marble double staircase, protected by wooden banisters, which gave access to the smaller apartments. The latter were composed of a great number of rooms, similar to each other, and separated by thick velvet and silk curtains, which, although considerably smaller than the others, were all furnished alike. A number of beautiful caskets, silver fountains, embroidered handkerchiefs, numerous vases of all shapes and sizes, a number of pretty little objects used by the women of the East, lay scattered about in all directions, which showed that these apartments were constantly occupied. In vain did I look around to find a book, not even an embroidery frame was to be seen; so that I naturally concluded that these distinguished persons considered it quite derogatory of them to do any single thing with their fingers. Thus it is almost impossible to conceive the *ennui* which those lovely beings must endure in these gilded cages; a most dreadful monotony, because the windows looked on to blank walls.

" Truth compels me to affirm, that most outrageous incongruities met the eye at every step we took in those splendid suites of rooms. Thus, for instance, scanty calico curtains were hung up at several windows, rush-bottom and cane chairs were placed side by side with some of the most beautiful inlaid drawing-room chairs, and the richest divans. The European chairs, in the Princess's drawing-room, were anything but in keeping with the magnificent decorations of the apartment. And I considered myself lucky even in finding a marble floor, where I expected to see but deal planks.

" The bad taste of modernizing had even been carried so far, as to paint the freestone of the outside, as is now the case with the palace of His Highness the present Viceroy, at Old Cairo. There were no signs of any bedchambers, as the inmates sometimes slept in one room, and sometimes in another. Mattresses, which are encased in satin cases, and piled up in an empty chamber in the daytime, were laid down upon the carpets, or on the top of long flat cushions, at night, on which the slaves sleep, ready dressed. Mosquito-curtains were suspended from hooks driven into the walls, over those occupied by the ladies of the Harem, which are removed in the daytime, when a bouquet of artificial flowers conceals the hooks from sight. There were no toilet-tables, or signs of any of the usual appendages; they sat upon the divans, and thus made their toilettes.

"The Princess's bath-room was large and well-arranged. The first room, or entrance into it, was furnished with a plain divan, where Her Highness reclined on leaving the bath. Marble baths were fixed in the second, or bath-room; and in the third one were taps of hot and cold water, combs, brushes, essences, scents, and the usual requisites of an Oriental lady's toilette. All these apartments were lighted by cupolas from the top. On entering, I observed several long marble tables, on which were placed a collection of small slippers, and plain yellow leather *babouchcs* (half-boots) appropriated for the use of the slaves. The Princess did not accompany me in this inspection, but every room showed signs of her personal surveillance, especially the bath-room, and consequently for me they had a peculiar attraction.

"Having thus run through the whole suite, I was conducted back again to the apartment which I had quitted with my *cicerone*. There I resumed my place near Her Highness, and my pipe was again replenished and coffee handed to me, by the beautiful Circassian slave. A short time afterwards, three white slaves sat themselves down, just as adroitly as if they had been Europeans, at the further end of the room, upon rush-bottom chairs—yes, upon wretched-looking rush-bottom chairs! One of them took up the oud (a kind of guitar, the strings of which she struck with a piece of shell; another played a long flute, resembling in shape that which the ancient painters always sketch Cecilia as placing to her lips; while the third one passed her small hand upon a tar (similar to a tambourine, but rather larger), which she beat hurriedly. The whole of these three instruments were out of tune, so that it was extremely difficult to catch any harmony, for the whole produced a most dull and monotonous, but yet not unpleasing sound. A fourth slave, the melody of whose voice Her Highness had much praised, ought to have sung to that accompaniment; but, I cannot tell how, the poor girl had been so imprudent as to catch a cold; so that it was utterly out of her power to sing a single note. She blushed deeply with confusion, trembled with fear, evidently foreseeing the storm that was about to break over her head; for she came and cast herself at the Princess's feet. How I longed to take her place! and kiss Nuzly's pretty little feet, to obtain pardon for the fault of which the slave had so unintentionally been guilty.

"But what right had a slave to catch a cold—to lose that voice which did not belong to her, but which was the sole property of her who had bought her? What an abominable crime! The haughty Princess, whom this untoward accident had greatly disconcerted, more especially as it had disarranged the fantasia that her Highness had prepared for a foreign visitor, frowned most darkly at the prostrate girl; her eye-brows almost met, and her countenance assumed an expression of fiendish cruelty. Then well did I see that she was a fitting consort for the Nero-like Defterdar. 'May thy voice' said she to the poor slave, in a threatening tone, as she kicked her from her, 'remain forever dumb!' She clapped her hands twice; then two eunuchs appeared, and led away the poor innocent victim of her malevolence.

"Whether it was my imagination or reality I know not, but it seemed to me that I soon after heard stifled cries and a cracking of the *courbache* (or native whip, made from strips of buffalo hides); but those mournful shrieks were soon drowned by the discordant sounds of the instruments.

The countenance of the Princess, which had borne such a sombre aspect, now appeared all radiant with smiles.

" After the concert was terminated, then the ballet began. Four dancers glided into the apartment, holding copper *saganets* (castanets), from which vibrated a complete rush of sonorous notes. All four of them had recently been sent as a present to the Princess from Constantinople. They were attired in red silk trousers, trimmed with gold, and elegant blue damask jackets, open at the chest, and which set off their fine figures to the greatest advantage. Their black raven hair hung down their backs in long curls, like that of the other slaves ; but one of them was quite fair, and her hair was cut in the Savoyard fashion. The most beautiful of the four, a charming creature of about twenty years of age, led the dance *à la mode* Taglioni. Nothing could possibly surpass the agility, nimbleness, and grace of all her attitudes ; her whole contour was the personification of elegance itself. Her head was thrown back, her small mouth half open, the eyes half closed, as she bounded about the room like a graceful gazelle ; and every time that her artistic enthusiasm led her in front of one of the immense mirrors which reached from the ceiling down to the floor, she glanced coquettishly at her own figure—most assuredly excusable in so lovely a creature ; for it was impossible to conceive a more exquisite specimen of feminine beauty and symmetry.

" The ballet was the ' lion ' of the fantasia, and its representation took place amidst a breathless silence, only broken at intervals by the clinking of the *saganets*, and it occupied a whole hour.

" The Princess scarcely bestowed any attention upon an amusement which was no novelty to her, and with which she had entertained me as being a foreigner of distinction. As Her Highness reclined indolently on her divan, her red lips were placed from time to time to the beautiful amber

15

mouth-piece of her *chibouk*, from which she puffed forth light clouds of perfumed smoke. Occasionally she seemed as if lost in deep thought; but those piercing dark orbs of hers never took their glance off me; and even when they were withdrawn, I still felt their fascinating influence upon me, for the very marrow in my bones appeared to become frozen within me.

" The slaves who were unemployed stood at the end of the saloon, but many of them kept constantly moving about; and from the number that I saw that day, I should think that Her Highness must have had not less than a hundred white, and a much greater number of black ones. Some of them were not more than six years old. While the dancing was going on, several of them were employed in handing us violet, jasmine, and rose sherbet, with various kinds of confectionery, but especially that of *Rahat-loukoun* (so much prized by the Turks, and which had been sent to Her Highness from Constantinople, where it is made in perfection), which had been served up in beautifully embossed silver vases.

" Still that lovely, tall, graceful Circassian kept kneeling and handing me sweetmeats in silver-gilt spoons, and sherbet in large gold cups encrusted with diamonds. I drank it very slowly, which gave me an opportunity of gazing upon her beautiful features; and when I had drank it, she presented me with a fine Indian muslin napkin, fringed round with a very deep border of gold and silk, of which a European lady would have made a head-dress for the opera or masquerade. During which, and, in fact, all the time my visit lasted, Abyssinian slaves, with their white ivory teeth, kept constantly fanning me with large ostrich plumes.

"I think I have already mentioned that some other strangers came to visit the Grand Princess during the time that I was with her. Two Coptic ladies, dressed in deep mourning, mother and daughter, the former a widow, passed through the saloon, with slow, theatrical carriage, like two spectres. As soon as they had reached Her Highness, they knelt down, kissed her slipper, and then sat themselves down at the bottom of the room near the slaves. Ten minutes after they had seated themselves, they returned, faced the Princess, and again went through the same salutation; after which they retired with the same solemnity as they had entered.

"The Princess did not even deign to exchange words with them; consequently she had not the trouble of replying to any questions, and the most death-like silence followed that ceremonial introduction. This is the manner in which all official visits are paid in the East. My reception, as I have already described, was of a very different character; but then I was a foreigner, a stranger of rank, in the East! for here, as elsewhere, such individuals are always received with marks of great distinction.

Although my visit had been prolonged the greater part of the day, still it seemed to me but a second, and I was quite delighted to think that my adventure had hitherto been so successful. Everything has its end, but especially lucky adventures.

"At length the hour of departure arrived. Accordingly I submitted with the best grace possible to the final ceremony, which terminates all visits to distinguished personages in the East. Two slaves advanced towards me; one held in her hands an incense-burner (in which was burning the wood of aloes,) with which she wafted the smoke into my nostrils, and perfumed me as if I had been a holy person; the other held a small silver urn, pierced with small holes, filled with rose-water, which she sprinkled over my whole person.

"I received this double attention in the most impassable manner possible, and thus, anointed with strong perfumes, I slightly touched with the tips of my fingers the Princess's hand, and then put them respectfully to my lips; which is the mode in which persons of rank take leave of distinguished Orientals. The Princess bowed gracefully to me; then rising up all at once, just as I had reached the door, she advanced towards me : —

" 'Stop,' said she to me, 'I must show you my garden. And I will accompany you myself.'

" We passed through the reception room, then descended a staircase, passed through a hall into a beautiful kiosk, but as empty and unadorned as a Dutch Protestant church, but delightfully cooled by a large marble fountain, which played in the centre. Then we passed into the garden. A whole troop of eunuchs preceded and also followed us; while the group of black and white slaves kept at a respectful distance. I remained by the side of the Princess, whose long robe trained along the ground. Her Highness took hold of my hand as we descended the staircase, and lucky was it for me that I had a very small hand, totally unlike that of a man, or else it would have betrayed me.

" While I was seated on the divan, I maintained my new character extremely well; but when I began to walk, I experienced considerable embarrassment, and although I possessed the features, the height, and even a most feminine voice, as I have already explained, still I had not the shuffling deportment. I endeavored as well as I could, to take short steps, so as to avoid treading upon my elegant long velvet dress, which I held up, as a sapper does his leather apron.

" Fortunately, the Orientals, being naturally of sedentary habits, do not shuffle along very quickly, unless when in a passion, and then they glide about as swiftly and noiselessly as serpents; and I imagine that there could not be anything so peculiar in my walk, awkward as it must have been, to have excited the slightest suspicion of my sex. The advanced guard of eunuchs, and that of the slaves who followed us, kept at such a respectful distance from us that it was utterly impossible for them to overhear our conversation; we, however, maintained an interminable silence, but it would have been all the same if we had been conversing with each other.

" The gardens into which we had entered, might be denominated very beautiful; but I confess that I was so dreadfully agitated, that I am quite unable to give any description of them; I was so entirely occupied in taking short steps, and so fearful lest I should catch a sunstroke, that I did not bestow the slightest attention upon the flowers, flower-beds, or fountains which were scattered about, and which played into marble basins. All that I remember is, that we walked for some time along, very slowly, under a very shady avenue of sycamore trees, and where I must have been least noticed.

" ' The silence that both I and the Princess observed towards each other at length became unbearable. So at last I took upon myself to break it, and began to praise, in as pure Turkish as I was master of, the perfume of the flowers, which I had neither noticed nor smelled; the gentle murmuring of the waters, that I had not listened to: and was proceeding in the same strain, when the Princess interrupted me rather sharply, without the least allusion to the effusions of my poetical rhapsody :—

" ' I hope that you do not for a moment imagine I am your dupe ? ' said she in a curt manner, at the same time letting fall my hand, which she had held in hers up to that moment. ' If my husband, Defterdar, whose anger knows no bounds, had seen you, and had had but the slightest inkling of your audacity in thus presenting yourself before me, he would have had you impaled upon the spot, and most assuredly you would have deserved it.'

" ' I flatter myself,' said I, ' that I have shown you, and I will prove to you again shortly, that I possess no fear, and that I am no coward.'

"Nevertheless, I cannot but confess that those words gave me such an electric shock, that the whole of my limbs shivered and trembled violently. The bare idea of empalement is far from being agreeable at any time. I was so thunderstruck that I remained speechless. Fortunately, the Princess gave me no time to offer any reply.

"'But luckily for you,' replied she, in a more subdued voice, 'my terrible husband is not at home, and I am as much mistress of my own actions as a woman can possibly be in any Mussulman's country. Adventurous mortals are far from being displeasing to me; I admire courage, no matter what form it takes; even if it borders on temerity or rashness. If then you are as brave and bold as the enterprise which you have now undertaken makes me give you credit for, you will come to the *Mogreb* to-morrow, to the Elfy Gate; a tall negro, dressed in red, will pass you, touch you on the left shoulder, as he walks along. Follow that slave if you wish to know anything more.'

"Saying which she again took hold of my hand as if nothing had happened, and led me on without uttering another syllable to the foot of the staircase. There she took leave of me in the most cordial and graceful manner imaginable, saying in a loud tone, so that all present might overhear her, that she was exceedingly grateful at having had the pleasure of conversing with such a lady-like specimen of my countrywomen, all of whom she trusted resembled me both in manners and habits.

"Preceded by the eunuchs, and followed by the slaves, I was led to the outer gate of the palace with the same ceremony as had been observed on my arrival. A devil of a tall black, armed with a most formidable-looking *courbache*, was present as sentry at the gate as I took my departure, for fear lest any of the slaves should take it into their heads

to take French leave and quit the palace. I propitiated
that sovereign of Egypt, Prince Baksheesh, by handing the
Grand Eunuch several purses of gold coins. Entering my
carriage, perhaps a little more hastily than ladies generally
do, I was driven straight to the residence of my charming
friend, the lovely Levantine, in whose clothes I was dressed;
there I exchanged my habiliments and put on my own
attire. She had been very uneasy during my absence as to
the result of my daring and dangerous exploit. I assured
her that my success had even been far greater than I had
anticipated, and that I had satisfied my curiosity very easily. But true it is, that I did not think it prudent to let her
into the secret of the manner in which my stratagem had
terminated. When I say terminated, I am in error, for it
was scarcely in its zenith, and the actual *finale* of it was at
that moment quite enveloped in mystery.

"You are not young, it is true, but you were so once;
consequently you will believe me when I affirm that I never
closed my eyes the whole of the following night. My brain
kept thinking of all the good and bad reports which I had
heard about the Princess Nuzly, and my mind became extremely uneasy. Was it really a meeting or a snare?
Was I to be the hero of some good fortune or the victim of
vengeance? My position appeared to be of a most embar-
rassing nature, especially as I well knew the reputed character of that Princess, and the dreadful things which were
recounted of her. Good fortune does not shield us from
vengeance, nor vengeance from our enjoyment of it; the
question was, if it were possible to avoid the one and to enjoy the other. My mind was employed in trying to solve
that difficult enigma. The finale of my adventure, however, will give you a key to the solution at which I arrived.
You must also bear in mind that I was then only twenty
years of age.

"Early in the morning I repaired to Khan-el-Khalyly;

there I purchased at the shop of one Barakat, who knew me intimately, an excellent Damascus scimitar, as fine as a hair, and which was so highly tempered that it would have cut an eider-down pillow in half. This I concealed beneath my cloak,—for I now wore my male habiliments—this was my life protector; and placing a six-barrelled revolver in my pocket, I walked up and down the Mogreb in front of the Elfy Gate.

" It was not long before the negro clad in red made his appearance and touched me on the shoulder as he passed. As that gate of Cairo is one of the most frequented, I did not attract the curiosity of any of the passers-by as I turned round and followed him. This I did and continued to do at about twenty paces' distance, still keeping him always in sight. Walking at first in the direction of Boulac, my guide soon proceeded along a path to the left, and after having taken several windings which always led nearer to the banks of the Nile, he stopped short, which I did also, at the foot of a high wall which seemed to block up our passage.

" As night had suddenly closed in I did not at first perceive the small low door, which had all the appearance of being the postern gate of some old castle, of which the negro possessed the key. While he was in the act of stooping down, for he was full six feet high, I scanned the height of the wall, and kept thinking whether, in case of need, it were possible for me to scale it by dint of a gigantic feat. That is what is called, in military parlance, taking a reconnoitre in case of emergency. I was just on the point of measuring it more accurately with my eye, not having any instruments with me, when the tall slave interrupted my calculations by touching me on the shoulder as a token that the door was open. I crossed the threshold with a firm step, at the same time feeling that my revolver was safe in my pocket, and my Damascus blade by my side. The slave quickly shut the door after me, and I continued to follow him.

He passed across a long garden, which I shall not stop to describe, for the best of all reasons that the darkness of the night prevented me from being able to discern how it was laid out. My guide maintained an imperturbable silence.

"I really believe (may God forgive me!) that he was a mute, and I will not swear but that he was deaf also, for he did not reply to a single question which I put to him. · The grating of our footsteps echoed on the hard sandy paths of the avenues as we passed along. After making several detours, we at length reached the door of a kiosk concealed beneath some large trees, which must have formed a most grateful retreat in the daytime. My mute of a guide did not enter therein, but pushed me rather than introduced me into it, and there I was within that mysterious retreat alone in the dark, and without being able to grope my way. My first care was to find out my position as best I could. All that I was enabled to discover was that I trod on a thick carpet, strewn with the softest cushions, and that the hangings were of silk. It was surrounded with a large divan. I had just finished taking this inventory of the *penates* when I felt something clasp my neck. Do not be alarmed, my friends, it was not the classic silken cords of the mutes of the Seraglio: it was only the two soft arms of a lovely woman.

"This mode of reception was adopted to banish all my fears. I returned the embrace as any young man would naturally have done, without waiting to identify the person of the individual who had thus honored me with a private interview, and my approaches were returned with a corresponding alacrity. It was not long before I knew perfectly well who my unknown Venus was.

"Now I must beg that you will allow me to draw the curtain upon the scene which followed. ·

"The night passed away as rapidly as if it had been but a few seconds; the stars were still shining most brilliantly, when that awful word, 'Farewell,' was pronounced by the sweetest lips I had ever pressed, and by a woman who was much more mistress of her own actions than I was of mine. I felt half inclined to have translated for her edification that beautiful balcony scene in Shakspeare's 'Romeo and Juliet,' into the purest Turkish that I could command; but she appeased my regrets by breathing into my ear the fond hope that I would come again to-morrow at the same hour, and in the same manner; and then, embracing me, the lovely phantom vanished, in the twinkling of an eye, like an ethereal being.

"I did not remain long alone; a heavy hand was placed upon my shoulder and I hastily retreated. My safety, however, was not yet secured. I was not long in discovering that, instead of returning by the way he had conducted me, my guide, still the same black, dressed in red, took me quite a different direction. He walked straight towards the Nile which lay before us, as the creaking of the *sakias*, 'water-wheels,' confirmed.

"'Good,' said I, as my heart beat with its usual promptitude. 'This is like having passed a quarter of an hour as Rabelais did. Now comes the forfeit. I am doomed to pay for the happiness I have enjoyed.' And all the dreadful tales which I had heard of the baseness and treachery of the Princess Nuzly presented themselves to my imagination.

"When a collegian, my tutors taught me to believe that Queen Cleopatra possessed such charms, that many thought themselves happy in passing an evening alone with her even at the sacrifice of their lives. I remembered that I was in Egypt, and if I had not quitted the presence of a Queen, I had at least left the arms of a Princess, who, if she were not equally beautiful, seductive, and powerful, still was quite as inhuman. The only difference was that I had not given her any right to take possession of my person, and most assuredly I was not fool enough to sacrifice it for the love I bore her beauteous orbs.

"But how and by what means was I to escape from the snare into which she had entrapped me? This second Margaret of Burgundy's black Orsini was six feet high, his frame Herculean, and I should have stood but little chance had I wrestled with such an antagonist. That Goliath would have crushed me with his thumb, and I possessed not the prowess of David.

It is true that I was armed with one of the keenest of Damascus blades ever made, and a six-barrelled revolver; but then the report of fire-arms would have brought a legion of eunuchs to his rescue, and as to the scimitar, well-tempered as it was said to be, I placed no confidence in it, as I had never used such a warlike weapon before. If my blow had missed I was a dead man; and yet I was obliged to adopt some plan; time pressed, or else in a few short moments all would be over with me, and I should never again drive or walk along the Cascine at Florence.

"The creaking of the *sakias* became more distinct; the Nile was evidently not far from us. The first dawn of the day, which gives such a very indistinct light in the East, hardly allowed me to distinguish any more than the lofty wall beyond the trees, which on that as well as on the other sides encircled the garden. Soon afterwards I saw the gate which opened on to the river, and you may rest assured that I was taken aback when I saw that it was guarded by three tall phantoms, three devils of blacks, placed there most unquestionably to seize hold of me and to cast me into the Nile, like a kitten, as they had done many a European before.

" At the sight of those formidable opponents, I resolved to put into execution the project I had been meditating. Slackening my pace, I took advantage of an angle of masonry-work, which concealed me from observation, to rush upon my guide with the agility of a man who struggled for his life, and to plunge my Damascus blade up to its very hilt into his body. My trial stroke proved a *chef-d'œuvre.* It must have pierced his heart, as the poor devil dropped down dead instantaneously without uttering a groan. I then rifled his pockets, expecting to find there the key of the gate by which I had entered the grounds. I was fortunate enough to put my hand upon it, and leaving others to bury his body, I turned about quickly and ran along as fast as my legs could carry me.

"In a few minutes I reached the opposite wall; the same the height of which I had taken the precaution to measure. On arriving there I found to my dismay that I had overrated my gymnastic abilities, and was baffled. A squirrel could not have bounded over it. I was then obliged to seek for the gate, which I was unable to discover. Was it on the right hand or the left? I could not tell. By mere chance I proceeded to the right, that side appearing the most likely; and, Heaven be praised! I had hardly gone thirty steps before I found the gate which had been anxiously sought for.

"Scarcely, however, had I put the key into the lock, when three tall black eunuchs, who had concealed themselves behind the opposite door, and who had given chase after me, came suddenly upon me from different directions. They were the same three eunuchs whom I had seen mounting guard at the door to which the defunct negro was proceeding. The first one who approached me brandished a tremendous large sabre, a blow from which would have cleft my body in twain, but the first ball from my revolver laid him prostrate on the ground. It had however, only broken his arm, but that was quite enough for the moment, as it was his right arm, and his sabre fell from it. That slight chastisement for his insolence produced a most salutary effect upon his companions, who thought that they would receive a similar correction, as they were also armed with formidable scimitars. As they drew back I passed through the door, and in so doing fired at them two farewell shots, without stopping to see what mischief I had done.   But it is most probable that they were killed, as I proceeded quietly on my way, and reached my own house safe and sound before sunrise.

"I assure you, however, that I hastened to quit Cairo as soon as possible, as I had killed a eunuch.   But it was passed over in silence, for people in Egypt are not so particular when a murder is committed as in Europe.   The East is the land of silence as it is also of mystery.

" Soon afterwards I proceeded on my journey to Jerusalem, and on my return to Cairo I called upon my charming Levantine friend, when she informed me that during my pilgrimage to the Holy Sepulchre, H. H. the Grand Princess had invited her to see her; on which occasion she had treated her most graciously, and made numerous inquiries about me, 'her amiable friend,' as Her Highness termed me.   The Grand Princess, who had no wish that the adventures in the Harem and the Kiosk should be bruited about, very quietly pocketed the trick which had been played her, and nothing more was said about it."

Then I pondered in my own mind, how many lovers, in that apartment in which I then stood, had paid the penalty of their audacity by their being plunged into the Nile, or allured to meet a watery grave, perhaps beneath those very windows from which I then beheld the lovely moon shining so brightly, and had thus been sent to their "last account with all their imperfections on their head!"   It was natural that my imagination should dwell upon such thoughts ; not because the old Frenchwoman had related the above incidents to me, on whose veracity I might have placed some doubt, had I not heard the ladies of the Harem and slaves repeat to me many a time and oft similar histories not only of the Grand Princess, but of other Egyptian Harem celebrities, that had made

"My hair stand on end, like quills upon the fretful porcupine," which proved to me what a mysterious abode a Harem is.

CHAPTER XXI.

THE next morning I was awoke at four o'clock by the three Germans, the laundry-maid, needle-woman, and cook (the latter of whom had only arrived at Ghezire a short time previous to our departure, and had not as yet been able to enter on her duties, there being no kitchen in that Harem, or any *batterie de cuisine* for her use) knocking at the door of my room, as they had only just arrived from Cairo.

Upon making inquiries of them, it appeared that they did not leave the Harem at Ghezire until nine o'clock at night, although their beds, &c., had been taken away from them at the time all the others were packed and sent away. I learned that they had also been treated most shamefully; and had their fellow-countryman, Mr. C. H. (his Royal Highness's civil aide-de-camp), been present when they rushed into my chamber, he would have learned how little they were disposed " to accommodate themselves to *such* circumstances," pressing though they were.

Getting up, I hastily enveloped myself in my flannel dressing-gown, unbolted my door, and gave them admittance. I shall never forget their gesticulations when they looked at my pallet on the floor, and the large empty space around. They held up their hands in perfect amazement:—" *Mein Gott Mein ! Gott ! was müszen wir thun ?* " " My God! My God! what must we do ? " The despair, the horror which was depicted on their countenances I shall never forget. They all burst into tears, and cried most bitterly. I endeavored to soothe their feelings, but to no purpose.

Then I inquired of them why they had come there to disturb me (knowing that I was powerless to help them,) instead of staying in their own room? You may guess my surprise when they told me they were all ordered to take up their quarters in my room; which, in short, was to be *not* the hospital as *yet*, but the European ward. Now I really became annoyed; for I could not possibly imagine for a moment that the English governess in the family of a Vice-regal prince of Egypt ought to submit to such an indignity as to have her chamber turned into a "nightly refuge" for Ismael Pacha's domestics. Thanks to the legislators of English jurisprudence, a poor governess is not a menial (drudge though she too often is made to be): and one thing is quite certain, and that was that no English family ever treated a Prussian institutrice as a domestic servant, although had I not battled against it, the Prussian *million-aires* in Egypt would have had me served and held in no better estimation than a slave!

Well, what could I do for those poor creatures, who had not had food between their lips from the hour I had left Ghezire on the previous day? Nothing—absolutely noth-ing! No propitiation on the altar of that all-powerful sovereign ruler of Egypt, Prince Baksheesh (for my heart bled for them, and I tried it in spite of the Princess's orders), at that hour in the morning, could procure them a crust.

I told them that they could lie upon the divan, but that it was very damp. They asked—nay, they positively cried to me for bread (hated Englishwoman as I was), poor help-less creatures! and yet the laundry-maid, who spoke Turkish very well and had been in Egypt much longer than myself, ought to have taken the precaution; as I did, to have had their breakfast and dinner before they left. True, I had only been enabled to obtain the former meal, but then I found that a great support to me in my present state of health.

I then despatched them down to the eunuchs, with bak-sheesh in their hands, in quest of some refreshment; and soon afterwards they returned, bringing with them some Arab bread, and a small tin-pot of coffee, of which they partook most voraciously, after which they threw themselves down upon the divan, damp as it was, and fell fast asleep.

Rising at five o'clock (for I could not sleep after the Germans had disturbed me), I summoned the slave, Senana, to take away my bed into the bed store-room (for it will be recollected that in every Harem there is such a repository); then partook of my breakfast, which consisted of Arab bread, as no European had as yet been provided for me, and several *findjans* of coffee.

Having heard salutes fired announcing the arrival of the Viceroy, I ordered the head-nurse to dress the Grand Pacha; and, being desired by their Highnesses the Princesses (who had arrived late at night in company with the Validè Princess) to take the little Prince early in the morning to visit his illustrious *Baba, Ras-el-Tin,* I walked across the court-yard into the palace of "Cape of Figs."

As we entered the grand entrance, it reminded me at that time of the floral arcade adjoining the Italian Opera, at Covent Garden, except that it was much more diminutive in size, and narrower in compass. It was now all arranged for the grand ball, the "lion" of the season, which the Viceroy was about to give to the Turkish *noblesse* and the *élite* of the European population of Alexandria and Cairo, who were assembled there on account of the excessive heat at the Capital.

The basement was covered with sawdust, over which was laid a handsome Brussels carpet. Colored globular lamps were suspended from the glass roof, which was concealed from the eye of the spectator by white lace and crimson silk curtains, interlaced and looped together in the centre by a crimson silk rosette, in the centre of which were placed artificial bouquets of flowers. On each side, raised in the sawdust floor, was an imitation *parterre* of blooming exotics, the fragrance of whose perfume was delightfully grateful to the senses.

A great variety of small colored illumination lamps were hung in festoons suspended from the gilded pillars. Large, handsomely-gilded mirrors hung down the sides, in which the exotics were reflected. At the bottom, on each side, were two pure white marble fountains, whose waters, as they played, formed representations of peacocks, with their superb tails. Around them were placed variegated evergreens and prettily-constructed rockeries. Over the door of the entrance to the palace hung a very handsome crimson cloth curtain, embroidered with gold crescent, and fringed with a deep gold border. At the top of the door were placed the Sultan's arms, and two standards with gilt spears.

We then descended two marble steps, which led us into a small marble-paved hall, which, owing to the large orange-trees and shrubs and exotics it contained presented a very sombre appearance, but which, when lighted up by means of the superb lustre that hung suspended from the ceiling, which was dome-shaped and most beautifully painted and gilded, gave it a truly fairylike *coup d'œil*.

It was such an entrance into a palace as the polishing of Aladdin's wonderful lamp might really have produced, but not outvied; in short, an Arabian Night-like creation. It was covered with mirrors which reached from the ceiling down to the floor, between all of which hung white lace and crimson silk curtains, which gave them the appearance of windows.

Upon numerous gilt brackets stood white marble vases, filled with moss and artificial flowers. Between the evergreens stood several marble statues, some bearing colored globes in their hands, and others bouquets of flowers. Here and there were placed gilded chairs, the cushions being covered with crimson velvet.

The effect, as the spectator entered, was extremely pleasing, and the gentle trickling of the water from the fountains in it produced a most delightful sensation.

Then we passed into an immense marble-paved hall, hav-

16

ing raised banks all around it covered with beautiful velvet-looking green moss, interspersed with natural and artificial flowers most tastefully blended together. The walls were hung with large mirrors, which reached half-way down them and rested on the raised banks, and a hanging terrace of flowers ran round the apartment on the top of the mirrors. On the banks were placed vases of the rarest exotics, interspersed with statues, on whose heads were placed rustic carved baskets of blooming flowers, each holding in his hand colored globular lamps. Down the entire centre of the room ran a huge bank covered with moss interspersed with flowers, creepers, and orange-trees, amidst which, dotted about, stood numerous statues, and which divided the apartment into a double promenade, at each end of which was a pure white marble fountain, bordered with flowers. The ceiling was magnificently painted, surmounted with a deep gilt beading. The room was lighted with twelve huge silver candelabras, fixed in the sides of the walls. Here and there rout-seats were scattered about, all covered with crimson velvet to match the hangings, which were of crimson silk.

Then we proceeded into another apartment similarly arranged, but having a double marble staircase covered with fine Brussels carpeting. The banisters were richly gilded. On the first landing stood two statues holding globular lamps in their hands, and a basket of flowers on their heads. Behind them were superb gilt mirrors, reaching from the top of the ceiling, which was also richly gilded, and elegantly painted down to the floor. The walls were covered with rich crimson satin-paper, ornamented with a broad gilt beading both at top and bottom. All up both the sides were placed boxes of blooming flowers.

"Then we ascended seven stairs, and soon reached the top of the second landing, on which stood two veiled, life-size statues holding gilt branch candelabras in their hands.

There the rooms branched off right and left, but I and the Grand Pacha first proceeded into those facing the staircase.

The first apartment that we entered was an immense round drawing-room, which commanded a most extensive marine view.

The floor was of highly-polished brown and white marqueterie, the ceiling beautifully painted, having in its centre a battle-scene, commemorating one of Mehemet Ali's victories, and very pretty vignettes of other warlike engagements in squares. A magnificent lustre was suspended from the centre. The walls were covered with crimson satin-paper, against which hung several rich cut-glass lustres. The hangings were of crimson silk and white lace, looped up with heavy bullion cords and tassels. The chairs and sofas were of ormolu and gold, covered with crimson satin. Mirrors hung from the ceiling down to the floor. In the centre stood a large round mosaic-table on gilded legs.

Opening a door on the left we passed into the Blue Drawing-room, furnished in a similar manner, but the hangings and furniture were of sky-blue satin. This led us into the Pink Drawing-room, the hangings and furniture of which were of pink and white satin.

Opening a door we entered the dining-room, a very heavy-looking apartment with green velvet hangings and black ebony furniture covered with velvet to correspond.

In the centre stood a long highly-polished ebony dining-table. The floor was of the same material, in black and white chequers, and as slippery as glass. Thence we proceeded into another apartment, similarly arranged, only with crimson hangings, and the coverings of the furniture to match. In the centre stood an inlaid-mosaic table, with gilt legs, and here and there stood several console-tables. The flooring was arranged in red and white chequers.

Passing out of it we entered the Viceroy, Ismael Pacha's bedchamber. The walls were covered with plain white satin-paper, with a roseate hue. The ceiling was painted and gilt, the flooring was arranged in brown and white chequers, with a strip of Brussels carpet down the centre, and also across the bottom, at the foot of the sofa, the frame of which was gilt, and the squabs were covered with red-figured silk.

On the left-hand side stood the gilt iron bedstead, with rods and poles to correspond. The hangings consisted of crimson Persian silk mosquito-curtains. At the foot were placed handsome thick Persian rugs. The bed was arranged *à la Européenne*, with bolsters, pillows, and covered with the usual linen. The Turks and Egyptians never use but one wadded coverlet, and nothing else on their beds, the coverlet being lined with thin white calico, which when dirty is unpicked, replaced by a clean one, while the soiled one is sent to be washed.

On the right hand stood a black ebony chest of drawers, with a cabinet to correspond, and those two articles, with a few chairs, constituted all the furniture. True it is, however, that the Viceroy does not reside much at this Palace, as he is a Prince who cannot endure to be annoyed with state affairs, and prefers spending his time on board his yacht, steaming up and down the Nile, as then he is free from the unwelcome visits of those " other eighteen Princes who govern Egypt," whose calls are not always of the most agreeable kind.

Leading out of this room, we entered the dressing-room, then the bath-room, the floors of both of which were of marqueterie. In it were two large marble baths, one being for fresh, and the other for sea-water. Facing these were the suite of apartments used by the Ministers of State, and Ismael Pacha's suite.

CHAPTER XXII.

LEAVING these apartments we passed along a marqueterie corridor of brown and white chequers, and entered that memorable apartment, in which Mehemet Ali, in March 1811, determined on the extirpation of the Mamelukes, whose powerful influence had thwarted his plans of aggrandizement.

It was an immense room, supported in the centre by three colossal green agate pillars, against the first of which stood a double marble fountain; round the second pillar was placed a tier-ed conversational sofa. At the third pillar was a beautiful cascade, where the water fell trickling over the rocks, interspersed with large white and yellow water-lilies, ice-plants, violets and beautiful ferns, amidst which was that species called "*Maiden's hair*," all then in blossom, which had originally been brought from the Island of Arran, and numerous other exotics, in full blossom.

Along one side was a gallery formed by twelve small white Corinthian pillars, on which were alternately placed silver candelabras and vases. Round the bottoms of them were ranged baskets of flowers, the tendrils being twirled round the pillars in imitation of creepers entwining themselves around forest-trees. The gallery was entirely festooned with yellow silk and white lace curtains, having in their centres bouquets of flowers with large blue satin streamers hanging down from them. This apartment extended along the whole *façade* of the palace on one side, and contained about twelve immense windows, all looking on to the Mediterranean. It forms the Viceregal promenade in the winter season, and here it was that Mehemet Ali gave his Kehia Bey (Mohammed Laz) his instructions for the decimation of the Mamelukes, which took place after he had at Cairo invested his son Tussom (Tussam)

Pacha with the command of the Egyptian army, when on the eve of his departure for Arabia.

On the left-hand side of it stood a yellow satin sofa and a few chairs covered with the same material. It also contained two large mirrors, one placed at the top and the other at the bottom, in which were reflected both the cascade and fountain, on each side of which hung the full length portraits of the renowned founder of the present Viceregal dynasty, and his cruel and subtle son, or adopted son (for his parentage has never to this day been clearly explained,) Ibrahim Pacha, the present Viceroy's father, both allowed by all old Turks and Egyptians to be most striking likenesses. One thing is certain, and that is, that they are beautifully executed.

It is a most regal apartment, replete with highly interesting historical reminiscences; and as I stood therein, holding by the hand *my* prince, the grandson of that remarkable man, I could not help looking intently at the child, and wondering what his future destiny will be. There he stood, that little "dot of humanity," the heir to almost countless wealth, (whose guardians, in case of his illustrious Baba's death, prior to his majority, I hope may not be any of the clique belonging to the Prussian Jews' fraternity,) endowed with talents which if properly cultivated would carve for him a name in the annals of Egyptian history, inheriting most unfortunately the combined vices of the founder of his dynasty and those of his grandsire, and spoiled, petted, humored, and inflated with pride.

His probable chance of succeeding to the Viceroyalty is at the present time very remote; but the Viceroy and the Validè Princess would, or I am much mistaken, both give every *para* they possess to every slave and dependent in their suite, whether Turk, Moslem, or Christian, and shed, too, the last drop of blood which flows in their veins, if they could but induce Her Sovereign Majesty to nominate the

Grand Pacha to be the next Viceroy (*Gouverneur de l' Egypte*). Then like another Jacob he would supplant his brother (but not by the same mother), Mustapha Pacha. It has been, and still is, " their thought by day, their dream by night; " and presently, when I come to describe the visit of the Crœsus-like viceregal family in 1864 to Sultan Abdul Aziz, " the poor," my readers will regard with peculiar interest the following clause in the Firman of Investiture, dated May 22nd, 1841, under which the Pacha of Egypt rules—

" Henceforth, when the post shall be vacant, the Government of Egypt shall descend in a direct line, from the elder to the elder in the male race among thy sons and grandsons. As regards their nomination, that shall be made by my Sublime Porte."

Continuing the historical reminiscences of this gallery, I must add that it was from that spot that Mehemet Ali reviewed that formidable fleet which he sent forth to the Morea, and which afterwards almost rotted in the roadstead, when he had nurtured in his ambitious mind the vain idea that he would be able to make himself the independent soverign of Egypt.

On the right hand are three doors, the first of which leads into a very pretty and tastefully-arranged boudoir. It was formerly the favorite cabinet of Mehemet Ali, and here he held his private Council. This consisted of his wife, who died at Constantinople in 1864, in her sixty-seventh year, at the palace of her daughter Zeneb Hanum, wife of Kiamil Pacha, President of the Grand Council, to whom she bequeathed her almost unrivalled collection of jewels and all her vast estates in Egypt, and the beautiful, wanton, gifted, but cruel Princess Nuzly, who acted as her aged father's *Bach-Kiatibi*, " Private Secretary."

Here it was that the better and cooler judgment of this able Turkish female politician often checked many a dire scheme of her ambitious parent.

The second was fitted up as a buffet on the occasion of the grand state ball on the 8th of June, 1864; and here it was that the *Kopecs* "dogs" of Christians, drank freely of those choice wines which the quondam Crimean suttlers knew so well how to select, and to charge for too. At the time we visited it, it was arranged for that forthcoming *fête.* In the centre stood a long table; in each corner a case of stuffed birds. Chairs covered with plain crimson morocco were placed in a row down each side.

We then proceeded to the ball-room, a circular apartment, which is well lighted by a handsome stained-glass cupola. The floor was of red and white marqueterie, highly polished. The walls were covered with white satin-paper, having a roseate hue. White lace and pink silk curtains hung in festoons from the cupola, fastened with bouquets and white and pink silk rosettes, having long streamers attached. The windows were similarly arranged. Most magnificent cut-glass lustres hung down from each side of the cupola, and several lustre candelabras were fixed to the walls. A semi-circular orchestra, covered with crimson cloth, occupied one half of the circumference, which, as well as the whole of the apartment, was decorated with vases filled with real and artificial flowers.

The artist who had fitted up these apartments for this state ball, happened to be in the Palace as we were making our tour of inspection, and he presented both myself and H. H. the Grand Pacha with several artificial flowers and bouquets of most fragrant exotics.

Here it was, that on the 8th of June 1864, the Viceroy Ismael Pacha gave the grand state ball. On that occasion the whole line of the route leading from the Place de Consuls to the Palace was most brilliantly illuminated with thousands of flambeaux, and the police arrangements were admirably conducted. My pen-drawing must necessarily fall very short of the splendid *tout ensemble* of the fête, *par excellence*, of the Alexandrian season. Still, I cannot but observe, that as the powerful rays of those torches fell upon the well-appointed equipages which rolled along to the festive scene, they brought out in bold relief the animated countenances of their fair, elegantly-dressed female occupants, whose hair was ornamented with many a lovely spray and brilliant tiara of diamonds, which formed a most becoming addition to their well-selected yet variegated colored costumes and elaborate toilettes.

I have not of late years amused myself by a perusal of any of the numerous beautifully illustrated editions of the ' Arabian Nights' Entertainments ' which have been published, although I must plead guilty to having been a resident within those " gilded cages," where such are narrated nightly, and believed in most scrupulously. Yet, as I gazed on the busy turmoil (for on that day I took no official part in that festivity,) as it was being rapidly whirled past me, I almost fancied that I had been carried away by some genii, and was at that moment an inhabitant of one of those spots, that the " rubbing up " of Aladdin's Wonderful Lamp is said to have the gift to call into existence.

I have already described the decorations of those splendid suites of apartments as I walked through them in the daytime; but when I entered them on this night, the *coup d'œil* that burst upon my sight as I most carefully walked up and down that beautiful mosaic pavement, was magnificently imposing. The stewards, quite ignorant of their duties as masters of the ceremonies, had forgotten one of the most essential precautions in a ball-room, but most especially where the flooring is of highly-polished marqueterie —to have it strewn with finely-powdered perfumed chalk.

I observed a good-natured smile cross the fine features of the Viceroy Ismael Pacha, as he graciously received the homage of his ministers and brilliant staff, closely attended by that small circle of Europeans yclept *the clique* who have the entrèe at Court. His condscending salaam was given with all that grace of deportment and suavity of manner which we should only have expected to see displayed by a Prince who had been educated in the school of the *first* gentleman of Europe (George the Fourth of England,) when he received the presentations of that bevy of European ladies (*kopeks*, "dogs" of Christian women,) who were presented to him by their own "Special Princes," many of whom officiated as masters of the ceremonies.

This fête will ever be remembered as a most remarkable occurrence in the annals of Egyptian history, as it is the first time that any Mussulman Prince gave audience to the fair daughters of Christendom. We did not perceive any of the dark-eyed daughters of Israel, although there was a pretty fair sprinkling of members of the Hebrew persuasion.

His Highness the Viceroy acknowledged the attendance of such a numerous body of his European population with much apparent satisfaction, walked about the rooms, showed considerable attention to the officers of the United States frigate, *Constellation*, and appointed them some attendants to escort them about the Palace; seemed much pleased at the *entente cordiale* which appeared to exist among the different classes and nations of Europeans; expressed his entire approbation of the whole of the arrangements that had been made to carry out his princely hospitality; and remained until a late hour, evidently gratified and amused most thoroughly at the dancing and hilarity of his guests.

I was crebibly informed that this entertainment cost no less a sum than 40,000*l.* to 50,000*l.* A few days afterwards the Viceroy visited the vessels in the port of Alexandria belonging to the Pacific and Oriental Company, and the *Messageries Impérials*, and presented the officers and crews with rings and baksheesh respectively; but his crowning and princely gifts were a tiara of diamonds, each valued at

1200*l.*, to each of the wives of the agents of these companies, Mrs. B. and Madame L., in consideration of the polite *personal* services rendered to His Highness by their husbands. The morning after the state ball, their Highnesses the Princesses ordered me to take the Grand Pacha to see his illustrious *Baba*. On our arrival at the palace we had to wait a considerable period, as the Viceroy had not yet risen. As soon as His Highness had dressed we were ushered into his bedchamber, which I have already described; there we remained a considerable period. The Viceroy was sitting on the sofa smoking a cigar, the Prince approached and salaamed. I curtseyed and was on the point of leaving the apartment, when His Highness exclaimed, "*Approachez ! approachez ! madame.*"

I did so, took my station in the centre of the room, and there remained, leaving the hangings of the door drawn aside, which gave the officials in attendance an opportunity to overhear all that transpired; and luckily I did so, for I soon found on my return to the Harem that the inmates had already begun to make "mountains of mole-hills." The little Prince soon became tired; for singular to add, as I have previously stated, he never liked remaining long with the *Baba*. The Grand Pacha salaamed the Viceroy, I curtseyed, and we both returned to the Harem. As soon as I reached the Prince's apartment I was surrounded by a whole host of ladies of the Harem, *Ikbals*, and slaves exclaiming, "Oh, madame! oh, madame! you have been in the *Baba's* bedchamber. Now you must ask this, and this, and this, for me," naming all their requests simultaneously together.

I listened very coolly to them, and neither smiled nor said a syllable; but at length, when their hubbuh had subsided and they were silent, I replied, "Well! and what of that?"

"What of that!" repeated the whole body in a chorus, "You are the Baba's *Ikbal*."

"No, indeed," added I: "you are mistaken, I have no desire to please the Viceroy in that manner; that is an honor I do not covet; so I cannot and will not ask any favors either for myself or for any of you."

They stared again at me; they believed me, yet could scarcely credit their senses; all were amazed and dumbfounded. Shortly afterwards their Highnesses the Princesses sent for me. On entering the apartment, which was quite as miserable in appearance as that of the Grand Pacha's, they inquired of me,

"Where was the Viceroy? Was he dressed? What was he doing? What did he say? When was he coming over to see them?"

To all these interrogatories I replied most truthfully, "In his bed chamber. Yes, dressed and sitting on the sofa. Smoking a cigar. He told me to draw near to him. He is coming over here at one o'clock."

Their Highnesses had previously questioned the little Prince. He was truthful, a virtue which he inherits from his mother the Princess Epouse, who always spoke the truth, and had already given them the same information. They smiled, sent me some coffee, sweetmeats, and a bundle of cigarettes. I partook of the former but declined the latter.

Their hitherto restless fiery orbs resumed their habitual calmness. The crisis had passed. I had been tried and found to be faithful and trustworthy, and from that hour confidence, esteem, and respect for me rose to par. Had I but yielded to the opportunity that presented itself for me to make—perhaps my fortune—what should I have gained? most assuredly only what the cunning creature does who is well up in the knowledge of this world, "who dodges past Prince Baksheesh in the antechamber of the Viceroy." Nothing! absolutely nothing! Indeed, I should have acquired something more lasting—the jealousy of their Highnesses the Princesses the three wives, and the mortal hatred of all the ladies of the Harem, *Ikbals* and slaves. And my life, what would it have been worth ? A few brief hours' purchase, perhaps not even long enough to have made my peace with my Maker !

God be praised that was the first and last time that I ever entered the precincts of the bedchamber of Ismael Pacha, the Viceroy of Egypt. For although His Highness behaved to me on that occasion with the same respect with which he had always treated me, still the effect that the telegraphic announcement (for no sooner had I crossed the sill of that apartment than the fact was known all through the Harem) produced on the minds of their Highnesses the Princesses, placed me in so painful a position that my life was jeopardized, and its preservation or forfeiture hung, as it were, upon a thread—the truthfulness of a mere child of barely five years old.

When I retired to my chamber, I returned thanksgiving to the Almighty, who had so wonderfully instilled into my Prince the virtue of truth, and I prayed that I might never again be thrown into such a dilemma.

God be praised ! my prayers were granted; for I was never again placed in a similar position, and I felt the full force of the Turkish expression, "Whatever is written is written."

<hr>

CHAPTER XXIII.

On the evening prior to the departure of their Highnesses the Validè Princess, the Princess Epouse, and the Grand Pacha (as none of the other Princesses accompanied them) for Constantinople, the whole of the ladies of the Harem and slaves were up all night.

I had been on a visit for three days at the Peninsular

and Oriental Hotel to some friends who arrived from Europe; and in the morning of that day, when in company with one of them, I had met Mr. B. of Cairo, near the British Post Office, and then told him that I protested against being sent to Constantinople, as it was a violation of my contract, which simply specified that my services were for Egypt only, and not for any other part of the Ottoman dominions.

He replied, "But, madam you must go, as we have no time to procure anybody else."

I replied, "No, No!"

"But you will return to the Harem this evening?"

My answer was, "Yes!" and that was the last time I had the pleasure of conversing with the banker; although when I afterwards returned to Alexandria, broken down in mind and body, I frequently saw him pass my Hotel, as I was sitting in the balcony to inhale the fresh sea-breeze.

Between three and four o'clock in the morning, the bed-scene similar to that which had taken place on our departure from Cairo, was enacted, and the beds, bedding, and baggage were shipped on board the steam-tenders, and then transferred to the *Mehemet Ali* frigate.

At five o'clock an eunuch came and called me, as he wanted to have my bed, &c., packed up. I arose, dressed myself, and admitted him. When I came to inquire for my breakfast I was met by the reply, "*Malesch*, Madam! *Malesch*, Madam! You shall have it in an hour's time." I perfectly understood what that meant, and I obtained nothing—no, not even a crust of bread, nor a cup of coffee!

Shortly afterwards the barber came into the Grand Eunuch's room, and cut the Prince's hair, which was picked up and thrown out of the window into the Mediterranean Sea, as the other had been into the Nile, and with the same ceremony. It was a most imprudent act, but done at the express desire of the Viceroy, and was the cause of the

Grand Pacha falling ill soon after his arrival at Constantinople.

As soon as the *perruquier* had quitted the palace, we were hurried upstairs to put on our things; and on our return into the Grand Eunuch's room, I found all the Ministers of State waiting, *en grande tenue,* to pay their respects to the little Prince.

As soon as this *besa los manos* was finished, the Grand Eunuch came and told me that I was to accompany the Prince on board the frigate. I was astonished—nay, electrified—at receiving such an intimation. I declined to go. I requested to be allowed to proceed into my chamber to fetch my travelling-bag, keys, and parasol, which I had left on the divan. But no; that "spectre of a man" told me that his orders were imperative not to leave me until he had seen us safely on boaad the frigate; and thus, without having had anything between my lips since I quitted the *salle à manger* at the Peninsular and Oriental Hotel on Saturday evening, and although it was my Sabbath, still, *nolens volens,* I was forced to go on board the Egyptian frigate. I had fully expected that when the levée was over I should have found my breakfast in my room; but I was egregiously deceived.

"Well," thought I to myself, "if this is a specimen of the treatment I am to expect on my voyage, and during my sojourn at Constantinople, I shall be heartily glad when I have finished out the term of my contract with the Viceroy!" which was, however, much nearer its conclusion than I then dreamed of.

Entering the carriage in the courtyard, we drove round to the Viceroy's bath-room, from which a marble-paved corridor led us on to the palace landing-stairs; there we embarked on board a small steam-tender, under a salute of five guns for the Grand Pacha.

There we were received with the usual honors. I inquired

for my breakfast, but no kind genius came to administer to the cravings of my hunger, although the Grand Pacha had, previously to leaving his head-nurse, been well supplied with symmets and boiled milk.

The whole of the quarter-deck was partitioned off by a thick canvas screen, which prevented the officers and crew from being able to catch a glimpse of any of the females. No! not even as they ascended the gangway ladder, the sides of which were closely covered in with similar material.

About twenty minutes after we had reached the frigate, the Princess Epouse, accompanied by the other two wives, came alongside, attended by their suite. They were all closely veiled.

Ten minutes later, the Validè Princess embarked in Her Highness's small yacht, under a Viceregal salute of eleven guns from the fort and frigates, the yards of which were dressed and manned as she ascended the gangway-ladder. The band of the regiment on board struck up the " Sultan's march," one of Donizetti's noisiest pieces. She remained on deck, chatting to their Highnesses the Princesses, while her suite went below and arranged her berth and their own.

Twenty minutes afterwards, Ismael Pacha, the Viceroy, came on board to take leave of those members of his family who were going on a visit to the Sultan. It is utterly impossible for my feeble pen-drawing to sketch with fidelity this parting scene; still I will do my best to convey to my readers a delineation of its leading incidents.

The Viceroy, who was received with the usual honors (a salute of twenty guns) on reaching the frigate, proceeded into the saloon. He was soon followed by his illustrious mother, the three wives, the Grand Pacha, and myself, the ladies of the Harem, *Ikbals*, and slaves. Then began a blubbering scene; for the whole of the women, from the highest to the lowest, commenced, not crying, but absolutely howling. Had they been the professional mourners at a Caireen's obsequies, they could not have enacted their parts better.

His Highness the *Baba* took it very coolly, and, if I might judge from his countenance, which is rather a difficult thing to do, as Turks seldom or ever show whether they are pleased or vexed, I should say that this scene did not affect him in the least.

After their Highnesses had given vent to their chagrin, the *Baba* rose up, approached his mother, kissed and embraced her most affectionately. He then kissed the Grand Pacha, patted him on the back, as also Her Highness, the Princess Epouse (who was crying most bitterly), wished her good bye, exclaimed, "Oh, *Zeneb-Nina! Zeneb-Nina!*" and when Her Highness turned away, sobbing as if her heart would break, His Highness turned towards me, looked intently at me, and as I caught the glance of his eye, he smiled most courteously, nodded to me, again looked at their Highnesses, turned round once more, appeared bewildered at beholding the scene before him, and left for the shore.

Soon this scene of woe and grief was changed into a marine picnic for *findjans* of coffee, sweetmeats, and cigarettes. These were handed round to their Highnesses, who partook of the former but sparingly, yet smoked away at the latter with great gusto.

Again I sallied forth, not like Cœlebs in "Search of a wife;" nor Dr. Syntax in quest of "The Picturesque;" but like a Bordeaux kopek, "dog" (for was I not looked upon as such in the eyes of the true believers around me? for the Germans were left behind, and I was the only unbeliever among this Moslem freight), who takes his morning rounds to find his *déjeûner;* for many a time and oft have I sat in the balcony of my residence in the *Cours d'Albert,* at that birthplace of our unfortunate sovereign, Richard II., watching *les chiens de cette jolie ville,* rummaging among

17

the heaps of offal, that are daily placed in the road, and selecting their dainty morsels; but, like many of them, who sniffed at the inviting mounds and found nothing to suit them.

On my return I found that the ladies of the Harem, and slaves, had stolen a march upon me: that, being as hungry as hunters themselves, they had eaten and drunk all up. At half-past eight o'clock, the frigate steamed away out of the roadstead of Alexandria, and then began my experience of life on board of an Egyptian frigate, especially when freighted with such a precious cargo as a Viceregal party.

The *Mehemet Ali* was a forty-two gun screw steamer, manned with a motley crew of Turks, Egyptians, Maltese, &c., and having a regiment of soldiers on board (most assuredly not a fitting escort for a Harem, if all that I have heard is true of those most moral Turks); but I saw quite enough to make me wish never to see more of it.

The upper deck, as I have previously described, had an awning over it, if I may be allowed the expression, thick canvas, and most appropriately so, as a promenade for their Highnesses and their suites, and comfortably fitted up with sofas and easy-chairs, but on which they never promenaded, or lolled about once during the whole voyage; so that I and the Grand Pacha Ibrahim had it all to ourselves.

The saloon was divided into three parts, having on each side six smaller cabins, in four of which were placed the ladies of the Harem, in attendance on the Validè Princess of Egypt; the other two were occupied by the Princess Epouse, and one of the little Princesses, Zeneb, who accompanied us. It was carpeted and furnished with pretty china vases, filled with growing exotics, tables, sofas, chairs, and divans. From the top of the panels hung large mirrors.

At the stern-end was a round cabin similarly fitted up, which was appropriated to the use of the Viceroy's mother, from which steps led up to the poop-deck, on which was ranged a large divan.

The poop-saloon was enclosed with large plate-glass windows, which were made to slide back at pleasure, and to which were affixed iron shutters. The hangings were of lace and crimson silk; branch silver candelabras were fixed to the panels.

The smaller cabins were similarly fitted up, having, like the saloons, boxes of Huntley and Palmer's biscuits, to which the slaves helped themselves; and large baskets of *bonbons*, besides two earthenware bottles, filled with water, with gold stoppers.

His Highness the Prince, together with his little sister, slept on the floor of the end saloon, surrounded, as I have already described him at Ghezire, by his slaves and nurses. Descending a staircase, I proceeded to the lower deck, which was so dark, that it was requisite to light it day and night.

This saloon was uncarpeted, and contained a deal table, a few wooden stools, and some rush-bottom chairs. On each side of it were ranged six berths, each of which was fitted up with a three-feet bare board, having two cotton coverlets placed thereon, not a mattress, or any other kind of bedding, or toilet utensils of any description. One of those most comfortless berths was appropriated to me; so that I found, while steaming on the bosom of the Mediterranean, I was deprived of the order of precedence which had been assigned me in Egypt on the banks of the Nile, which promotion was given to the ladies of the Viceregal Harems, while I took up my place among the lowest slaves on board (except the coffee and cigarette makers and scullery maids,) as the low-caste black slaves occupied the other eleven berths.

This was a change of position and scene I had not contemplated; however I held my peace. I knew that, cooped up in that wooden barrack, I had no chance of redress; so that I abided my time. Still I could not help thinking that my visit to the Viceroy in his bedchamber, although their

Highnesses, the wives, sent me there at that early hour, well knowing that the *Baba* could not have risen, as he had scarcely arrived more than two hours from Cairo, and the presence of that overbearing dame, Ibrahim Pacha's widow, had something to do with this rude treatment.

At the end of this (the second saloon) a flight of steps led up on to the deck. About half-past eleven o'clock the eunuchs brought the Princesses' breakfast to the door of the saloon; but as they were all suffering from *La Maladie de Mer*, as also the whole of their retinue, it was removed. I made another attempt to get some refreshment, but all in vain; and, unwell and fatigued, I retired to my miserable berth, rolled up my paletot, placed it under my head for a pillow, and laid my weary limbs down upon the wadded coverlet, having then been no less than sixteen hours fasting. Thus, though the table of the Princesses was covered with Arab and Turkish delicacies, I was left without anything.

There I lay, with numbers of slaves snoring like grampuses around me, until nine o'clock at night, when the eunuchs came down to lock up the hatchets, just as if we had been a band of slaves on a voyage across the middle passage. I then appealed to the humanity of that phantom of the stronger sex, who, possessing a little of the milk of human kindness within his breast, brought me a cordial cup filled with chicken broth, and a piece of European bread, so stale, that it was almost as hard as a stone, with a cup of bad-tasted water; and this was my feast after a fast of more than twenty-four hours! I think on that occasion I can safely say I had accommodated myself to circumstances. The fast I had been obliged to endure, added to my bad state of health, confined me to my almost unbearable berth (situated close to the chain of the rudder) the whole of the following day.

Her Highness the Princess Epouse now visited me, and

after expressing her surprise at finding me so ill, inquired if all the " *à la Franca* " ladies suffered in that manner.

The doctor, who was an Italian, attended me, advised me to make an effort to rise, which I did, and went on deck. My usual refreshments while on board that detestable frigate chiefly consisted of a cup of tea in the morning, without any milk, a piece of dry bread, a few Palmer's biscuits, which the Grand Eunuch had the kindness to send me.

In the middle of the day I had a little chicken-broth, thickened with rice, and the fowl, of which it had been made, served up with it, and a little fruit; and at six o'clock similar rations were given me for my dinner. Then did I wish I could have sent a *Mektoub*, "letter," to the Viceroy, in which I should have appealed to his feelings as a Prince and a gentleman; for Ismael Pacha, into whose service I had entered, finished his education in France, was courteous in his general deportment towards me, and well knew what were the requirements of a European lady; for had he not one "caged up" in the Harem in the citadel, with whom I had conversed? Besides, there was a *chef de cuisine,* and staff about him, and had His Highness himself adopted proper means, that intelligent Frenchman or his assistants, would have gone on board the frigate before our embarkation, and have arranged everything for my comfort, but it was all *Boosh! Boosh!* But the *clique* were endeavoring to supplant them, and as an exodous of French attendants took place after my departure from Alexandria, in all probability they have been replaced by Frankfort *Dienst boten,* "servants," and *Deutsche Küche,* "German cookery."

There was an under-current in motion as regards myself, but neither the source nor mouth of it could I as yet discover; later, however, both were clearly developed. Had I but then been able to send forth a missive by the hands of a trusty messenger—I always had one at hand in the

Harem (one over whom Prince Baksheesh had no power, and with whose actions that Sovereign Prince of Egypt dare not and could not interfere,) my Prince—the Grand Pacha Ibrahim would not have left me in this state.

As I was constantly perambulating the frigate from stem to stern, I had an opportunity of seeing the ample provisions that had been laid in for the creature-comforts of their Highnesses and suite, who were sumptuously served every day.   It was only the *Nazarani kelb*, " the creeping Christian dog," my unbelieving self, that was left to feed off the crumbs that fell from the daughters of the Prophet's table, at which, however, my heart turned sick, and I found the scanty diet I had prescribed myself more palatable.

Daily did the Prince run up and down the deck.   One day I had observed that several of the port-holes were left open, and that the Prince had approached close to them. By them were sitting the two Grand Eunuchs smoking their *Tchibouks*.   I told them to order them to be closed— they only smiled.   Nevertheless, I insisted upon its being done, for well did I know that if that " dot of humanity " had fallen into the sea, neither my life, nor that of the Grand Eunuchs, were worth ten minutes' purchase after that event had taken place.   I had now gathered such an insight into the mysteries of Harem life, and the manner in which, in this the nineteenth century, Viceroys of Egypt and Egyptian Princes had been launched into eternity, that I kept, as the sailors say, " my weather eye open," and the Grand Pacha was hale and sound when I took my leave of him in the old Palace at Bebek, in 1864.   If the port-holes had been left open with any sinister purpose, *Allaha chukur*, " God be praised," the fish gained not their prey.   What is written, is written, *Bismillah ! Bismillah !*

Often did the Prince stop and amuse himself by looking at the almost countless number of fowls, pigeons, turkeys, quails, and sheep being fed.   He had a perfect mania, as all the inmates of the Harem seem to have, for eating crude vegetables, so that he looked most wistfully at the basket-loads of vegetables, gourds (which were actually piled up like cannon-balls,) bushels of onions, hundreds of lettuces, thousands of cucumbers and lemons, of which they were particularly fond, baskets of cherries, sour green plums, green tamarinds, strawberries, cans of sour milk, and im-mense lumps of ice. It is almost impossible for me to give an estimate of the immense quantities of all the above eatables which were consumed by the Viceregal party.

Close to the *caboosh*, " kitchen," were ranged several wooden benches, on which the cooks were engaged daily, arranging their fruits and pieces of melon in glass dishes as their Highnesses the Princesses, and in fact all Arabs, have a particular *penchant* for them, and will consume the contents of six of them daily, although each is as large as the round part of a common-sized crockery pan.

Their Highnesses amused themselves by stuffing and gormandizing (especially munching fruit and crude vegetables) from four o'clock in the morning until twelve at night : The crew and soldiers were frequently in a state of inebriety, which was caused by the quantity of *araki*, " a spirit distilled from dates," that they drank. This rather surprised me, as I had always understood that it was contrary to the Mahometan religion for Moslems to imbibe spirituous liquors —that is what they termed their *kef*, " dolce far niente." Sometimes they would amuse themselves by singing their favorite Bacchanalian song.

During the whole of our voyage, which lasted seven days, when it might easily have been accomplished in four, a deputation of women consisting indiscriminately of both rich and poor, from the numerous places at which we stopped, came off, bringing with them large baskets filled with fruit of every kind then in season, especially oranges, lemons, gourds, cherries, plums, sweetmeats, cucumbers, cakes, jams, candied fruits, besides presents of native earthen jars, toys (some of which were very ingeniously made), superb open-worked silk stockings, native stuffs, shawls, gums in large jars, the greater portion of which were filled with the Turkish Delight," the *Lentiscus,* or "gum mastic," of Scio (the sale or traffic in which is "a monopoly, and is a fruitful source of illegal action and crime in many a form"); also a kind of porridge made of flour, water, sugar, almonds, both green and blanched, limepips, &c., which was, for I often tasted it, as sweet as syrup.

When we arrived off the island of Scio, their Highnesses the Princesses, who were unveiled, were in the saloon, amusing themselves by looking at silk stockings and various other articles that had been presented to them by some of the deputation. A number of boats put off from the shore, most of them full, among whom were the Governor and his officials, as also hucksters, who had brought things off for sale.

So intent were their Highnesses looking at *les nouveautés,* that I did not heed the approach of the boats. I was standing near the windows of the saloon (which, as previously explained, had been drawn back), when I noticed a number of boats glide round and round the frigate. All at once they approached so near that the men, had they felt disposed, could have put their hands in the openings and have jumped in. I observed the Validè Princess and the Princess Epouse smile, when they looked at the occupants in the boats, and kept asking whether I did not think some of them "*Guzel*" and others "*Batal?*" But as the men (perhaps thinking that they were only some of the ladies of the Harem, or slaves) drew nearer, the Princess Epouse shrieked out and drew back; the Validè Princess jumped up on a divan, and then placing myself before them while they played "bo-peep," and acting according to their orders, I returned the salaam of the men in the boats, who all placed their oars upright and salaamed me. This afforded the Princesses great amusement, as they enjoyed the sport amazingly, and every now and then kept asking me if I did not think it great fun, as they were sure that those officials would go back and report that they had seen their Highnesses the Princesses, when they had only been salaamed by the Grand Pacha's governess.

I only smiled; but it is a fact that those individuals had gazed upon their Highnesses, and that, too, when they were (believe it whether you like it or not, ye sons of the Prophet, Moslems and true believers) *unveiled !*

The moment that the Princess Epouse screamed, the farce was ended, for down rushed the eunuchs and drew the curtains across the opening, while those on deck with drawn swords, warned the intruders off. How little did they suspect that the Peris of the Harem had been gazed upon by other eyes than theirs and those of their liege Lord and Prince ! For, had they but known it, the boats and their live freights would have been fired upon by the frigate's guns until they had gone to their last account. One old Turk, thinking that I was one of the Peris destined for the seventh heaven, seemed quite in ecstacy when I returned his salaam by the Princess's orders, at which his Highness smiled; but as he was well advanced in years she exclaimed *" Batal, Madame ! Ihtyar, Madame !"* "He is ugly, he is old Madame."

The Princesses accepted of such presents as took their fancy, in return for which they gave baksheesh of gold Egyptian coins.

Often and often did I think that I should never leave that cockpit of an Egyptian frigate, and vowed if ever the Almighty vouchsafed that I should land on the lovely shores of the Bosphorous, nothing should induce me ever again to tread the decks of the *Mehemet Ali* frigate. At that time I often glanced in the mirrors of their Highnesses' splendid saloon, at my attenuated frame, sunken eyes, and blanched cheeks, and thought of the misery and discomfort I had suffered, but little dreamed that I had yet to endure much more before I was released from my unprofitable, irksome, and thankless task. I had, however, found out the utter worthlessness of my " Special Prince's " assertion, that, if the Viceroy Ismael Pacha was polite to me, I had but to ask, and nothing would be refused me. Well, the last time I had the honor to see the Viceroy (which was, as I have already stated, on board that detested frigate) he was polite to me ; and, acting up to the advice of one of those "Eighteen other Princes " who govern Egypt, I have asked for my just rights since my return to Europe, but they have not been accorded to me.

So beautiful beyond conception is the approach to Constantinople (the Byzantium of the ancients, the *Eis-tin-polin* of the Greeks, and the *Is-tam-boul* of the Turks) that I dare not attempt a pen-and-ink drawing of the wonderful panorama displayed to me in all directions. That prince of French writers of travels, Theophile Gautier, has painted that varied landscape with fidelity, when he states that " never did outline more magnificent display its undulation and indentations between sea and sky. It is one of the favorite spots of the world's history ; another scene in which she loves to engrave in perishable matter, *imperishable* words."

As soon as the frigate reached *Bebek,* " Babec," it came to anchor off the Sultan's palace at that village, which is beautifully situated on the water's edge. Then salutes were fired by the Turkish frigate that lay off it. There we remained full two hours, during which time the Validè Princess received the deputation sent by the Validè Sultana. It consisted of twelve ladies of the Imperial Harem, who came off in three caïques, unattended, however, by any eunuchs. They were by no means beautiful in appearance, and were attired in different colored silk dresses. Their feet were encased in white cotton stockings, which hung down about their heels, over which some wore yellow boots, and others *babouches*. Round their faces was wrapped one end of a piece of white net, and the other was passed over their heads, which it quite enveloped, so that the whole of their features were distinctly visible. On their shoulders they wore colored stuff cloaks, with sleeves, and two large capes.

Leaving their shoes at the door of the saloon-stairs, they descended into the saloon. On entering, they salaamed the Validè Princess, after which coffee and cigarettes were handed round. They did not remain much longer than a quarter of an hour.

After they had taken their departure a whole bevy of ladies from the different Harems of the Imperial family, as well as those of the Ministers of State and nobility, came on board; and after they were gone, a host of females belonging to the Turkish merchants and Imperial shopkeepers, bringing with them numerous rich and costly presents, and some of the most curious description. After these receptions had taken place, the Sultan's Grand Eunuch, dressed *à la Européenne*, and wearing one of the most superb diamond rings perhaps ever seen, valued at 125,000*l*., on the little finger of his right hand, came on board. He descended into the cabin of the Validè Princess's Grand Eunuch; there, in company with the Princess Epouse's Grand Eunuch, he sat down, smoked a pipe, and sipped a *findjan* of coffee.

Scarcely, however, had he finished this refreshment when was heard the cry, "Men overboard!" for seven of the Viceroy's soldiers, who were being lowered into a caïque from the side of the frigate, were upset into the Bosphorus. Fortunately they were soon picked up, and sustained no bodily harm, but were much frightened at their ducking, which is not to be wondered at, as the clear blue waters of that lovely river swarm with sharks. After tranquillity had been restored on board, the Sultan's Grand Eunuch proceeded into the saloon to pay his respects to the Validè Princess and her Viceregal Highness. There that important functionary was received with all the honors due to his rank and position. *Findjans* of coffee, served in elegant gold filigree *zarfs*, encrusted with precious stones, placed upon a gold salver and covered with a violet-colored silk velvet cloth, one mass of gold embroidery ; and a *kanum kaloun*, filled with fragrant gold-leaved tobacco, was then served him, which he remained smoking until their Highnesses were ready to land.

In the mean time three caïques had been drawn up to the gangway ladder, which, as well as the whole of the deck, had been covered with fine Brussels carpeting. All being ready the Sultan's Grand Eunuch rose up off the sofa and led the Princess Validè to the gangway. He took hold of the front of her robe, on one side walked her own tall stately sinister-looking creole of a Grand Eunuch, and on the other our own noble Grand Eunuch, who was followed by the Princess Epouse. Behind walked three of our other Eunuchs, dressed *à la Européenne* in black, as they all doffed their Egyptian costume while in Turkey, holding drawn swords in their hands.

On each side of the gangway stood the naval and miltary officers. Behind the Princess Epouse walked the ladies of both those princesses, who, on reaching the gangway, formed themselves into a double line.

Then the two Princesses descended into the Viceregal caïques, each of which were about ten yards long, pointed at the stern and prow, of a very deep build, drawing a considerable depth of water. At the bottom of the caïque were placed several mattresses covered with satin, which, as also the cushions that were placed round it, and which formed a divan, were covered with violet velvet cloth richly embroidered with gold. Their Highnesses seated themselves in the centre, near the prow.   On a raised deck was placed a piece of carpet, on which knelt the eunuchs, who had divested themselves of their patent leather overshoes, in which silver spurs were fixed, those of the Grand Eunuchs being of gold, as whenever the Princesses take carriage exercise they ride by the side on horseback.

All of them had swords belted round their waists : those of the Grand Eunuchs being gold hilted, with crimson velvet scabbards inlaid with gold.   The Turkish standard floated at stern and prow.

Each caïque was manned by four caidjis, attired in white crape silk open-worked shirts, blue silk trousers, which reached a little below the knee, sky-blue velvet jackets, embroidered in gold, and wore fezes on their heads.   The Caidji Bachi, a very old, grey-headed man, sat in the stern and steered the Viceregal party.

Then I and the Grand Pacha and the young Princess, his sister, attended by his suite descended into our caiques, which were similarly fitted up to that of the Validè Princess, only that they were furnished with crimson drapery, and the caidjis being dressed in crimson.   After us the Grand Eunuch descended, holding in his hand a black silk velvet bag completely covered with silver, which contained the jewels of the Validè Princess.   He was attended by another eunuch, carrying her Highness's cash box, which was similarly covered.   It had a silver handle in the centre.   Both of these caskets were carried in a separate caïque, and covered with a cloth of gold.

The yards of the frigate were dressed and manned, the band struck up the Sultan's March, and a Viceregal salute was fired.   Then the water procession commenced ; the caïque containing their Highnesses the Princesses led the way, and our own followed in its wake.   After them the ladies of the Viceregal Harem descended into six caïques, which were fitted up with red silk ; then followed in other caïques the whole of the slaves, and all were rowed to the steps of the grand entrance of the Sultan's palace at Bebek.

This is an immense long two-storied stone structure, facing the Bosphorus, of which it commands most extensive and beautiful views, having pavilions at each end, which are occupied by the eunuchs. In the centre is the grand entrance, which is reached by a flight of marble steps. The portico is supported by four Corinthian pillars, at each end of which are two large gilded lamps.

The centre of the palace projects considerably forwards, over which run three square balconies. The promenade before it, which is paved with stone, forms (oddly enough, as it destroys the privacy of the place) the fashionable rendezvous of the *élite* of Bebek, a very pretty village, and its suburbs ; and on which hundreds of persons also land from their caïques, and lounge up and down in the evening.

CHAPTER XXIV.

HERE we landed, and were received with full honors, the military band playing at a distance the Sultan's March, and the frigates booming away their Viceregal salute ; while, drawn up in double line, stood a host of the ladies of the Imperial Harem, who on that occasion were richly clad in silk robes, wearing a profusion of diamonds and other precious stones. Their hair hung down their backs in two long plaits, like Polish women, and the ends tied with broad rich ribbons of various colors. Then their Highnesses the Princesses passed through an immense marble hall, the floor of which was covered with matting, with long strips of handsome Brussels carpet laid over it in the form of a square. The walls were papered. From the ceiling, which was beautifully painted with views of Egyptian and Turkish scenery, and bordered with the representation of numerous musical instruments, hung suspended several magnificent chandeliers.

Ascending a flight of marble stairs, similarly covered, we entered the Grand Reception-room. The floor was matted, having pieces of Brussels carpet laid down along the sides, and across the top and bottom. The walls were painted in drab color; a large chandelier hung suspended from the ceiling, which was also painted with landscapes.

In the centre stood a long, narrow, plain white marble table, standing on gilded legs, on which was placed a superb beautiful Sèvres china painted vase, with jugs to match, similar to those used as ale tankards in England, but as large as ordinary toilet ewers; also a small bottle containing otto of roses; two cordial cups, with lids and saucers, which are used to contain water, and serve the purpose of glasses; and two very elegant damask napkins, richly embroidered in gold, with deep bullion fringe.

Opposite to it, but against the wall, stood a similar table, on which rested a large mirror. In the centre stood an enormous vase, on each side of which were placed colored fancy wickerwork baskets, lined with crimson and blue silk, filled with bonbons. They were covered over with pieces of silk of the same color, which were looped up at the handles with bunches of ribbon and artificial flowers. On each side stood silver candelabra.

On the opposite side, facing it, stood another table similarly arranged. At the bottom of the room was a divan, covered with stamped red velvet, ornamented with gold leaves, ranged underneath the four great windows that looked into the garden, very small, and anything but cheerful-looking, which also commanded a view of the lovely heights.

On a fancy table was placed a superbly-gilded musical-clock, indicating Turkish time, which played tunes instead of striking the hours, half-hours, and quarters.

About half-a-dozen chairs, covered to match the sofa, were placed about in various parts. At the top stood another divan, having cushions as large as mattresses at each end (on which squatted the ladies in attendance), much smaller than that which we had previously described, but similarly covered. This was arranged under the three large windows, from which the *mucharabiehs* were removed, and overlooked the Bosphorus, commanding one of the finest views the eye ever looked upon.

Out of this large room branched off four corridors, two leading to the right hand, and two to the left. One of the rooms on the latter was appropriated to the Validè Princess, as her private sitting-room. And here I may as well remark, that I was extremely fortunate in having accompanied their Highnesses; for, otherwise, I should never have had the opportunity of entering the Imperial Harems, this being the first time in the annals of Turkish history that any Egyptian Princess had had the honor of having one of the Imperial Palaces appropriated for her reception, and of a *Nazarani kelb,* "Christian dog," having defiled them with her presence.

Why such a mark of favor was shown to the widow of Ibrahim Pacha, I know not, unless, indeed, it was that the *poor* sovereign, who on his flying visit to Egypt, on his accession to the throne, had looked with a jealous eye upon the riches of his Crœsus of a vassal; for then, if report speaks truth, His Majesty urged that wealthy Prince to give him more tribute. That request was met with a most courteous negative; and the expediency of which was based upon the following clause of the Firman of May, 1841—viz. :—

"As each of the conditions settled as above is annexed to the privilege of hereditary succession, if a single one of them is not executed, that privilege of hereditary succession shall forthwith be abolished and annulled," so Ismael Pacha, Viceroy of Egypt, had no idea of acting contrary to the letter of that document.   We know that large presents were made to the Sultan at that time; and there is not a shadow of a doubt but the Validè Princess, whom His Majesty Abdul Aziz on this occasion " delighted to honor," was invited as an Imperial guest from political as well as personal motives; but what they were, time will, no doubt, disclose.

Well, to continue our description of the Viceregal guests' apartments.   The hangings were of yellow stamped velvet, embossed with several leaves and flowers.   The furniture of the divans and chairs corresponded.   The floor was matted, and covered with the usual pieces of Brussels carpet.   The walls were covered with embossed velvet of the same kind; the ceiling, which was very lofty, and from which hung suspended a massive silver chandelier, was beautifully painted.   In the centre of the room stood a round inlaid table, supported on gilded legs; on each side were ranged two similar ones, on one of which stood a superb gilt clock, that chimed the hours; and each side of it was similarly ornamented to that which we have previously described as being in the Grand Reception-room, with the exception that a large mirror, reaching down from the ceiling, rested on each table.

Crossing the Grand Reception-room, and passing into the second corridor, we entered, on the right hand, Her Majesty's bed-chamber.   The floor was matted with the usual carpeting.   The gilded iron bedstead was ornamented with sky-blue silk hangings, bespangled with silver crescents; at the foot and sides were gilded crescents, holding plumes of ostrich feathers.   Rich Persian rugs were placed at the sides of the bed, and by that of the divan, which stood underneath the three large windows which overlooked the garden and heights.   The divan, chairs, and cushions were covered with sky-blue satin, fringed with silver.   An inlaid console-

18

table stood on one side of the room, on which rested a large mirror, and on the top of the table were placed three inlaid caskets on gold legs, the largest of which contained Her Highness's treasure, and the others, jewelry, essences, and narcotics. On another table, facing the foot of the bed, stood a handsome gilt clock, having on each side a small elegantly-painted Sèvres china jug and basin, used for holding the perfumed water which is poured over the hands.

Then we passed into the room on the left hand, which was assigned to Her Highness's Lady of the Bed-chamber, whose office it was to relate tales to her, rub or champoo her limbs, until she fell off to sleep, which operation had a mesmeric effect upon the Validè Princess.

In the row of rooms that led straight along on the left-hand side, were placed the ladies of her Highness's suite. The room on the right-hand side, adjoining that of Her Highness's, contained her wardrobe. Her wardrobe-women slept in it, and there were ironed out daily the crumpled dresses, linen, &c. belonging to the Princess and her retinue.

The bath-room, which was fitted up with a marble bath, arranged with taps for cold and hot water, was situated opposite Her Highness's chamber. A small door opening out of it led into the boudoir, which was a moderate-sized room. Out of that a door led into the *cabinet d'aisance,* arranged *à la Turque,* having a small marble fountain in the centre; on a table stood two silver basins, one empty and the other filled with small calico napkins, fringed with gold thread, and on a silver rod hung several towels embroidered with gold. Passing along the other corridor on the same side, we entered the Princess Epouse's apartments. The sitting-room was similarly fitted up to the Grand Reception-room, the folding-doors in which led into another sitting-room similarly arranged, only having the hangings and furniture covered with pink satin. Then we passed into the bed-chamber, arranged like that of Her Highness the Validè Princess, the hangings and furniture of which were of crimson silk bespangled with gold stars and crescents. The cases of all the beds, which were left in the bedsteads without any coverlets, were of blue satin interwoven with bouquets of flowers.

Then we entered the Grand Pacha Ibrahim's sitting-room. The hangings and furniture were of red embossed satin with white lace curtains. Over the doors and windows were elegant gilded cornices. The floor was covered with matting, and round the sides were placed pieces of Brussels carpet. In it stood an English fireplace with a bright steel registered stove; on the chimney-piece, which was of white marble, rested a large mirror, and at each end stood a silver branch candelabra. In the centre was placed a large elegantly painted Sèvres jug, on each side of which stood two essence-bottles and drinking-cups of the same material. The walls were covered with red embossed paper. On the ceiling was painted Mazeppa and the wild horse, and beautiful vignettes of the fine arts filled up the corners.

Half-a-dozen elegant light fancy gilded occasional chairs, of English manufacture, as also twelve rosewood ones, covered with embossed crimson satin, corresponding with the *musnuds* which fitted up each corner of the room, were scattered about the apartment. In the centre stood a round marble table.

Then we passed into the Hall of Audience, which was lighted with ten immense windows. The floor was matted, the walls plainly painted, as also the ceiling, from which was suspended a large chandelier. A marble table stood in the centre; and two dozen heavy-looking square-seated chairs, covered with silk and ornamented with figured gilt-headed nails. In a square recess stood three marble fountains, used for ablutional purposes, and up to which the slaves climbed as the sun set, and washed their feet. Leading out of it was a double staircase, covered with matting, which led down into another hall running parallel to it. Passing into a corridor having rooms on both sides, like the saloon of an American steam-packet, (which were appropriated for the use of the upper slaves,) we entered at its extremity another spacious hall, and crossing that proceeded into other corridors.

The first on the right hand led into my chamber, and here, as had elsewhere been my fate, one of the worst furnished rooms in the palace was set apart for me. In fact, the apartment was similar in every respect to those occupied by the ladies of the Sultan's Harem, who were attached to the suite of their Highnesses the Egyptian Princesses, some of whom might, for aught I knew to the contrary, be His Majesty's *ikbals*. So that I should most unquestionably have been called fastidious, since I murmured at being treated as if I were one of the Sultan's favorites, which, *Dieu merci!* I was not; although, perhaps, for many reasons, they might have wished I had been. But, as Harem life had no charms for me, there was no more chance of my pleasing "the Sovereign of Sovereigns, the Light of the World," than there had been of my pleasing the Viceroy Ismael Pacha, in the sense that the sister of His Highness's civil aide-de-camp evidently meant.

The floor was matted, and the ceiling painted. The hangings of the doors and the two large windows which overlooked the Bosphorus, together with the furniture, were of brown and black cotton, giving it a most dismal appearance. Everything European was excluded from it, as it was furnished with a divan, and on the floor lay two thin mattresses covered with the same fabric. These, with the addition of two silver-gilt candlesticks with glass shades, constituted all the effects; and, as usual, I had to do battle for the deficiencies, which I did, and came off victorious.

Proceeding across the hall, and facing my apartment, were the chambers of the ladies belonging to the Sultan's

Harem, the floors of which were matted, and the walls and ceilings painted. The hangings of the doors and windows, which overlooked the Bosphorus, were of figured cotton. The only furniture in each were two mattresses laid on the floor, which served them as divans by day and beds by night.

We then returned to the double staircase from whence we had descended. Opening a door on the left hand, we passed through a large room, then through another on the right, and thence down a long corridor; then we ascended six stairs, and entered the apartments occupied by the Validè Princess's Grand Eunuch, which comprised a sitting-room, the floor of which was covered with matting, and the walls and ceiling whitewashed. The hangings of the windows and doors were of white and crimson striped satin, the divans and chairs were covered with the same costly material.

At the side stood a marble console-table, on which was placed a handsome gilt clock, two beautiful Sèvres china jugs, two essence-bottles, and two drinking-cups to match, and two silver branch candelabras; leaving which we passed along another corridor to the right, the first door in which opened into the Grand Eunuch's bed-chamber. The floor was matted, and had strips of Brussels carpet laid down around the sides. In it stood a gilt iron bedstead with crimson silk hangings, on which was laid a wadded coverlet of the same material, and at each side was spread a fine Persian rug, a crimson figured satin divan, chairs with gilded backs covered with the same material, an ebony chest of drawers with white marble top, on which stood an elegant gilt clock and two large silver candelabras, a marble-top washing-stand with Sèvres china toilette service, two water-bottles, and drinking-cups to correspond.

Quitting this apartment we entered that of Khoorshid Pacha, the Validè Princess's Chamberlain's bedchamber, similarly arranged, and opening the door opposite, we walked into his sitting-room. The floor was covered with matting, the walls papered, and the ceiling beautifully painted. The divan and chairs, which were of ormolu and gold, were covered with faded blue satin, and the console-table was similarly fitted up to that in the Grand Eunuch's room.

Then descending down a flight of steps we reached the promenade, proceeding along which we entered the apartment of the Princess Epouse's Grand Eunuch's house, which was detached from the Palace, the basement floor of which was occupied by the officers belonging to the Sultan's household, who were in attendance on their Highnesses the Princesses and the Grand Pacha.

Ascending a flight of stairs, we entered the sitting and bed-rooms of our Grand Eunuch, which were similarly arranged to those of the Validè Princess's Grand Eunuch, except that the furniture and hangings were of plain red satin. The other rooms, both on the right and left, were occupied by the other eunuchs and male attendants.

Leaving this house, we ascended a steep, chalky hill, and opening a large pair of gates, we entered the grounds belonging to the Harem, which consist of a long walk lined with avenues of plane-trees, under which were placed two square marble baths, and at the extremity of the walk we passed into a large neglected kitchen-garden, which is situated upon the heights, and commands a view of the Palace, and one of the finest views of the Bosphorus and the city of Constantinople.

Then descending a noble avenue, we entered a small garden adjoining the Palace, in which stood two marble baths. It contained an immense number of lime, orange, almond, and tamarind trees; also beds of double-headed poppies. Then descending down a noble flight of marble steps, we crossed a large courtyard covered with sand like shingles. Then ascending another flight of steps, we re-entered the Palace by the grand entrance hall.

As soon as the Grand Pacha and myself had finished our inspection of the royal Palace and grounds, we returned to Her Highness's sitting-room, where I found dinner served up upon a large round tray with a silver rim.   It contained the usual viands, but was placed upon a large table, at which the whole party was seated.   This comprised not only the Viceregal children, but also the black nurses, all of whom made a most ludicrous group ; for they were seated on chairs with their legs cocked up like hens at roost, the seats not being wide enough to admit of their doubling themselves up like clasped knives, *a l'Arabe.*   Had the chairs, however, been as large as those which the late Viceroy Said Pacha was accustomed to sit in, they might have indulged in that mode, for all of them are of an enormous size.   Now and then the slaves kept swinging one leg about, and after the lapse of a few minutes, they wound it round the leg of the chair, but becoming tired of that operation, they all rose up and changed their legs, sat down again, and then resumed their hen-roost postures.

The little Prince and myself could not help bursting out into a fit of laughter at their *gaucherie.*   The table not being furnished with either knives, forks, or spoons, the whole of the party, except the Viceregal children (whose spoons, &c., had been unpacked) set to work at their dinner like savages, dipping their fingers into the dishes, helping themselves to whatever they liked, and then conveying those tit-bits to their mouths in a disgusting manner.

After I had witnessed these barbarians partake of their meal, I waited to see what had been provided for me, and, on inquiry, was told nothing ! that I must " pig " it with the nurses in that manner, " sans fourchette, sans couteau, sans rien."

I quitted the room in absolute disgust, nay, in anger.   I could not but think that this insult must have been pre-meditated, for there were about us the same domestics as we had had in Egypt. The Grand Eunuch was with us, the nurses all knew how I had been treated in the Palace at Ghezire—how my meals had been served up to me—what complaints I had made at being obliged to sit down at table with the European menials; and therefore there really was no excuse for my being placed upon a par, and made to hob-nob it with black nurses of the lowest caste.

As I have stated before, I knew that there had been an under-current at work; still it worked steadily on; but my patience was not exhausted, and I was resolved to stem against it. I perceived that the impetuosity of its course was becoming much more rapid since my arrival in what is styled, *par excellence*, the Ottoman dominions, and now I resolved to crush this hydra on the head, if possible. Leaving the room, I proceeded to the Princess Epouse, to whom I complained most bitterly, and point-blank told Her Highness that I could not, and would not, partake of my meals in that disgusting manner.

At first the Princess began to remonstrate with me, alleging that the slaves had not had time to unpack my luggage; for all the glass, china, plate, &c., which had been provided for me in the Harem at Ghezire had been sent on in the other frigate that had accompanied us, and therefore I must put up with it; and as to my viands, why no others could be cooked, and I must partake of the leavings of those slaves. "*Malesh, Malesh !*" "Madame, what does it matter !—what does it matter !"

But I now knew the character of the individual with whom I had to deal, so I replied, "*Mafesh, Mafesh, hanem Effendi !*" "Nonsense, nonsense, your highness !" and as I still insisted, orders were instantly given to have the knives, &c., unpacked, and other viands served up to me; and at the same time she instructed the slaves to go and fetch my dinner, and place it upon the table, and never again attempt to take their meals until I had finished.

I salaamed, and left Her Highness; but not until she had given orders that the Grand Eunuch should go and purchase me articles of the same furniture that I had had provided for me at Cairo, all of which had been left behind; and when I obtained them, my chamber soon assumed a European aspect.

Her Highness was, as I have already shown, ever ready to do her utmost to contribute to my comfort—she did all that lay in her power; so that it was not she who set the under-current in motion (oh, no, not she, indeed!—I had been tried and found "true as steel," and she placed the greatest confidence in me), but it was the clique about Ismael Pacha who had been setting it running all this time, and ignoramuses as they were, they thought I had not sense enough to know it. It was to them that I was indebted for all my sufferings, both mentally and bodily, while an inmate of the Harems of Egypt and Constantinople.

Cui bono? Woman is an enigma, and so I proved to them. I had been cajoled and flattered into the belief that when I went to Constantinople all would be "*Guzel! guzel!*" "Pretty! pretty!" but I had found it "*Batul! batul!*" "Bad! bad!"

Well, things went on rather more satisfactorily for a few days; but as Arab and Ethiopian nurses are like our neighbors on the other side of the water, who invariably *reviennent à leurs moutons*, so did those black denizens. For they soon took every opportunity of annoying me by bringing a host of the low-cast slaves into my room, dipping their fingers into the dishes before they were placed upon my table, squatting themselves down upon the divan in and on the floor of my chamber; in short, making it "the servants' hall," where they smoked and chattered away in high glee, to my extreme discomfort and abhorrence. Often when I held my finger up to them, as was my custom at Ghezire, and told them to leave my room, instead of obeying my injunction, they stared and grinned at me like idiots.

Things went on in this manner for some time, until I was obliged to call in the interposition of the Grand Eunuch, who ordered them to leave the room, and desired them not to repeat such conduct. Then for a while they would discontinue making my room "a liberty hall," and I was freed from all annoyance; but after a lapse of time they would break out again into their vagaries, slip slily into my chamber, whenever they could gain access thereto, and repeat their annoyance.

The sovereign ruler of the Ottoman dominions, Prince Baksheesh, was the instigator. In Egypt, they obtained baksheesh, through my means, because I never despoiled the Grand Pacha, as Shaytan did, but then distributed a portion of her purloinings among them, and they were content; but now they did not obtain any, as the Prince had no *Baba* near him to fill his pockets with silver or golden coins. So Shaytan could not propitiate her host of evil spirits, and they thought that poor I should be made to do so; but as I received no baksheesh, I had none to dispense.

Our daily life at Bebek was not quite so monotonous as it had been at Ghezire, and, but for my falling ill, it would have passed away most agreeably; for the Viceroy had sent a pony for the Prince, and a sweet pretty Arab steed for myself; both of which were never used during my sojourn at Istamboul.

We rose (I am speaking of myself and the Prince) at six in the morning; when, through the kind attention of one of the ladies of the Sultan's Harem, whom I will call Selina, I was served with a bottle of new milk, and a salver of *symmets*, "rings of milk-bread," like that which is so delicious in Italy, but having seeds on them, which taste like fresh pork.

At half-past seven we breakfasted, and at nine we went for a walk on the promenade, then passing along a road on the left hand, we proceeded through a large gate, which led us into the Palace grounds, which were laid out as a fruit and kitchen-garden. They were kept in a high state of cultivation, and being, in fact, neither more nor less than a part of the Heights, presented a most picturesque appearance, many of those elevations being covered with strawberry beds.

Here we used to purchase for a few *paras*, a plentiful supply of fresh-gathered fruit every morning from the *bostandji*, " gardener," as those grounds did not, as I first imagined, belong to the Sultan. Here, seated on mats, on which the *bostandji* laid Persian rugs, which, when he knew that our visits were almost diurnal, he procured from the Grand Eunuch, I often passed many hours with the Prince, he playing and enjoying his fruit by my side.

After we had partaken of what the Grand Pacha called his *Yorton Cilék*, " Strawberry Feast," we wandered about the Heights, on the top of which stood a small Greek *café*, which commanded an extensive and lovely view of the Bosphorus, and the cluster of picturesque villages which stood on its banks—there we rested.

We afterwards passed on to a market-place, which was in a most filthy and dilapitated condition ; but in rambling about it the Grand Pacha took great delight.

At twelve o'clock we returned to the Palace, then partook of dinner, the Prince dining with me, to the utter horror of the nurses, who did all in their power to prevent, as they termed it, such an abomination as the believer and the unbeliever eating together. But the Princess Epouse's *Malesch! Malesch!* frightened them out of their superstitious horror, and so far enlightened them, that they were obliged ever afterwards to look upon such as being perfectly orthodox, which perplexed and puzzled them not a little ; and then they thought that wonders would never cease, and would often exclaim, " What is written, is written ! " *Bismillah! Bismillah!* " In the name of the most merciful

God!" *Allah! il Allah! Mahomet Resoul Allah!*
"There is but one God, and Mahomet is His prophet!"

CHAPTER XXV.

ONE day, after the Grand Pacha had dined, he told the Grand Eunuch to send up into his apartment an immense chest, which had just arrived in a caïque. Upon being opened, it was found to contain some magnificent toys mechanically constructed, the value of which must have been upwards of 100*l.* I did not learn the name of the donor, but I think they were presents from one of His Highness's reputed partners. With these the little Prince often amused himself in the afternoons.

At five o'clock he supped; after which, we again sallied forth, sometimes on the promenade, and at others we went for a row in a caïque on the beautiful Bosphorus.

At eight o'clock we returned; but it was quite impossible to get His Highness to retire to rest at any stated period, so that I was obliged to request the *Hekim Bachi*, the Physician to the Viceregal family, who, unknown to the Viceroy, was also the medical attendant on Mustapha Pacha's family, to give the Grand Eunuch instructions that the little Prince should retire at nine o'clock.

These pleasant and agreeable times, however, soon came to an end; for, as I had foreseen, when the *Baba* had ordered his hair to be cut, on the eve of the departure of the Viceregal party from Alexandria, the Prince caught a slight cold during the voyage. This could have been easily cured had I been permitted, as I suggested, to give him a cordial-cup full of arrow-root at night, and a warm bath before retiring to rest. To this however the Princess Epouse would not consent, but called in the *Hekim Bachi*, who immediately placed him on starving diet, and ordered him to live on chicken broth, bread, and milk. He then gave me a packet of tasteless powders, some magnesia, and a bottle of syrup, with strict injunctions not to give the Prince more than a teaspoonful at a time; to put his feet in hot water, to let him have a basin of arrow-root when he retired to rest, and to have his chest and back rubbed with green oil.

The *Hekim Bachi* was a strange character; it was only of late years that he had resumed his professional pursuits; for finding that medicine did not bring sufficient " grist to the mill," he had turned his attention to farming. He was a clever man, but considered "the germs " of a disease quite beneath his treatment. In desperate cases he was extremely skillful; but he was not a proper person to be called in to attend upon any person with whose constitution he was unacquainted. How he managed to hold the appointment of *Hekim Bachi* to the Viceroy's Harem, while he was the medical adviser to Mustapha Pacha, the brother of Ismael Pacha (between whom there existed at that time a most deadly animosity) I am at a loss to know.

Preparatory to retiring to rest, Shaytan undressed him, and the Princess Epouse, accompanied by the ladies of both Harems, and a host of old crones, entered the room. Then a large brass basin was brought into the room by several slaves.

On one side of the foot of the Princess' bed sat his illustrious mother, the Grand Pacha sitting in the centre, and on the other side was the governess. A slave then advanced and cast some fuller's earth into the brass basin, while the whole assembly exclaimed *Bismillah! Bismillah!* Then hot water was poured upon it after which a thick wadded coverlet was drawn over the whole party, and thus they had the pleasure of nothing more or less than a vapor bath, while His Highness kept sipping some lime-flower tea; then his feet and legs, which had remained in hot water for some time, were taken out, and rolled up in the coverlet, which had served the purpose of a vapor bath. After this a brazier of live charcoal was brought in, into which some ground coffee was thrown, white candied sugar, aloe-wood, myrrh, some peculiar aromatic resin and gum, the fumes of which were wafted into the Prince's face by the Princess Epouse, and his night attire was held over it. Some large pieces of cotton wadding were now held over the brazier until they became thoroughly impregnated with its fumes, and then placed on his chest and back; and in that state His Highness was put to bed. The whole of the spectators present kept continually exclaiming *Bismillah! Bismillah! Bismillah!* which brought to my recollection the celebrated incantation scene in Webber's opera of "Der Freyschutz."

The next day Shaytan, the head-nurse, contrary to the strict injunctions of the governess, carried the Prince down into the apartment of one of the black slaves, where he caught a fresh cold, owing to the windows being open. As soon as I entered my chamber I missed the Grand Pacha, and proceeded·down the grand entrance-hall, in quest of the Prince. That vestibule at the moment looked as if harlequin with his magic wand in a Christmas pantomime had been at his handiwork; for there stood huge bales of the most costly silks, rich satins, soft velvets, fine French merinoes, nets, lawns, linens, calicos, muslins, both white and colored, India and Cashmere shawls, silk stockings, huge bales of Parisian boots and shoes of almost every size and description. There were rich chased caskets, whose contents comprised tiaras of magnificent diamonds, almost peerless in value, ear-rings, bracelets, belts, clasps, chains, rings, necklaces, sword-hilts, amulets, zarfs of unparalleled beauty, encrusted with most precious jewels, and numerous other gems of art, the brightest and most elegant of which the Grand Eunuch kindly handed to me to feast my eyes upon. All of them were most unique specimens of the handicraft of man and of the mineral kingdom. In short, not being an *artiste*, I cannot give pen-and-ink drawings of them.

Boxes covered with silks, containing Japan china *findjans* gold filigree *zarfs*, most richly encrusted with diamonds and precious stones, gold salvers, silver ewers and basins, caskets of jewels, and a host of magnificent miscellaneous objects of *vertu*. In short, the sight of them made me think that I stood on fairy ground. It seemed as if the Viceroy Ismael Pacha had suddenly become the master of Aladdin's Wonderful Lamp, which he must have found in one of the newly-excavated caves on the banks of the Nile, and, having rubbed it as the genii of old did, had become possessed of untold wealth, and thinking perhaps that His Majesty the Sultan Abdul Aziz ought at least to have a share of the treasure-trove, he despatched the precious coin dug out of the bowels of the earth of Egypt to England, France, Italy, in short, all over the continents of Europe and Asia, which enabled this Sinbad of the nineteenth century to collect tegether the most costly manufactures of the world, and had sent them as presents to his suzerain the poor Sultan, from his Crœsus of a vassal—for the estimated value of them, now. a well-established fact, was upwards of half a million of English pounds sterling. It is, indeed, no fiction when I say that were it possible to strike the spades upon the right spots, the whole sod of Egypt would, if turned up by manual labor, become a rival to California—for the cotton mania has sent such heaps of gold into the land of the Pharaohs, which the Arabs have buried in the earth, that it may be said to be coated with that precious metal.

The supposed object of these valuable presents was not an ostentatious desire to display the prosperity of Egypt under the paternal administration of the Viceroy Ismael Pacha, but to manifest that prince's paternal solicitude that His

Majesty Sultan Abdul Aziz, " the light of the world, the sovereign of sovereigns," would take into his holy keeping (for is he not the Commander of the Faithful ? the Pacha, the Head of the Mahometan religion !) that " dot of humanity," the Grand Pacha, and bestowed upon him the coveted nomination to the Viceroyship.

All these commodities had been shipped in Alexandria on board the frigate *Ibrahim*, that had accompanied us. The Prince I found busy examining several beautiful articles ; and holding up some elegant diamond branches, made in the shape of small parasite plants, to me, he exclaimed, *Ay, Madame, Guzel ! Guzel ! Ay, Madame !* " Beautiful, Madame ! Beautiful, Madame ! " I kissed him on the cheek, but scolded him for having left his room, which imprudent act of the head-nurse rendered him an invalid to the time that I quitted the Old Palace.

The domestic life of the odalisques in the palace commenced at four o'clock in the morning, when the ladies of the Sultan's Harem left their couches, repeat their *namuz*, which they did every two hours during the livelong day, (for all of them were fanatics and most religiously inclined,) partook of *findjans* of coffee, and smoked cigarettes. At five, the whole of the inmates rose; at six our Grand Eunuch (I call him such in contradistinction to that cunning, crafty " spectre of a man," the Validè Princess's) said prayers to the ladies of all the three Harems, touched the centre of their foreheads with his finger, in which *kohl* had been placed, which left a small black spot upon it like a piece of sticking-plaster. One morning when he drew near toward me, for I had risen much earlier than usual, and happened to be present in the room with the Prince, he was on the point of bestowing upon me the caste-mark of the believer, but I drew back : he smiled and passed on. It was always after she had attended this prayer meeting that Selina, the lady of the Harem to whom I have already alluded, like a charitable geni came with new milk and hot bunns, exclaiming, " Eat and drink, in every bit and drop life's essence burns." At seven the Grand Pacha, his sister, and myself breakfasted together. At eight we took a promenade, but generally returned at ten. Sometimes we walked up and down the Esplanade, where we amused ourselves by gazing at the hundreds of pretty caïques that passed up and down the river freighted with numberless beautiful odalisques, wealthy merchants, well-to-do shop keepers, bustling Europeans, calculating *Ichondis*, " Jews," and crafty Armenians. Steamers passed along, with their decks covered with passengers of all classes and nations, steaming along at a rapid rate towards the different *Scales*, " landing-places," of the Turkish Babel. *Mashallah !* *Mashallah !* " How wonderful is the wisdom of God," exclaimed the little Prince, clapping his hands with delight, as he stood still every now and then gazing upon the animated scene before him.

Once when he saw a caïque upset its living freight into the river, and caught a good view of the occupants drenched to the skin, who had jumped into it again, he cried out, " Allah is great ! " then he added in Arabic, " *Allah ! il Allah ! Mahomet Resoul Allah* "—" There is but one God, and Mahomet is his prophet." Then we saw many a well-trimmed *Sandul* dash along full of odalisques, whose lovely dark orbs were fixed upon the little Prince as he stood near to the edge of the azure water of the lovely Bosphorus. And often, ah ! too often to be pleasing to the sight, baskets came floating past, most of which, gentle reader, in all probability contained the heads, and many of them the trunks, of human bodies. For it is no uncommon sight in Turkey, " where women always pay the penalty of their misdeeds " by a most severe and summary punishment, which, horrible to say, is privately enforced. Their bodies then are invariably placed in large baskets or sacks, which are thrown into

19

the lovely sapphire-looking river to feed the fish, which swarm here in shoals, against the catching of which there is an Imperial edict.

May not that injunction of the Padishahs have been occasioned by their Majesties' knowledge that the depths of that clear, bright stream is but too often converted into an immense city of the dead? And yet both I and the Prince had often watched with intense interest the singular manner in which the Moslems catch those forbidden tenants of the dreaded Bosphorus. Their mode of taking them is by smearing a piece of calico about the size of a table-cloth with the roe of some fish, then launching it into the river, and after the lapse of a few moments hauling up a most miraculous draught of fishes. But Europeans eschew them as they do the prawns out of the Ganges, which feed on the corpses cast into it, and which float past the ghauts at Calcutta as the wicker baskets do down the Bosphorus.

When the Grand Pacha saw those baskets float rapidly by the edge of the Promenade, he inquired of me what they contained? I informed His Highness that they contained the corpses of culprits (but what culprits I did not mention) who had been killed, as I supposed, for some crimes that they had committed. And yet most likely many of those baskets contained the murdered bodies of persons perhaps almost as innocent as the little Prince himself.

The basket and the sack in Turkey contain the victims of jealousy, which the handiwork of the Eunuchs has sent to their last account! for these spectres of men are, like the Thugs in India, adepts at strangulation. It is no uncommon thing in the Harems to hear them relate to each other, if not their own exploits, at least those of their predecessors in office, and I have often seen the elder ones give their fellow-phantoms illustrations of the manner in which those deeds have been accomplished. This they do, with the utmost *sang froid*, while the spectators exclaim, *Aferin ! Aferin !* "Well done! well done!"

The little Prince also took great delight in looking at the *Kachambas* as they glided along filled with *galiondji*, "sailors" belonging to some of the different European vessels at anchor off Galata; for contrary to the general custom of the Turks, he did not possess such a hatred for all who differed from him in point of faith.   He did *not* dislike the Franks, but he abhorred those unclean beasts! those misbelieving dogs!—the Jews; and on one day when he pointed his little hand to a headless corpse that we saw floating by a caïque which lay at anchor in the stream, he imquired of me, if that were not the body of a *kopek*, "dog of an Israelite?"   I replied that I did not know.   *Basham itchiam*, "By my head! " *jehenum*, "Hell" "will be the portion of that accursed band, as there is but one Allah," added the little Pacha, clapping his tiny hands.

Time after time, barges passed close to the promenade filled with *araki*, "corn-brandy," and freighted with that harmless-looking white colorless liquid, the wine of Carnabat, for which Carnabat merchants find a ready market, and many a cask of which is kept lodged in the well-secured cellars of wealthy Turks, although it was the *Kishmet* of that extract not to be drunk by all good Mussulmans.

After that we went and climbed up to the Greek café, and there we sat gazing with wonder and delight on the surpassing loveliness of the picturesque scenery by which it is surrounded.

At noon their Highnesses the Princesses dined; but if (which frequently happened) they went out in the morning in caïques or carriages, and did not return until late, none of the ladies of the Harem were allowed to partake of either dinner or supper, as the case might be, until their return. If they were absent much beyond the usual dinner-hour, the ladies of the Harem would pay a visit to the governess *(cocana,* "lady," as they termed her), and ask her to allow them to partake of her dinner, which being cooked *à l'Arabe*, they enjoyed with much *gusto ;* and then the Grand Pacha's and my own slaves had short commons.

I am always ready to bestow praise where praise is due, and must acknowledge that while a guest within the precincts of the Sultan's palace at Bebek, there was abundance of everything, and the Turkish and Arab *cuisine,* for its kind, was exceedingly good.

When dinner was finished, the ladies of the Sultan's Harem went about their usual occupations. They had no slaves to attend upon them—I am only speaking of those who resided with us at Bebek. They employed their time in filling the Sèvres china jars in the apartments with fresh water, setting up the wax candles in the chandeliers and candelabras, arranging their chambers, decorating the rooms with fresh gathered bouquets ; in short, their lives may not inappropriately be likened to those of nuns in a convent.

The younger slaves officiated as chamber-maids. The aged ladies, however, did nothing ; but were waited upon most attentively by the younger ones.

The washing and ironing of the linen of the Viceregal family and suite was carried on at the old palace, on account of the badness of the water for that purpose ; so that on Wednesdays and Thursdays the whole of the slaves belonging to the Egyptain Harems went over to the palace, which greatly inconvenienced the Grand Pacha and myself, as then we had not a single attendant to wait upon us. On these two days the whole establishment was up and about at break of day, the rooms were turned topsy-turvey, the matting taken up off the floors, and the whole of the interior of the palace swept and garnished, " when disorder reigned throughout the Harem's curtained galleries."

The slaves belonging to the Sultan's Harem washed and got up their own linen in the Harem. The general appearance of this bevy of ladies was not, as Tom Moore, in his " Lalla Rookh," describes,

> "Maids from the West, with sunbright hair,
>   And from the garden of the Nile,
>   Delicate as the roses there;"

for they were indeed very plain—nay, ordinary, and some absolutely ugly.

His Highness the Prince and myself dined punctually at twelve o'clock, at which repast we were waited upon by slaves belonging to the Sultan's Harem. The Validè Princess always took her meals alone, and the ladies of her Harem and her suite regaled themselves off the scraps. Sometimes the Princess Epouse would invite some of the aged ladies of the Harem to dinner; but the ladies of her Harem and slaves were also fed with the scraps. So that as regards "the table" (to use a sea-phrase), there was but one, which showed that strict economy was the order of the day in the Imperial as well as the Viceregal household.

It was highly amusing to see the ladies of the Harem and slaves squat themselves down upon the floor in a circle, holding most elegant Sèvres china cups and saucers, with gold spoons, in their hands; while the freezing pail of lemon ice stood in the centre, into which they dipped their spoons, filled their cups, and even their saucers (as most undoubtedly they thought that it was impossible to have too much of a good thing), with that refreshing condiment, and handed them round to each other; and ever and anon they dipped the gold spoons into the pail, and regaled themselves to their hearts' content.

Their Highnesses, both before and after dinner, went out for an airing, either in caïques or carriages, down to Stamboul, each attended by their respective Grand Eunuch, and other attendants. Sometimes they were accompanied by a few of the ladies of the Harem; they then went shopping. At other times they would receive visitors, both rich and poor; give audiences to their dressmakers, to whom all their dress-pieces were sent from Egypt to be made up; and also to to their boot-maker's wife. At four o'clock they lay down, after having smoked their pipes.

> " Then their pure hearts to transport given
> Swell like the wave, and glow like heaven.'

At six o'clock they rose, dressed themselves in their evening toilette, and went out in caïques on the beautiful Bosphorus; sometimes to pay visits to the different Harems, and at others they accompanied their visitors to their Harems. (The Validè Princess very seldom went out in the evening, but often sent for the governess and the Grand Pacha.) At eight o'clock they supped.

The ladies of the Sultan's Harem were much more civilized than those of the Viceroy's; for they amused themselves of an evening singing songs to their own accompaniments on castanets; while others sat quietly in a group, not like the dames of olden times, plying at their distaffs and spindles, but industriously employed in useful needlework, repairing their own garments; others again played at cards and dominoes;—all smoking, and sipping *findjans* of coffee out of *zarfs* of gold, encrusted with diamonds.

At ten o'clock our Grand Eunuch, who appeared to have taken upon himself the office of Mufti ever since our arrival at Bebek, shouted forth the call to prayer; " and down upon the fragrant sod kneels with his forehead to the east, lisping the eternal name of God." After that the Harem's gates and doors were locked.

One morning, soon after our arrival at Bebek, and when the Viceregal children were suffering from severe colds, they were playing in the Grand Pacha Ibrahim's apartment, which was filled with white and black slaves, both of the upper and lower class, some running about the room like mad creatures, others squatting down in dirty crumpled muslin dresses, of the introduction of which heterogeneous assembly into His Highness's room I had already complained to the Princess Epouse, but without effect, as it was always stated that they came to pay their respects to the Grand Pacha.

After the young slaves had been romping about for some time, one of them came running up to me, and informed me that the large diamond in the waistband of the little Princess, which had only been fastened on a few moments before, by her own nurse, was missing. That seemed to me rather a singular incident, as the Princess had never quitted the apartment. Search was immediately made for the *elmas*, " diamond," but it could nowhere be found. The matting and carpets were removed, the divans, chairs (their cushions), tables, corners, crevices, and every place were examined, and the room swept, but still no traces of it could be discovered. The slaves were questioned, but denied all knowledge of it.

The head-nurse, Shaytan, with all the effrontery in the world, walked up to me, and with one of the cunningest leers imaginable, inquired of me whether I had taken it ? I replied, very coolly, " No ! I have not ! and what is more, I have never set eyes on it to-day, as I did not see the little Princess after her nurse had dressed her."

Her Highness the Princess Epouse was sent for, and as soon as she became aware of the loss, she burst into a flood of tears, for that *elmas* had been the gift of the Viceroy to her before they were married, and therefore she prized it greatly, and not for its intrinsic value, which was, however, estimated at 500*l*. The Grand Eunuch was sent for, and then another search was made, but with no better success. At length it was given up as a bad job.

The little Princess's nurse, who was an honest, upright woman, cried most bitterly ; upon seeing which, the Grand Eunuch approached her, exclaiming, *Malesch ! Malesch !* but the poor creature continued to weep, as she well knew that if it were not found she would be most frightfully branded. Shaytan looked most artfully at her, but uttered not a syllable.

At length the Princess put herself into a towering passion, and told the eunuch, that if it was not forthcoming on her return (for she was then on the eve of her departure, to accompany the Validè Sultana in her yacht,) she would have the whole of the nurses and slaves flogged.

Then a slave approached the Princess, and handed her a *zarf*, with a *findjan* of coffee. She sipped it, but not relishing the taste of it, or else not having overcome her passion, she spat into it, as was invariably her custom when she disliked anything, threw the beautiful Japan *findjan* with its contents on the floor, and stamped her feet upon it which broke it into a thousand pieces, which the slaves quickly removed.

I was quite aware in my own mind that Shaytan had wrenched the diamond off the band. I said not a word, as that would have been dangerous to myself; but told the Princess's nurse, that she had better watch an opportunity, and look into the head-nurse's *sarat* "trunk," when she found it open. Poor thing, she cried for days and nights, most piteously. About two days before I left the Palace, the Princess's nurse made another search, "swept and garnished" the apartment, and lo and behold! by the side of Shaytan's *sarat*, there lay the diamond, just as if it had been dropped there by pure accident. The artful Shaytan, not feeling inclined to undergo a flogging, for she knew that the Princess Epouse always kept her word, whether for good or evil, had disgorged her prize. But it is impossible for me to describe the excessive delight of the Princess's nurse when she found it—then indeed did she "weep for joy."

Another day we sauntered up the flower enameled heights, and the lovely view which I there beheld will never be effaced from my memory. As I scanned the horizon, at one moment I caught sight of the Muezzins on the balconies of the minarets, taking their Asmodeus-like observations of the doings of the denizens who were perambulating about the three cities; for they are the most arrant spies and busy-bodies alive, scarcely any thing or object escaping their observation. This knowledge they are ever ready to turn to the most profitable account, for they are devout worshippers of the Sovereign Prince Baksheesh, who here reigns as dominant as in Egypt.

Here I gazed on the crowds of people embarking in caïques from the numerous *scales*, now and then several *arobas*, " covered carts," drawn by bulky bullocks, ascending the various steep, elevated ascents; I saw also closely-veiled figures, flitting about the *Cities of the Silent*, to which I observed numerous processions depart from the *scale* of the *Meit Iskellese*, " Ladder of the Dead." Then, listening to the various sounds that vibrated on the clear atmosphere, I heard the *improvisatori* chanting of the *cackdjis*, one of which commenced with—

> " My childhood's home was 'mid the isles
> That gem the bright Ægean sea; "

then the rude singing of the sailors hauling up the anchors of their ships, at the mast-heads of which floated the Blue Peter, that signal of departures to distant lands ; the buzzing of the dense population of the bay's three cities (Stamboul, Pera, and Galata) ; the howling of the legion of mongrels that prowled about in all directions; the booming of distant cannon ; the soft music of the military bands at the different barracks, floating on the rippling waters ; the hallooing of the *Hamalls*, as they wended their way with their heavy loads up the steep ascents ; the bleating of the sheep grazing hard by; the trampling of the horses' hoofs; the words of command, as the troops were being drilled on the parade grounds; and now and then the stentorian howling of those incorrigible beggars, the Howling Dervishes, with whom it is almost as dangerous for a Frank to trust himself alone (unless well armed), as it now is for a tourist to perambulate about the environs of Naples, lest he fall into the hands of the Italian banditti.

Sometimes the Prince partook of his supper at five o'clock, as he was not made to conform to the rule laid down by the precept of the *Suna :* "Eat not till the planet of the fourth heaven, the all-beneficent sun, hath hidden his rays behind the mountain Kaf." When that was the case, we sallied forth for an evening ramble on the Esplanade, which was generally thronged with loungers at that period of the evening. But whenever their Highnesses the Princesses and *Kadines* ("the ladies of the Sultan's Harem") thought proper to frequent it, then the *Kislar Agaci*, and his formidable guard, with their drawn scimitars, stationed themselves on the heights, and no individual was allowed to approach there, which was on other occasions a public promenade. Sometimes they entered one of the caïques, and took an excursion on the Thracian Bosphorus, when the beautiful moonbeams reflected their soft light on the sparkling waves.

At other times they visited the lovely shores of Beshic-Tach, and its palace; Istenia, with its beautiful suburbs; Therapia, and the splendid palaces of the foreign ambassadors; nor did they omit to wander about Buyuk-Deri.

We often entered some beautiful and large gardens belonging to some of the wealthiest Turks, which were laid out in the Oriental style; and as it was summer-time, the air was impregnated with the delicious and powerful odors of citrons, roses, myrtles, jasmines, azalias, lovely passion-flowers, almond-flowers, rose laurels, pomegranates, cedars, &c. The well-kept avenues were refreshingly shaded with large bananas, lofty palms, tall cypress, and the banian-spreading *tchinars* (plane-trees). Dotted about were several gilded aviaries, full of birds of most superb plumage, and lively songsters; and here and there the air was cooled by the flowing of the waters which were spurted forth from numerous elegantly-sculptured fountains. While gazing upon this scene, the Prince prattled away, asking me the names of the exotics that bloomed around them, and inquiring if I had such lovely flowers in my own country.

At times he would go and seat himself in one of the kiosks, in which he generally found a crimson satin cushion, which the owner, who had watched the little Prince at the time of his first visit to his pleasure-garden, had ordered to be placed there, as also one for the *Khanum Inglese,* "English lady," as he designated me.

On the last occasion when he went there, a short time before he fell sick, he found a basketful of strawberries, and porcelain cups filled with iced sherbet, in his favorite kiosk. Then he ran up to me, exclaiming, "Oh, madam, pray do not laugh at me, but only see! My *dgin,* 'spirit,' fairy-like, has laid luncheon for us in the kiosk; and I have placed all the chocolate buttons, that you are so fond of, on a plate for you!" Upon which I followed His Highness; and, true enough, there I found the frugal repast, of which we both most cheerfully partook.

Frequently we were rowed in a caïque, which transported us to the beautiful Asiatic shores, where His Highness loved to sit down upon his Persian rug, beneath the wide-spreading and luxuriant *tchinars,* at Hunkiar Eskellesi; and often under the shade of the noble *tchinars,* "plane-trees," I also sat and contemplated the beauties of nature as well as the Grand Pacha, Ibrahim; for, young as he was, he possessed that inherent characteristic of his race, the study of Nature in all her pristine loveliness, and which was here presented to his gaze in most variegated shapes and forms.

Sometimes we selected the Valley of the Grand Seignior as our retreat, and then the banian-like foliage of the great walnuts afforded us most grateful shelter. Now and then he would climb the Giant's Mountain, which commands one of the most incomparable panoramas ever beheld; and when he caught sight of the tapering minarets of the white marble mosques, on the balconies of which stood the muezzins, ready to chant the *Esan*, "call to prayer," then, in an ecstasy of delight, he would clap his tiny hands, and exclaim, "Oh, madam, look! the mesjed!—the mosque!" Calling attention to the steamers on the river, he would begin to imitate the captains, and shout out, "*Aivali! Aivali! Di! Imote!*" "Bravo, boy! Courage! Go on!"

At other times he would look up at the cloudless sky, and then inquire of me if I did not think that the heavenly Paradise Mahomet had promised to the faithful must not indeed be "*Pek quiyis! pek quiyis! Mashallah! Allah karim!*" "Very pretty! very pretty! How wonderful is the wisdom of God! God is merciful!" But then added His Highness, "No *kopek* (dog) of a Jew can enter there;" for he had an abomination of the Hebrew race.

One day the Grand Pacha took it into his head to have the whole of his little female slaves dressed in male attire, and, sending for the Sultan's *terzi-ile*, "tailor," he ordered him to take their measures for two suits. After that was done, he had his own taken for half-a-dozen private suits, and for all the uniforms of various regiments in the Sultan's service, the patterns of which were placed before him. Then his male attendants underwent the same ordeal.

The Validè Princess's Grand Eunuch being in the apartment at the time, but not understanding French, could not speak to the *terzi-ile*, so he requested me to have the kindness to become the interpreter, and to explain that he required him to make several suits of clothes, also a mantle, which he wanted to wear on the approaching state occasion of his having to attend the Validè Princess on her visit to the Sultan. I accordingly made the tailor understand that the Grand Eunuch had seen the portrait of the late Prince Consort, dressed in his Field-Marshal's uniform, and wearing the blue mantle of the Knights of the Garter, and that he desired to have one of a similar shape, only of crimson instead of blue velvet; and, it should be added, the *terzi-ile* executed the order with great ability.

After His Highness had amused himself by looking attentively at the minuteness with which the "schneider" used his tape-measure, he turned round to me, and entreated me also to be measured for a suit; then coming up close to my side, and looking into my face with a most winning smile, he added, "Do, madam; you will look so *guzel! pek guzel!* ('pretty! very pretty!') in a richly-embroidered male attire." But I declined the honor he intended me, with many thanks.

One morning I was surprised, on entering His Highness's room, to find that the ceremony of breaking bread over His Highness's head was being performed. In a basket were placed about a hundred small loaves (similar in size to the five-centesimi loaves sold in Italy) of European bread, nine of which were broken by Shaytan—that very impersonification of the Angel of Darkness—over the Grand Pacha's head; the head-nurse counting their number in Arabic as they were broken up. Only seven were broken over the head of Her Highness the little Princess. This ceremony was performed with European bread, because no Arab bread was ever provided in the Sultan's palace; but I was unable to learn the origin of that superstitious rite.

One day His Highness the Prince perceived a very pretty small gold ring which I wore on my little finger. It was twisted in the shape of a serpent, having two rubies placed in the head for the eyes, and the scales were exquisitely enamelled. His Highness took a fancy to it, upon which I took it off my finger, made him *bokshalik*, "a present of it," and placed it on the second finger of his right hand, with which he salaams.

Her Highness the first wife having admired it, owing to

its being in the form of a serpent (as such is valued by the
Arabs as a token of immortality, because snakes shed their
skin annually), offered to give me a superb diamond ring,
valued at 500*l.*, off her own finger, if the little Prince
would let Her Highness have it; but that he most positively
refused to do, at which his mother, the Princess Epouse,
smiled. The head-nurse, Shaytan, having seen me place it
upon the Grand Pacha's finger, and hearing that her Highness the Lady Paramount had coveted it, as soon as she
took him into his bedroom, under pretence of changing his
pantaloons, began to wrench the ring off his finger, as it
fitted tight, and His Highness was reluctant to part with
it. In the struggle to accomplish her vile object of stealing
the ring, she tore away a piece of his flesh, as she lacked
the sense to moisten his hand with water, in order to slip it
off easily, and he shrieked out most lustily, which brought
myself, the ladies of the Harem, Grand Eunuch, and slaves,
into his apartment.

As soon as I looked at his finger, I perceived that the
ring was missing, when I immediately desired her to produce it. The Princess Epouse, who had by this time entered the room, glanced most angrily at the head-nurse, who
then handed me the ring, which the Princess took into her
own keeping, and ever after it remained in her jewel-case,
and was only worn by the Grand Pacha on grand occasions,
but it is highly prized on account of its shape, for anything
in the form of a crocodile is considered by the Egyptians as
a very lucky omen. Hence so many of the doors at Cairo
have figures of that animal sculptured over them.

CHAPTER XXVI.

LONG before break of day, on the morning after the loss
of the *Elmas*, the whole of the inmates of the Harem at

Bebek were up and stirring, as their Highnesses the Validè Princess and the Princess Epouse were going to pay their state visit to the Validè Sultana (the Sultan's mother), at the Sultan's Palace, as the Imperial Harem, at which the Validè Sultana was then staying, is situated within the palace. It is entered by two most exquisitely-gilded bronzed gates, the portals of which are strictly guarded by several eunuchs, who will not even allow the *Kislar Agaci* to enter therein without the express orders of His Sublime Majesty.

It is almost impossible to describe the hurry and confusion that reigned in the whole establishment. At five o'clock upwards of fifty caïques, of various descriptions, were ranged about the palace landing-place, and two regiments of soldiers, in full-dress uniforms, mounted guard. Then commenced the loading of the heavy caïques with those costly treasures of which I have previously given a description, as having been shipped on board the frigate at Alexandria.

Her Highness the Validè Princess wore on this grand occasion a most magnificently rich white satin robe, elaborately embroidered with gold thread, pearls, diamonds, and various colored silks. Her long train was trimmed with flounces of very deep point lace and flowers, and the bodice was ornamented with a rich point lace bertha and gold ribbons. The stomacher was composed of large diamonds, sapphires, and rubies, which matched the rich embroidery of the dress most admirably.

Her head was covered with a beautiful pink gauze handkerchief, around which was placed a splendid tiara of costly diamonds, composed of crescents, stars, and palm-leaves, forming the Sultan's crest. Her arms were ornamented with beautiful sapphire and spotless opal bracelets. Her feet were encased in white silk stockings, white satin shoes, embroidered with colored silks, pearls, gold and silver thread, with high gold heels, over which she wore a pair of yellow morocco boots. Her waist was encircled with a belt of sapphires. On her fingers she wore several diamond rings, many of the stones of which were almost as large as the celebrated Koi-i-noor diamond, since it has been cut. Her cloak was of rich sky-blue satin, lined with white satin, and over her face she wore a superb Brussels veil, one end of which was placed over the head, and the other crossed over the mouth and nose, then passed round the back of the neck and tucked down under the cloak.

She carried in her hand a very handsome blue silk parasol, lined with white satin trimmed with rich bullion fringe, and having a gold handle, encrusted with agates, amethysts, corals, diamonds, emeralds, hyacinths, jaspers, opals, pearls, rubies, topazes, and turquoises.

Her Grand Eunuch carried over her head a rich sky-blue silk umbrella, with a mother-of-pearl handle, quite as large as those used for carriages in Europe. Her eyelids were blackened with kohl, and on her forehead was the sectarian kohl spot.

Her Highness the Prince Epouse wore a most superb thick white moiré-antique silk robe, with a long train, trimmed with handsome point Alençon lace, having rich ruches of tulle and pink artificial daisies all round it. - The body and sleeves were also trimmed with silver ribbon and daises. The bertha was composed of rich lace, ribbons, and daises. Her slender waist was encircled with a ceinture composed of sapphires and diamonds.

On her arms she wore diamond bracelets. Around her neck was clasped a superb diamond necklace. Her head was adorned with a tiara of diamonds, arranged in the shape of Indian wheat, the weight of which was very great. An immense branch, forming a geranium flower in full blossom, composed of opals, diamonds, emeralds, rubies, amethysts, formed the stomacher of her dress. A pink satin Turkish cloak, with sleeves and cape, was placed on her shoulders. Her face was covered with a rich Brussels lace veil, one end of which was placed over the head, the other end crossed over the mouth and nose, passed round the back of the neck and tucked down behind the cloak. Her feet were encased in white silk stockings, white satin shoes, richly embroidered with colored silks, pearls, and gold and silver thread, with high gold heels, over which she wore a pair of yellow morocco *papooshes,* " slippers."

In her hand she held a rich pink silk parasol, lined with white satin, trimmed with a deep silver fringe, with a gold handle inlaid with a great variety of precious stones. On her fingers were a large yellow diamond and a beautiful sapphire ring. Her Grand Eunuch held over her head a handsome large pink silk umbrella.

I assisted at Her Highness's toilette, and when she was dressed, she turned round and asked me if her costume was *à la Franca,* and like those worn by any of our European Princesses. It is almost impossible for me to give a correct pen-and-ink drawing of the costumes of these Princesses, who looked the impersonification of

"Blooming May and bright September,"

for the appearance of the Princess Epouse was that of

> " A beauty for ever unchangingly bright,
> Like the long sunny lapse of summer day's light,
> Shining on, shining on, by no shadow made tender,
> Till love falls asleep in its sameness of splendor; "

while that of Her Highness the Validè Princess, the idol of Ibrahim Pacha's devotion, was

> " Like the light upon autumn's soft shadowy days,
> Now here, and now there, giving warmth as it flies
> From the lip to the cheek, from the cheek to the eyes;
> Now melting in mist and now breaking in gleams,
> Like the glimpses a saint hath of Heaven in his dreams."

These two beauteous courtly dames were "the stars of Egypt."

20

When their Highnesses entered the Grand reception-room, prior to taking their departure, they were joined by the ladies of both the Sultan's and Viceregal Harems, to whom

> " They turned, and as they spoke,
> A sudden splendor all around them broke,"

for the whole of them were dressed in most magnificent variegated colored brocaded silks of the costliest kind, wearing large Turkish cloaks, *feridges,* of the same materials.

Their heads were covered with small colored gauze handkerchiefs; their faces veiled with superb Brussels net veils; their foreheads were ornamented with tiaras of diamonds, emeralds, rubies, sapphires, turquoises, pearls, and other precious stones ; their arms, fingers, and ears, were ornamented with diamond bracelets, rings, earrings, and their waists and necks were encircled with ceintures of precious stones and diamond necklaces.   Gold watches hung at their waistbands, suspended from massive gold chains.   Many of them wore two chains attached to them, all of which marked the Turkish time.   Their fingers were tinged with the scarlet *henna*, their eyelids dyed with *kohl*, and the sectarian *kohl* spot was on their foreheads.   Their feet were encased in white silk stockings, and embroidered white satin slippers, over which they wore a pair of yellow morocco *papooshes*.

Each carried in her hands a colored silk parasol to match her dress, with gold ferrules and mother-of-pearl handles, inlaid with precious stones.   There, as they stood, they looked like a galaxy of beauteous sprites, the denizens of a fairy land, and the attendants of two fairy queens.

At ten o'clock their Highness's caïques, with the Turkish standards floating at the prow and stern, were hauled along the side of the landing place, the whole length of which, from the threshold of the grand entrance, was covered with rich Brussels carpet.   The•Caidjis who rowed the Princesses were dressed in richly-embroidered sky-blue silk velvet jackets trimmed with silver buttons, and white silk trousers. They wore on their fingers beautiful diamond rings, their baksheesh from their Highnesses, and sat on cushions of blue satin, fringed with gold, and ornamented with gold tassels.

At the grand entrance two regiments of infantry were drawn up in full uniform, and as their Highnesses descended the staircase and passed out on to the landing-place (which was covered over with an awning), attended by their elegantly attired suites, the band struck up the Sultan's March, the soldiers presented arms, and shouted "Long live the Princess Validè Kanum Effendi, the Princess Epouse!"

Her Highness the Validè Princess entered her caïque first, then Her Highness the second wife followed. They were both attended by their Head Eunuchs, who were dressed in European costume, each wearing over his shoulders, a large crimson velvet cloak, embroidered with gold, lined with white satin, trimmed with ermine, and fastened round the throat with bullion tassels and cord, the tassels hanging over the right shoulder, similar in shape and form to that worn by the Knights of the Garter, wearing their diamond-hilted swords sheathed in gold scabbards, hanging from gold belts fastened with diamond clasps. Each had a pair of gold epaulets upon his shoulders. They took with them no less than ten different suits of habiliments, each suit having gold cords and tags to correspond, in order that they might appear in a new uniform daily during the Viceregal visit to the Sultan's Harem. They were also accompanied by their attendants. They knelt in the stern, each holding the large umbrellas over their Highnesses' heads. Then followed the ladies of the Harem, four of whom occupied a caïque.

Then followed a caïque with four officers, two Turks and two Arabs, holding drawn swords in their hands. The rear guard of this river procession was brought up by numerous other caïques containing the guard of infantry and the attendant slaves. The Princesses and attendants also took with them upwards of ten different kinds of new dresses, all of which were worn during their visit.

Then they proceeded to the Sultan's palace, the new one, or Palace of the Bosphorus, as it is called *par excellence*. It is an immense pile of buildings, the marble steps by which it is entered bathing in the sapphire and rapid-flowing river. It is of *plateresco* style of architecture, and resembles a huge model of the finest workmanship of a Lisbon goldsmith. Its windows, balconies, pilasters, festooned frames, sculpture and arabesque work, remind one of the beautiful Palazzo Doria of Venice, except that the former is a large, stately structure, and the latter hut a diminutive model. The hybrid composite front is rich and elegant in appearance, and to sum up all, it is, as that gifted author Gautier has stated, "a palace which might be the work of an ornamentist who was not an architect, and who spared neither the hand, nor labor, nor time, nor yet expense."

The wings of this enormous building are neither so lofty, nor in unison with the centre piece. A noble terrace runs along the whole extent, "bordered on the side toward the river with a line of columns, linked to each other by an elegant rich wrought-iron balustrade railing, in which the iron curves and twines in a thousand arabesques and flowers, like the figures which a bold penman traces with free hand upon the paper."

Landing on this terrace their Highnesses were received with all the honors due to their exalted rank. The steps were covered with Brussels carpet, a guard of honor consisting of eunuchs lined the approach, and their band struck up the Sultan's March as they landed and proceeded across a spacious marble hall, the floor of which was covered with matting and strips of carpet, the ceiling was beautifully painted in fresco, as also the walls.

Proceeding up the grand staircase they were ushered by the *Kislar Agaci* into the Grand Reception Saloon of the Sultana Validè, which is a lofty room looking upon the Bosphorus. The ceiling is in elegant and fresh colored fresco, and is, as Gautier has most naïvely and accurately described it, " a perfect marvel of elegance and ingenuity ; for now they are skies of turquoise, streaked with light clouds, that form depths of inconceivable profundity in their intervals ; then immense veils of lace of marvellous design ; next, a vast shell of pearl irradiated with all the hues of the prism, or imaginary flowers hanging their leaves and tendrils through trellises of gold." The floor was covered with handsome Brussels carpet, the walls hung with immense mirrors, which reached from the ceiling down to the floor. The whole of the furniture, which is ormolu and gold, is of French manufacture; the covers of the chairs and sofas are of white satin, embroidered with gold crescents and bees. The hangings of the doors and curtains correspond, and are lined with rose-pink silk. The tables are similarly ornamented to those in the palace at Babek (Bebek).

Her Highness the Validè Sultana, who was richly but plainly dressed in a pink satin robe elegantly trimmed, and wearing a profusion of diamonds and other precious ornaments, received the homage (for here the Viceroys of Egypt have only the rank of Viziers, and their mothers and wives are placed on a footing of equality with those of the other Viziers) of the " Stars of Egypt," and pointing to them to be seated on the divan on each side of her. She is rather handsome, about the same age as the Validè Princess of Egypt, equally as shrewd in character, and bearing a family resemblance to her. Then the usual refreshments were handed round, and pipes smoked. After the Princesses had remained here some time sipping coffee, eating *bonbons,* " Turkish sweetmeats," and puffing away at their pipes, the

Sultana Validè rose up, and followed by her Viceregal guests and staff of attendants, passed into another reception-chamber, which Gautier has most accurately described as being "a casket, the jewels of which are spread about in picturesque disorder; necklaces, whose pearls have broken from their chain, and rolled forth like drops of hail, while a perfect flood of diamonds, sapphires, and rubies forms the basis of the decoration. Censers of gold painted upon the cornices, send forth the blue or clouded smoke of their perfumes, and cover one ceiling with the varying tints of their transparent vapor."

There they were received by the Sultana of the year, who was doubled up on a divan like a clasp knife; by her side lay the ivory sceptre, the emblem of her rank. She pointed to her guests to be seated; the Validè Sultana occupied the seat of honor, and the "Stars of Egypt" sat on the other side.

In this apartment were assembled the Ladies of the Harem, who are divided into five classes. Those of the highest rank, who are called *Kadens*, chiefly natives of Salonica and Circassia, are the Sultan's mistresses; close by stood the *Odalisques*, about seventy in number, all of whom attend upon the Sultan, and form, as it were his personal staff. The favorite of the period is termed the *Ikbal*, who if she became *enceinte*, is raised to the rank of a *Kadan*, and behind them were a whole host of *Oustas*, "upper domestic slaves," who form the Validè Sultana and the Harem's household staff. A little in advance of them stood the *Dadas*, "nurses," with the children, and bringing up the rear where the *Ghez-Metkian*, "the lower-cast slaves," who perform all the drudgery in the household.

The census of the Imperial Harem must be about three hundred souls, the majority of whom are of Circassian, Greek, Caucasian, Egyptian, and Ethiopian origin. Most of them are totally unacquainted with their parentage, or even the land of their nativity.   They are all subservient to the *Kadens*, who in their turn pay implicit obedience to the commands, whims, and caprices of the Sultana of the year, " the lady with the ivory sceptre," whose exalted position is by no means an enviable one, as the other Odalisques adopt all kinds of intrigues, plots, and often have recourse even to poison to supplant her; but the moment that she becomes *enceinte*, all their vile machinations cease, and they bow their knees before her with submission and respect.

The usual refreshments, pipes, and cigarettes were served round to their Highnesses.   I then accompanied one of the Ladies of the Harem into one of the large corridors, and entered her apartment, the door of which, like those of all the others, led into it like the cells of nuns in a convent, and at the end of each corridor were the eunuchs' quarters.

Then we passed into another reception-room, where Phingari bursts through the opening of the cloud, and displays the silver bow, so dear to the Moslem ; Aurora tinges with blushes a morning sky ; or farther on, a piece of embroidery, glowing with light, shows its golden texture, confined by a clasp of carbuncles.   Arabesques with countless interlacements, sculptured caskets, masses of jewels, wildernesses of flowers, vary these subjects in innumerable ways, totally beyond the reach of description.   In short, it is impossible that my feeble pen-and-ink drawings can give the imagination of the reader a correct idea of the gorgeous and fairylike magnificence displayed here.

Amidst the luxury of this regal splendor, and the enjoyment of profuse hospitality, their Highnesses the Princesses and the numerous suites whiled away a fortnight.   The time was passed in paying visits, making excursions on the Bosphorus in caïques, promenading about the gardens, and shopping ; for the reader must know that the ladies in Turkey go about freely, and are not caged up in Harems as they are in Egypt.

All the Ladies of the Harem soon fraternized together, and accompanied their Highnesses the Princesses in their per..u.bulations.

I and the Prince soon took our leave, and returned to the Palace at Babec, and on my arrival I was informed that I must get ready to accompany the Grand Pacha and his suite to pay their state visit to the Sultan. Next morning I was rather surprised at the Grand Eunuch entering my room very early. He apologized to me, and hoped that I would not feel offended, but I was not to accompany their Highnesses to the Sultan's, as he would take charge of them, and I was to go *alone* to pay my respects.

Very early the next morning, the Grand Eunuch came into the reception-room for their Highnesses. He was in one of his best humors, and amused me very much by the droll manner in which he attempted to salute the Prince according to our European mode. He advanced close to him, then bowed most respectfully, at the same time exclaiming, "Gud mourning, gud mourning, your High—ness, your High—ness"—drawing back until he reached the door.

Another eunuch, the second in rank, and who would become the Grand Eunuch should that official die or retire, had picked up a few words of English, and he also saluted the Prince in the same manner, at which he was quite pleased; but he had that morning been guilty of a breach of etiquette for which I reproved him. The fact was, that in the hurry of the moment he had forgotten to leave his overshoes at the door, so I sent him back, knowing full well that no European should ever allow a native to show less respect to him than he is obliged to show to persons of rank in his own country, or he would abuse his calling, and treat him contemptuously, if not with positive disrespect. It was, however quite an oversight on the part of this eunuch, whose name was Southcote, for he always behaved most kindly to me.

In a few moments Shaytan entered the room with the

Grand Pacha, who was dressed in the splendid uniform of a Grand Pacha of the highest rank. He wore a dress black coat, the front of which was completely covered with one mass of gold embroidery, trimmed with gold buttons. The corners of the tails were richly embroidered, having two gold buttons fastened behind at the waist. It was buttoned np close to the neck, the collar also being embroidered with gold. His trousers were of black cloth, decorated with strips of gold lace down each side ; his feet were encased in silk stockings and patent-leather boots, with high heels and gold spurs : on his shoulders were placed two gold epaulets, his small diamond-hilted sword was sheathed in a gold scabbard encrusted with diamonds, and girded round his waist by a gold belt, fastened with a diamond clasp in the shape of a crescent.

A small diamond star hung on his breast, attached to a blue ribbon, which was placed across his left shoulder. His head was covered with a *fez*, and on his forehead was placed the sectarian black spot, which was *not* made of *kohl*, as it ought properly to have been done, for the head-nurse not having any of that pigment by her, was obliged—oh! " say it not in Gath, tell it not in Ascalon ! "—to make it with the *black ink* taken out of the Dog of a Christian's inkstand, miscreant " *Giaour*," though she was. His overcoat was of black velvet, lined with crimson silk.

He was accompanied by the young Princess, his sister, who wore a white satin dress, with a long train richly embroidered with gold leaves ; round her waist was a gold belt, fastened with a diamond clasp in the form of a crescent; her tiny feet were encased in white satin embroidered shoes with gold heels, like those of their Highnesses the Princesses, over which she wore " *papooshes* " of yellow morocco. Her head was covered with a small sky-blue velvet *fez*, encircled with a band composed of small pearls, diamonds, and gold thread, the tassels being made of similar stones. Their cloaks were of light mauve-colored silk, lined with pale green satin. In her hand she carried a parasol of the same material with a pearl handle, studded with pearls and diamonds. Her beautiful jet black hair hung down her back in long curls.

She was accompanied by her own young slaves, and the Prince's attendants, all of whom were dressed in male attire, made expressly for the occasion by the Sultan's *turzi-ile.* The female slaves were attired in most costly silks of various colors. Then they descended into the grand entrance-hall, and I accompanied them down to the terrace, where I saw them safely seated in their caïques.

Upon their Highnesses' arrival at the Sultan's palace they alighted at the terrace, were received with due honors, and then ushered by the Grand Eunuch into the Sultan's apartments. These are all superb rooms, and furnished in the most costly modern manner, in imitation of those at Versailles, only considerably Orientalized. The whole of the ceilings are painted in fresco, and from them hung suspended magnificent gilt chandeliers : the floors are covered with rich carpets, the walls decorated with beautiful mirrors, the tables in the rooms are all inlaid with mosaics, and similarly arranged to those in the Palace of Bebek, but with richer ornaments. The doors and framework of the windows, the hangings of which are of rich silk to correspond with the furniture, and fine white lace curtains, are of the finest cedar, violet, ebony, and mahogany woods, beautifully carved, and the shutters are handsomely gilded. But the view is the most beautiful that has ever gladdened the sight of man, the picturesqueness of the panorama is unsurpassed in the whole universe.

Looking out of those immense windows we behold the Asiatic coast looming from amidst a mass of superb dark cypresses; then Scutari comes forth with all its pretty objects ; the rapid azure waters of the dreaded Bosphorus flowing swiftly on, bearing on its sapphire-looking bosom vessels of all denominations, from a caïque to a steamer, above which, poised up in the balmy air, are seen flights of albatrosses, gulls, mews, &c. Then, as we stretch forward, a fine view of both shores is obtained, lined with pretty country-seats, kiosks in almost all the hues of the rainbow. Over those terraces of fairy palatial structures the most singular rays are cast, both by the sun in the day and the lovely moon at night, which "lend enchantment to the view."

As Abdul Aziz was closeted with some of his ministers, their Highnesses had to wait for their audience, and in the mean time the Grand Eunuch undertook to escort them through several of the other apartments. At first he led them into the Red-glass Saloon, which is without exception the most extraordinary apartment in the whole pile, and which should be seen as Gautier saw it: "When the sun streams through this dome of ruby, then all things within blaze with strange light; the air seems to be on fire, and you almost imagine yourself breathing flame; the columns shine like lamps, the marble pavement reddens like a floor of lava, a fiery glow devours the walls, and the whole wears the aspect of the reception-hall of a palace of salamanders, built of metals in a state of fusion."

The pictorial "hell" of a grand opera, or the glare of a mass of Bengal lights, can alone convey an idea of this strange and startling effect; and in order that the visitor should behold everything in keeping, it only wants the owner of this most singular-looking apartment, the Sultan, to be seated there on the magnificent divan, when, like Zamiel in Weber's opera of "Der Freyschutz" (and which · is the custom in Turkey) the scarlet-clad odalisque with her flaring red turban glides alone, and lifts up the flaming colored hangings of the doorway, standing like a phantom before him. Her visit warns "the light of the world" that the lugubrious cry of *Stamboul hiangiuvar!* "Constantinople is on fire," resounds from street to street, and that he must do his duty and proceed to assist at extinguishing the flames. Then, indeed, it might well be designated " the palace of the prince of salamanders."

Their little Highnesses were not in the least frightened at the singular appearance of this chamber; on the contrary, they appeared delighted at it. Then that good-natured functionary took them into what has been considered by some writers, who went over this noble pile of buildings when in course of construction, as the *bijou* of the place (such, however, is not my opinion, now that the whole of the rooms are occupied,) the bath-room. Theophilé Gautier has described this so accurately that I shall quote his account of it. " It is in Moresque style, built of veined Egyptian alabaster, and seems as if carved out of a single precious stone, with its colonnades, its pillars, with graceful, overhanging capitals; and its arch, starred with eyes of crystal which sparkle like diamonds. It is in those transparent flags, shining like agates, that the ' sovereign of sovereigns ' surrenders up his frame to the, to him, delicious and skillful manipulations of the *tellaks*, ' rubbers,' surrounded the while by a cloud of perfumed vapor, and beneath a gentle rain of rose-water and benzoin ! "

Then the Grand Eunuch, leading their Highnesses by the hand, retraced his steps back to the apartment into which he had first introduced them. There they found the Sultan Abdul Aziz seated *à la Turque* on a divan, attended by a whole host of Houris, who were most assuredly no Peris of loveliness.

He was about the same age as the Viceroy, a noble-looking personage, of middle height, piercing dark eyes, but most courteous and amiable in his manners. His costume was simplicity itself; it consisted of a frock coat of dark blue, almost black; white trousers; patent leather boots; and a fez in which the imperial aigrette of heron's feathers was fastened by a large button, formed of diamonds of the first water. He received the homage of their little Highnesses with a smile, and pointed to the Grand Eunuch to seat them by his side on the divan. Then coffee and sweetmeats were served, but not pipes, as both their Highnesses were as yet too young to indulge in the luxury of the weed. The Sultan, however, puffed away at his pipe.

At the end of an hour their Highnesses took their leave, salaamed, and were conducted by the Grand Eunuch into the Harem, where they found the Validè Sultana, together with their Viceregal grandmother and mother squatting on the divan, puffing away at their cigarettes, while a whole host of Kadens, Odalisques, Ladies of both the Viceregal Harems, Oustas, Dadas, and low-caste slaves were ranged about the apartment in the form of a crescent. Then they went and fraternized with the bevy of little children, whose relationship to the late or present Sultan I was unable to ascertain; they appeared to have formed on that day at least, a joyous group.

At eight o'clock at night their little Highnesses returned to the Palace of Bebek. As to myself, after I had witnessed the departure of their water pageantry, as it glided swiftly in the basin of the Bosphorus, I roamed about the beautiful heights, then rested myself on the green sward near the Greek café, gazed in raptures at the picturesque and extensive views before me and as evening drew near, returned to my solitary chamber, pondering on my strange position, and wondering how soon I should be released from my gilded cage.

The scene I had witnessed put one in mind of the Lord Mayor's procession on the Thames on the ninth of November, only with this difference, that the lovely sky was azure bright, the river of a sapphire color, and the weather warm and cheerful.

CHAPTER XXVII.

AFTER the lapse of ten days, their Highnesses the "Stars of Egypt" and suite returned to the palace at Bebek, with the same pageantry as they had left it. The Grand Pacha was still suffering from a severe cold, brought on, as I have previously stated, by having his hair cut, and considerably increased by the dampness of the rooms in which we were located, as the Palace, being of stone, was always damp. In short, the furniture had become quite covered with mildew, and the divans and sofas were spotted all over with it.

The Hekim Bachi ordered the Prince to be removed to the Old Viceregal Palace, which stood further up the Bosphorus, and orders were given for our immediate departure. Well, thought I, so then the Old Palace is to be our dwelling! and those words tell me enough of misery, as I fully expected to enter another "mansion of discomfort;" and not feeling in good health myself, I regretted our removal.

Before the necessary preparations for our flight were completed, I fell sick, and finding that the Hekim Bachi, whom the Princess had sent to attend upon me, did not treat me properly, I became alarmed, and informed the Princess Epouse that I must quit my post. Her Highness having told the Validè Princess of my determination, the latter, contrary to all precedent, sent for His Excellency Khoorshid Pacha, the Chamberlain, who entered the Harem, and proceeded to have a conversation with the widow of Ibrahim Pacha. I add conversation, because His Excellency did not see that Princess, for she held the door of the room ajar, and keeping in the background gave him her instructions, Her Highness being the Lady Paramount here.

His Excellency informed me that Her Highness wished me to have every attention shown me, and asked me to remain; saying that when we removed to the Old Palace I should soon recover, as the place would not be so damp.

I yielded to Her Highness's remonstrances, although I felt quite convinced that, lacking the necessary "creature comforts" (for even in Constantinople I had been obliged to live upon bread, fruit, and a little pigeon or fowl, those being the only eatables that approached to anything like European diet), her kindness and sympathy would avail but little, and that the change to the Old Palace would not benefit my health, whatever it might do that of the Grand Pacha.   He would have remained in robust health, had I been allowed to treat him as I wanted to do; but no, the Hekim Bachi thought that was a capital opportunity to reap a golden harvest, and so he made the most of that accommodating disease—a cold.

Many a time and oft would the Validè Princess come into my chamber, sit upon my couch, and do all she could to cheer me.   One day she ordered her jewel keeper to fetch her jewel caskets, and showed me all the costly presents that the Sultan had sent her.   They were most beautiful; some of them superb tiaras of diamonds, consisting of large sprays of the lotus flower; magnificent stomachers, made in the shape of jasmine, myrtle, and rosebuds.   Then she would place before me her trays of rings, which comprised sapphires, diamonds, opals, emeralds, rubies, &c.

At length I managed to leave my bed, and then I began to pack up my *penates*, for removal to the Old Palace.

About six o'clock the next morning I was awoke by the eunuchs, who had brought several slaves to my room to remove the furniture, bed and bedding, out of the chamber. I was in so weak a state, that I requested them to let them remain a few hours longer; but, as they explained to me that the Grand Pacha would leave at eight o'clock, I dressed myself as quickly as possible, and let the slaves enter, who stripped the apartment of everything except the divan, and left it in the same state as I had entered it on my arrival from Alexandria. Soon afterwards Zenana brought me my breakfast; but as spoons, knives, &c., were all packed up, I dipped my bread in my coffee, and partook of it in that manner.

Looking out of my window, I beheld a complete fleet of sailing-boats at anchor off the Palace landing-place, into which I watched the slaves put the *penates* of the Princess Epouse, the Grand Pacha, and the Princess, his sister, and the whole of *my* Princess's suite. The Validè Princess did not accompany us, but remained behind at Bebek, until she returned to Egypt, which did not take place for some time after I had quitted Constantinople.

Scarcely had the boats been loaded, when the wind began to rage with great fury, the clouds lowered, the hitherto sapphire-looking Bosphorus assumed the dark, indigo-colored tinge of the angry ocean; and yet, amidst the warring of the eternal elements, the flashing of the forked lightning, and the rolling of terrific thunder, the hardy *galiond-jis* weighed anchor.

The storm continued to rage for many hours with unabated fury, so that the Viceregal party had to remain at Bebek until six o'clock in the evening before they could start for the Old Palace. I had just descended the landing-stairs, and was on the point of entering the caïque in which I had placed H. H. the Grand Pacha, when I had to stand back and allow His Excellency the Chamberlain (who had just come out from Egypt), to take my place, as he wished to accompany the Prince. I therefore entered another caïque, and, after a smart row of twenty minutes, the whole party arrived in front of the Old Palace.

It is a most singular-looking, tumble-down structure, closely resembling in its exterior appearance an old English gable-ended farm-homestead, *minus* the thatched roof; for it was slated. The caïques came to an anchor off a dingy-looking wooden pier, about 14 feet long by 10 feet wide, lined with lofty iron palisades, the spikes of which were richly gilded. It was entered by the everlasting iron prison-gates, richly ornamented with the gilded crescents, which led to the grand entrance.

It must be confessed that a kind of shudder thrilled through my veins as I gazed upon that mean, common-looking, wooden barn of a place. It looked like the den of a miser. It was composed of two long-storied tenements, the interior of which was admirably in keeping with the exterior, which was in a most dilapidated condition. It evidently looked more fit to be burned down to the ground, which I afterwards most fervently wished it had been before I had ever set my feet within its miserable walls.

Opposite to it lay at anchor a noble-looking new screw Turkish frigate, her port-holes bristling with heavy guns, the salute from which always shook the rickety old palace—oh, what a misnomer! " barn " would have been the proper appellation—to its very foundation.

Landing on the pier, we entered an immense door, or gate-way (not unlike the Traitor's Gate, in the Tower of London, as it was thickly studded with huge nails); then we passed into a magnificent marble-paved hall, lined on both sides with rooms. The apartment on the right-hand was appropriated as the Grand Eunuch's reception-room, ever memorable, as the reader will presently learn, as the hall in which I was forced by one of the Viceroy's reputed partners to sign the resignation of my appointment, in order to gain my liberty, not from " a gilded cage," but from this old barn.

The only furniture it contained was a divan and a large table. The floor, like that of all the other rooms, was mat-ted, and the windows (which commanded a full view of the pier, and its prison-looking gates) were, together with the doors, hung with dark-brown curtains.

21

On the left hand were the rooms appropriated to the use of His Excellency the Chamberlain, his secretaries, the officers, and male attendants on their Highnesses the Princesses and the Grand Pacha.

Turning round an angle in the hall, we approached a doorway, just like the entrance to a cellar, but so low that the men were obliged to stoop to pass through it. Then, descending two steps, we passed into a long underground apartment, in which were located the male attendants, who were obliged to remain almost bent double, on account of the lowness of the ceiling. It was so dark, that a lighted lamp hung suspended from the roof both day and night.

This subterraneous vault reminded me most forcibly of the underground cavern into which the banditti led Gil Blas. It had evidently been used in olden times as a dungeon; for chains and rings were still hanging to the walls. It looked like the *carceri* of the palace of an Italian nobleman in the days of the Medici. The very sight of it was enough to give the spectator the horrors.

Facing the grand entrance was a noble flight of marble stairs, covered with new matting, and the walls had been freshly whitewashed. Ascending the stairs, we approached a large door, at which we were obliged to knock for admittance. On its being opened, it led us into the grand entrance of the noble marble hall of the Harem, along which ran a corridor, the entire length of which faced the Bosphorus.

It was lighted by five spacious windows, all of which commanded views of the sapphire-looking river, and the lovely heights on the opposite side, dotted about with trees from out of which peered forth the white tapering minarets of many a beautiful mosque and the variegated roofs of pretty country-houses. In the centre stood a large marble fountain; at each end the rooms branched off both right and left.

On the right-hand of the entrance were the Grand Pacha's suite of rooms, and those of his little sister. They were all most wretchedly furnished (the noble reception-room was the only apartment carpeted); the walls and ceilings were whitewashed; the hangings of both the doors and windows were of blue and white cotton chintz, as was also the divan, which was placed under the windows that looked into a very tiny garden. Such parsimony and meanness in the furnishing of this palace was totally incompatible with the dignity of Ismael Pacha, as Viceroy of Egypt; but I am fain to believe that he thought that the Grand Pacha's visit to Constantinople was an excellent opportunity for him to learn an apt lesson in practical political economy.

On the left hand were the attendants' apartments, all destitute of furniture except divans. On the right hand was the Princess Epouse's sitting-room, which was covered with matting. In it stood a divan covered with old worn-out faded crimson damask. A door led into the bedchamber, which was furnished with a plain iron bedstead, with crimson mosquito-curtains, a large mirror, and a divan covered with dark-brown chintz. The hangings of the doors and windows were of the same material, with the addition of white muslin curtains; no other furniture of any kind.

It is almost impossible to imagine the bare and miserable appearance of this barn, or the parsimony displayed in the arrangements in this " Mansion of Wretchedness." The accommodation that had been afforded to us in the palace at Bebek, where merely necessary comforts for the Egyptian Princesses, and plenty of discomforts for the miscreant of a Christian, had been provided, was superfluous compared with the fitting-up and *mènage* arrangements of this Turkish work-house for the Egyptians. And this, reader, was the Elysium, the Abode of Bliss, which was to restore health to my shattered constitution, and prove a sanatorium to His Highness the Grand Pacha.

At the extremity of the hall was a large apartment, used as Her Highness's wardrobe-room, in which the "*Kaftandji Ousta*," "Mistress of the Wardrobe," slept. Across it hung several lines on which were placed the Princess's jackets, dresses, &c. It was matted, and contained a divan covered with faded damask. Opening a door on the right, we entered another large room similarly fitted up. Passing through it I reached my own miserable chamber; it was, like all the others, the worst in the whole building, except the subterraneous cavern. It was of very small dimensions, not a quarter of the size of that I had occupied at Bebek, about 12 feet long by 12 feet wide, having four windows all destitute of hangings, but with cotton blinds. The floor was matted, the walls white-washed, and it contained an old worn-out divan, covered with washed-out chintz.

The furniture which had been supplied me at Bebek stood outside the door, and when it was placed therein I found it very difficult to move about, especially when I was attired in a walking-dress with a moderate-sized crinoline on. Two of the windows faced the door, and looked into a square piece of a wilderness of a garden, which divided the two tenements forming the palace. Among the weeds were grazing two very old lanky-looking sheep, perfect skeletons, who now and then found shelter beneath the shade of the sycamore and cherry-trees which stood therein.

Privacy was out of the question in that chamber; for one of the two windows looked into the corridor, and the other into another room. When I first put my feet in it, I entertained some slight misgiving that I should not find the comfort and repose the Princess Epouse had promised me, as I soon found that everybody had to pass by both my door and windows, so that the constant flitting to and fro of human forms past the double frames of the windows, (the old ones being broken were left, and the new ones placed over them,) together with the trampling of the heavy feet of the attendants, increased instead of lessening the nervous fever under which I was then laboring, and which made me much worse.

Passing along a short passage, I entered the room into which one of my windows looked, which was similarly furnished to the others, but having in the centre a marble fountain, with water laid on to it. Then turning to the right I proceeded along an extensive corridor, having numerous rooms leading off from it on the left-hand, in several of which I observed piled up quantities of beds, coverlets, iron bedsteads, &c., and at the extremity of this was another chamber, the door of which led into a short corridor.

Passing along this I entered a noble-looking reception-room in the second tenement, as it were, of the palace. It was similarly furnished to the others, only having two or three console tables, and branch candelabras standing on them. Other rooms branched off both right and left. In the centre stood the grand staircase, which was well lighted by a handsome stained glass cupola; and in the corridor, round which stood several marble fountains, the windows were decorated with dark-brown hangings.

Descending this marble staircase, which was matted, we entered a large hall. On the right we passed into the most singular apartment in the whole palace; the atmosphere of which, on entering it, struck so icy cold, that I turned round to the little Princess's Greek attendant who had accompanied me, and asked him what made it feel so cold. He then, as he had visited this palace before, warned me that some of the marble slabs with which it was paved were removable at pleasure, like the flooring at Sadler's Wells Theatre. This proved correct. One day, when I was in that room with some of the eunuchs, I asked them to show me how the water was let in, when Southcote pressed the springs, slid the bolts back, and then one of the largest marble slabs sank down, as it were, into the river. This, however, was not the case, as it rested upon a marble flooring, so that all persons standing on the sunken slab found themselves suddenly let down into an immense room of marble, like a swimming-bath, filled with the water of the Bosphorus, which flowed into it through the five upright iron gratings outside, which are fastened by bolts, and if those bolts were drawn back, the individuals bathing, if they were not expert swimmers, would be carried away into the dreaded Bosphorus, and inevitably drowned.

I stared vacantly at that abyss, wondering how many a beautiful slave, the victim of jealousy or treachery, had in that manner found a watery grave. I was then suffering from nervous fever, and my imagination became troubled and diseased. I remembered the sad fate of poor Amy Robsart in Sir Walter Scott's beautiful novel of "Kenilworth"—how she had crossed the treacherous planks and had been suddenly launched into eternity. My blood curdled in my veins, my debilitated frame shook like an aspen-leaf, and it was several moments before I could recover strength of mind to know that it was a reality—that the yawning water-abyss lay at my feet. But there it was, . sure enough.

Recovering my self-possession, I remembered the story a Russian nobleman had related to me, of his having been inveigled into a palace on the Bosphorus, and after having passed some hours with a Princess, had been let down into the river by means of a similar trap, but being a good swimmer had escaped unhurt. Then I thoroughly understood that I was an inmate of one of those old yet mysterious palaces whose rooms are built over the Bosphorus, and down which river I had seen sacks and baskets floating almost daily. I hastily returned to my own chamber, and a kind of presentiment came over me that I must quit that palace as soon as I could gain strength enough to enable me to do so. I had been advised by the Hekim Bachi to take baths, but I declined, for I had seen quite enough of the bathing establishments of the Viceregal Palace.   I conversed with some of the aged women of the Harem, and when I told them of the marble slab, they shook their heads and uttered that significant word, " *Malesch, Madame, Malesch, Madame ;* " and they told me horrible tales of that room, into which none of them would ever venture.   It was suggested that the Grand Pacha and I should have our meals laid there, as it was so cool, but I refused to allow the Prince to do so, and would never permit him to enter that apartment unless I was with him, and we were accompanied by the Grand Eunuch.

One day, prior to my taking to my bed, I took a walk accompanied by the Grand Pacha.   We passed the subterraneous dungeon I have previously described, and there I saw through the dark iron-grated windows congregated together the Grand Eunuch, not, reader, with his band of forty thieves, but his corps of forty " spectres of men " like himself, to whom he was reading the *Koran* as was his daily custom.   Then we proceeded along a covered-in stone passage, and shortly afterwards we entered the gate of a small flower-garden, most beautifully arranged, in which stood a square marble bath.   At the further extremity was another large square marble bath, and also an immense shed (boat-house), under which were moored the caïques, up to which the river flowed.

Adjoining was a large *kiosk* and a lofty pair of gates which constituted the back entrance to this palace, as the attendants and slaves embarked in the caïques from the flight of stone steps that led down from it into the river. Both sides of the walk down it were pleasantly shaded with a great variety of beautiful trees, and one side was lined with a number of arbors, having small divans around them, and *soofras* in the centre.   They reminded me of the tea-gardens in England, especially those at the Spaniards' Inn, on Hampstead Heath.

Traversing the grounds we ascended the lofty hill, at the top of which stood a pair of large lofty gates, and these being open I passed through and entered the stables, which contained accommodation for fourteen horses. There were also several loose boxes and two immense carriage-houses.

At the side of the outer gates stood a large well-built modern house, in which the coachmen, grooms, and helpers lived. The stable-yard led into the Stamboul Road, which was down hill, but one of the most execrable imaginable, much worse than that from Haverfordwest to St. David's, full of ruts, loose stones, and clods of hard mud, up and down which the carriages were constantly bumping, so that the Viceregal family but seldom traversed it. The rides and drives about the vicinity were excedingly picturesque, as all of them commanded most lovely and extensive views of the Bosphorus.

CHAPTER XXVIII.

THE morning after my arrival at the Old Palace I found myself so weak as to be obliged to lay myself down upon my bed on attempting to unpack my trunks. In short, I was obliged to get Zenana, the slave who waited upon me, to do it. Previous to placing my body-linen in the chest ot drawers, she laid it upon the divan, from which I had only a few moments before risen up, and when she went to remove it, she found the whole completely covered with a family of the Browns, who rejoice in the patronymic of bug. Not only were the pieces of linen the slave held in her hand covered with them, but the whole of the divan swarmed with them. It put me in mind of an ant-hill in the interior of India, and if the reader has ever been the tenant of a mud-built hut in any of the suburbs of Bombay, Madras, or Calcutta, he will be able to form some idea of the spectacle which was presented to my sight.

Like most people I have a most intolerable aversion to all the members of that disgusting family. Fortunately I had taken the precaution to provide myself with several tin cases of Keating's Insect Powder, which I strewed upon the divan, and after having left it there a few moments I had the satisfaction to find that it had so stupefied them that Zenana was enabled to sweep them away in her dust-pan. Whenever I began to write a letter, the whole of the paper was covered with them. To sum up all, I was never free from them all the time I remained there. Their Highnesses the Princesses were equally tormented. Glancing at my mosquito curtains, which were as white as the driven snow when put up, I found them perfectly brown, as the bugs clung to them as tenaciously as a miser does to his gold, and the slaves were obliged to sweep them off into pan after pan.

One night the whole of the Palace was besieged by them, and their Highnesses, who could not sleep for them, ordered a regular hunt, which the slaves continued until daybreak, using their dust pans to take them up and slop-pails to drown them in. The next morning, after we had all been employed in that manner, we were doomed to be completely besieged by them; for, owing to its being the anniversary of the accession of the Sultan to the throne, it was a gala day; in honor of which the frigate fired a royal salute, when down came the whole race of Browns like a flight of locusts—rooms and persons were all covered with them. It was a sight I never shall forget were I to live for a hundred years. Their Highnesses shuffled about the place as if they were mad, and the poor slaves worked, as the expression is, "like niggers."

Preparations had been made for several weeks for the illumination, which took place that evening. It was a most lovely sight. The whole of the iron palisades and gates of the landing-place was covered with innumerable variegated colored lamps; scaffoldings were erected in front of the Palace, which being ornamented with various Turkish devices, all lighted up with those lamps in festoons, gave it a beautiful appearance. On the iron palisades, which extended along the whole length of both tenements, hung colored glass lanterns, lighted with wax candles, many of which were knocked down into the Bosphorus by the two old lanky sheep which grazed in the small garden by my room; for not being able to reach their usual provender, the vine leaves, they butted their heads against the lanterns and sent a score of them into the river, scattering the *débris* of several others about in all directions.

Facing us lay the frigate, which was one mass of light, for she was decorated and festoened with variegated lamps up to her royal mast-head. The military bands played the Sultan's March, polkas, and other noisy airs, the officers and crew were all *en grande tenue*, and on the other side the palace of the Sultan's nephew, which was most brilliantly illuminated, gave enchantment to the scene, as it was beautifully reflected in the river.

The scene up and down the Bosphorus all day long was exceedingly enlivening, at night grand and picturesque, for there on its azure blue bosom lay thousands of caïques, with lamps at prow and stern, all filled with elegantly-dressed Turkish ladies. The steamers, brilliantly illuminated, were plying up and down, decorated with flags; bands of music played on their decks, which were thronged with crowds of well-dressed persons. It was a brilliant sight.

I have omitted to mention that the Sultan passed up early in the course of the day in his elegant yacht. He was standing on the deck, and the Prince and I being at the pier had a good view of His Sublime Majesty as the boat drew very near to the Palace. As soon as I perceived the Padishah, I made the Grand Pacha salaam His Majesty three times, and I curtseyed to him. He most graciously returned it by waving his hand several times, a mark of very great honor, as the Sultans are seldom in the habit of returning any salutations. The frigate, which was dressed and decorated, fired a royal salute and manned yards, and the band played the Sultan's March, and the whole of the crew vociferated with stentorian lungs, "May he live a thousand years, and may he see his grandson's hairs as white as the driven snow." Late at night the Old Palace pier was absolutely swarming with caïques full of musicians, who serenaded their Highnesses, from whom they received baksheesh. The Princess Epouse, attended by a bevy of the ladies of the Harem, and accompanied by the Grand Eunuch, went in caïques down the river to witness the illumination, which is the sight *par excellence* of the year, and were thoroughly gratified at that display of Turkish patriotism, if I may be allowed the expression.

The next day, happening to be in the reception-room where we had had such a levee of the Browns when the frigate fired the royal salute, I saw Her Highness give the Grand Eunuch a handful of sovereigns, which I perfectly understood was baksheesh for having accompanied her to see the illumination.

And now I must explain to my readers, that it is almost impossible for them to know the power the Chief Eunuch of every Harem possesses, whether he belong to the Viceregal or to a plebeian one. The whole of the women, Princesses, ladies of the Harem, and slaves, are entirely under his control. His word is law, his smile sunshine ; and that is always obtainable by bestowing a proper amount of baksheesh. Well do I know it, for often and often have I seen the Kislar Agaci salaam their Highnesses the Princesses, smile, and hold out his hands to them, exclaiming, Sish ! Sish ! "baksheesh," when they invariably sent for their cash-box, and, opening it, placed handfuls of bright new sovereigns into his hands.

His frown, however, is dark as a stormy cloud; for if he declines to allow them to go out either, into the grounds, in the caïque, or carriage, they have no remedy, but must, like all poor prisoners, submit to his will and pleasure. As regards myself, they are almost powerless; I repeat almost, because on my wishing to return to my chamber in the Harem at Ras-el-Tin, when on the eve of my departure for Alexandria, he positively refused to allow me to do so; and again I experienced the force of their power when in the Old Palace, as I shall presently have occasion to relate. They all had orders given them by the Viceroy to allow me to do as I liked, and I shall not soon forget the astonishment of some of the inferior eunuchs, when one day the Viceroy ordered the Grand Eunuch belonging to the Harem at Ras-el-Tin to have a carriage ready for me to take the Grand Pacha out for an airing; whereupon that functionary turned round to His Highness, and inquired if it were to be a close one, whether the blinds were to be drawn down, if the governess (meaning myself) was to sit outside on the box with the Arab coachman, while he himself sat within? The Viceroy looked at him for some time, then burst into a fit of laughter, and told him very curtly, " No, you are not to accompany them; never to interfere with Madame; the carriage is to be an open one, and whenever it is a close one, the blinds are not to be pulled down, unless Madame orders them."

It was utterly impossible to obtain any candles in the Harem on the evening after the illumination, as the whole quantity in store had been consumed in the lanterns, so that the Prince and myself had to burn whatever few pieces could be collected out of the lanterns. Not a drop of oil was to be had, and, extraordinary as it may appear, all the sugar had been consumed, so that even the Princess Epouse had to sip her *findjans* of coffee minus that condiment, for the slaves, being on the alert, had taken advantage of the fête, and had purloined all they could lay their hands on.

The *mènage* in His Majesty the Sultan's Palace at Bebek was admirably conducted, but here it was carried out in the most harum-scarum manner imaginable; there was neither order nor regularity; all was discomfort, confusion, and disorder. There were times when neither bread, meat, coffee, sugar, candles, nor oil could be obtained; and then everybody, even from the Princesses, the Prince, and myself, down to the slaves, had to go without whatever articles were deficient, until an arrival of bum-caïques—for caïques plied at the palace gates with almost every article of consumption, from a sheep down to a lemon, so many times weekly (which put me in mind of the bum-boats at Portsmouth) —from whose owners the Grand Eunuch made purchases.

Here we partook of our daily meals at the same hour as we had done in Egypt. The Princess squatted herself down upon the divan, made the slaves do needlework, and partook of cigarettes and coffee, refreshed herself with her siesta, enjoyed her kef, went out on the river in her caïque, paid visits to the Validè Princess at Bebek, and to numerous other Harems.

Soon after the illumination was over I fell so ill as to be obliged to take to my bed. The Hekim Bachi was called in by the Princess Epouse to attend me, but I gradually became worse. A thorough prostration of body, loss of appetite, spinal complaint, and nervous fever had all preyed upon me, until I was reduced to a mere skeleton, and I found myself sinking fast. The Hekim Bachi either did not know how, or would not treat me properly. When the Princess asked him what ailed me, he replied, "Nothing; that it was only a cold." I then asked Her Highness to allow me three months' leave of absence, promising to return as soon as my health was re-established. This Her

Highness granted me, and accordingly I began to prepare for my departure for Alexandria, whither I purposed returning, in order to place myself under the care of Dr. Ogilvie, Physician to H.B.M. Consulate.

One day, prior to my departure, as I was dressing, Her Highness, accompanied by the Grand Eunuch and a lady, came and knocked at my chamber-door. I opened it; but being at that time *en deshabille*, Her Highness did not enter my room, but stood at the door. Then the lady in question asked me if I would return at the expiration of that time? to which I replied in the affirmative. Soon afterwards, that lady left the corridor, without showing the Princess the slightest respect as she marched away before Her Highness, and left her to close my door; but that I prevented, as I took hold of it myself, and that was the last time I had the pleasure of seeing my Princess, that kind lady who had always treated me like a sister, for the next morning she went in the Sultan's yacht to his summer palace at Ismid, in company with the Validè Princess, the Validè Sultana, and attended by the Grand Eunuch.

Ill as I was, I rose early the next day, packed up my *penates*, resting every now and then; and when I had finished I descended into the Grand Eunuch's room, and ordered one of the eunuchs to fetch me a caïque. I asked, but asked in vain—none came, not a eunuch stirred. This was the second, but it was the last time that any of those spectres of their race had shown me their teeth. At length I was quietly told that I could not leave the Palace until His Excellency the Chamberlain came from Bebek; that they had sent for him, and that he would soon arrive; and thus I was checkmated; but not for long, however. After the lapse of a considerable period, Khoorshid Pacha made his appearance, accompanied by the Hekim Bachi and Mr. H., the Viceroy Ismael Pacha's reputed partner; now I know that the under-current was flowing rapidly towards its mouth. To sum up all, Mr. H. positively refused to let me leave the palace, unless I would resign my post. So to save my life and release myself from perpetual imprisonment I signed, under protest made to my own " Special Prince " at Constantinople, the form of resignation that Mr. H. himself drew up, glad to escape from Harem life; and proceeded to Alexandria, where I placed myself under the treatment of Dr. Ogilvie, who gave me a medical certificate, although the Hekim Bachi, who attended the Harem at the Old Palace, had said in my presence, before His Excellency, that there was nothing the matter with me. Yet he had previously told me in my own chamber, that I wanted rest and good European diet, and had himself been prescribing for me. Dr. Ogilvie ordered me to Europe as soon as I was in a fit state to undertake another sea voyage.

All my attempts to lay a statement of the treatment I had received before His Highness the Viceroy failed during my sojourn at Alexandria. I petitioned His Highness for redress, since my resignation was not a free, but a coerced one, brought about by " one of those diplomatic manœuvres which occur nowhere so suddenly, nor so fatally as in the East," and I am up to this moment ignorant of the result.

Brilliant as are the pen-and-ink sketches that our poets have painted of Harem life, I have visited and resided in three of them, which ought to have been, and most undoubtedly are, the most magnificent of all those gilded cages, and I have no desire to visit or live in a fourth. I did not set my foot in the second with the same interest which my ignorance of daily life therein had inspired me on entering the first.

I found, when I became acquainted with their language, that the conversation of the Odalisques was most indelicate, and when bearable, was directed principally to external matters. I soon discovered that it would be most impolitic for me to ask any questions; but, as I have previously stated, I learned by indirect means all that I required to know, and everything that interested me. Their conversation, which becomes absolutely tiresome, continuing from hour to hour, invariably touched upon things which in Europe are regarded as criminal, abominably indecent, filthy, and disgusting.

It is almost impossible to conceive how difficult it is to talk with individuals, who usually contemplate the world only from behind grated windows, or the curtains of carriages, or caïques, and who so far from being removed from worldly interests, are, to all intents and purposes, living in, and stirring in them. For here even more than the body is the female mind immured. Existence in the Harems becomes frightfully monotonous; it engenders melancholy madness; an utter carelessness of worldly things creeps over the senses, a total indifference to everything around you, and a lethargic stupor enshrouds the mind. From what else can this arise, but from breathing an atmosphere redolent with the perfume of tobacco, and the powerful narcotics with which the air is impregnated?

I have minutely detailed their daily social and domestic life. They did not seem to experience any *ennui* in their monotonous seclusion, which robbed them of all participation in the life of their liege lord and master. They knew very little of his daily life. And His Highness shared nothing with them, but yet they shared him with his slaves —of which sensual intercourse the *Ikbals*, " favorites," made no secret, for they would very coolly approach and inform me whenever they were commanded to attend His Highness the Viceroy in his pavilion—which they considered a great honor.

The Princesses never took the slightest notice, nor made any allusion to me about such visits; but I have already explained how I knew when they took place. If I had asked them if they were weary to death of so degrading an

existence, they would have answered, *Mafesch, Madame!
Mafesch, Madame!* "What does it matter! What does
it matter!"

True it is that they have at their command that *succeda-
neum* of all women who lack interest in life, that which
European society avails itself of as readily as do the inmates of the Turkish and Egyptain Harems,—I mean, intrigue; which in the East, and especially within the halls
of the "Enchanted Castles," in which I have been lately
immured, commences "below stairs," among the slaves;
but within these secret institutions for the corruption of
women, a hundred, nay, a thousand by-ways and cross-roads
are taken to secure the object in view, even if it be the
supplanting of an *Ikbal;* especially if such occurs within
the splendid halls of the Imperial "Bower of Bliss," where
no fair Sultana reigns paramount for a longer period than a
year, for the Sovereign of Islam has no consort. The
Sultan's mistresses are but purchased slaves—(he is himself
the son of a slave)—the more fortunate of whom by beauty,
intrigue, or the birth of sons, raise themselves to be *Ikbals,*
"favorites;" or, as it often happens, the single favorite has,
many a time and oft, governed the Empire.

Petticoat-government, as history tells us, is nothing new
here. And not only under weak governments and in times
of decline, as for example, under Murad III., who had for
his mistress, the charming Venetian, Baffa; and under
Achmet I., whose favorite was the high spirited Greek,
Kosseus—women who, in the seventeenth century, misused
and abused their power—both were strangled in insurrec-
tion: but when Suliman I. the Great, the conqueror, the
lawgiver, was so completely in the chains of his beloved and
darling French actress, Roxalana, that he murdered his two
sons by another slave, in order to secure the throne to those
of Roxalana.

The downfall of a Minister, the spoilation of the goods
22

and chattels of an Egyptian Prince, the removal of an hated rival, the substitution of one infant for another, the sending of an heir apparent to his last home, the poisoning of the reigning Sultan or Viceroy, in short all crimes are hatched in the lower regions. It is probable, that the very condition of slavery renders the practice of trickery, subtlety, and artifice, unavoidable, and makes easy the science of weaving nets which cannot be broken through; that dreadful science not so well understood where the relations of mankind are more free. In all this you may be satisfied that the women of the Harem evince the same deep interest in the private affairs of their neighbors, as we in civilized society are accustomed to feel.

CHAPTER XXIX.

IT is very easy to understand how Harems become the very hotbeds of every wicked quality, the seeds of which are already slumbering in the heart of woman. The inmates are surrounded by rivals, always watched, for the surveillance surpasses even that of the secret police in Russia, where the very walls have ears, and spies, most emphatically termed by our neighbors the French *les mouches*, buzz about as thick as mosquitoes in India and Egypt. They are encompassed by those cunning, shrewd, and merciless monsters of humanity, the eunuchs; and being always without any profitable or suitable occupation, jealousy, envy, asperity, hatred, an innate love of intrigue, a boundless desire to please, inflamed with sensual passion, must blaze up like flames. One will vanquish a hated rival, either by a display of personal charms, the poisoned cup, or by the all-powerful influence of baksheesh over the human spectres that guard those " Castles of Indolence," and who, as I have shown, like the once dreaded Thugs of India, are adepts at strangulation.

Is not all this natural to the heart of Eastern women? especially in marble halls, where many a Lucretia Borgia abides her time to turn to account her intuitive knowledge of poisons and acts of cruelty. And say as often as you please that Eastern Houris are accustomed to the Harem, and that " custom makes all things tolerable," nay, light and easy, I look upon the assertion as one of the many thread-bare phrases which are current. Yes, reader, they come under the yoke of the Harem, and they are by degrees habituated to its form ; but against its essence their very instinct revolts. I cannot say their conscience, for that may sleep in all but a very few, but their untamable and all-powerful instinct.

Since there is no culture of the intellect or soul to restrain or regulate its aspirations, how is it possible that there should not be violent outbreaks, shameless coarseness, great barbarity? And this is the opinion I have formed, after having witnessed both Egyptian and Turkish women at home, and their deportment towards each other and strangers. I have taken part in their daily life; observed their bearing towards each other, and how far the dominion of lawful wives (for with the exception of the Sultan, every Turk has one or two) extends over the female slaves, which amounts over their own to life or death, but over those belonging to their liege lords none, absolutely none. They, in like manner, possess no control over theirs, with whom they must not attempt to intrigue, except at the penalty of a divorce, ah! and perhaps the certainty of being sooner or later the victims of their own audacity (as has but lately been the case at Constantinople) and the instant disappearance of that slave who has so boldly coveted the honor of becoming the *Ikbal* of her lord, and so heedlessly attempted to supplant her mistress in her lord's affection.

It is an incontrovertible fact that the walls of the Harems have, and still do conceal, sad and terrible secrets. One most wretched fruit which has grown out of the Harems, and mainly contributed to the decadence of the Ottoman dominions, is the result of the neglected education of the Princes, or, properly speaking, their very existence in the State. To sum up all, the wings by which we are enabled to raise ourselves from the dust, and to develop which is, or ought to be, the end and aim of all culture and of all education, are crippled by the Turk.

Turkish history shows us that no Sultan brought up by Turkish Thugs (the mutes,) intriguing lewd women, and those spectres of mankind, the eunuchs, in or out of the Princes' Cage ever attained to that development which at the same time discerns and wills. And the same will be the result with all Egyptian Princes nurtured within the baneful influence of the Harems, even in this the nineteenth century.

It is true that heavenly gifts the free grants of God, are chiefly needed for such consummation and that the regenerating genius of a Prince depends as little upon inclination, caprice, and education, as the genius of a financier, or artist, or any other character; nevertheless, having lived in the Harems, I am satisfied that the soil is capable of producing only crippled plants, and we know that almost all the Sultans and heirs presumptive to the Viceroyship vegetate upon it until they are called from that noxious atmosphere to the throne; and although the Egyptian Princes quit that institution for the corruption of women and young princes at ten or twelve years of age, still the recollection of the indelicate scenes in which they daily took a part have become too deeply rooted in their minds ever to be eradicated.

But if their Highnesses were removed at the tender age of four years old from the Harem, and placed, together with the Moslem nurse, under the care of a European with a European staff of attendants about them, and had an establishment suitable to their rank and position assigned them, then we might look forward to such a course producing more healthy plants, from which, in each succeeding generation, would spring lasting benefit; but until some such measures are adopted, all hope for the future regeneration of the Sultans or Viceroys of Egypt is vain.

The same observation is applicable to the whole of the *noblesse* of both those countries. Most of the great functionaries of both Egypt and Turkey are, at least their forefathers were, but purchased slaves. A slave, we know has no fatherland, and can have none. He lives for himself, as all the Moslems do. He must in some degree keep himself within the circle of his obligations; but whence shall he obtain the incitement to activity and efficiency which refuses to be bound within the old beaten track? If the wheels of the state machine which for so many years have kept affairs in motion, should, through age, be tottering and feeble, not turning with due regularity and vigor, he takes good care to leave them as they are. If, in addition to this, you consider that the population of Turkey diminishes every year, as is always the case in all ill-governed countries; and here it is positively alarming, partly from polygamy, and partly from infanticide—(for women in the Harems who have had one or two confinements, and have grown tired of child-bearing, as they soon do, especially if they have been daughters, think it no sin to destroy their unborn offspring,) for I have known even Princesses to leave their only sons when they were dying to the care of Moslem nurses for a whole week together, while they went out visiting;—if you consider this, I say, does it not become natural to ask, How is it possible for future hopes to knit themselves to young branches, to fresh roots, when the pith of the tree has lost all its vital powers?

THE END.

T. B. PETERSON AND BROTHERS' PUBLICATIONS.

NEW BOOKS ISSUED EVERY WEEK.

Comprising the most entertaining and absorbing works published,
suitable for the Parlor, Library, Sitting Room, Railroad or
Steamboat reading, by the best writers in the world.

☞ Orders solicited from Booksellers, Librarians, Canvassers, News
Agents, and all others in want of good and fast selling
books, which will be supplied at Low Prices. ☜

☞ TERMS: To those with whom we have no monthly account, Cash with Order. ☜

CHARLES DICKENS' WORKS.
☞ GREAT REDUCTION IN THEIR PRICES. ☜

CHEAP EDITION.—IN BUFF PAPER COVER.
Each book being complete in one large octavo volume.

Our Mutual Friend,	$1.00	Sketches by "Boz,"	75
Great Expectations,	75	Oliver Twist,	75
Lamplighter's Story,	75	Little Dorrit,	75
David Copperfield,	75	Tale of Two Cities,	75
Dombey and Son,	75	New Years' Stories,	75
Nicholas Nickleby,	75	Dickens' Short Stories,	75
Pickwick Papers,	75	Message from the Sea,	75
Christmas Stories,	75	Holiday Stories,	75
Martin Chuzzlewit,	75	American Notes,	75
Old Curiosity Shop,	75	Pic Nic Papers,	75
Barnaby Rudge,	75	Somebody's Luggage,	25
Dickens' New Stories,	75	Tom Tiddler's Ground,	25
Bleak House,	75	The Haunted House,	25
Joseph Grimaldi,	75		

PEOPLE'S DUODECIMO EDITION.—ILLUSTRATED.
Reduced in price from $2.50 to $1.50 a volume.

*This edition is printed on fine paper, from large, clear type, leaded, Long
Primer in size, that all can read, and each book is complete in one large
duodecimo volume.*

Our Mutual Friend,	Cloth, $1.50	Little Dorrit,	Cloth,	$1.50
Pickwick Papers,	Cloth, 1.50	Dombey and Son,	Cloth,	1.50
Nicholas Nickleby,	Cloth, 1.50	Christmas Stories,	Cloth,	1.50
Great Expectations,	Cloth, 1.50	Sketches by "Boz,"	Cloth,	1.50
Lamplighter's Story,	Cloth, 1.50	Barnaby Rudge,	Cloth,	1.50
David Copperfield,	Cloth, 1.50	Martin Chuzzlewit,	Cloth,	1.50
Oliver Twist,	Cloth, 1.50	Old Curiosity Shop,	Cloth,	1.50
Bleak House,	Cloth, 1.50	Message from the Sea,	Cloth,	1.50
A Tale of Two Cities,	Cloth, 1.50	Dickens' New Stories,	Cloth,	1.50

Price of a set, in Black cloth, in eighteen volumes,	$27.00
" " Full sheep, Library style,	36.00
" " Half calf, sprinkled edges,	45.00
" " Half calf, marbled edges,	50.00
" " Half calf, antique,	55.00
" " Half calf, full gilt backs, etc.	55.00

☞ Books sent, postage paid, on receipt of the Retail Price, by
(1)   T. B. Peterson & Brothers, Philadelphia, Pa.

CHARLES DICKENS' WORKS.
ILLUSTRATED OCTAVO EDITION.

Reduced in price from $2.50 to $2.00 a volume.

This edition is printed from large type, double column, octavo page, each book being complete in one volume, the whole containing near Six Hundred Illustrations, by Cruikshank, Phiz, Browne, Maclise, McLenan, and other eminent artists.

Our Mutual Friend,.....Cloth,	$2.00		David Copperfield,.......Cloth,	$2.00
Pickwick Papers,.........Cloth,	2.00		Barnaby Rudge,..........Cloth,	2.00
Nicholas Nickleby,......Cloth,	2.00		Martin Chuzzlewit,......Cloth,	2.00
Great Expectations,......Cloth,	2.00		Old Curiosity Shop,......Cloth,	2.00
Lamplighter's Story,....Cloth,	2.00		Christmas Stories,.......Cloth,	2.00
Oliver Twist,.............Cloth,	2.00		Dickens' New Stories,...Cloth,	2.00
Bleak House,.............Cloth,	2.00		A Tale of Two Cities,...Cloth,	2.00
Little Dorrit,.............Cloth,	2.00		American Notes and	
Dombey and Son,........Cloth,	2.00		Pic-Nic Papers,........Cloth,	2.00
Sketches by "Boz,".....Cloth,	2.00			

Price of a set, in Black cloth, in eighteen volumes.....................$36.00
   "   "   Full sheep, Library style..................................... 45.00
   "   "   Half calf, sprinkled edges.................................. 55.00
   "   "   Half calf, marbled edges................................... 62.00
   "   "   Half calf, antique.. 70.00
   "   "   Half calf, full gilt backs, etc.............................. 70.00

ILLUSTRATED DUODECIMO EDITION.

Reduced in price from $2.00 to $1.50 a volume.

This edition is printed on the finest paper, from large, clear type, leaded, Long Primer in size, that all can read, the whole containing near Six Hundred full page Illustrations, printed on tinted paper, from designs by Cruikshank, Phiz, Browne, Maclise, McLenan, and other artists. The following books are each contained in two volumes.

Our Mutual Friend,......Cloth,	$3.00		Bleak House,..............Cloth,	$3.00
Pickwick Papers..........Cloth,	3.00		Sketches by "Boz,".....Cloth,	3.00
Tale of Two Cities,......Cloth,	3.00		Barnaby Rudge,..........Cloth,	3.00
Nicholas Nickleby,......Cloth,	3.00		Martin Chuzzlewit, ...Cloth,	3.00
David Copperfield,.......Cloth,	3.00		Old Curiosity Shop,......Cloth,	3.00
Oliver Twist,.............Cloth,	3.00		Little Dorrit,..............Cloth,	3.00
Christmas Stories,.........Cloth,	3.00		Dombey and Son,.........Cloth,	3.00

The following are each complete in one volume, and are reduced in price from $2.50 to $1.50 a volume.

Great Expectations,......Cloth,	$1.50		Dickens' New Stories, ...Cloth,	$1.50
Lamplighter's Story,.....Cloth,	1.50		Message from the Sea,...Cloth,	1.50

Price of a set, in thirty-two volumes, bound in cloth,.................... $48.00
   "   "   Full sheep, Library style,................................. 64.00
   "   "   Half calf, antique,....................................... 96.00
   "   "   Half calf, full gilt backs, etc............................. 96.00

GREEN CLOTH—AND GREEN PAPER COVER EDITION.

Each novel of this edition will be complete in one octavo volume, illustrated, and bound in Green Morocco cloth, at $1.25 a volume, or in Green Paper cover, sewed, at $1.00 each. "Our Mutual Friend," "David Copperfield," "Great Expectations," "Tale of Two Cities," "Bleak House," and "Little Dorrit," are now ready.

☞ Books sent, postage paid, on receipt of the Retail Price, by T. B. Peterson & Brothers, Philadelphia, Pa.

CHARLES DICKENS' WORKS.
THE "NEW NATIONAL EDITION."

This is the cheapest complete edition of the works of Charles Dickens, "Boz," published in the world, all his writings being contained in *seven large octavo volumes*, with a portrait of Charles Dickens, and other illustrations, the whole making nearly *six thousand very large double columned pages*, in large, clear type, and handsomely printed on fine white paper, and bound in the strongest and most substantial manner.

Price of a set, in Black cloth, in seven volumes,........................ $20.00
"   "   Full sheep, Library style,........................... 25.00
"   "   Half calf, antique, ... 30.00
"   "   Half calf, full gilt backs, etc...................... 30.00

☞ No Library is complete without a set of Charles Dickens' Works, and either edition of Charles Dickens' Works will be sent to any address, free of transportation, on Receipt by us of the advertised Price.

MRS. E. D. E. N. SOUTHWORTH'S WORKS.

The Bride of Llewellyn,..........	1 50	Love's Labor Won,................	1 50
The Fortune Seeker,..............	1 50	Deserted Wife,.....................	1 50
Allworth Abbey, ...	1 50	The Gipsy's Prophecy,...........	1 50
The Bridal Eve,....................	1 50	The Mother-in-Law,..............	1 50
The Fatal Marriage,..............	1 50	The Missing Bride,................	1 50
Haunted Homestead,..............	1 50	Wife's Victory,.....................	1 50
The Lost Heiress,..................	1 50	Retribution,.........................	1 50
Lady of the Isle,..................	1 50	India; or, the Pearl of Pearl	
The Two Sisters,..................	1 50	River,...............................	1 50
The Three Beauties,..............	1 50	Curse of Clifton,....................	1 50
Vivia; Secret Power,.............	1 50	Discarded Daughter,..............	1 50

The above are each in paper cover, or in cloth, price $2.00 each.

Hickory Hall,........ .... 50 | Broken Engagement,............. 25

MRS. CAROLINE LEE HENTZ'S WORKS.

The Planter's Northern Bride,..	1 50	Rena; or, the Snow-bird,........	1 50
Linda; or, the Young Pilot of		The Lost Daughter,................	1 50
the Belle Creole,..................	1 50	Love after Marriage,..............	1 50
Robert Graham. The Sequel		Eoline; or, Magnolia Vale,....	1 50
to "Linda,".......................	1 50	The Banished Son,................	1 50
Courtship and Marriage,.........	1 50	Helen and Arthur,................	1 50
Ernest Linwood,...................	1 50	Forsaken Daughter,...............	1 50
Marcus Warland,..................	1 50	Planter's Daughter,..............	1 50

The above are each in paper cover, or in cloth, price $2.00 each.

MRS. ANN S. STEPHENS' WORKS.

The Soldiers' Orphans...........,	$1 50	The Heiress,.........................	$1 50
The Gold Brick,...................	1 50	Fashion and Famine,.............	1 50
Silent Struggles,...................	1 50	Mary Derwent, ...	1 50
The Wife's Secret,.................	1 50	The Old Homestead,.............	1 50
The Rejected Wife,...............	1 50		

The above are each in paper cover, or in cloth, price $2.00 each.

☞ Books sent, postage paid, on receipt of the Retail Price, by T. B. Peterson & Brothers, Philadelphia, Pa.

BEST COOK BOOKS PUBLISHED.

Mrs. Goodfellow's Cookery as it Should Be,.. 2 00
Petersons' New Cook Book,.. 2 00
Miss Leslie's New Cookery Book,.. 2 00
Widdifield's New Cook Book,.. 2 00
The National Cook Book. By a Practical Housewife,................................... 2 00
The Family Save-All. By author of "National Cook Book,".......... 2 00
Mrs. Hale's Receipts for the Million,.. 2 00
Miss Leslie's New Receipts for Cooking,.. 2 00
Mrs. Hale's New Cook Book,... 2 00
Francatelli's Celebrated Cook Book. The Modern Cook. With
    Sixty-two illustrations, 600 large octavo pages,................................ 5 00

FREDRIKA BREMER'S WORKS.

Father and Daughter,............ 1 50	The Neighbors,..................... 1 50
The Four Sisters,................... 1 50	The Home,............................ 1 50

The above are each in paper cover, or in cloth, price $2.00 each.

Life in the Old World; or, Two Years in Switzerland and Italy. By
Miss Bremer, in two volumes, cloth, price, ... $4.00

WORKS BY THE VERY BEST AUTHORS.

Colonel John W. Forney's Letters from Europe. Bound in cloth,.... 2 00
Harem Life in Egypt and Constantinople. By Emmeline Lott,...... 1 50
My Son's Wife. By author of "Caste," "Mr. Arle," etc................. 1 50
A Woman's Thoughts about Women. By Miss Muloch,................. 1 50
The Initials. A Story of Modern Life. By Baroness Tautphœus, ... 1 50
The Rector's Wife; or, the Valley of a Hundred Fires,.................... 1 50
The Rich Husband. By author of "George Geith," 1 50
Woodburn Grange. A Novel. By William Howitt, ... 1 50
Country Quarters. By the Countess of Blessington,...................... 1 50
Out of the Depths. The Story of a "Woman's Life,".................... 1 50
The Coquette; or, Life and Letters of Eliza Wharton,.................... 1 50
Self-Sacrifice. By author of "Margaret Maitland," etc................... 1 50
Flirtations in Fashionable Life. By Catharine Sinclair,................... 1 50
Family Pride. By author of "Pique," "Family Secrets," etc.......... 1 50

Gemma. By Trollope,.......... 1 50	Love and Duty,..................... 1 50
The Lost Beauty,................... 1 50	Bohemians in London,........... 1 50
The Rival Belles,................... 1 50	The Man of the World,.......... 1 50
The Lost Love,..................... 1 50	High Life in Washington,...... 1 50
The Woman in Black,............ 1 50	The Jealous Husband,............ 1 50
The Pride of Life,................. 1 50	Belle of Washington,............. 1 50
The Roman Traitor,.............. 1 50	Courtship and Matrimony,..... 1 50
Saratoga. A Story of 1787,... 1 50	Family Secrets,..................... 1 50
The Queen's Favorite, ... 1 50	Rose Douglas,...................... 1 50
Married at Last,.................... 1 50	The Lover's Trials.................. 1 50
False Pride,......................... 1 50	Beautiful Widow,.................. 1 50
Self-Love,........................... 1 50	Brother's Secret,................... 1 50
Cora Belmont, ... 1 50	The Matchmaker,.................. 1 50
The Devoted Bride,............... 1 50	Love and Money,.................. 1 50

The above are each in paper cover, or in cloth, price $2.00 each.

The Story of Elizabeth. By Miss Thackeray. In one duodecimo volume, full gilt back. Price $1.00 in paper, or $1.50 in cloth.

CHARLES LEVER'S BEST WORKS.

Charles O'Malley,	75	Knight of Gwynne,	75
Harry Lorrequer,	75	Arthur O'Leary,	75
Jack Hinton,	75	Con Cregan,	75
Tom Burke of Ours,	75	Davenport Dunn,	75

Above are each in paper, or finer edition in cloth, price $2.00 each.

Horace Templeton,	75	Kate O'Donoghue,	75

MADAME GEORGE SAND'S WORKS.

Consuelo,	75	Fanchon, the Cricket, paper,	1 00
Countess of Rudolstadt,	75	Do. do. cloth,	1 50
First and True Love,	75	Indiana, a Love Story, paper,	1 50
The Corsair,	50	Do. do. cloth,	2 00
Jealousy, paper,	1 50	Consuelo and Rudolstadt, both	
Do. cloth,	2 00	in one volume, cloth,	2 00

WILKIE COLLINS' BEST WORKS.

The Crossed Path, or Basil,	1 50	The Dead Secret. 12mo	1 50

The above are each in paper cover, or in cloth, price $2.00 each.

Hide and Seek,	75	Mad Monkton,	50
After Dark,	75	Sights a-Foot,	50
The Dead Secret. 8vo	75	The Stolen Mask,	25
Above in cloth at $1.00 each.		The Yellow Mask,	25
The Queen's Revenge,	75	Sister Rose,	25

MISS PARDOE'S WORKS.

Confessions of a Pretty Woman,	75	Rival Beauties,	75
The Wife's Trials,	75	Romance of the Harem,	75
The Jealous Wife,	50		

The five above books are also bound in one volume, cloth, for $4.00.

The Adopted Heir. One volume, paper, $1.50; or in cloth, $2.00.

The Earl's Secret. One volume, paper, $1.50; or in cloth, $2.00.

MRS. HENRY WOOD'S BOOKS.

Elster's Folly,	1 50	Lord Oakburn's Daughters; or,	
St. Martin's Eve,	1 50	the Earl's Heirs,	1 50
Mildred Arkell,	1 50	Squire Trevlyn's Heir; or,	
Shadow of Ashlydyat,	1 50	Trevlyn Hold,	1 50
Oswald Cray,	1 50	The Castle's Heir; or, Lady	
Verner's Pride,	1 50	Adelaide's Oath,	1 50

Above are each in paper cover, or each one in cloth, for $2.00 each.

The Mystery,	75	A Life's Secret,	50

Above are each in paper cover, or each one in cloth, for $1.00 each.

The Channings,	1 00	Aurora Floyd,	75

Above are each in paper cover, or each one in cloth, for $1.50 each.

Red Court Farm,	75	The Lost Bank Note,	75
Orville College,	50	Better for Worse,	75
The Runaway Match,	50	Foggy Night at Offord,	25
The Lost Will, and the Dia-		The Lawyer's Secret,	25
mond Bracelet,	50	William Allair	25
The Haunted Tower,	50	A Light and a Dark Christmas,	25

Books sent, postage paid, on receipt of the Retail Price, by
T. B. Peterson & Brothers, Philadelphia, Pa.

ALEXANDER DUMAS' WORKS.

Count of Monte Cristo,	1 50	Memoirs of a Physician,	1 00
The Iron Mask,	1 00	Queen's Necklace,	1 00
Louise La Valliere,	1 00	Six Years Later,	1 00
Adventures of a Marquis,	1 00	Countess of Charney,	1 00
Diana of Meridor,	1 00	Andree de Taverney,	1 00
The Three Guardsmen,	75	The Chevalier,	1 00
Twenty Years After,	75	Forty-five Guardsmen,	75
Bragelonne,	75	The Iron Hand,	75
The Conscript. A Tale of War,	1 50	Camille, "The Camelia Lady,"	1 50

The above are each in paper cover, or in cloth, price $2.00 each.

Edmond Dantes,	75	Sketches in France,	75
The Marriage Verdict,	75	Isabel of Bavaria,	75
Felina de Chambure,	75	Man with Five Wives,	75
The Horrors of Paris,	75	Twin Lieutenants,	75
The Fallen Angel,	75	Annette, Lady of the Pearls,	50
The Corsican Brothers,	50	Mohicans of Paris,	50
George,	50	Buried Alive,	25

SAMUEL C. WARREN'S BEST BOOKS.

Ten Thousand a Year, ...paper,	1 50	Diary of a Medical Student,	75
Do. do. cloth,	2 00		

Q. K. PHILANDER DOESTICKS' WORKS.

Doesticks' Letters,	1 50	The Elephant Club,	1 50
Plu-Ri-Bus-Tah,	1 50	Witches of New York,	1 50

The above are each in paper cover, or in cloth, price $2.00 each.

Nothing to Say, cloth, ... 75

GUSTAVE AIMARD'S WORKS.

The Prairie Flower,	75	Trapper's Daughter,	75
The Indian Scout,	75	The Tiger Slayer,	75
The Trail Hunter,	75	The Gold Seekers,	75
The Indian Chief,	75	The Rebel Chief,	75
The Red Track,	75	The Smuggler Chief,	75
Pirates of the Prairies,	75	The Border Rifles,	75

GOOD BOOKS FOR EVERYBODY.

The Refugee,	1 50	Currer Lyle, the Actress,	1 50
Life of Don Quixotte,	1 00	Secession, Coercion, and Civil	
Wilfred Montressor,	1 50	War,	1 50
Harris's Adventures in Africa,	1 50	The Cabin and Parlor. By J.	
Wild Southern Scenes,	1 50	Thornton Randolph,	1 50
Life and Beauties Fanny Fern,	1 50	Memoirs of Vidocq, the noted	
Lola Montez' Life and Letters,	1 50	French Policeman,	1 50

Lady Maud; or, the Wonder of Kingswood Chase. By Pierce Egan, 1 50

Above are each in paper cover, or each one in cloth, for $2.00 each.

Whitefriars; or, The Days of Charles the Second. Illustrated, ... 1 00
Southern Life; or, Inside Views of Slavery, ... 1 00
The Rich Men of Philadelphia, Income Tax List of Residents, ... 1 00
Political Lyrics. New Hampshire and Nebraska in 1854. Illust'd.   12

GECRGE W. M. REYNOLDS' WORKS.

Mysteries of Court of London,	1 00	Mary Price,	1 00
Rose Foster. Sequel to it,	1 50	Eustace Quentin,	1 00
Caroline of Brunswick,	1 00	Joseph Wilmot,	1 00
Venetia Trelawney,	1 00	Banker's Daughter,	1 00
Lord Saxondale,	1 00	Kenneth,	1 00
Count Christoval,	1 00	The Rye-House Plot,	1 00
Rosa Lambert,	1 00	The Necromancer,	1 00

The above are each in paper cover, or in cloth, price $2.00 each.

The Opera Dancer,	75	The Soldier's Wife,	75
Child of Waterloo,	75	May Middleton,	75
Robert Bruce,	75	Duke of Marchmont,	75
Discarded Queen,	75	Massacre of Glencoe,	75
The Gipsy Chief,	75	Queen Joanna; Court Naples,	75
Mary Stuart, Queen of Scots,	75	Pickwick Abroad,	75
Wallace, Hero of Scotland,	1 00	Parricide,	75
Isabella Vincent,	75	The Ruined Gamester,	50
Vivian Bertram,	75	Ciprina; or, Secrets of a Picture Gallery,	50
Countess of Lascelles,	75		
Loves of the Harem,	75	Life in Paris,	50
Ellen Percy,	75	Countess and the Page,	50
Agnes Evelyn,	75	Edgar Montrose,	50

WAVERLEY NOVELS. BY SIR WALTER SCOTT.

Ivanhoe,	50	Red Gauntlet,	50
Rob Roy,	50	The Betrothed,	50
Guy Mannering,	50	The Talisman,	50
The Antiquary	50	Woodstock,	50
Old Mortality	50	Highland Widow, etc.,	50
Heart of Mid Lothian,	50	The Fair Maid of Perth,	50
Bride of Lammermoor,	50	Anne of Geierstein,	50
Waverley,	50	Count Robert of Paris,	50
St. Ronan's Well,	50	The Black Dwarf and Legend of Montrose,	50
Kenilworth,	50		
The Pirate,	50	Castle Dangerous, and Surgeon's Daughter,	50
The Monastery,	50		
The Abbot,	50	Moredun. A Tale of 1210,	50
The Fortunes of Nigel,	50	Tales of a Grandfather, vol. 1,	25
Peveril of the Peak,	50	Life of Sir Walter Scott. By	
Quentin Durward,	50	J. G. Lockhart, cloth,	2 50

"NEW NATIONAL EDITION" OF "WAVERLEY NOVELS."

This is the cheapest edition of the "Waverley Novels" published in the world, all of them being contained in *five large octavo volumes*, with a portrait of Sir Walter Scott, the whole making nearly *four thousand very large double columned pages*, in good type, and handsomely printed on the finest of white paper, and bound in the strongest and most substantial manner.

Price of a set, in Black cloth, in five volumes,			$15 00
"	"	Full sheep, Library style,	17 50
"	"	Half calf, antique,	25 00
"	"	Half calf, full gilt backs, etc.	25 00

The Complete Prose and Poetical Works of Sir Walter Scott, are also published in ten volumes, bound in half calf, for $60.00.

W. H. AINSWORTH'S BEST WORKS.

Life of Jack Sheppard,	50	Tower of London,	1 50
Guy Fawkes,	75	Miser's Daughter,	1 00
Above in 1 vol., cloth, $2.00.		Above in cloth $2.00 each.	
The Star Chamber,	75	Court of the Stuarts,	75
Old St. Paul's,	75	Windsor Castle,	75
Court of Queen Anne,	50	Desperadoes of the New World,	25
Dick Turpin,	50	Ninon De L'Enclos,	25
Life of Davy Crockett,	50	Life of Arthur Spring,	25
Life of Grace O'Malley,	50	Life of Mrs. Whipple and Jes-	
Life of Henry Thomas,	25	see Strang,	25

G. P. R. JAMES'S BEST BOOKS.

Lord Montague's Page,	1 50	The Cavalier,	1 50

The above are each in paper cover, or in cloth, price $2.00 each.

The Man in Black,	75	Arrah Neil,	75
Mary of Burgundy,	75	Eva St. Clair,	50

WAR NOVELS. BY HENRY MORFORD.

Shoulder-Straps,	1 50	The Days of Shoddy. A His-	
The Coward,	1 50	tory of the late War,	1 50

Above are each in paper cover, or each one in cloth, for $2.00 each.

BY THE BEST AUTHORS.

Illustrated Life, Speeches, Martyrdom and Funeral of President Abraham Lincoln. Cloth, $2.00; or paper, ... 1 50

Illustrated Life and Campaigns of General Ulysses S. Grant. Cloth, $1.00; or in paper, ... 75

Illustrated Life and Services of Major-General Philip H. Sheridan. Cloth, $1.00; or in paper, ... 75

Life, Speeches and Services of President Andrew Johnson. Cloth, $1.00; or in paper, ... 75

Trial of the Assassins and Conspirators for the murder of President Abraham Lincoln.   Cloth, $1.50; or cheap edition in paper, ... 50

Webster and Hayne's Speeches in Reply to Colonel Foote, ... 75

Roanoke; or, Where is Utopia? By C. H. Wiley. Illustrated, ... 75

Banditti of the Prairie,	75	Mysteries of Three Cities,	75
Genevra,	75	New Hope; or, the Rescue,	75
Tom Racquet,	75	Nothing to Say,	75
Red Indians of Newfoundland,	75	The Greatest Plague of Life,	50
Salathiel, by Croly,	75	Clifford and the Actress,	50
Corinne; or, Italy,	75	Two Lovers,	50
Ned Musgrave	75	Ryan's Mysteries of Marriage,	50
Aristocracy,	75	Fortune Hunter,	50
Inquisition in Spain,	75	The Orphan Sisters,	50
Flirtations in America	75	The Romish Confessional. By	
The Coquette,	75	Michelet,	50
Thackeray's Irish Sketch Book,	75	Victims of Amusements,	50
Whitehall,	75	General Scott's $5 Portrait,	1 00
The Beautiful Nun,	75	Henry Clay's $5 Portrait,	1 00
Father Clement, paper,	50	Violet,	50
do. do. cloth,	75	Montague; or, Almacks,	50
Miser's Heir, paper,	50	Tangarua, a Poem,	1 00
do. do. cloth,	75	Alicford, a Family History,	50

☞ Books sent, postage paid, on Receipt of the Retail Price, by T. B. Peterson & Brothers, Philadelphia, Pa.

T. B. PETERSON AND BROTHERS,

PUBLISHERS AND BOOKSELLERS,

PHILADELPHIA, PA.,

Take pleasure in calling the attention of the public to their Choice and Extensive Stock of Books, comprising a collection of the most popular and choice, in all styles of binding, by all the favorite and standard American and English Authors.

To Collectors of Libraries, or those desiring to form them.

Many who have the taste, and wish to form a Library, are deterred by fear of the cost. To all such we would say, that a large number of books may be furnished for even One Hundred Dollars—which, by a yearly increase of a small amount, will before long place the purchaser in possession of a Library in almost every branch of knowledge, and afford satisfaction not only to the collector, but to all those who are so fortunate as to possess his acquaintance.

For the convenience of Book buyers, and those seeking suitable Works for Presentation, great care is taken in having a large and varied collection, and all the current works of the day. Show counters and shelves, with an excellent selection of Standard, Illustrated, and Illuminated works, varying in price to suit all buyers, are available to those visiting our establishment, where purchases may be made with facility, and the time of the visitor greatly economized. Here may be seen not only books of the simplest kind for children, but also exquisite works of art, of the most sumptuous character, suitable alike to adorn the drawing-room table and the study of the connoisseur.

Our arrangements for supplying STANDARD AMERICAN BOOKS, suitable for Public Libraries and Private Families, are complete, and our stock second to none in the country.

☞ Catalogues are sent, on application, and great attention is paid to communications from the country, and the goods ordered carefully packed and forwarded with expedition on receipt of orders accompanied with the cash.

To Booksellers and Librarians.

T. B. Peterson & Brothers issue New Books every month, comprising the most entertaining and absorbing works published, suitable for the Parlor, Library, Sitting Room, Railroad or Steamboat reading, by the best and most popular writers in the world.

Any person wanting books will find it to their advantage to send their orders to the "PUBLISHING HOUSE" OF T. B. PETERSON & BROS., 306 Chestnut St., Philadelphia, who have the largest stock in the country, and will supply them at very low prices for cash. We have just issued a new and complete Catalogue and Wholesale Price Lists, which we send gratuitously to any Bookseller or Librarians on application.

Orders solicited from Librarians, Booksellers, Canvassers, News Agents, and all others in want of good and fast selling books, and they will please send on their orders.

Enclose ten, twenty, fifty, or a hundred dollars, or more, to us in a letter, and write what kind of books you wish, and on its receipt the books will be sent to you at once, per first express, or any way you direct, with circulars, show bills, etc., gratis.

Agents and Canvassers are requested to send for our Canvassers' Confidential Circular containing instructions. Large wages can be made, as we supply our Agents at very low rates.

Address all cash orders, retail or wholesale, to meet with prompt attention, to

T. B. PETERSON AND BROTHERS,

306 Chestnut Street, Philadelphia, Penna.

Books sent, postage paid, on receipt of retail price, to any address in the country.

All the NEW BOOKS are for sale at PETERSONS' Book Store, as soon as published.

☞ Publishers of "PETERSONS' DETECTOR and BANK NOTE LIST," a Business Journal and valuable Advertising medium. Price $1.50 a year, monthly; or $3.00 a year, semi-monthly. Every Business man should subscribe at once.